I0763510

Dragon Tooth Gold

Volume 3 – Pay Dirt

By

Kent J. McGrew

Dragon Tooth Gold – Volume 3 – Pay Dirt

ISBN 978-1-7336650-1-8

Cover Image by Night Raven Illustrations
www.deviantart.com/nightravenillust
nightravenillustration@gmail.com

Kent J. McGrew

Meet and Contact the Author @

https://kentjmcgrew.com/
Printed in the United States of America

First Printing: Aug 2019
Dragon Tooth Publishing

In Remembrance

I dedicate this book to memory of my first mentor in the mining business, Walter J. Scott. Walter was an interesting mix of scientist and charlatan. He signed his name followed by M.E. A naïve public eager for help with mining issues, assumed this meant Mining Engineer. A mining Engineer signs his name E.M. – Engineer of Mining. Walter was a Master Photo Engraver.

His chemistry was the world of vitriol, hypo, and pyro silver. Mine was the world of the periodic table, molecular weights, stoichiometry, and chemical reactions. Together, and with the mechanical genius of my father, we stumbled through the remnants of the California gold and mercury industry. Walter went to heaven after five years of our friendship with the aid of the cigars he smoked as he poured over mining and metallurgy books, finding mysteries for me to solve.

Walter and wife Fern, may you rest in peace in the light of your God; may you rest with my most sincere thanks. Your love and guidance were the best start possible a boy could have for a lifetime of rich, rewarding work.

Table of Contents

Prologue

It was hard for the young Callahans to imagine that they had reached their destination on the west coast of their troubled nation. Each of them had months to think about what they would do after the journey's end. The travel seemed endless while they were on the trail. Now the time to act on what each decided to do next had come. In Los Angeles, the reality that they would soon part ways shaded their moods as heavy as the Pacific fog that hugged the coast. Eli, the oldest of the four siblings, accepted the role of patriarch of the family after the tragic death of their parents in a tornado that swept their home away in Independence, Missouri. He knew that a new role and responsibility arrived when he took charge of the wagon train at the beginning of the trek west. He wasn't sure, however, of where that role stood now with his grandmother still alive. She was a remarkably strong woman, and very much still acting like the leader of their family. Eli felt it was time to break away from that influence and be on his own.

His twin brothers, Jacques and Roland, had made big decisions on the road west. Jacques, the adventurer, was joining Major Hancock's growing regiment as a civilian scout. Roland had married quite unexpectedly in Bernalillio and was already on the way to becoming a father. Roland, the deep thinker and visionary of the family, seemed to have his hand on an invisible tiller. Eli learned that, when needed, Roland was quietly steering the family ship into some unknown distant port.

Suzette, still fourteen, was the family enigma. Eli left home, still calling her his baby sister. She wasn't a baby anymore. She was a hardened young woman, trail tough and able to take care of herself. Suzette was the smartest young woman Eli knew. Her eidetic memory and ability to learn were extraordinary. Until the tornado that killed their parents, she was training to be a doctor in the hospital in Independence. She made up her mind to go to San Francisco to continue that education. She at least wouldn't be traveling alone. Roland and his wife Lia would be taking her north. Mr. Sue, their lifelong friend from the trail, would see her safely there and maybe even stay with her through medical school. He had family in San Francisco, but all along their journey west, it never seemed like Mr. Sue was returning home.

Denise, the unstoppable grandmother, would be waiting in San Francisco, delivered by their uncle Connor on his whiskey schooner *Blessed by the Wind*. Denise, the overbearing family matriarch, Eli had to get out of her shadow and find his way in the world. It seemed odd to him that he was the only one that didn't have a future planned out to the minute. He would go back to Yuma with Moses, the slave that he freed when they reached the crossing on the Colorado River. From there, he wanted to find a mysterious hill marked on a map, a map they recovered from the Peralta family envoy whom the Apaches wiped out on the San Pedro River. Eli had no idea what he would do after that. His father had taught him well that it was his responsibility to shape his destiny. Whatever came next would be good, because he would make it so. He resolved to do that day-by-day as he said goodbye to his family and friends and headed east with Moses.

As he left the Los Angeles basin, an overwhelming peace of mind overtook him unexpectedly. He realized he found something on the trail west. He had something new. He had his father's faith in the future, and that alone would carry him forward.

Yuma Crossing

It took Eli and Moses more than two weeks to return to Yuma with the rope necessary to rebuild the ferry. Eli was amazed at how long it took him to prepare meals and care for the mules without Mr. Sue's chuck wagon and the rest of the crews the wagon train provided. When he left Los Angeles to backtrack along the trail to Yuma, his family was ready to go their separate ways. Roland, Lia, and Suzette were still waiting for Juan Pedro's shoulder to heal enough to travel safely. Jacques left with a squad of Hancock's company to find a good trail over Pacheco Pass that could be widened out for a passible road into the Imperial Valley area. Denise and Irwin were long gone for San Francisco with their Uncle Connor on *The Blessed*. It was the first time Eli had been separated from his family and completely on his own. Besides suffering cooking for himself and eating the consequences, loneliness for his family burned with a new intensely. He also missed the security of the heavily armored wagon train he headed up on the journey west.

Moses made a good traveling companion, and his cooking was a lot better than Eli's. After a few days of travel, they settled on a more convenient and comfortable agreement. Eli would hunt and take care of the animals; Moses would cook. One day south of the Vallecito Mountains, Eli was north of the trail hunting deer. He pulled his mount up short when he came across the strong putrescence of decaying flesh. Instinct told him to see what was dead. The stench was strong and widespread. Riding upwind about a quarter mile, he found three wagons around a foul-smelling waterhole. The hapless travelers no doubt had come off the Mojave Desert from the east and found the water, thinking their long-dry trek had finally ended. Ended, it did indeed. Bodies lay in the shade of the wagons, and dead oxen lay around the waterhole. Eli was choking on the stench of rotting bodies and on the verge of losing his breakfast, but he searched through the wagons until he found a diary and logbook. Three families, fourteen people altogether, eight of them young children or teenagers. He kept the diary and logbook to hand over to Major Jenkins in Yuma. By the time he left the deadly pool, he reeked with the smell of death and didn't think he would be able to eat again for several days.

That night Moses roasted two rabbits over their open campfire. Eli ate sparingly and still wanted to stock up on venison before crossing the Mojave. The next morning, he headed north again before the sun rose, but swung well upwind of the poison water. It wasn't long before he was on the track of a herd of deer, and within another hour, he had a handsome buck dressed out and tied across the back of his saddle. He headed east of their last camp to intersect the trail and finally saw Moses in the distance. He didn't want to push the horse hard because it was at least another fifteen miles to the last water hole before they entered the Mojave. It took him till noon when Moses stopped to catch him. Moses smiled and broke out his carving knives, and bone saw, looking forward to eating better for the rest of the crossing to Yuma.

It took seven more days to reach Yuma, the whole return journey taking fifteen days overall from Los Angeles. They arrived late on November tenth, three days after the national election. Eli and Moses found Major Jenkins in his office deep in thought. "Hello, Eli. Hello, Moses. I wasn't expecting ever to see you back here again."

Eli spoke up first, "We came back with a rope, and we're going to fix the ferry. After that, I am going back to find my friend in the Hopi village on the Gila."

"Where's the rest of your family? Especially that pretty little sister of yours."

"Scattered to the winds for the time being. Jacques signed on as a scout with a battalion that Major Hancock is building up at Fort Moore. Suzette, Roland, and Lia are on their way to San Francisco. Our grandmother is probably already there. She is going to settle and buy a newspaper. I expect you will be seeing some of her print passing through here before long. She is making war for women's rights and other issues. Tensions are pretty high over the election. I don't suppose you have heard anything yet?"

"No, it will be four or five more days before the news reaches here. There is trouble already, though. The soldiers from the South are demanding to be in a platoon of their own. If Lincoln is elected, I expect there will be a lot of desertions among their ranks. For my part, I will be glad to see them go. If there is going to be a civil war, I sure don't want it here on my doorstep." Jenkins shuffled some papers on his desk, "Here are all the papers we have received over the last month. Every one of them is predicting a Republican win and civil war if the South succeeds from the Union. I think it is naive, but both sides are also predicting that the war will be over in weeks! Can you believe that?"

"Thanks, Major. If there is a war, we are a long way away. California will side with the North since it joined the Union as a free state. I have a suggestion for you. Why don't you send the southerners to Texas or anywhere east of here? There are other southern sympathizers in California. You won't want them to join forces. I think it would be wise to keep them separated from each other. I could take them as far as the bend in the Gila River. Then I am heading north."

"Not a bad idea. I take it you will be here for several days fixing the ferry. I'll get the southerners together and send them east with you. I appreciate the help. By the way, the ferry is still running with sail and a lot of strong backs pulling oars. The little steamer that pulled it up from the gulf didn't stick around. It was a southern boat and wanted to be in Mexico before the election. It will be great to have the ferry rigged up again. Hit the mess hall for a good meal before you turn in for the night."

The Major was right; it did take several days to rig up the ferry with the hardest job being splicing the eyes into the ends of the rope. By the time Moses and his men finished, there were sixteen soldiers from the South outfitted and ready to head east with Eli. The Major also provided a supply wagon, a chuck wagon, and a cook. The food was pretty ordinary compared to Mr. Sue's cooking, but Eli still appreciated not having to take the time to feed himself. On Monday morning, Eli said his goodbyes to Moses, Amos, and the rest of the river crew and set out for Gila Bend. It must have been that he was now familiar with the trail, or maybe he just liked traveling. He didn't have the feeling that the journey was as endless as he did when crossing the continent for the first time. He had a letter pouch for the trading post at Agua Caliente, and they reached that first destination in five days.

The stage stop for the Butterfield Overland Mail was on the Flap-Jack Ranch. Two men, Martin and Woolsey, owned the stage stop and eked out a modest living trading with the Tonto Apache that surrounded the Agua Caliente hot springs and tending the horses for the stage line. Eli handed them the mail pouch and asked if they had any news about the election. No, was the response, but there was a stage due within the hour. It didn't matter where the soldiers spent the night, so Eli had them make camp back down on the Gila. He was talking with Mr. Martin when some of the soldiers walked in and started to look over the goods. Mostly they wanted candy and other foodstuffs to supplement the bland diet from the chuck wagon.

Woolsey had fresh beef steaks cooked on an open spit fired with dry mesquite. Eli finished with an enormous piece of steak, and it was nearing dark when the sound of the stage could be heard coming up from the river road. More people gathered around the trading post to see what news the stage would bring. The Butterfield Overland Mail originated in two cities. One was Memphis, Tennessee, and the headline on the Memphis Times read,

JOHN C. BRECKENRIDGE SWEEPS THE SOUTH.

Some soldiers that were in the crowd cheered wildly, but the devil is always in the details. Results from California and Oregon had not yet reached the east, and it would not have made a difference anyway. The St. Louis Daily Missouri Republican's headline ran,

ABRAHAM LINCOLN WINS THE ELECTORAL COLLEGE.

Likely some of the southern soldiers didn't understand that the Electoral College was the entity that elected the president to office. The soldiers were ready for a party, though, and the drunken celebration carried on well into the night. Martin, Woolsey, and Eli just shook their heads at the stupidity, but Martin pointed out, "Let them celebrate. We have plenty of whiskeys to sell."

The next morning the soldiers were hungover and wasted. Most of them wouldn't even get out of their bedrolls. There was a total disregard for military discipline, and Eli was completely disgusted. He hitched up his teams and decided to leave without the soldiers. He could easily enough follow the river east on his own. Mr. Martin came to him in the pre-light of dawn and posed an interesting appeal. "Son, you look like a virile young man, and I would greatly appreciate it if you would do me a tremendous favor."

Eli raised his eyebrows and looked pensive, but he at least agreed to hear Martin out. "There is an Indian woman here; she is different from the rest of them. She is from back east. You won't see her until you get away from the soldiers. She can speak all the local languages and can double as a guide and a hunter. I want you to take her with you."

Eli asked, "If she is so useful, why do you want to get rid of her?"

"Well, to be honest with you, she has some quirks. Her nickname is *Walks Naked*. She is nothing but trouble around white people. Woolsey and I want to stay married, and I'll tell you it is damn tough when she is walking around in the buff. Look, she has some sheep and pigs of her own. They won't be any trouble for you. There is plenty of feed along the river. I beg you, if she follows you out of town, please don't send her back."

"What tribe is she from?"

"Humm! I don't know, but it is back east somewhere. New York, I think."

Eli didn't think she wouldn't follow him, but he did tell Martin that he wouldn't turn her back if she did. Little did he know how much this Indian woman would change his life. His loneliness for his family was intense but taking on an Indian woman to ease that problem certainly wasn't in his plans. He finished hitching up his team, saddled his horse, and quietly pulled away from the Flap-Jack Ranch. He was on his way back down to the river when he saw several pigs rooting in the wash and about a half-dozen sheep above on a grassy bench. The woman sat on a log in the wash, and she looked like she had been waiting for him. She got up and whistled, and the pigs left their diggings and walked over to her. The sheep were a little slower but did the same.

The woman at least wasn't naked. She had on buckskin clothing with soft boots and leggings and had a large pack on her back with what looked like a machete sheathed on the side. She started walking behind Eli's wagon. Eli could see she wasn't a bad looking woman at all and understood that her standing around naked could certainly drive a happily married man to distraction. But Eli wasn't married, and while he wasn't immoral by nature, he also wasn't bound by priggish mores of a more strait-laced society. He was literally in the middle of nowhere; he would do as he pleased, and right now, he was more intrigued as to why she had chosen him. It didn't matter; he would stop later on to eat and show her the map with the hill with the X marked on it upstream on the Hassayampa River. More than anything, he just wanted someone to talk with along the trail.

The morning rolled around to midday, and Eli pulled up in the shade of a cottonwood grove along the river for some lunch. He had an ample supply of venison jerky, and he waved the woman over to join him. She walked up from the river bottom, wary at first, but then friendlier as Eli held out a thick slab of jerky for her to eat. She sat down just out of his reach and gnawed a strip of the dried meat off and chewed with a look of contentment on her face. She looked at Eli with her dark eyes, and he looked back. She wasn't a big woman, but certainly not elfin either. Eli thought of her as an Indian version of a gamine woman, a term used by his mother to describe the young Suzette. This woman was lean. Not the lean that comes from starvation, but the muscular lean that is inherited down hundreds of generations of people who hunted and foraged for survival. He was beginning to realize that she was a very attractive woman. Long shiny raven hair hung in waves, longer than her shoulders. There was something else; she didn't smell bad. She smelled of a herb that Eli knew grew on the desert. She caught him looking at her muscular legs as she stretched out in the shade of the cottonwood.

"What is your name?" he asked. "Where do you come from?" After a considerable pause, he asked more gruffly, "Do you speak English?"

She nodded her head, *yes*. *A good start, at least*, Eli thought. He offered her some water, and she accepted that too. *Real progress,* Eli thought. He could push along and make it to the Pima village in two days, but he decided to take it easy. He was a little afraid that the Indian woman would leave him and stay with the Hopi or wander off somewhere else without him. He would rather she stayed with him. In all honesty, he wanted to see her live up to her nickname, but he wouldn't touch her unless she came to him willingly.

Eli spent three days getting to the Pimas. He allowed ample time for the pigs and sheep to root and graze. Grass and roots were in ready supply along the river, and he had no set schedule, and nowhere, in particular, he had to be. Nonetheless, he was glad to reach the home of his friend, Deep Rivers, the Indian guide who guided the wagon train over from New Mexico. The settlement was healthy this visit, and Deep Rivers welcomed him heartily and settled him in his lodge. A host of happy children and some of the neighbors all flocked around Eli wanting to know where his sister, the doctor, was.

"What about the woman?" his friend asked as they drank a round of agave liquor.

"She followed me out of Agua Caliente. I don't know if she will stay with me. She nodded that she could speak English, but she doesn't talk. I don't know anything about her except that she is good with her animals, and she is pretty too."

Deep Rivers punched him on the arm and said, "It's about time you noticed there are women in the world. You were much too serious of a young man when you passed through here with the wagon train." Deep Rivers' wife went out, and with her help, the Indian woman put the pigs and the sheep into a make-shift corral made from mesquite limbs and the dried spines of ocotillo cacti. She brought the Indian woman into the lodge and was talking to her in the Pima language. Deep Rivers listened in and then said, "The woman speaks French, English, my language, Yavapai Apache and her native tongue – Algonquin! Where is that?"

Eli could speak some French, but he was nowhere as skilled as his sister. He looked at the woman and asked, "Est-ce que tu parles français?"

The woman averted her eyes and said just above a whisper, "Oui Monsieur. Español aussi y Inglés."

Eli was amazed and asked a question in English that sounded more like a statement. "You are from back east. How long have you been in the west?"

"More than five years," she answered in perfect English. Eli was more intrigued than ever, especially when she looked deep into his eyes when she answered.

Deep Rivers asked her in his native tongue, "How old are you? What is your name?"

Again, she was embarrassed but answered, "Veintidós. My name is Abàgamibìsàn. It means *Warm Rain* in English. Most white people call me Abby. They can't remember the rest of it."

Now, Deep Rivers was truly amazed and looked at Eli in all seriousness. "My young friend, if you don't keep this one, I will!"

"I'll keep her if she will have me. I want to go up the Hassayampa and find the hot springs on the map with the X we got off the Peralta's men back on the San Pedro." Eli took the map out of his shirt and unfolded it on the floor of the lodge. "Would you go upriver with me?"

Deep Rivers looked troubled and said, "I'll take you up there, but I won't go up on that hill. I told you before, that is a bad place: bad spirits, bad medicine, bad everything. You should find a different place."

"I want to leave in the morning. I have to see it for myself. I need to know what is up there. I want to leave word here though, if my brothers or Suzette come looking for me, would you guide them up there?"

"Of course, I would. But you should reconsider. There is a lot of good lands up above there. Go, make it your own. You don't need the hill. Just leave it alone. Settle where you can farm. Live a happy life. Make a lot of babies with this woman, and the spirits will smile on both of you."

The two old friends talked into the night. There was a bed for Eli in the lodge, but Abby was more comfortable sleeping out by the corral. The full moon was starting to wane, but the air was clear, and the moonlight still shone brightly. Deep Rivers' wife gathered Abby up after midnight and led her into the lodge and made her sit on Eli's pallet. The older woman gave Abby a blanket of her own and turned and walked out of the lodge. Abby was scared. She didn't want to wake Eli, but the night was cold, and so was she. Slowly and quietly as possible, she lay down next to the sleeping Eli, wondering if he truly would keep her. She finally fell asleep and, in the morning, awoke with Eli's arm around her. She slept in her blanket separate from Eli, so she rolled away quietly without waking Eli and went back out to her animals. She sat stoically facing the east and waited for the first light of dawn with some thoughts and feelings she had experienced before but didn't trust.

They left early with Deep Rivers, and about twenty children followed them as far as the road that wound its way north on the west side of the Gila. Some of the older children stayed with them until they reached the mouth of the Hassayampa, but none would go any farther than that. Deep Rivers rode on the driver's seat with Eli, but Abby walked along with her animals, leading Eli's horse by the reins. Each night Abby would put her blanket next to Eli, and while Eli never touched her first, when she cuddled against him for warmth, he didn't push her away. Abby grew more comfortable sleeping with Eli's arm around her.

After four days of travel, they entered a canyon carved out by the fickle Hassayampa. Water flowed on top of the rocks and sometimes on top of the sandy bottom. At the north end of the river gorge, there was only a dry-sandy bottom that made for easy travel. Eli knew they were growing close to the hill. The next day the canyon opened into a wide valley. There was a red hill, high enough to be a mountain, just like the map indicated. It was about five miles away, but in the cold morning air, a wisp of steam could be seen rising from the rounded top. Deep Rivers apologized and said, "This is as far as I go, my friend!" He hugged Eli and turned and walked back into the canyon without another word or even a wave goodbye.

In another hour, Eli and Abby were standing at the bottom of the hill. Hot water flowed down the southeast side, making its way to the Hassayampa. Ancient mesquite covered the hill with cottonwoods growing where the hot water ran. Mesquite trunks tangled and twisted within each other, and brush made climbing the hill almost impossible. Where cottonwood trees lined the hot water stream, the brush was thin, shaded by the big trees. Everywhere the mesquite grew, a deep layer of mesquite beans covered the ground. The pigs loved it; they had arrived in heaven. The sheep nibbled at the beans but preferred the green grass lining the hot water stream. Eli tethered the mules and fed them. He took some supplies from the wagon for a trek up the hill. He wanted to see what was at the top.

They followed the stream up the side of the hill and found a hot springs pool at the top. The hill stood six hundred feet high, and even in the cold air, Eli and Abby raised a healthy sweat before they reached the top. The water rose from the bottom, clear and almost uncomfortably hot. Ten feet in diameter and four to five feet deep, the pool was nature's bathtub in the wilderness. Abby looked at Eli and then started removing her clothes. She started with her soft boots and leggings then started unlacing her buckskins. Eli didn't know what to do, but she reached up and slid his vest off his shoulders and unbuttoned his shirt. His heart pounded, and that wasn't all. More in a rush now, both naked and happily submerged in the water. Eli was relieved that his erect member was now out of sight. The gentle upward current felt good, and where the hot water flowed out of the top of the mountain, it broiled the sand covering the bottom of the pool. They relaxed to the sound of light wind in the trees and the babbling of the stream as it started the tumbling journey down the hill.

Abby came to Eli and pressed against him with her arm around his neck. They kissed passionately, and both of them thought that this was the best place they had ever been. It wasn't the first time for either of them, and it was slow and deeply satisfying. They spent several hours in the pool and on the grass along its sides. Finally, they were sated and dry. They dressed and ate, and then made their way back down the hill. There was a game trail, and they followed it down from the top and reached the bottom about one hundred yards away from where they left the wagon. On the way down the hill, Eli said, "I don't know why Deep Rivers says this is a bad place. It is a wonderful place."

They would stay the night under the wagon. In the morning, Eli would move the wagon to the bottom of the game trail and carry their belongings to the top. For the first time since he left Independence, he felt a deep sense of home.

Abby had no trouble building a fire; there were dry mesquite limbs on the ground everywhere. Eli cut mesquite limbs to build a roasting spit over the fire, and Abby went hunting with nothing more than her machete. She came back about an hour later with four rabbits tied to her belt. Eli didn't know how she did it. She had only a hunting knife and the machete. It was apparent to Eli that those two tools were all she needed to keep them fed. Eli set up a crude spit and had the rabbits turning over a low fire. They sat side by side, hand in hand, and watched the sunset off to the west. They ate their fill and made their bed under the wagon. That night and many more nights to come, they weren't cold or lonely ever again.

It took several days to carry all their goods from the wagon to the top of the hill. Eli turned the mules loose, but they didn't go far. He kept his horse and saddle and walked the big gelding up to the top of the hill. The pigs were nowhere in sight, but Eli could hear them rooting out in the mesquite forest that covered the hill. The sheep didn't leave either. There was grass all along the hot spring's creek and down to some grassy plains on the banks of the Hassayampa. Eli and Abby stayed too. They started scavenging boards from the wagon to build a cabin. Eli was going to survey off a square mile with the summit of the hill in the exact center. He didn't know if there was a land office as yet in this part of the territory, but he would stake his claim to the land and wait to see what developed. He did expect that sooner or later, homesteading would come of age to his mountaintop. His father used the 1841 Pre-emption Act to take up land in Missouri. He would stake out and survey the corners of four one-hundred-sixty-acre claims for the members of the Callahan family and wait for the homestead acts to catch up with him.

He and Abby were the quintessential pioneers. They worked hard and bathed in the pool every evening. Eli was more content than he had been since his parents died in the tornado. He figured that they would stay on the hilltop and watch the world go by until the North and South worked out their differences over states' rights and slavery. There wasn't another human being within sight of the hill. That suited him fine. He held the world at bay; he would take it in small increments as he wanted it. He couldn't think of a reason that would cause Deep Rivers to think the hill was a bad place. At that moment he didn't care if it was a bad place. He felt some new and deep emotions. He wanted to stay on the hill for the rest of his life, as long as Abby stayed with him.

Young Doctor Suzette

It was weeks before Suzette was able to depart from Los Angeles. Juan Pedro was healing nicely, but influenza had set into the Angelinos, and Suzette had her hands full treating the worst of the victims, struggling to bring down the temperatures of the youngsters. Of more concern, Lia contracted the flu before the hard onset of the epidemic. Suzette wouldn't leave Los Angeles until Lia was healthy again. She was more concerned that Lia's baby would be safe. The epidemic wasn't the worst in the history of the young nation, but some of the elderly died, and some young pregnant women lost their unborn babies.

Denise was probably safely in San Francisco by the time Suzette and her troop got on the El Camino Real to head north. Jacques was up north with a platoon of soldiers searching for a pass over the mountains into the California Central Valley. Eli lost himself back into the wild backcountry of the New Mexico Territory. Suzette missed her two brothers deeply, but she had her destiny to pursue. Before she left Los Angeles, she made sure that the letter from the Doctors Way in Fort Union was safely in a mail pouch in Roland's wagon.

They were making their way up the El Camino Real, one Franciscan Mission at a time. Each mission was strangely bereft of the Indians to which they were supposedly administering. Suzette and Roland wanted to know more about the history of the missions. There were twenty-one missions altogether and seventeen between Los Angeles and San Francisco. The Franciscans who ran them were friendly, and most provided corrals and guest rooms for travelers. It helped that Lia looked Hispanic along with Señor Francisco and Juan Pedro. Roland and Suzette were the minority Anglos in their small entourage.

Lia wanted to visit every one of the missions. The missions were built to be a one day's walk from one another to facilitate foot travel and door-to-door safety for the weary traveler. The problem was there were several of them not on the main route of the El Camino Real. They left the Real and went toward the coast after leaving the mission at Santa Barbara. They were glad they did. The Mission La Purisima was one of the best they had encountered so far on their trip north. The California coast was spectacular with grasslands stretching right down to the sea and sandy beaches and coves that it would take a lifetime to explore. The mission itself lay about eleven miles inland on a plain covered with rich-deep grass. The vegetable gardens there were the lushest they had ever seen. The mist and fog from the ocean kept every living thing watered and thriving in the cool but sunny days. The soil was deeper than a man could dig in a day. It would have been easy to spend more than a day there, but Suzette was anxious to get to San Francisco.

The only other trip they made off of the main route was into a valley to visit Mission San Antonio de Padua. Again, this was a rewarding side trip. The valley was perched high in the Santa Lucia Mountains. It was nearly thirty miles long with deep grass, endless herds of deer, numerous small animals, hawks, and the occasional Golden Eagle. The San Antonio River ran through the west side of the valley, and Mission San Antonio de Padua sat in the flat at the north end of the valley. Close to the mission, vaqueros tended to a modest-sized herd of cows. The valley was the most abundant in wildlife they had yet seen, and they thought it was probably more abundant in wildlife than any other place in California. Again, they could have spent days in this out-of-the-way paradise, but Suzette, ever pressing to get to San Francisco, would hurry them along every time they tarried. As it was, it took them more than two weeks to make the trip to San Francisco. A Franciscan in his prime, motivated and walking forty miles a day, could make the trip in ten days, a challenge even for a person on horseback.

It was a cold, wet winter evening when the weary travelers reached Hunters Point on San Francisco Bay. There was a hotel with a livery stable on the south side of Mission Bay called the Racetrack Inn. Roland went in and arranged rooms for everyone before he and Juan Pedro put the wagon, mules, and horses in the livery. Mr. Sue was anxious to get to the Chinese community in San Francisco. He wanted to excuse himself and walked into the fading evening light to find his way north. He would find them later at the medical school Suzette sought to find. Roland pulled Mr. Sue into a fierce bear hug and told him, "Don't get lost, my friend." Mr. Sue just smiled and nodded his head in consent, turned, and walked north bathed in the last dim light of dusk. It was cold, and it was raining hard. Mr. Sue seemed impervious to the weather. He left with nothing more than his staff, his Chinese hat on his head, with no concern for money or belongings.

Lia and Suzette immediately sought the comfort of a hot bath; the men settled for libations in the bar adjoining the restaurant. Talk in the bar all ran to betting on the races and gold and silver mining. Betting on the horses was popular, but betting on investments in the newly developed Comstock Lode raged like wildfire. Rumors were rampant, and stock certificates commonly changed hands several times a night. There was a broker who was selling shares in George Hearst's Ophir Mine. The silver lode lay under the streets of Virginia City. There was another venture in Gold Hill, which lay down the mountain and to the south of Virginia City's Main Street. Roland, Señor Francisco, and Juan Pedro looked like they just arrived off the trails. The hucksters, harlots, and pickpockets left them to their drinks. Roland, though, was adsorbed in the chatter and amazed at the zeal with which the peddlers talked about the riches of the Comstock.

All chatter stopped when Suzette and Lia came to join their men for a good dinner. As the girls entered the bar to find the fellows, all eyes turned their way. The patrons of the bar were more or less the upper crust of San Francisco society, so advances toward the ladies were respectful and easily declined. The barroom returned to its wild chatter and deal-making as Roland, and Juan Pedro stood up and took their ladies by the arm and led them into the dining room. The fare was exquisite with fresh salmon and Dungeness Crab. Lia poked skeptically at the unfamiliar pink fish but then ravished the meal with the hunger of the weary traveler after discovering that the pink fish tasted exquisite. Señor Francisco was particularly impressed with the red wine served with the meal. Roland noted that the wine was from Sonoma, California, produced by the Buena Vista Winery. Now here was an industry Roland could understand. He wondered if any of the brokers in the bar were selling shares in wineries?

The next day Señor Francisco and Juan Pedro set out for the east side of the bay. Señor Francisco was looking for his sister and her family. Supposedly, they had acquired a ranch on a land grant from the Mexican government before control of California fell to the United States after the Mexican American War. Suzette, Roland, and Lia saddled up their horses and rode up to San Francisco. Suzette checked several times to make sure she had her letter of introduction to Dr. Cooper.

It only took a couple of hours to ride around Mission Bay and find the University of the Pacific, a stately four-story brick building located on Mission Street. Suzette entered alone and asked a petite girl with flaming red hair if she could meet with Dr. Cooper. The nameplate on her desk read Miss Bridgette O'Malley, *a fellow Irish woman*, Suzette thought. Miss O'Malley told Suzette that Dr. Cooper was in surgery, but if she wanted, she could watch from the gallery. "By the way, your grandmother came here more than a week ago and left this for you." It was an envelope with nothing more than an address in it. When the girl saw the address, her eyes opened wide, "It's the mansion on Rincon Hill!" After that, she was speechless and just stood and looked at Suzette.

Finally, Suzette broke the spell and asked, "Where is the gallery?" The girl pointed down a hall and indicated it was the last door. Suzette thanked her and walked down the hall and climbed a narrow set of stairs and found her way to a seat in the gallery. The operation in progress was on a man's foot. Dr. Cooper was correcting a congenital deformity commonly called *clubfoot*. The patient was a young man, probably in his early twenties. He was unconscious, sedated with chloroform. There were other doctors and students in the gallery watching the operation and writing notes with determination and talking quietly amongst themselves.

Suzette must have appeared quite the anomaly dressed in her buckskins with the Lefaucheux strapped to her hip. One of the doctors noticed her and likely wanted to embarrass her so she would leave. He asked, "Do you know the name of this condition?"

Suzette smiled at him graciously and answered, "Talipes equinovarus. She could only see the one foot the surgeon was working on, so she asked, "Is it just the one foot, or is he unfortunate enough to have the congenital disability on both feet? Is the operating surgeon, Dr. Cooper? I want to see him. How long do you think this is going to take?"

"Yes, that's Dr. Cooper. I am Dr. Lane, Dr. Cooper's nephew. It is only one foot, so I think Dr. Cooper will be done around two this afternoon. We usually go down to the Willows for a drink after a long surgery. You could meet us there this afternoon." He didn't say a word about Suzette's use of the Latin name for the young man's condition, but it did get his attention.

Suzette left the gallery, said goodbye to Miss O'Malley, and rejoined Roland and Lia on the street. They were watching a man juggling oranges while another man marched around him adorned in an impressive array of one-man-band instruments. A base drum beat loud every time his right foot hit the ground, and a pair of cymbals crashed when his left foot followed in time. There was a horn with a rubber bulb under his arm that he could squeeze, moving his arm in and out like a chicken wing. He wore a harmonica on a holder around his neck and strummed a banjo that was loud enough to echo off the buildings. Every time he passed the juggler, the oranges would fly from the juggler's hands and hit the drum and bounce back in a rapid staccato that fit seamlessly into the rhythm of the song and thrilled the audience — shouts of gaiety and clapping along with coins dropping into an iron stew pot rewarded the duo.

They asked directions to Rincon Hill and were told to go toward the bay, where they would then turn up Second Avenue. Mission Street was teeming with commerce, and the travelers were amazed at the size of the city and the myriad peoples who crowded the streets. Second Avenue climbed up gradually out of the flats of Mission Bay. At the top of the hill, the most beautiful house they had ever seen set on an acre of well-groomed gardens and lawns. It was a mansion indeed, three stories high with a garret built into the roof with windows overlooking the bay and the rest of San Francisco to the north. Suzette hoped this was the right house; she could picture herself up in the garret with her books studying deep into the nights to come.

There were hitching rails in the street in front of the mansion, and further up on the manicured lawn was a polished block of granite with an ornate brass nameplate that said LATHAM. They tied their horses and took their rifles and saddlebags with them as they opened the wrought iron gate and ascended the stairs. Denise opened the door before they reached the top and once again exuded great joy that they completed the trek up the El Camino Real safe and sound. Suzette asked, "Grandmother, how did you come by such a magnificent place to live in such a short time?"

"The owners are in Europe for six months. They were leaving just as I got here. We both use the same bank, and the banker rented me the house while they are away. I have the whole second floor for our living quarters and Suzette; I'm going to put you in the attic. The garret serves as a study, and I think that is what you will want to do. Did you find Dr. Cooper?"

"Yes, but he is in surgery until this afternoon. I was told by his nephew to meet them in a place called the *Willows* at around two o'clock."

"My dear, the *Willows* is one of the seediest bars in the Mission. You can't go down there alone. You will need an army to protect you."

"I think I can manage. Roland and Lia can take me down. It's not like I can't take care of myself!"

Denise backed off. She could see that Suzette was quick to get her back up to anyone who treated her like a child instead of a woman. She had to admit, the young woman standing in the foyer of the mansion wasn't anything like the girl she knew back in Independence. The trials of the trail certainly did make her stronger. Irwin came in and could sense that the reunion was already turning tense. He eased the moment offering to show Roland and Lia to their bedroom. He took Suzette up to the garret. When they got to the top of the stairs, Suzette threw her arms around him and held him in an affectionate hug for a long time. She finally let him go and looked around the attic. There was a simple bedroom with a chamber pot and washbasin, but it was the garret that caught her attention. The view from the windows was spectacular. There were hundreds of ships lined up from Mission Bay up around the crest of the peninsula as far as she could see. Everywhere, there were buildings, houses, and the amazing hustle and bustle of people. It was like a scene out of storybooks about the biggest cities in Europe or the metropolises on the east coast of the US. She thought that she could easily spend the rest of her life here.

There were pen and ink on the writing desk in the garret, and Suzette asked Irwin for a little time. She sat down and wrote a letter to Maria in Bernalillo. She had promised to send for her, and she was making good on her word. She didn't know if Lia's family would send the orphan to San Francisco, but she had to try. She sealed the letter and took it downstairs. She gave it to her grandmother and said, "I want to mail this to New Mexico." Denise took the letter and said she could mail it the next day.

It was approaching two o'clock, and Suzette and Roland were riding down Mission Street looking for the *Willows*. They learned it was a bar and grill and famous for being a rough place. It couldn't be too rough, or Dr. Cooper would have found a better place for an afternoon libation. They found it several blocks down from the University and tied up the horses in front of it. Roland paid a lad a dime to watch the horses, and the boy said, "For a dime mister, you will have all my friends in the neighborhood watching." They drew the Henry rifles out of the scabbards and walked into the bar. Suzette had her rifle on her shoulder, and Roland carried his casually over the crook of his arm. Suzette asked about Dr. Cooper, and a man well into his cups pointed to the back of the bar.

The aisle was narrow with burly men bellied up to the bar, and others packed in small groups, swearing, drinking, smoking cigars, and as usual, lying to one another. As Suzette threaded her way down the aisle, a hush fell over each of the groups as they noticed her. She didn't look like a barroom floozy, but the men couldn't figure out just what she was either. About halfway down the aisle, a big man with a full black beard stepped away from the bar to block her way. Suzette stopped and spat on the floor. That wasn't something anybody expected, even Roland. She just said calmly, "You are in my way."

The big man had a wicked smile, and his eyes glazed with wicked intent. He didn't move, he just said with the slurred words of the inebriate, "You' al will be spending some time with me, honey." Then he made the worst mistake of his day; he tried to grab Suzette. She stepped back, and his badly timed grope closed on thin air.

Suzette said again, this time with more emphasis, "You are in my way. Let me by!"

The drunk tried to touch her again. Suzette turned the Henry on her shoulder, so the stock was horizontal and rammed the butt of it into the man's chin. He staggered back a step then fell to his knees. The man was angry and red in the face. When he tried to sit up, Suzette put him on his back with a kick to his chest. The bar was quiet, and then the bar cheered. Some of the patrons wanted to call her the *top dog*. But a female dog is called a *bitch,* and they thought better of it. Suzette and Roland walked by the man on the floor. He was struggling to draw a breath. She walked up to the table in the back where Dr. Cooper and his nephew were sitting.

There were some other doctors and students there, none of them women. All had been watching Suzette confront the drunk in the aisle. Suzette pulled her letter of introduction out of her shirt and handed it to the nephew. Dr. Cooper was sitting with an expression of extreme pain on his face. The left side of his face looked distorted like he was a stroke victim, and his right hand was shaking spasmodically. The nephew formally introduced himself. "I am Dr. Levi C. Lane. Dr. Cooper, here is my uncle. He has a neurological illness, and right now, he is having an attack." He opened the letter and read it. "Very impressive," he commented. "Why haven't you just declared yourself an M.D. by now? You are certainly qualified."

"Two reasons: first, it is almost impossible for a woman to break into the field without a formal degree, and second, I want to learn surgery -- all kinds of surgery. I understand that Dr. Cooper is at the forefront of his field. I want to enroll in his medical school and study under him."

"I am the administrator of the Medical College. Come in first thing in the morning, and I will admit you. After that, you will have to work out your program with my uncle. I expect that if you set yourself to the hard work, you can finish here in a year."

"I'll see you in the morning." Suzette turned and walked back through the aisle to the front door. This time no one got in her way. She stopped at the front door and smiled back at the barroom. She knew all about turf and territory. She just made a substantial claim on this part of Mission Street.

She didn't return directly to the mansion with Roland and Lia. She stopped at the University and had the receptionist show her to the library. She got down a large tome titled *Human Circulatory System, Illustrated*, and another on human bone anatomy. The books must have weighed five pounds. She rode back to Rincon Hill with the books under her arm. Roland was at the street, busy sending for the rest of their belongings from the Racetrack Inn. She put Patches up in the stable next to the mansion and went up to her garret to begin the work on her formal medical degree. Today was the best and happiest day of her young life. She already forgot about the incident in the bar.

The next day Suzette was up early and begged a bowl of oatmeal from the housekeeper long before anyone else stirred. She intended to walk to the medical school, not wanting to worry about her horse on the streets during the day. Denise and Roland had an appointment at the Wells Fargo Bank on Montgomery Street. They would go by carriage; the Latham mansion had a number of them at their disposal. The bank was going to give them a summary of the assets of the Callahan estate.

Mr. Sue had returned from the city and already was ensconced with the kitchen staff. He learned from the Chinese grapevine where the Callahans were staying without having to meet Suzette at the medical school. He always rose early, ready to walk Suzette to the medical school. They arrived at the University too early and found the doors still locked. Mr. Sue went across the street to a vendor that had an open window in the corner of a small granite block building and returned with two cups of tea and some dumplings. Suzette commented that it was a lot better breakfast than oatmeal.

She sat on the steps and reviewed the names of the blood vessels in the foot and leg that she committed to memory last night. She was interrupted by a man who introduced himself as Dr. Fillmore. He had the young receptionist on his arm and went up the stairs to unlock the door. Suzette followed him inside and then had Miss O'Malley direct her to Dr. Cooper's office.

She was surprised to find Dr. Cooper asleep on a couch at the side of the room. Suzette was concerned that Dr. Cooper wasn't over the seizure of the previous day and gently shook him by the shoulder to wake him. He moaned and woke up, acting like he didn't realize he had fallen asleep in his office. He rose, struggling to be fully awake and said, "Good morning. I assume you are the young woman that wants to enter the program here. I am Dr. Cooper, President of the University of the Pacific Medical School."

Suzette realized that he had no memory of their encounter at the bar the previous day. She introduced herself again and handed him the Way's letter of introduction. She didn't want to usurp his authority and remind him that Dr. Lane said yesterday that he would admit her this morning, but she didn't have to. Dr. Lane put his head through the door and said, "Dr. Cooper, uncle, I see you spent the night here again, and you have met Miss Callahan, the young lady I told you about that looked us up yesterday down at the Willows. I'm impressed with her qualifications and accomplishments. She wants to study surgery under you. With your approval, I'm going to sign her up."

Dr. Cooper seemed distracted and just uttered, "Humm! Lea Way and her husband are in Fort Union. Interesting!" He looked at Suzette, sizing her up as if for the first time. "Do you always walk around armed?" he asked.

"Yes, it's safer for a woman, especially at night. Is that going to be a problem?"

"No, maybe I will assign you as my bill collector." Dr. Cooper laughed at his feeble attempt at humor. "You know your grandmother has already assured your enrollment here with a generous donation. She also tells me that you are very wealthy in your own right. Is that true?"

"My brothers and I are the heirs to the Callahan Meadows brewery and complex south of Independence, Missouri. We came west after a tornado killed our parents. My brother Roland takes care of our money along with my grandmother. You would have to ask him for an exact accounting, but yes, one could say I am a woman of considerable means."

"Why didn't you go abroad to study? You certainly have the means, and women are more readily accepted in the medical schools in Europe."

"Is that what you want me to do? Lea Way encouraged me to come here. Was that a mistake?"

"No, not at all. It's just that I don't know where to place you in the program. Have you ever performed a surgery?"

"Well, yes. On the trail, I set many compound fractures and even performed an appendectomy. All my patients lived if that is your next question."

"How about I convene all the doctors this morning, and we give you an oral exam to evaluate where to place you in the program. Would you be willing to submit to that?"

"Certainly, but usually, I would have more time to prepare for an exam. But I will try my best, and then you and your staff can decide what to do with me."

"Good, let's go see if breakfast is ready. You can meet the rest of the doctors, and after we eat, we'll move up to the big lecture hall for your review."

Suzette was uneasy with the plan but had little choice than to agree. Breakfast was quite good with fresh bacon and eggs and an inexhaustible supply of rich black coffee. She sat at Dr. Cooper's right with the rest of the doctors introducing themselves and chit-chatting about cases they would see that day. There were about thirty students in the dining hall, and most of them looked on, giving Suzette some hard stares of disapproval. There were no women among the doctors or the students. Dr. Cooper announced that they would all meet in the lecture hall on the third floor.

As she was leaving the dining room, Bridgette gave her a notebook and an ornate fountain pen engraved with U of P Medical School. It was a small gesture, but Suzette was grateful and felt more welcome. As Bridgette walked down the hall, Dr. Fillmore emerged from the men's room and put his arm around Bridgette and pulled her into a brief hug. He groped her breast but turned her loose when he saw Suzette watching.

After a short break in the restroom, the staff convened in the lecture hall. Dr. Cooper stood at the podium and signaled Suzette to join him. Her stomach was a nervous ganglion of un-reconciled loose ends. She wondered if the oral exam was a standard for entrance to the university. She imagined the hundreds of questions the doctors might ask her. Dr. Cooper started the proceedings by delineating the dilemma of not knowing where to place Suzette in the program. He then opened up the floor to questions.

The first question had nothing to do with medicine. It came from Dr. Fillmore. "You arrive here with quite a reputation. How many people have you killed, and how do you reconcile seeking to join a healing profession considering your background?"

Suzette wasn't intimidated. She walked out to the front of the podium and answered. "I didn't keep count. It was a matter of survival. If you were there, I expect that you would have been thankful for my protection. And if you were injured, I would have taken care of you the best I could."

The next question was easy, "What's this little bone here below the sternum?"

"The xiphoid process."

"Can you spell it?"

"Yes, X-I-P-H-O-I-D." Suzette was beginning to enjoy this. Before another doctor could present the next question, she added, "In Latin, it is *processus xiphoideus*. Do you want me to spell that one too?" The doctor asking the question shook his head no.

Dr. Fillmore again, "Is it true you shot a man in the back."

"Yes."

"How do you justify that as self-defense?"

"He was a scout for a larger band of Apache that wiped out a Peralta Family patrol less than a mile from our camp on the San Pedro River.

Fillmore wouldn't let loose of it. "Yet you shot him in the back, and the newspaper said he was running away. That wasn't self-defense!"

Suzette had enough. She walked out from behind the podium again and up the stairs to the row where Dr. Fillmore sat in the aisle seat. "Let me ask you a question, Dr. Fillmore. Have you ever spent a night in the dark in the wilderness waiting for the Apache to attack? Have you ever even treated an Indian of any American tribe? Have you ever been the object of someone who desired to molest you sexually? I have, and I'm still here because I made the right decision at the right time. If you are so interested in my time on the trail, read the memoir my grandmother is publishing. I'll answer any more medical questions, but Dr. Fillmore, I won't put up with any more of your bias, anti-woman bullying." Suzette turned and went down to the podium. Fillmore was turning red with anger as the rest of the staff clapped and gave her a rollicking here-here.

Dr. Cooper got the exam back on track. "How many bones of the foot can you name?"

"All of them; all twenty-six." She listed them and then named all of the blood vessels. She was halfway through the muscles and tendons when Dr. Cooper stopped her.

"Young lady, that is more than adequate. Any more questions from the staff?"

The doctor Suzette sat next to in the gallery above the surgery the day before asked, "What did you think of the surgery yesterday?"

"I don't mean to offend, but your surgery isn't clean and a long way from sterile. Several doctors and students that were on the floor yesterday weren't even wearing masks. The survival rate in the US for surgery right now is only fifty percent. Some of those unfortunates die of their ailments, but the rest die of infection. I operated on the trail in the worst of conditions, and I didn't lose anyone. I discovered a treatment for infection that I intend to introduce into medical practice. It comes from some herbal medicine, first discovered by the Comanche. It's called aspergillus, I brought an ample supply with me from New Mexico, and I want to study it while I am here at the university."

Dr. Fillmore again, this time with an outburst, "So you want to change what years of medical practice deems their best methods. Who exactly do you think you are?"

Suzette had enough of this arrogant prick. She walked up the aisle again to where Fillmore sat like a little god in the aisle seat. She got right in Fillmore's face. "How many of your patients die from infection, Dr. Fillmore? And another thing, how many young women like Bridgette have you molested?" She drew her revolver, cocked it, and put it to Fillmore's forehead. "You try that with me, and I will kill you." Filmore paled and kept quiet, cowering in the chair.

Dr. Cooper rose to diffuse the confrontation. "That will be quite enough, Miss Callahan. Put the gun away. More than seventy-five percent of Dr. Fillmore's surgery patients have died from infection. He has, however, taken on some of the most difficult cases that have come to our attention, so we have allowed him some leeway there. Leave us now, and when you come back, please check your weapon at the front desk with Miss O'Malley."

Suzette holstered the revolver, and the color returned to Dr. Fillmore's face. She left the lecture hall looking one last time back at Dr. Fillmore. Bridgette was at the door listening. Her terrified eyes told all. Suzette tried to reassure her, "Maybe he will leave you alone now."

Suzette's attempt at reassurance didn't help, Bridgette broke down crying. "I – I – I need this job. I am the only one in my family that works. It is hard for the Irish here. If I get fired, my family will starve. Please don't aggravate Dr. Fillmore any farther. He will take it out on me. Please, please, I beg you."

“Don’t worry, Bridgette. No one is going to fire you. If they do, I will hire you at twice what they pay you to carry my books.”

Bridgette relaxed and smiled at the joke, but she didn’t quite believe Suzette. Suzette exited the front door of the Medical College. Mr. Sue was waiting on the steps and asked her, “How did it go?”

“Not good. I doubt that the good doctors will let me in; they were expecting a meek, subservient woman. I don’t think I came anywhere close to meeting their expectations. Let’s go back to grandma. I’m not even sure I want to stay in San Francisco at the moment. They walked down toward the bay and turned up to the mansion. Before they reached the front door, a runner hailed them from the street. Breathlessly, he ran up and handed her a note. Suzette smiled; it was from Dr. Cooper. It read, “You are accepted if you still want to join us. I put Dr. Fillmore on a probationary leave. Please see me first thing in the morning.” Mr. Sue gave her two thumbs up, and they went in to tell Denise the good news.

Sierra Nevada Mother Lode

A few days later, when Suzette returned from the university, she found Roland and Denise sitting in the parlor with a stately looking gentleman who introduced himself as Jim Parish, the Chief Financial Officer of the Wells Fargo Bank. Denise was trying her best to put the man at ease, but he was either nervous by nature or intimidated by a successful, wealthy businesswoman who was making some heavy demands on him. Suzette listened for more than thirty minutes while the banker tried his best to talk her grandmother out of a hostile takeover of the *Alta California* Newspaper.

Finally, the sparring got around to a summary of the Mercier and Callahan fortunes. Denise had sold her newspaper conglomerate in Missouri along with several other interests she owned, like the mansion in Independence and was sitting on approximately eight million dollars. Her cash made up a healthy percentage of the assets in the Wells Fargo Bank of San Francisco. Then Mr. Parish started to list the assets of the Callahan heirs. There were some properties in Missouri, including the original three thousand acres of *The Meadows,* the railroad, and the brewery. Mr. Parish largely spoke to Roland and only acknowledged Suzette with a glance her way from time to time.

Suzette was getting a little annoyed but let the banker ramble on through the asset list. There was stock in the railroad and steel companies, and minority positions in some coal and lead mines in Missouri. The brewery account alone had over twelve million dollars in it. Mr. Parish concluded with the estimate that each of the four Callahan heirs was worth a little over fourteen million dollars. Not all of that was cash. If they wanted the fourteen million in cash, they would have to liquidate all the assets.

Suzette was fed up with being ignored. She set off towards a corner on a settee with Irwin. Lia had come in and sat with Roland. Suzette got up and went over and sat down next to her brother. Mr. Parish stood up out of politeness, thinking that the meeting was drawing to a close. Suzette caught Mr. Parish with several questions before he could make his exit. "What would it take to restore the brewery in Independence? You seem to know a lot about the assets. How many of the people are still left there? What are the proceeds from the sawmill, and how many of the other cottage industries are still intact?" Roland beamed at his sister with pride. Lia was quite amazed at what she heard, not sure what her role in this would be. She was relieved, though, that Suzette was speaking up for herself and asserting a role for the female side of the family.

Mr. Parish seemed to ratchet up one more level of nervousness. He wasn't used to being questioned and thought his presentation was adequate for the time being. He answered honestly, however. "I truly don't have that much detail. Our agent in Independence could be contacted and tasked with finding answers to all your questions."

"Good; please do that, Mr. Parish. I want a full accounting, and while your agent is busy with his research, I want a full report on the status and financial strength of the hospital in Independence. If it is for sale, I want to buy it. Have your man inquire if you would."

"Miss Callahan, I have to remind you that you are a minor, and while the provisions of your father's will did not appoint a trustee, it would be most irregular for you to make decisions concerning your money until you at least reach the age of eighteen. Twenty-one would be better."

That did it. Suzette stood up to make her next point. Mr. Parish suddenly realized that he had gone too far. He looked to Denise for support but only found the same look of pride that her brother used to encourage his sister. "Mr. Parish, please take what I say next to heart." Suzette smiled to ease the banker and continued sweetly. "None of us but Eli are *'of age'*, on which you seem overeager to capitalize. Perhaps you wish to use that to stay in control of our money. Make no mistake; we will not accept you or any other member of your bank as our overseers. All decisions concerning mine and my brothers' holdings will be made by us and us alone. Is that clear?"

"Most irregular, but yes Miss Callahan, that is abundantly clear."

"My first request is that you put all of my money that you hold in your bank or anywhere within the Wells Fargo system into gold. If you can't find enough gold, you can supplement with silver. Hold out ten thousand in a checking account. I want to make some improvements to the surgery at the University of the Pacific Medical School. I will be there at least six months, maybe a year. If you have any questions, you can contact me at the college, or send word here through my grandmother." Suzette held out her hand to indicate the meeting with Mr. Parish was over. "Thank you, Mr. Parish. I will expect another report in a week." Suzette shook his hand, then turned and walked out of the room.

Everyone was amazed, especially Denise. She was thinking, *who is that woman, and what has she done with my granddaughter*? Mr. Parish left after a short discussion with Roland, and he was feeling lucky that he still had the account. Denise found Suzette in the kitchen, making a sandwich to carry up to her garret. She had to ask, "You said that you would be at the university for six months. Aren't you going to do the whole four-year program?"

"Sorry, grandmother. That banker was a total surprise. I went through the oral exam today, and the result is I only have to take a couple of courses and attend and assist at all of Dr. Cooper's surgeries. If I complete those requirements, the university will grant me my M.D. in June with the graduating class."

Denise pulled her granddaughter into a hug, "I'm so proud of you. Jessica always said you should already be a doctor. What are you going to do with the money you set aside for the university?"

"First, I am going to enclose the gallery above the surgery in glass so that we can sterilize the operating room. If there is money left and they will let me, I'm going to build a greenhouse on the roof to grow astragalus and other herbs I learned about from the Indians."

There was a ruckus in front of the house. Roland came running into the kitchen, "You got to come to see this." There was a parade in the street. At least a thousand Chinese people led by a huge red dragon, twenty feet high and a hundred feet long were arriving from the north. At least a hundred men carried the dragon along on long poles, and the long body weaved back and forth like a huge snake crawling down the street. They must have come down to the Mission from Chinatown. Firecrackers and fireworks of all kinds were banging and throwing sparks into the sky. Behind the dragon was a rickshaw gilded with gold. The dragon passed the house, and the rickshaw turned into the drive. More firecrackers, drums, and Chinese crash cymbals kept the people in the street in step. The dragon turned around and came to a stop at the gate, ready to lead the parade back up to Chinatown.

Mr. Sue stepped out of the rickshaw, and an older Chinese woman in a beautiful white Zhongshan suit with elegant silk embroidered gold trim got out with him and kissed him. She got back in the rickshaw without a word and joined the parade that started back up the street. Mr. Sue was embarrassed at the spectacle, standing there in the drive at the bottom of the steps dressed in his usual casual clothes, his staff, and satchel, his only possessions. "My sister," he said apologetically. "She has a real penchant for the outrageous."

Suzette skipped down the steps and drew Mr. Sue into an affectionate hug. "We have missed you; when you left me at the college a couple of days ago, I wasn't sure you would return. I'm glad you are back."

"Where else would I be. My sister's life is not mine. She is flamboyant and ostentatious, and when I told her you were living in the mansion, she organized this parade to bring me back. She loves making a spectacle of herself. I love her dearly, but I have to live at a distance. By the way, I am hungry. What's for dinner?" Everyone laughed, and they welcomed him into the mansion. He had only been away a short while, but already there was a lot of catching up to do. Everyone wanted to know about the sister.

Mr. Sue was impressed with the mansion and was particularly pleased that Suzette had a private place to study and keep to her schedule. He would accompany her to school and back every day. Maybe the university kitchen needed a cook. If they couldn't afford one, he would offer his services for free so that he could keep the same hours as Suzette. He cautioned that she should not be walking back and forth by herself. It wasn't that he was worried that she couldn't take care of herself. He was worried that even a small incident would increase her visibility in the Mission District. She was already famous enough, and all agreed that if word got out about her wealth, she would be a prime target for a kidnapping.

The next day Roland booked passage for himself and Lia on the *Empire City* steamboat to a town on the Tuolumne River that bore the same name as the steamboat. Their horses would make the trip across the bay and up the rivers on a stable barge, towed by the boat. The *Empire City* was a small boat, only one-hundred sixty feet long. There were hundreds of small boats like it servicing all the tributaries of the Sacramento and San Quaquin rivers. He and Lia would be leaving in two days. They would find John Gould and Mary, then head south to round the Sierra Nevada and make their way across the Mojave into New Mexico Territory. They expected to find Eli on his hill by early spring. If he weren't there, they would return and wait for Suzette to finish with her medical training.

The two days went by quickly. Mr. Sue volunteered at the University kitchen so that he came and went with Suzette any time of the day or night. He was quick to point out that she was followed by a group of thugs, to and from the school. Figuring out the intent of the men following her was not hard. Mr. Sue told Suzette not to worry about it; she should focus on her studies; security was his and only his concern.

The morning that Roland and Lia were due to leave, Suzette and Mr. Sue were up early and had to wait an hour or so to say goodbye. Suzette hated wasting time. She pushed herself hard, taking two extra courses over and above what Dr. Cooper required. One was German, and the other was medical jurisprudence. Walking back and forth to the University, along with eating and sleeping, was the only time through the day she would take off from her studies. She often had a textbook out at the dinner table and worked late into the night, seven days a week. She was determined to not only earn her M.D.; she was determined to be the best doctor possible.

Roland and Lia were enjoying the steamboat ride. They left from Steamboat Point by eight in the morning and stopped in Benicia on the Carquinez Straights. The Captain had them up in the wheelhouse and was giving them a tourist guide's narrative of the sights along the way. They all went ashore for the lunch break; the rest of the day would be spent steaming up the San Joaquin River and then taking the Tuolumne River to Empire City. It was dark when they reached their destination, and they spent the night on the riverboat. Their horses were off the barge and on the bank at dawn, and they set out to make their way to Amador City, the last known location of John Gould. In the few letters that they received from him over the years, he never mentioned Mary or anything about family. His news was always about work and engineering projects at the mines.

Roland checked them into the Imperial Hotel in Amador City. There was an Irish girl at the front desk. A small woman, elfin in appearance. Roland asked, "Where would I find a friend of mine, John Gould and his wife, Mary?"

"John Gould, heh? He's a strange one he is. His office and residence are upstairs in the back. We seldom fill the hotel now that the gold rush has come and gone, so we rent him four rooms up there. He has built them into a fine suite. Mary and the children are nice, but I can't understand John. He comes and goes; sometimes, he goes for weeks at a time. I think he is home at the moment. His boys are grown and live and work in Jackson, underground at the Argonaut. Mary spends most of her time down here with us when John is gone."

"Thanks, we'll be staying for several days. I'll get my wife Lia settled and put the horses in the livery and then go up and see him."

Lia helped with the horses. The stable hands couldn't take their eyes off of her. They didn't see many women passing through, let alone one as unique and beautiful as Lia. She said to them, "Take good care of my horse gents," as she slid her Henry rifle out of the scabbard. She also untied her saddlebags and slung them over her shoulder as the men watched, completely enthralled. Roland just tolerated the attention they were lavishing on his wife. Every time it happened, he just remembered how lucky he was to have married such a beautiful woman.

They climbed the back stairs of the hotel and knocked at the door. A burly man with a long graying beard answered. He had no idea as to who the handsome young people were. Roland was quick to set his perplexed expression at ease. "You're John Gould, I assume?"

"Yes, lad, and who might you be?"

"I, sir, am Roland Callahan, and this is my wife, Lia."

John just stared in silence, taken aback that anyone from Independence would care to look him up after all these years. Mary pushed him to the side and drew the Callahans through the door. "Please excuse John, he is a great engineer, but his social skills are way on the negative side of the equation." She led them to a small living room and pushed the chairs around so they could sit comfortably facing one another. "I haven't seen you since you were an infant. Please tell me how your father and mother are? They are two of the most generous and loving people I have ever known."

Mary cried as Roland told of the tragedy that the tornado wrought on their lives. John asked about the railroad and their oldest boy, who returned to Independence to operate it. It took hours to relate all that had transpired since John and Mary left Independence. It was getting late in the day, and Lia asked if she could help with dinner. "Oh, I don't cook, dear. We eat down in the dining room. We'll all go down there now and order up a big meal. I bet you're famished after that boat ride."

Down in the dining room, they were the only patrons until a well-dressed man took up the table next to them. Mary was shaking her head *no* at John with a look that said – *you better not*! The man turned to them though and said, "Hello, John. Hello, Mary. Who are these young people you are entertaining tonight?"

Roland got up and shook the man's hand. "I'm Roland Callahan, and this is my wife, Lia."

The man recognized the last name because his eyes flashed to dollar signs as he held Roland's hand longer than customary and introduced himself. "My good sir, I am Steven R. Peterson, mining entrepreneur, and a stockbroker. Welcome to the Mother Lode. What brings you to town?"

Mary was shaking her head *no* again while Roland explained why they had traveled across America and found their father's old friends, John, and Mary here in Amador City. Mr. Peterson couldn't be more pleased as he connected the dots and thinking about how he could take the best advantage of new money in town. Mary broke into the conversation, "Steven, Roland, and Lia are busy with dinner now and tired from their trip up the river from San Francisco. I am sure that you will see them around town tomorrow, but for tonight you should leave us in peace so we can eat without having to digest your myriad mining deals."

Mr. Peterson took the hint and sat down at his table with his back to them. Mary gave her husband a stern look. There was much more to this story, but Lia turned the conversation to her pregnancy, and the men knew that any more discussion about mining was an absolute taboo at Mary's dinner table. They finished their meal and bid goodnight to Mr. Peterson and retired to their rooms for the night.

In the morning, Mary knocked on their door quietly as not to wake them if they were still asleep. Roland and Lia were up, however, and ready to go down to breakfast. Mary filled them in how Peterson was a smarmy character, and swindled John out of most of his money in wild stock promotions and deals up and down the Mother Lode. "John is a respected engineer and has built many of the hoist houses and compressor works on the hard rock mines. But he is a bad judge of character and an even worse at investments. We get by here really well, but John has wasted a lot of money chasing the next big strike. Peterson has an office down the street. He will sell you stock in any company you express an interest in, even ones that are privately held and not traded on the San Francisco Exchange. Don't give him a dime. He will only keep coming back for more and more. I had to threaten to leave John to get him to break the cycle. I manage all the money now. If I could get him to leave here, I would go in a minute."

Roland responded with caution, "I don't have anything going on at the moment, but if I do, I will send for you and John in a heartbeat. We are going to travel down the Sierra Nevada and cross over to go back into the New Mexico Territory. Eli is staked out on a hill up in the wilderness. I think we can find him, but as far as I know, there is no gold there. We will write and stay in touch. If I can, I will come up with something to get John to leave here, but I know that is going to take something extraordinary and challenging. Let's see what some time brings us."

After breakfast, Roland and Lia walked down Main Street. Amador City wasn't a city at all but a well-established town. There was only one street with a few houses off the main drag along the alleys that paralleled Main Street. As expected, Peterson saw them passing his office and ran out into the street to welcome them in. Roland was amused, but Lia was cautious. As Roland crossed the porch, he saw a flyer for a bare-knuckles championship fight taking place in Angels Camp in several days. The prize money was one thousand dollars for anyone who could go three rounds with the reigning champion, a bruiser named Robert Day, who went by the moniker *End of Days* to advertise his unblemished record. Roland was interested; he hadn't been in a fight since the bout with Bent's Brawler back in Fort Wise. Lia saw him reading the flyer and was immediately the worried wife. She wasn't with Roland yet when he fought at Fort Wise, but she had heard about it and how Suzette broke Bent's bank, putting down a hundred dollars on their friend, the long odds Chinaman, Mr. Sue.

Peterson all but pulled Roland off the porch and into his office. He had a board posting all the stocks he was an agent for, along with the last known price for each from the San Francisco Exchange. A number of the offerings had two or three gold stars behind their names. Peterson explained that these were mines where he had inside information that the mines were on the verge of big strikes or expansions that would send their stock prices through the roof. He was fervent and overzealous, and Roland could easily see how people would be taken in by his sincerity and enthusiasm but could also identify with Mary's depiction of smarmy. Roland sat in a chair in front of Peterson's desk, and Lia stood behind him with her hands on her husband's shoulders. Peterson was mesmerized by the beautiful Mexican woman and kept returning his gaze to her attractive cleavage. Lia helped him out by unbuttoning the top two buttons of her blouse and fanning herself with one of the brochures off Peterson's desk.

As Roland kept declining the deals offered, Peterson got more and more into the hard sales pitch. "Son, I know you probably aren't familiar with gold mining, but I assure you, you are missing an opportunity of a lifetime here."

Roland kept declining regardless of how badly Peterson was trying to make him feel about missing out. He finally asked, "How far is it to Angels Camp?"

"Only about thirty-five miles. Why? Are you going up there for the fights?"

"Maybe. Thanks for the presentation. I don't want to invest in any gold mining opportunities at the moment, but I will keep some of the offerings in mind." With that, Roland got up and walked out of the office without shaking Peterson's hand. Lia smiled at him as they walked up and down the street, window shopping, and buying a few items they would need on the ride over the Sierras.

Roland did find his way to Angels Camp. Lia wouldn't beg him not to fight; she knew that if Roland decided to fight, she would not be able to stop him. She was thinking about how much money she had to bet on him if he was going to go into the ring. They found Robert Day's training camp in a park on the edge of town. Roland watched the champ sparing with a few contenders. He wasn't very impressed with the boxer's ability. Mostly he was like Bent's blacksmith. Big and strong with a long reach but slow on his feet and soft in the middle. Roland looked at his wife and smiled. He didn't have Mr. Sue to stage a farce to drive up the odds, but maybe he and Lia could pull something off on their own. They settled into a poker game in the Frog Jump Bar, and Lia worked her magic again with her extraordinary looks. Roland won about five hundred dollars in gold while the other players spent all their time looking at Lia instead of concentrating on the game. Mostly they placed large bets on bad hands. It was easy for Roland to take their gold.

He bought several rounds of drinks for the table and brought up the subject of the fights. Every man at the table believed that there wasn't a man in this part of California that could beat Day. They believed that when Day went back east, he would come back as the national heavyweight champion. Only the ignorant would bet against him. Roland thought to himself that only the ignorant would bet on an untrained boxer with a soft middle, but that was good for the odds. He asked about the odds. The standard was ten to one. The betting and the purse based on the odds was a sophistication that hadn't arrived at the Mother Lode yet. Lia knew Roland was going to fight. She stepped in and did her part. "I'm going to bet my winnings from today's game on the fight tomorrow. I'm going to put my money down on a boxer from out of town. He's not that great of a boxer, but he is damn tough. I'll give you all a chance to get your money back. Who is holding the purse?"

All the men were falling over themselves to show her to Utica Park and get her to Day's manager. Roland watched from the sidelines as Lia baited the manager into something higher than ten to one odds. The manager was no fool. He asked, "How much will you bet?"

"I'll put down five hundred dollars if you will give me twenty to one."

"I can't go that high."

Lia smiled at the greedy man and started to walk away. A smartly dressed man at the manager's elbow told her to wait and pulled Day's manager into a private conversation. Day himself was up in the ring, bouncing around and throwing roundhouse punches at the air that even a child could duck. Roland took it all in watching the man's moves and noticed that after a minute of his antics, he was breathing hard. Day's manager turned back to Lia and said, "We can cover your bet. Mr. Reimer here has the money down in the bank. Who is your boxer anyway?"

Lia nodded towards Roland, who was trying to make himself as small and weak looking as possible. Lia said, "I am betting gold. If my man wins, I want gold for my payment."

More conferencing with the banker and Day's manager said, "Done. I want the money now."

"No, I will bet the money before the fight, as is the custom. For all I know, your 'boy' will run away with the money and not even show up for the fight. Day's manager turned red, but that was a weak response compared to Day's reaction. Mr. Day was a true berserker. He had overheard the conversation and was turning purple with rage. Roland thought he would even foam at the mouth with a little more encouragement. The setting couldn't be more perfect. He followed Lia out of the park, and they walked down the street and took a room in the Long Jump Hotel. The stable boy took their horses and put them in the livery.

Roland and Lia went into the dining room and ordered two steak dinners. Lia took out the bag of winnings from the poker game and counted out the money. There were some double eagles and around ten ounces of free gold, mostly nuggets and one fair-sized vial of flakes and powder. She kept out the free gold and made up the five hundred dollars with double eagles from Roland's money belt. There were a lot of onlookers, but none would approach the young couple with their Navy Colt 0.44's on the table and their

Henry rifles leaning against the wall within easy reach. Between them, Roland and Lia had more firepower than the law enforcement and most of the miners in Angles Camp combined.

The next day the town was abuzz with the news of the big bet. There were a dozen boxers on the docket, so of course, Roland signed up to be last. At noon, they walked down to the park. Robert Day was strutting around the ring; his hands taped ready for the first fight. Lia placed her bet, putting down the bag of gold. The manager and the banker counted out the coins. Lia asked, "Where's your money, gents?" The banker said, "I am not coming down here with ten grand in gold with no security. If your man wins, we'll go down to the bank, and I will pay you there."

Lia picked up her bag of gold. "Not good enough. I put down my money; I believe it is custom that you put down yours to cover the bet. I am a patient woman, go get your money, or my *'man'* is off the docket." To emphasize her point, she chambered a round in the Henry and stood there at port arms. There was nothing but hesitation on the banker's part. Lia kept up the taunting. She flicked her hair in the wind and asked, "What's the matter gents? Are you afraid I'm going to steal your gold? I don't need to. I am going to win it fair and square. That is if you have it. I will believe it when I see it." The chagrined banker was trapped. If he didn't produce all the money currently wagered, his ability to pay would be in question. They didn't have any intention of paying any winnings, let alone ten grand in one fell swoop, but now their credibility was on the line.

Roland was distracted, watching a small man struggling to pedal a velocipede up the gentle road to the park. The weird bicycle had a large wheel in front and a very small one trailing. It was easy to see why it was hard to peddle. The large front wheel sported red, white, and blue cloth streamers that must have made a colorful pinwheel when the bicycle was moving fast, but just offered more air resistance as the man peddled up the hill. A man to Rolands left muttered in his ear, "It's the mayor, and he has his bike decorated for the victory parade after the fight."

The mayor had arrived in time to hear the last of the standoff between Lia and the banker. The mayor was a small man named John Sedlack, but he spoke with authority. "Reimer, go get the money, or you two will refund all the bets and get your boxer out of town. I'll send the sheriff and his deputies to escort you up here with the gold."

The banker finally agreed and left with the sheriff to get the gold. Sedlack approached Lia. "You are quite the young woman. How did you get so tough?"

"None of your business." Sedlack made to touch her, but she stopped him with a glare and said, "Touch me, and I will hurt you." Sedlack was content to join back into the crowd and wait for the gold to arrive and the fights to start.

The sheriff and the deputies arrived with the banker carrying two bags, each containing a little over fifteen pounds of gold. They put the bags on the table, but Lia said, "Open the bags and count the coins."

Again, the money man was reluctant, but he opened the bags and stacked the coins in fifty piles, ten coins to a pile. "Ten thousand dollars. Where is your gold?" Lia lifted her buckskin skirt and unhooked a bag that hung on a belt around her waist, which drew gasps from some of the women in the crowd and lascivious stares and some hoots from the men. She threw the bag down on the table, indicating for the banker to count it out. He arranged the double eagles in five stacks of five coins each. He was starting to question the wisdom of backing the bet looking at his large pile of gold compared to Lia's.

Sedlack yelled out, "Call the first fight." Day was in the ring, throwing punches in the air again. The first boxer went down after about thirty seconds. Money was changing hands at the betting table and in the crowd. The second boxer did a little better, but Day suckered him with a feint and then landed a crushing roundhouse with his right. The next seven fights all went his way, but Day was winded, and despite the breeze, he was sweating profusely. He had taken several strong blows to his stomach and was rubbing his belly, trying to catch his breath as Roland stepped into the ring.

Roland was stripped to his waist and had his hands taped. He was a little smaller than Day, but his broad shoulders and ripped stomach gleamed in the sun. Lia had rubbed him down with some olive oil while the rest of the fights progressed. Roland bent over the ropes and kissed his wife and said, "Keep your eye on the gold and get ready to collect."

Both men stepped to the center of the ring, and the referee recounted the rules of engagement for the sake of the newcomer. Lia noticed that hers was the only bet placed on Roland. Everyone else had bet against him favoring their champion. Roland stepped back, and the timekeeper rang the bell. Both men circled one another for about twenty seconds until Day stepped in to throw a punch. Before Day could even lift his arm, Rolland slapped him in the face open-handed, the slap sounded like a gunshot as the crowd fell silent. Day turned red, and his eyes turned evil. He threw several more punches at Roland, but Roland sidestepped the first two and blocked the third. He responded with a crushing blow to Day's midsection. The wind wheezed out of the big man, and Day stood there helpless until the bell rang a few seconds later. *Perfect timing,* Roland thought as he returned to his corner. Lia held a cup of cold water up for him to drink, but Roland hadn't even broken a sweat.

Round two. Day came at Roland head-on, but Roland stopped him with a jab and ducked under the roundhouse right. As Day straightened up again, Roland landed another slap. This time Day turned purple. One more level up and he would foam at the mouth. Now Day came on like a raging bull, trying desperately to land a punch. He was breathing hard and not doing a very good job of defending himself. Finally, he landed a glancing blow that slid off Roland's forearm and landed on his shoulder. The big man would have to do better than that, but the crowd went wild, shouting their encouragement. Day came on again, and Roland landed another slap, louder and stronger than the first two. Day's face was already red, but now his mouth leaked blood at the corner. His eyes bulged, and finally, he did foam at the mouth. Roland landed another crushing blow to Day's midsection and left him again, standing helplessly in the middle of the ring as the bell sounded ending the second round.

Day's manager started to pick up the money and put it back in one of the bags. Lia just swung the Henry over and pressed the barrel between his eyes. The sheriff started to reach for his revolver, but Lia stopped him with a shake of her head and a swing of the Henry to the middle of the sheriff's chest. The Henry was cocked, and the sheriff knew he couldn't beat her. She could kill them both before he even cleared leather. The two men stood down and waited for the last round to start.

Day was almost staggering when he came out into the middle of the ring. Roland walked up to him casually and let the big man try to hit him. Day knew this wasn't going to end well. Roland bobbed left and right, always just far enough for Day's punches to miss. The crowd was quiet. The handwriting was on the wall. Their undefeated champion had met his match. Roland landed two quick blows to Day's stomach. He didn't let up but continued, left-right, several double blows in a row. The big man was going to go down anyway, but Roland finished it with a roundhouse right to the jaw. An audible crack sounded out through the crowd, and Day fell on his back and didn't move. He was counted out with thirty seconds left to go in the round.

Roland and Lia were ready to leave with the money. The stable boy from the Jumping Frog had their horses tied off at the edge of the park. Lia handed Roland a towel, and he wiped himself down and put his shirt back on. The stable boy came running up to Lia with her saddlebags. She kept her Henry at port arms while Roland scooped the money off the table. Ten thousand dollars in Double Eagles in the pot plus the five hundred dollars they won in the poker game, and another thousand for staying in the ring with the champion for three rounds. He thanked everyone kindly; Day was moaning and coming to in the ring behind them. Lia flipped the stable boy a double eagle as they walked out of the park. It was a fortune for the boy, and he just looked at her in awe as they mounted up. "Were ya'll a go'in?" he asked.

"Back to Amador City," Roland announced in a voice loud enough to be heard by at least half the crowd in the park. They did indeed leave out on the road back to Amador city and rode to beat hell for several miles. Then they left the road and struck out to the southeast. Walking the horses through an oak forest, careful not to leave too clear of a track as they picked their way through the trees. They pulled up to rest the horses after they were sure no one followed. Roland looked at Lia, and they both started to laugh. Their memories of the Mother Lode were sure to be fond ones.

It took days, but they were in the south end of the San Joaquin Valley. There was a trail over the mountains to the southeast. Roland knew the Mojave would stretch to the Colorado River on the other side. They weren't equipped yet to cross the Mojave, but that was a problem he would solve on the east side of the mountains.

The Storm's Golden Gift

Eli found it impossible to cut lumber from the cottonwood lining the sides of the hot spring creek. The wood was too hard to saw by hand, and the mesquite was even harder yet. He needed to find some pine and knew it would be in the higher mountains to the north, but no roads were going north or anywhere for that matter, within sight of his hill. Finally, in need of a shelter for Abby and himself, he resorted to the Indian ways and built a structure with the spines of dried cacti, tied together and covered with deer hides. With boards from the wagon forming the frame, they had a strong and waterproof shelter.

There was no lack of food, however. Abby's pigs prospered in the mesquite forest, and there were already two litters of piglets doubling and tripling the size of the pig population on the hill. Abby's sheep were slower to produce offspring, but all of the ewes were pregnant, promising a good yield of spring lambs. Life was easy, and the only problem was finding enough feed for the mules and horses. Eli knew the mules could fend for themselves if he turned them loose on the desert, but the horses were another matter. Every few days, he would saddle up the horses, and he and Abby would take them down to the Hassayampa to water and graze.

They would see the occasional lone Indian or even a small group from time to time, but none would talk to them or follow them onto the hill. Eli knew there was a story behind the hill being a bad place, but he knew that was a mystery that he might not ever understand. Indian superstitions were just that, he couldn't even get Abby to tell him her story -- until one stormy night when a strong winter front could be seen blowing onto the desert from the northwest. Eli and Abby huddled over the firepit in their makeshift shelter, and when it started to thunder and rain, Abby started to talk.

"I was born to a chieftain of the Algonquin tribes in what is now New York. I attended a mission school, and at age fourteen, was wed to the son of a chief of a neighboring tribe. Our parents were avid for us to have children to weave the destiny of our two tribes together. I tried for three years to have a child, but it was not to be. I was living with the neighboring tribe but was banished when the chief's son took another wife, who quickly bore him children. My parents would have taken me back, but my tribe considered me a failure, a cursed woman, so to say, unable to bear children. I chose to leave, and I walked west. I have spent four years here in the desert with the Apache, the Maricopa, and the Pima. I speak French that the missionaries taught me, Spanish that I learned in Santa Fe, and the local dialects here in the desert."

"I will never be able to bear your sons or daughters. If you want that, you will have to find a different woman."

Eli's anger bridled at her comment about a different woman. "I want you to stay with me. I never planned on having children, and maybe parenthood is not for everyone." Just then, the storm intensified. Lightning filled the evening sky, and it started to rain harder than Eli had ever seen, even harder than the storm he remembered on the Santa Fe Trail. The two of them fed the fire and huddled together for warmth through the night. The warmth of the hot spring was inviting, but the wind and lightning in the trees and the sound of a limb crashing to the ground now and then, made Eli think he should have dug a cave. The shelter couldn't protect them from a falling tree limb, but it did offer a sense of security from the wind and rain. The warmth of the fire felt good on the cold winter night.

It seemed impossible that the rain could become more intense than the first night, but it did. They kept feeding the fire, and on the second day of the storm, the last of the dry wood was burning away. That night one of the huge cottonwoods on the edge of the hot springs toppled over and hit the ground with a crash that shook the hill. *That was close*, Eli thought. Abby felt that their lives would end soon and was more frightened than she ever thought possible. Wet and cold, they made their way in the dark over to the hot spring. The hot water was soothing, but the storm still raged around them. By sunrise, however, the storm broke. The winds died, the rain fell to a drizzle, gradually the sun started breaking through the clouds.

Looking off the hill, Eli could see a desert that looked like a sheet of water. The washes and rills were still swollen and overflowed their banks. In the distance, the Hassayampa roared. They had to find some dry wood, which seemed to be an impossibility, and cook up some fresh meat and eat. Eli went down the hill with his Henry rifle on his shoulder. Abby started searching the hill for her flock of sheep. There was one ewe that was her favorite and would usually come to her when she called. Abby called her Rosie, another mystery to Eli, but this morning, Rosie would not answer her whistles or calls. Abby found the sheep about halfway down the hill, but Rosie wasn't with the flock. She kept looking with a feeling of dread and finally found Rosie sprawled dead across the stream that ran down from the hot springs. Rosie had a burnt patch of wool on the back of her neck, and it was obvious she had been struck by lightning during the storm. Abby could see that there was no bloating of the stomach yet, so she took out her knife and skinned the animal. She sadly took the hide and the two hindquarters back up to their camp. At least the problem of how they would feed themselves was solved.

Abby climbed the hill and hung the hide in the hot spring, wanting to wash the red mud out of the dirty wool. When it was warmer and dryer, she would stretch and cure the hide in the sun. For the moment, though, her only concern was to start a fire and get some warm food into their starved bellies. Eli returned empty-handed. There was water standing everywhere on the desert floor; the deer didn't need the water from the spring. He had released the mules to fend for themselves and fed the last of his grain to the horses. The only benefit he could see from the storm was that there would soon be plentiful grass on the desert for feed. Abby gathered up dead mesquite branches and was trying to dry some kindling; Eli sat down beside her and asked her why she had tears in her eyes. "We are going to have Rosie for our first meal after the storm – if I can get a fire started."

Abby sent Eli down the hill for the rest of the meat from the carcass. He looked at the hide hanging in the hot spring as he passed but dismissed its odd color to dirt in the wool. He found the flock of sheep standing in a spot of sunshine trying to get dry. He gathered the rest of the meat from the carcass and was sad to see that Rosie was carrying two lambs that now would never be born. By the time he got back to the top of the hill, Abby had a meager fire going. Smokey and struggling to burn, the fire was not yet big enough to cook on, but warm enough to dry more wood. It took an hour, but Abby finally had one of the hindquarters on a spit over the fire. She was grinding mesquite beans for flour and had to tell Eli to be patient when the smells of roasted leg of lamb started wafting around the campsite.

Eli walked over to the hot spring. The water was still somewhat muddy from the storm, but it was clear enough to wash the dirt out of Rosie's wool. As the red dirt of the hill was washed out, Eli became more and more intrigued at the golden color of the wool on at least a quarter of the hide. He kept washing the wool as long as red dirt left trails in the water, then he rung out the water best he could. The golden color, however, did not wash out. Eli carried the hide over and showed it to Abby. She was as puzzled as Eli. Eli was trying to remember the story of *Jason and the Golden Fleece*, but literature was not his strong suit. He needed his mother, the scholar in the family, or Roland. He was thinking of his mother and her school as he stretched the hide on a crude wood frame he had made from dead mesquite limbs. For the moment, he forgot about the strange coloring, all he could think about was eating. It was the third day without a good meal, and both their stomachs were crying for food as Rosie's hindquarter roasted and dripped grease into the fire.

When Abby finally declared the roast done, they ate, slowly at first, then with ravishing big mouthfuls to sate their hunger. That task finished, they walked around the hilltop, assessing the damage from the storm. Thankfully, the giant cottonwood that fell before the wind had fallen away from their shelter. Mud had washed from the huge root ball by the rain. The mud was still clouding the usually clear water in the hot spring. It had quit raining, and the spring would eventually clear. More importantly, their clothes would dry, and by nightfall, they would have dry firewood again. Everything would dry out and return to normal. They counted the sheep; all were there except for Rosie. They couldn't count the pigs, but they could hear them rooting around down the hill. They walked back to their shelter; they needed to hang what few clothes they had to dry.

When they walked over to where the hide was hanging, Eli turned the drying rack around to dry the wool in the sun. Remarkably, the golden color was more brilliant, more gold in color. Eli finally concluded that the golden color was gold, Jason's golden fleece. He walked back down to where Abby had found Rosie. He looked at the mud in the bottom of the stream. It was nothing but mud. If there was gold here, it was indeed too small to see. He had a gold pan down in the wagon at the bottom of the hill. He told Abby he was going down to get it.

Trying over and over again, he worked his way up the rill from the hot spring, panning the mud from the bottom of the stream on his way up. He didn't find any gold. When he got to the top of the hill, he showed Abby the gold pan and told her he couldn't find anything. She watched him work the gold pan and then took it away from him and started over with a fresh pan of red mud and the now clear water in the spring. Abby worked a lot more patiently and much more slowly. She kept floating the mud and washing it away a little at a time. When the red mud was finally gone, she had a thin thread of gold powder in the crook of the pan bottom. She handed the pan to Eli. He looked at the streak of gold and looked back at the golden stripe on Rosie's wool. There wasn't any doubt; there was gold in the hill.

The violent storm had uprooted the giant cottonwood; the gold had to have come from the root ball. Eli scooped some of the dirt out of the root ball and panned more patiently. When he finished, the streak of gold in the bottom of the pan was twice the size of when Abby had finished. Ok, it was definite; there was gold in the hill or at least a trace. There was little he could do at the moment about the gold discovery. Even if they had handfuls of the yellow metal, there wasn't a store or trading post within a hundred miles or more. There was a more important job at hand, and that was survival in this treacherous and unpredictable land. They could deal with the gold later when they were safe. For now, Eli dubbed the hot spring the *Oro Caliente Mine.* In his mind, it was nothing more than a curiosity.

On their next ride to the Hassayampa, they discovered that the storm had left the riverbanks covered with pine logs floated down from the high country. Here was wood Eli could saw and split into a cabin for Abby. Being a man of considerable energy, he rounded up the mules and started hauling logs from the river to the base of the hill. He had the tools to fashion logs for a crude cabin, and he set to that task with a vengeance. Abby found a cabin site in a clearing among the mesquite trees out of the reach of the giant cottonwoods surrounding the hot spring. She started gathering rocks for a simple hearth and chimney. Mortar for a chimney was going to be difficult; she would have to rely on Eli's ingenuity to provide that.

At least the weather was in their favor. Eli was hewing about a half-dozen logs a day for the cabin. Walls were rising quickly around a simple dirt floor. The days turned into weeks, and at last, Eli was splitting shakes for the roof. He solved the problem of mortar with a crude beehive oven, a miniature version of the ovens his father had built back in Independence. Finding limestone to roast was the bigger problem, but a vein of calcite on the mountain to the north served as a good alternative. Finally, with the cabin complete, and Rosie's golden fleece hanging on the wall, the young couple could turn their attention back to recovering gold from the hot spring.

Eli had brought a crate of books from Yuma. He never opened it and figured that all would be a loss from the storm but was pleased that only a few of the books had gotten wet. Most survived, wrapped in oiled paper. Abby found that all the books were practical manuals for survival in the desert wilderness. Some of the texts that survived covered foraging and cooking, medicines and treatments, and much to Eli's surprise, two books about mining. One was Edward Hitchcock's *Elements of Geology*, and the other was

De Re Metallica, written by Agricola in 1470 in Latin. They didn't have a Latin dictionary, but with Abby's command of two of the three romance languages and the illustrations in the book, an understanding of the basics was gleaned from the ancient text.

From Agricola, they learned that if they wanted to recover all of the gold from the red dirt and rock, they would have to grind the rocks to liberate the fine gold. Abby tried grinding the coarser red sand from the bottom of the hot spring in a metate she was using to grind mesquite beans. It was hard work to grind a whole gold pan of sand, but her efforts were worth it. She got a little bigger streak of gold than she got from panning the mud alone. Eli was impressed, but his first concern was providing food and shelter. You could have all the gold in the hill, but it wouldn't feed them or keep them warm.

Eli started cutting the smaller limbs away from the giant cottonwood that had fallen in the storm, and Abby spent her time in the hot spring panning for more gold. By the end of a week, she had more than an ounce of the fine powder. One day when she was digging in the pool bottom, she found a fossil that she first thought was a claw. She washed it off and showed it to Eli, who turned it over and over, studying it intently. "I think it might be a tooth, rather than a claw. It is really big for any animals that are around here now, though. Also, it is heavy like a rock rather than like a tooth. It has to be from an animal that died in the hot spring a long time ago." Abby thought little of it, but like her ancient ancestor, she fashioned it into an amulet that she added to the beads she wore around her neck. First found by an Indian woman and discarded, the petrified tooth was found again by an Indian woman who also made it into something to wear. The tooth, Eli called it a *dragon tooth*, was again taking its place in the history of man.

Every day, Eli scanned the desert with his binoculars looking for any signs of humans, Indian or otherwise. Once he saw a hunting party approaching the hill, they did not seem to be affected by the superstition that kept the local Indians away. They approached the hill from the north and found one of the numerous game trails leading up to the hot spring. The small party entered the trail and started up the hill. Eli couldn't see them through the mesquite forest, but he knew that the Indians would soon encounter the herd of pigs that had made that side of the hill their home. Armed with wooden spears and the traditional bows, they were no match for an angry boar. Abby had named the biggest boar Cornelius; he was constantly on guard and protected the rest of the herd. The big boar heard and smelled the Indians approaching. When they saw Cornelius, he must have looked like an easy meal for them. One of the Indians approached and threw his spear, wounding the big hog in the shoulder. Cornelius charged him. Others in the party tried to hit him with arrows but missed, and their curiosity turned to horror as the boar kept on coming, crashing through the brush like it did not exist. Cornelius ran the brave that had thrown the spear down and killed him with a vicious slash of his four-inch tusks. The rest of the Indians ran faster and escaped. Cornelius did a fine job of maintaining the superstition that the hill was a *bad place*.

Eli heard the scream of the fallen brave. He went down the hill with his Henry cocked and upon his shoulder at the ready, making his way down through the trees. He came across the body of the brave and gathered up his medicine bag and several arrows that were still in his quiver. Cornelius was close by, but Eli didn't see him. That was good; he didn't want to kill the big boar. Cornelius was proving to be a good sentinel and probably wouldn't taste that good anyway.

Eli showed the arrows and medicine bag to Abby. She studied them for a while and said, "These Indians are not from here. I think they are Utes. If the Apache find them, they will kill them. How many were in the hunting party?"

"At least a dozen. It was hard to count the hunting party when it was out in the brush, and once they entered the mesquite, I couldn't see them at all. I bet they have never seen a feral pig before, and they are probably hoping they never see one again. I think if we want to eat pork, we are going to have to hunt them from a blind. Preferably next to a tree, we can climb to get away from Cornelius."

"Don't worry about Cornelius. When it is time, I can slaughter a piglet without getting chased down and killed." Eli didn't know how she would do that, but he had seen her creep up on deer and slash a throat with the machete. There was no doubt in his mind that Abby could kill a pig just as easily. But Abby was more fascinated with the gold in the hot spring than hunting. She would hunt, of course, when their larders were nearly empty, but otherwise, she spent most of her time panning mud from the hot spring and recovering the gold. It was obvious to both of them that they could recover more gold if they ground the rock and sand. It wasn't difficult to grind by hand, but the production was really slow. Abby kept encouraging Eli to invent some way for them to grind the rock and sand. They would page through the mining book and try to make sense of the Latin, but all the machines depicted in the illustrations were well beyond their means to build out of the materials on their hilltop.

Eli remembered an apparatus he saw up in the mountains of Colorado that he didn't understand at the time. It was a simple machine with a center post and an arm that could be attached to an animal. A heavy rock was attached to the arm and drug around and around in a trough lined with flat rocks. It was a simple enough concept to build with what they could find around the hilltop. The cottonwood limbs were strong, so what they needed was two rocks of the right shape, and they could build some version of the machine.

The next day they saddled up the horses and rode up to the north, to the base of the granite mountains in search of just the right rocks. They had venison jerky and water in their canteens, so staying out all day to search was not a problem. There were plenty of flat rocks for the base of the mortar. But finding a rock for the part of the grinder that would serve as the pestle, was more difficult. Finally, Eli saw a pear-shaped boulder that looked a little too heavy but decided he could move it with the horses. He rigged the pestle rock behind his horse with a rope over the saddle horn and a lead down both sides of the horse to the rock. They moved over to the flat rock and rigged that one behind Abby's horse. These weren't draft animals, but they did reasonably well over the several miles to the base of the hill.

It was almost dark by the time they got to the north side of the hill, but Eli wanted the rocks around on the south side where the water from the hot springs flowed down from the top. It was completely dark by the time they corralled the horses and climbed the hill to their crude log cabin. Exhausted from their day's labors, neither wanted to build a fire and cook. They ate the rest of the jerky, and Abby promised that she would hunt the next day if Eli would build her the grinder. She also wanted a wooden trough, like one she saw in Agricola's text, to line with canvas so that she didn't have to do the slow and patient panning to recover the gold dust. Eli was wealthy, and he didn't need the gold, but he wanted to keep Abby interested in him, and mining gold seemed to be her insatiable obsession at the moment.

As promised, Abby went hunting the next morning, and she didn't go far. They would be dining on fresh pork that night. With a young weanling dressed and hanging to age in the cool winter air, Abby headed down the hill to see what Eli was doing with the rocks. She was amazed at his ingenuity. Eli had dug out a place in the hot water stream and had pulled the flat rock into it. He was sawing some pine logs to build a frame over it and already had two short posts buried in the ground to mount it on. He had parts from the wagon, a spare axle, and some other large nuts and bolts that held the axle blocks in place. He drew out a picture in the dirt of what he was building, and Abby asked what she could do to help. He didn't know why, but there was a rock drill in the tool chest. He showed Abby how to use it and had her sitting in the shade of a large mesquite tree as she worked with a hammer and the rock drill making two holes in the top of the pear-shaped rock.

It took Abby three days to finish the holes, but she finished by the time Eli had the frame completed with the tongue of the wagon securely tied to the axle. It took both of them to wrestle the pestle rock under the frame, but they finally got it in place. It must have weighed more than two-hundred-fifty pounds, but after Eli had it lashed to the axle, it rocked up easily when he pushed down on the other end of the axel. Perfect, the gentle slope at the bottom of the hill was the ideal place for a mule to circle the grinder. On the downhill side of the circle, the pestle would tilt up to let the red dirt wash under it. Eli still had to build the trough, but he wanted to round up a mule first and get it trained to pull in a circle. Abby volunteered to catch the mule. She knew where they grazed down at the river, so she set out the next morning on foot, a halter in hand. Eli smiled and was skeptical that she could catch one without a horse and a lasso, but the woman never ceased to amaze him.

He had the trough built and was wondering where he was going to get a piece of canvas for the bottom when Abby walked around the east side of the hill leading a light-colored jenny from the mule team. Amazing, she not only caught a mule but also had a suggestion for the bottom of the sluice. She would go up to their hide stretching racks and cut strips of deer hide to line the bottom of the trough. Before she left, she cut a stick just the width of the trough. By the time Eli came up the hill at the end of the day, Abby was sitting next to the fire pit, turning a pork roast on the spit. Eli didn't know if he would ever find a woman more perfect than Abby. She was smart and resourceful, and Eli didn't know what he would do if she left him; but beyond that, he knew that each day that went by, he loved her more than he ever thought possible.

Abby smiled at him and said, "You look hungry and tired. Thank you for building the grinder. I have fixed a good meal for you as a reward. After you eat, let's go bathe in the spring, and I'll give you the rest of your reward for as long as you can stay awake over in the cabin."

Eli sat down next to her and drew her close with an arm around her shoulders and talked softly into her ear, "You know I love you, and if you give me a chance, I'll build you much more than a grinder. I will build you or get you anything you ever want," then he kissed her while a soft wind rustled the leaves above them and the howl of a lone coyote reminded them how good it was not to be alone.

Abby kissed him back passionately and said, "What I want is for you to eat so we can get on with this evening." She got their plates and filled each with a good helping of roast and mesquite bread slathered with gravy she made from pork fat rendered in a pan at the edge of the fire. Eli ate his fill, and they didn't clean up the plates and utensils from their meal. Abby undressed and walked away on the trail to the hot spring. Eli dropped everything and followed. It was hours later when they returned to their bed in the cabin. They slept the deep sleep of exhausted lovers but still awoke at dawn. Abby's clothes were by the fire pit, but Eli had to walk up the trail to the hot spring to find all of his. He returned fully dressed, and by then, Abby had bacon frying and more bread baking. Sooner or later, they would have to go somewhere for supplies. Maybe they would get a cow for milk and butter. These were only fleeting needs in Abby's mind; she wanted to get down the hill and try out the grinder. She woke with a good case of gold fever working on her and wanted to remedy that.

Through the day, Eli brought mud and sand down the stream bottom to feed the grinder. Abby had fashioned a board to act as a feed chute, and while she sat on the rock wall Eli had built around the mortar, she would push more mud and sand under the pestle each time the mule was on the downhill side. Abby built up a mud barrier around the mortar to direct the finely ground mud into the sluice. Eli kept fiddling with a small dam he had built in the stream to get the flow of water through the mortar just right. They spent most of the day adjusting and learning how to mill the ore more efficiently. When it was time, they quit for the evening. Abby unhitched the mule and staked her out on a green patch of grass downstream from the mill. She went back to find Eli panning the cleanings from the deer hide. He handed her the pan to finish up.

Eli walked up the stream bed to where he mined through the day and estimated that they had ground over one yard of material. Tomorrow they could mill more, but for the first day, he was pleased with their efforts. He walked back down to watch Abby finish panning. Her eyes grew wide as she finished up with a healthy amount of gold dust at the bottom of the pan. They carefully added it to the small amount they had in the pickle jar from Abby's panning up in the hot spring pool. It would take more than a month to fill the jar, but that was remarkable, considering that one couldn't easily see any gold in the red mud itself.

Every night they would page through the Agricola text and try to translate another section that looked interesting to them. Eli was particularly interested in *Book V* that discussed and illustrated ovens used for assaying. He didn't know if he could build an oven that would get hot enough to melt gold, but it was something he was planning on attempting soon. Another thought he had was to mill ore from all over the hill. What he needed was a wheelbarrow, and he was looking at the wheels from the wagon as possible starting materials. Abby pointed out an illustration in Agricola of a wheelbarrow made completely of wood, even the wheel. She was beginning to think that Eli could do anything, and she wasn't far from wrong.

They mined every day, and slowly, the pickle jar was filling. Eli was encouraged by his sampling around the hill. Everywhere he picked up the red dirt and rock; he got a good return from the grinder. The whole hill was full of microscopic gold. He didn't have a scale, so he couldn't calculate exactly how much gold there was in the ore, but he knew it was significant. He thought a lot about John Gould and wondered if Roland and Lia found him over in the Mother Lode. He missed his brothers and Suzette desperately and cherished the times they had together. He wondered if there would be a time in the future that they would all be together again.

To that end, Eli kept watching the desert every day. He was expecting Roland and Lia to arrive, but the weeks were turning into months, and there was still no sign of them. It was a quandary. If he left the hill and they arrived, they wouldn't find him and go on to places unknown. If he stayed and they never arrived, he wouldn't know what happened to them or if he could have helped if he had gone looking for them. Too much country to search and too many unknowable catastrophes that could have befallen them, there was little he could do. He finally decided to stay and see just what the future would bring. He was also getting the feeling that Abby was as deeply attached to the gold mine as she was to him. That certainly wasn't a bad thing. Eli himself was attached to both of them too.

Beale's Crossing

Roland and Lia left the broad San Joaquin Valley and rode up a trail on the mountain slopes to the southeast. The going was easy at first but then more difficult before they reached a mountain valley that made almost a flat path across to the east side of the mountains. The air was cold, and there was snow in the high valley but not deep enough to hinder their travels. Before they left the valley, Roland had purchased a packhorse. Equipped with a small tent and heavier bedrolls, called soogans. The two days they spent in the high mountain pass were only mildly uncomfortable. When they came down on the east side of the mountains, they could see for a hundred or more miles across the Mojave Desert.

Soon they were on the rolling desert floor of the Mojave. Roland had a map that showed a settlement, Victorville, about sixty-five miles to the southeast. Victorville was on the Mojave River, and for pioneers headed to Los Angeles, it was the last stop on the Mojave before crossing the mountains to San Bernardino. Roland was hoping to buy a wagon there to ease Lia's travel across the desert. She was three months pregnant and beginning to show a bit. Roland wanted to do his best for her. It took three days to cross the Mojave to Victorville. Water wasn't a problem; there were plenty of small streams full of snow and rain runoff from the west. They needed the bigger Mojave River, however, to cross the rest of the desert east to the Colorado River.

Roland and Lia were expecting a small town at Victorville but came to only a few houses. One of them looked like a general store with a sign on the front of the building that read, *Lane's Crossing.* Roland walked into the store; the proprietor was behind a counter going over ledgers that looked like his inventory records. Roland reached over the counter to shake his hand and said, "You must be the Mr. Lane of *Lane's Crossing*. I'm Roland Callahan, and that is my wife Lia out there with the horses."

The storekeeper took his hand in a firm shake and said, "Yes, I'm Lane, but call me Aaron. What can I do for you?"

Roland was relieved that the store appeared to be well-stocked. He replied, "My wife and I are traveling back to a spot in the middle of the New Mexico Territories." Roland had sketched a map showing the position of the hill on the Hassayampa River. He unfolded it on the top of the counter and pointing at the hill said, "We want to get to here. We came across on the

Santa Fe Trail and crossed at Yuma on our way to Los Angeles. If we follow the Mojave to Beale's Crossing, is there a way down through the mountains to where we want to go?"

"There is, but those mountains are tough, and there aren't any wagon roads through there yet. I am not saying it is impossible; I think it would be easier if you went down to Yuma to cross and then up that river to the hill, just like your map shows."

Roland asked, "Is there anyone around here that knows the way down to the hill from Beale's Crossing? Also, I would like to buy a wagon and provisions to get me there. My wife is pregnant, and she thinks she will need a wagon to travel in before long. If you have the goods, I have the money. What can you do for us?"

"I can get you a wagon, and I have plenty of supplies. Your wife would have an easier time though sticking with her horse. A wagon is not a smooth ride. You must know that, though, if you came across on the trail. There is a fellow who came here and then lost his wife to yellow fever. He lives about a mile down the river, and since his wife died, he doesn't want to stay here anymore. He had sent for a couple of pre-cut cabins that are still on the wagons they arrived here on from the factory. He even has a buckboard with a spring seat. If you could talk him out of it, the buckboard would be the best ride for your wife. I'll take you down there if you want."

Roland thought that would be a good idea, and as they left the store, Hale slipped a padlock through a hasp on the door. Mr. Lane commented, "Going over to that part of the mountains, you might want to take some mining equipment with you. I still have some stuff left over from my days up in the Mother Lode. If you want it, you can have it. There is nothing around here but sand and rattlesnakes."

"Let's see if your friend down the river will sell his wagon and his cabins. If we take too much, I'll have to hire some mule skinners."

They rode down the river with Aaron and went to the bare bones homestead of one Finley K. McFadden. There were two wagons in front of a tent and some oxen that looked pretty scraggly in a corral a few yards away. Aaron called, "Finley, you around here, Buddy?"

A young man not much older than Roland pushed the tent flap back and stepped out. He was drunk and didn't smell good. His unwashed appearance had Roland and Lia skeptical that they would be able to make a good deal with him. Lia moved her horse upwind but didn't comment on the man's condition. Aaron broached the subject of McFadden selling his wagons and the cabins. "Finley, you're looking worse than ever. If you don't knock off the rotgut, you're going to kill yourself."

McFadden just stood in front of the tent and ignored what Aaron had just said. He was staring at Lia, his look half sad, half lascivious. Roland thought it would be better if they let Lia negotiate for the wagons and the mules, but Aaron continued. "Finley, I know it has been rough out here, but this young couple might be interested in buying your wagons and the teams if the price is right."

Again, McFadden acted like he didn't hear or didn't understand. Lia got down off her horse and walked over to the upwind side of McFadden. The top two buttons of her blouse showed ample décolletage that held McFadden's stare like a magnet. She cooed, "Finley, we want to buy your wagons, the teams, and the cabins. How much do you want for them?" She even moved a little closer to the man so he could enjoy the visual feast she was providing.

McFadden finally came out of his drunken trance. "Eight-hundred dollars," he slurred, still not taking his eyes off Lia.

Answering politely, Lia said, "Mr. McFadden, I can see from here that you have not been taking good care of your stock. The covers on the wagons are half-blown away, and the harnesses are just thrown down in the dirt over there. I understand that you have been through some hard times, but I can't let my husband buy you out for that kind of money."

"Well, how much will you offer?"

"I don't know, but my husband and I will talk about it tonight. Maybe you could meet us at Mr. Lane's mercado tomorrow morning." With that, Lia turned and mounted her horse. Without looking at Roland or Mr. Lane, she turned her horse and rode back up the river. Along the way back to Victorville, she asked Roland, "How much do you think we should pay?"

Roland answered, "In another couple of months, he won't have much left there to sell. Those animals have to be taken down onto some grass on the river. Right now, they are in no shape to even cross the Colorado, let alone try to make it into the middle of New Mexico Territory. I would go two-fifty for each of the wagons with the cabins and say one hundred for each of the teams and the harnesses. That would make seven hundred my top offer, but he might jump at anything you offer. He is going to need more whiskey soon, but you know, anything we give him will be enough for him to drink himself to death. There is just too much tragedy there for him to handle. I wonder if we could offer him a job and have him come with us?"

Aaron piped up, "I don't think that would be wise. He is drinking pretty hard. I haven't sold him any more booze in over two weeks, and he is still as drunk as a tomcat in a barrel of catnip. I don't know where he is getting his alcohol from, but I doubt you can dry him out."

Roland said, "Let's see what tomorrow brings. I want the wagons, and the cabins would be a good idea. If we bought the whole lot, though, we would need some drivers and maybe even one more wagon for supplies. I didn't see the buckboard; maybe he traded it for whiskey. It might be around here on one of the other farms?"

Mr. Lane was sure he could come up with everything they needed. He asked for a couple of days, and he would see what he could do. He had a small cabin they could stay in for a few days while he tried to round up some drivers and a buckboard. There was a scattered population around Victorville. He would put the word out and see what might avail itself.

The next morning McFadden was sitting on the porch of the general store. He was washed up and shaven but shaking hard and sweating from alcohol withdrawal. None the less, he greeted Roland and Lia cordially when they arrived at the Mercado. McFadden shook when he stood up, but with hat in hand, he was sincere when he apologized, "Ma'am, I wasn't myself yesterday, and I am truly sorry. I am as disgusted with myself as you are, but I hope you will give me another chance. If you and your husband are still interested in the wagons and teams, I will take the oxen down to the grass in the river bottom and get them fed properly."

Lia didn't even look at Roland; she told McFadden, "We are still interested; go graze your stock. We are looking for some other things and should be able to let you know by this afternoon. We will need some drivers, and we are looking for a buckboard and a draft horse. Know anyone who could help us with that?"

"I am a good driver, and I could take care of all the stock. I don't want to stay here. There are too many ghosts for me to handle around here. Where are you going anyway?"

Roland took out his map and unfolded it. "We're going down into the middle of the New Mexico Territory. If there is a way down through the mountains, we'll cross the Colorado River at Beale's Crossing and cut across the mountains, if that is possible."

Aaron Lane arrived to unlock the store and joined the conversation. "Good to see you up early and sober, Finley. There aren't any roads to the southeast off of the Beale Wagon Road on the east side of the river. The mountains are too rugged for wagons. There is a river, though, about forty miles south on the Colorado that will take you east into that country. Finding that hill, though, will be pretty tough. You would be better off going down to Yuma to cross and following the other rivers like the map shows. However, if you could stand having an Indian along with you, I think old *Walks Alone* could at least get you up the river to the east. If I can find him, I'll send him over to talk to you."

With that information, each went their separate ways. Lane opened the store; McFadden set out to walk back to his camp, and Roland and Lia saddled their horses. They were going to ride around the area and see the farms the settlers had started. There were quite a few, some more established than others. Most of the families were German immigrants who were tired of the long journey across America and settled the first viable-looking farmland they had seen since leaving the comfort of the Midwest. There was one family that invited them in for lunch. Roland and Lia related their story of going over into New Mexico Territory to find their brother. There were eleven children in this family, three to nineteen years, enough children to start a small school. The father, Burkhard, took Roland aside and told him they had too many children for the farm to support. His second youngest boy, Björn, was good with animals. If Roland promised to take good care of him and promised to send him back someday, he would send his boy with them to drive one of the wagons.

Roland spent some time with Björn and discovered that his father didn't have high hopes for him. Roland told Björn that it was a long way to where they were going, and there would be danger along the way. It was completely obvious that an adventure appealed to the boy. Roland offered to pay the boy twenty dollars a month and keep him with them until he could be sent back safely to his parents. This lad was only a couple of years younger than Roland, and he put out his hand like a man to shake on the deal. Roland told Burkhard what he offered the boy, and if it were agreeable to his family, Roland and Lia would send for Björn in a day or two. Burkhard thanked Roland and said, "Keep him safe, and we will pray for you."

By the time they returned to Lane's, the man had proved to be as resourceful as he claimed. An old Mojave Indian was sitting on his porch, and a fine-looking horse hitched to a buckboard stood tied to the hitching post. There was also an empty Conestoga that had seen better days next to the Mercado but with no team to pull it. Lane said that wouldn't be a problem; he had a team coming from further up the river. Lane introduced them to the Indian; his name was *Walks Alone*. Roland showed the old man the map; the old Indian deepened the lines in his brow and said, "The bad place. I can take you there, but I won't go there. It is a bad place."

Roland offered to pay him to guide them up the river to the east of the Colorado, but the old Indian didn't want money. He countered, "No money -- food, rifle, ammunition -- I will take you there." Roland offered his hand but Walks Alone just looked at it with a puzzled look on his face. "Your word Whiteman is what I want. I have a hand of my own." Lia smiled at the clash of cultures. She walked over to the older man and assured him that their word was good. Then she went into the store and bought him a 0.54 caliber Hawken rifle, powder, and a good supply of rifle balls and primers. When she gave the rifle to the old man, a broad smile spread across his face; and his eyes beamed startled amazement, like a child at Christmas.

It was another day before Aaron Lane came up with the third team of oxen to pull the supply wagon, which he packed with food, seed, and a cast iron cook stove. He also put in several iron-pipe flasks of quicksilver, an amalgam plate, a crude gold scale, and several other geological instruments. Before he put in an iron mercury retort, he took Roland aside and explained, "Never put the end of this condensing tube underwater. If your fire goes out, the retort will cool and draw water up the condensing tube, and when it reaches the retort, it will turn to steam, and the retort will explode like a bomb. My partner up in the Mother Lode died that way. Also, be careful with the mercury. It's poisonous, and mercury vapor will make you sick, and all your teeth will fall out." With that, he put the retort in the back of the supply wagon. Roland settled with Lane for fifteen-hundred dollars. Now they just had to wait for McFadden to come in to close his deal, and they would be off to cross the Colorado.

That night, Roland and Lia rode down to McFadden's and was pleased to see that the livestock looked much better with their bellies full after a day of grazing down on the river. McFadden had the harnesses hanging on the corral fence and was cleaning and oiling the leather. Lia got down and walked up to the corral to look over the oxen. McFadden knew she was there. However, there were none of the lascivious starings of the previous day. He didn't stop working on the harnesses but looked at Lia and said, "Are you here to make a deal?"

Lia said, "We are, but I am not going to pay your asking price."

McFadden stopped his busy work and looked at her for the first time. "I need the eight-hundred dollars to cover my costs."

Lia gave him a coquettish look and shook her head *no* with a smile on her face. Then she said, "I can offer one-thousand even, and that is my last offer."

McFadden opened his mouth to protest before he realized what she had said. Lia took fifty double eagles out of her pocket and handed him the money. Lia said, "Be ready to leave at dawn. We will bring a driver for the second wagon."

McFadden was standing there with his mouth open but finally managed, "Thank you, ma'am. I'll be there first thing; you can count on that."

That night Roland held Lia in his arms and told her again how much he loved her. She responded in Spanish. It would soon be their only language that their new companions wouldn't understand. "Siempre tendrás mi corazón, mi amor."

Roland answered, "Too complicated, say it in English, please." Lia didn't say anything; she just showed him. Privacy would soon be a rare commodity when they were on the trail again. She was making the best of the small cabin that Aaron had provided. Although the next leg of their journey would be short compared to the Santa Fe, it would still be the life of a pioneer with constant travel, danger, and little privacy.

Before dawn, Lia awoke to the sound of oxen lowing and gravel crunching under heavy wheels. She fumbled in the dark and lit a lantern at the bedside. She pulled on the rest of her clothes, noticing that she would need some larger things before they left the comfort of Lane's modest store. She went outside, and McFadden and Björn had already hitched and brought the wagons up to the Mercado. The old Indian was sitting on the porch and had a woman with him that looked to be as old as him. She had a burro packed with supplies. Lane was unlocking the front door of his store. The sky was only starting to lighten in the east and close by, roosters crowed, and the hoot of a barn owl welcomed in the dawn. Lia went back into the cabin and jumped on Roland to wake him. "Get up, Wagon Master; it is time to head east."

Roland moaned, still drowsy from his very active night, and said, "Not till after some breakfast."

Lia went over to the store. Mrs. Hale, Rebecca, was starting a fire in their outdoor cooking grill. She talked to Rebecca and told her she would need some bigger clothes soon. Rebecca told her she had just what Lia needed and took her inside while her husband was filling two large pans with bacon and potatoes. Lia went out the front of the Mercado and sat down next to Walks Alone. She asked, "Is this your wife?"

"Yes. Woman won't be any trouble. She doesn't talk; never has. She walks strong, hunts, and is a good cook. She won't be any trouble for you." It seemed a given that the Indian woman was coming with them. Roland came over from the cabin and eyed the old woman skeptically but said not a word when the two Indians got up and made ready to leave. Walks Alone said, "The first camp is thirty miles down the river. We meet you there tonight." With that, the two Indians walked into the first light of dawn, leading the burro like a couple of old trail hands.

They reminded Roland of prospectors he had seen up in the Mother Lode, lean and hearty and leading a burro. *Thirty miles,* he was thinking, *will that be a daily challenge.*? He turned to Lia and his two drivers. "We better eat and get going if we want to keep up with them."

Thirty miles in one day was a long way for the oxen but going down the river was easy. They had gone the first ten miles before the desert started to warm up. There was even time for a break where McFadden unhitched the ox teams and let them graze on a grassy patch in the river bottom. Lia was driving her buckboard with her horse tied behind. She let both horses drink their fill at the river, then broke out the lunch Rebecca had sent with them. The Indian guide and his wife were nowhere in sight.

Travel through the day went well with the oxen maintaining their slow, steady pace. Björn said, "It is the tortoise and the hare. I can't believe those old Indians can stay ahead of us." He was right; it was evening time when they saw the smoke from a fire up ahead. When they pulled up to the camp, it became obvious that the Indians had gotten there well ahead of them. There was a deer dressed out with venison steaks and part of a hind quarter roasting on a spit.

Walks Alone smiled and said, "I thought you were going to be late for your dinner." As Lia ate, she thought the investment in the Hawken rifle was one of the best she had ever made.

Roland, though, needed to talk to W.A., which was going to be his nickname for Walks Alone, which seemed to be a mouthful and a difficult way to start every sentence. "W.A., we can't push the oxen thirty miles every day, or we will kill them. Tomorrow let's go twenty. There is no rush, is there?"

"Yes, we must rush. A big rain is coming. Must cross the river before the big rain gets here."

They hadn't seen a cloud in the sky all day. Roland had to ask, "How do you know a big rain is coming?"

W.A. beckoned him to walk with him. Just outside of the campsite, there was a large ant colony. Big black ants were furiously building a wall of sand around the hole that was their home. The wall built of sand grains was at least three inches high and over a foot in diameter on the outside of the ring. The old Indian just pointed at the ants and said, "The ants told me."

The next day was still clear, but the day after that it started to rain long before they reached the river, and It didn't rain just a little bit. It was a huge winter storm, driven down from the northwest on high winds. The skies darkened and lightning started to light up the fading daylight. The rain was torrential, and soon Roland had to find a way to travel on the banks of the river rather than on the bottom. Now the old woman led the way through the sparse desert cacti, but even dry washes that joined the river from the south were flowing heavy and difficult to cross. The valley floor, where W.A. told Roland the Mojave usually disappeared into the desert sand, was turning into a lake. W.A. also told Roland, "We have to stop and stay on the high ground until the storm passes. My ancestors told me that this whole valley could fill with water. If we get bogged down in the middle, we will drown."

The old Indian was right. They didn't move for two days. When the storm finally started to clear, the valley was full of water; for twenty or thirty miles to the mountains east, there was nothing but water. They started to move again but were pushed far to the south of the trail, finding their way around the lake. Finally, days behind Roland's schedule, they came to the Colorado River. Their spirits sank. The shallow water of Beale's Crossing was a raging torrent, brown with mud and flowing fast. There was no other choice. They had to wait for the river to go down. Roland doubted they could even cross if they made the long trek down to Yuma. "Some desert," he railed, watching the raging waters.

One week turned into two. The water was going down but not very fast. The third week the water slowed, and the brown color of the raging torrent gave way to the blue water Roland and Lia saw when they crossed in Yuma months ago. Roland explored the river. The sandbar that made up the shallow bottom of Beale's Crossing was gone. He rode more than five miles down the river before he found a place shallow enough for the oxen to cross. It was still treacherous, and it took all day to take the wagons across one by one. The light buckboard threatened to float away, but Roland had hitched all three horses to the buckboard, and as it swept downstream, the horses kept moving through the current. Roland took his and Lia's horse back to the west side of the river. Lia was the last one there with the burro. The burro was much shorter than the horses and wouldn't enter the water. They tethered him between the two horses and literally drug the reluctant animal into the river. About halfway across, he must have realized that it was better to get to the other side. He quit fighting, and as the water started to get shallow towards the east bank, he bellowed and started to run for the dry ground.

Roland and Lia laughed and made a joke about a dumb jackass. W.A. was offended. "Burro not dumb. Burro scared of the river. Burro smart. We dumb, cross too early." He had a point; they spent the rest of the day drying out.

W.A. wanted to strike out to the southeast. The way looked clear; there was a long stretch of reasonably flat land in that direction with mountains in the distance. His wife, however, refused to go. She stood by the side of the trail and pointed south, down the river. That is the way Lane told him to go; Roland had to side with the wife. W.A. was adamant that they should head to the southeast. His wife shook her head *no* again and pointed at the wheels on the wagons and then pointed south again. Finally, W.A. got it. They could walk to the southeast, but the wagons had to make it to the other river before they turned east.

There were hills on the east side of the river, but no impassable mountains. In three days, they turned east into the mouth of the tributary. It was rich with fish and game, and the Indian woman provided them with lush meals each evening. It wasn't long that the water of the river was nothing more than a trickle, but the river bottom still provided an easy pathway for the oxen. Roland scouted out ahead, but there wasn't any need. They had not seen another human in the month since they left Lane's Crossing. He asked W. A. about that, and he said sadly, "All the Indians are on the reservation by Yuma. No more war is good, but peace on the reservation has evils of its own." He didn't elaborate on that, but Roland suspected that life under the white man's rule wasn't easy for the Indians to accept.

After several days they reached a fork in the river bottom. Again, there was a conflict between their guides. The old woman was pointing at the narrower south fork. The old man wanted to take the bigger river bottom that turned north. The old woman smiled and kept shaking her head and still smiling, turned, and walked up the south fork until she was out of sight. Roland led his miniature wagon train up the south fork and called to make camp where the old woman was sitting by a large fire ring. When they gathered around her, she pointed at herself and then, holding her hands spread wide, one far above her head and the other down on the ground, she lowered her upper hand down to the size of a small child. Then she pointed at herself again and gestured with both palms open and sweeping out forward. The crude sign language was plain. She was born here. The fire ring was her first home. Lia sat down beside her and swept her arm around the old woman's shoulder and pulled her into an affectionate hug. "I wish you could talk. I know you have a precious story to tell." The old woman grunted but didn't speak. She got up and walked out on the desert to gather wood for a cooking fire.

The next morning, they traveled up the creek bottom. The sand was easygoing for the oxen but hard on the horses. The two Indians just walked, the faithful little burro following behind without a halter. In two more days, they came to a mountain range that ran in a straight line, east to west. Here the old woman took them out of the creek bottom and walked toward the southeast. In a few miles, Roland could see a round hill in the distance. He got excited, but the W.A. calmed him. "Wrong hill," he said, "but we are close."

They made camp that night by the wrong hill. Roland and Lia climbed to the top of the small mound, and as the sun was setting, they could see a round-red mountain on the horizon to the southeast. They were almost there. That night they didn't bother to put up the tent. They fell asleep laying on their bedrolls, staring up at the stars. W.A. didn't sleep that night. He was standing guard. They were in Apache country, and while he had not seen any hostiles, he was sure that they had seen him. Around three in the morning, his wife walked out of the camp and took the Hawken Rifle out of his hands. He was dozing, but she didn't wake him. She just took over the job of guarding the camp. The sky lightened in the east, and their vigilance paid off.

When it was light enough to see, smoke from an Indian camp rose into the gray sky several miles to the west. W.A. woke the camp and told everyone to hitch up the teams quietly. By first light, they had moved well out of sight of the Indian camp. By that afternoon, the red mountain was right in front of them.

Roland rode forward, and Lia followed in the buckboard. They went north of the hill and then circled it to the south. There they found Abby tending her grinding mill. Eli was up on the hill mining. Abby called up to him, and when Eli came down out of the mesquite, he let out a whoop and ran the rest of the way to give his brother and his sister-in-law a huge welcoming hug. He introduced Abby, and she showed the new arrivals her jar of gold. It was half full and heavy. Roland's eyes got big, and then he and Lia laughed. Lia went over to the wagon and got the leather sack that still contained nearly seven-thousand dollars in gold. Eli and Abby were amazed at all the coins, but then Eli pointed at the mountain and said, "That is a lot of gold, but there is a lot more here."

Lia sat with Eli and Abby in the shade of the mesquites and related the story of Roland winning the fight in Angels Camp and their escape out of the San Joaquin Valley with the gold. Abby was fascinated with Lia's hair. After a while, she asked Lia if she would like to go up to the hot spring for a bath. Lia didn't think that was possible in the wilderness but followed Abby up to the top of the hill. Lia was thrilled to see the hot spring pool. She very much needed a bath and to wash her clothes and her hair. All she brought with her from the buckboard was a comb and a hairbrush. As she and Abby settled into the hot water, Lia thought that a red mountain in the middle of the New Mexico Territory wasn't such a bad place to be at all.

Roland rode out to bring the wagons and his new friends over to the base of the hill. Eli told him to stop at the bottom of the trail that led up to his cabin. He didn't want anyone else to know they were mining gold out of the red dirt. That night Roland had McFadden and Björn make camp at the bottom of Eli's path. As expected, the two Indians were nowhere in sight. They had left without a word. It was the "bad place" again; it couldn't be all bad; *there is gold here,* Roland thought. The next day he would send McFadden and Björn back with one of the wagons. He was anxious to have Eli show him everything he knew about the mountain, and he wanted to keep the gold discovery a secret for as long as possible. They weren't ready to defend the homesteads Eli had surveyed, let alone ward off a gold rush.

Roland had to get a letter to John Gould and Mary. He now had just the thing to get John away from the Mother Lode. That night he wrote the letter and gave it to McFadden and Björn to post to Amador City at their first opportunity. In the morning, he paid the two men more than they were expecting and told them to be careful on their way back to the Colorado. He watched them head out to the west from the top of the mountain. About a mile from the bottom of the mountain, he saw the two old Indians join them. He felt a little better for their safety and hoped John would eventually get the letter. Now he had some cabins to build and a niche to carve out of the wilderness for him and his wife. He was going to be busy for some time to come.

Doctor Callahan

Progressing through her coursework, Suzette was a textbook model for the workaholic. She completed the first two classes Dr. Cooper mandated necessary for her degree in eight weeks. She took on auditing several others in addition to her daily attendance to the surgery. There were three places she studied. One was her garret, and the other two were the library at the medical college and the closet/office there that she could call her own. Mr. Sue was her constant companion and always made it a point to know where she was, even when among the floors, classrooms and the hallways of the college. He walked with her to and from the medical college and volunteered there as a cook in the cafeteria. Dr. Cooper was pleased to have him help in the kitchen.

Suzette had become good friends with Bridgette, the receptionist. Bridgette was still sexually abused by Dr. Fillmore, but at least it no longer happened in public. One day Bridgette sat down next to Suzette in the gallery above the surgery. A contractor was there with his men installing the glass windows that Suzette had designed to isolate the gallery from the surgery floor. Suzette felt she had gotten to know the girl well enough to ask how she got involved with Fillmore.

Bridgette was reluctant to talk about Fillmore at first, but once she started, the floodgates were open. It started small at first, but then, after the occasional touch, Fillmore started asking her over to his apartment for dinner. It seemed innocent enough at first, and Fillmore was quite a lot older, but he was an eminent doctor and well respected around town. One evening at his apartment, he offered her an apéritif. She didn't know what was in it, but soon after she drank it, she was aroused and receptive to his every request. While reluctant to admit it, she was sexually excited beyond anything she ever experienced in her young life. She not only let Fillmore have his way with her, but she also confessed that she enjoyed it.

Now Suzette understood Fillmore's obsession with herbs. He had perfected a powerful aphrodisiac and had used it to seduce Bridgette. The young woman admitted that occasionally she would have dinner with Fillmore, and they would both partake of his wicked brew. That was about a year ago and ever since Fillmore had been getting bolder here at the college. Bridgette even confessed that she had sex with Fillmore at least once a week at the college. Usually late at night, up on the roof or down in the basement.

Suzette wished that Fillmore would make a move on her so she could carry out her threat in good conscience.

She focused on her future, though. She was in the third month of her six-month residency and wanted desperately to finish with her M.D. She talked the situation over with Irwin and Mr. Sue several times, and both of them strongly advised her to stay out of it. The fact that Bridgette continued with the relationship after the first time, which constituted nothing less than rape, made the situation legally complicated. On the way up to the roof to check the progress of the greenhouse, Suzette assured Bridgette if she needed her help, she would do what she could. As always, Bridgette needed the job, and for fear of being fired, let the situation ride. It was enough that Suzette got Fillmore onto a probationary status. Fillmore steered clear of Suzette and was even more careful with Bridgette around the college. Dr. Cooper and his nephew Dr. Hale were both keeping a sharp eye out for any improprieties, at least during the hours the college was open for business. Suzette got the idea that they would fire Fillmore, the first opportunity that availed itself.

To her credit and held in high esteem by both the doctors and students at the college was the fact that since Suzette started using her magic brown herb on closing the surgeries, death from infection ended. The college not only didn't lose any patients to infection in the clinical practice, but they also didn't have even one case of infection associated with the many surgeries they completed every week. Even Fillmore had to agree that Suzette was making a significant contribution to medical science. Suzette's work appeared in the San Francisco Medical Journal, and copies had been sent back east for comment and review.

The men who had been following Suzette lost interest and gave up on harassing her. They never found her alone on the streets, and even when she joined the doctors and students down at the Willows, Suzette and Mr. Sue were left completely alone. On one occasion, as Suzette was strapping on her gun belt at Bridgette's desk, the young woman asked if she could walk down to the Willows with them. Along the way, Bridgette told Suzette and Mr. Sue that she wanted to break away from Fillmore. Mr. Sue put his arm around Bridgette and said, "It is going to be hard after so long. When are you going to tell him?"

"In a few minutes," was the reply. Fillmore was at his usual spot at the table in the back of the bar. He saw Bridgette enter the bar with Suzette. Mr. Sue always waited outside. Suzette avoided Fillmore's table, but Bridgette walked back to him and said, "We have to talk." They went over to the bar, and Bridgette said quiet enough that only Fillmore could hear, "Doctor Fillmore, our affair is over. Do you understand me? Never again."

Fillmore turned purple and sputtered. He wanted to scream at her or slip her some more aphrodisiac, but that would have to wait till later. He stormed past Suzette with a look of hatred that could kill. He didn't say anything, but Suzette knew that he blamed her for Bridgette finally finding some backbone. Fillmore stormed out the front door and turned and gave Mr. Sue the same threatening glare of hatred. Mr. Sue just smiled; he didn't even get up. He just made the motion with both hands for Fillmore to come ahead and attack him. Fillmore turned more purple but turned and walked toward the bay before he did something that would surely put him in the hospital as a patient.

Inside the bar, Suzette walked up to Bridgette and put her arm around her, "If you need any help with that asshole, come and get Mr. Sue or me. How about you and I talk to Dr. Cooper or his nephew tomorrow." Bridgette agreed to let Suzette help. What Suzette wanted was to get Bridgette enrolled in training to have her certified as a surgical nurse. Suzette didn't intend to leave her in San Francisco when she went to find her brothers.

As Suzette and Mr. Sue were walking down Mission Street to return home, they could see a huge man several blocks away. Suzette thought that it couldn't be, but as she got a little closer, she could see that it was Uncle Tio from Bernalillio. Maria was following in his wake, amazed at the hustle and bustle around her, finding her first trip to the big city more than just a little intimidating. Suzette ran forward and jumped up onto Tio's chest to give him a big hug. She didn't notice that Fillmore was on the other side of the street talking to some thugs. Mr. Sue noticed, though, and he saw several of the thugs shake their head *no* and walk off at the sight of Tio. At seven-plus feet tall, Tio was easily the biggest man in the Mission, if not in all of San Francisco. When Mr. Sue caught up with Suzette, he found her and the young girl holding each other and crying; cooing to each other and carrying on in Spanish. Ever watchful, Mr. Sue saw Fillmore beating a hasty retreat off through a side alley. He was sure that the threat of Fillmore would manifest itself soon, but not tonight.

They walked past the medical college and then up Third Avenue to the mansion. Suzette took Maria in to meet Denise. Denise was upstairs in her office, and Suzette sent word to her to come downstairs. Tio stayed with Mr.

Sue. The two of them went to the kitchen. The ceilings in the house were high enough for Tio, but the doorways were way too low. Mr. Sue was glad to see the big man again. However, the kitchen staff shrank back, terrified of the giant who invaded their domain. Luckily, they had a huge pot of fish stew prepared for the evening meal. Tio was docile as a kitten, but the cook took credit for her good bisque being responsible for settling the big man down for a hearty meal.

Denise came down the stairs and into the parlor. Her smile reached ear-to-ear; she knew it was Maria, the girl Suzette found on the trail. She extended her hands to the young girl. "You must be Maria. Suzette has told me all about you. Bienvenido, a San Francisco."

Respectfully, Maria rose to her feet and with a small curtsy, said, "Muchas gracias, Señora."

Denise turned to Suzette and told her to let Maria know she was to call her Denise. Then Denise asked, "Where is the uncle?"

Suzette took Denise by the hand into the kitchen. Uncle Tio knocked his chair over, jumping up to greet Denise. Suzette told him to calm down in Spanish and then introduced Denise. By that time, Tio was on his third bowl of soup, but he put his dinner aside for the moment to be respectful to the Abuela. Denise was amazed at Tio's size. She asked Suzette, "Why is he so big?"

"*Homo Giganticus* is the official medical term. Fortunately, Tio is gentle as a lamb and mentally just a few years older than Maria. I am surprised that the family let the two of them travel alone, but then again, who would be dumb enough to mess with a man Tio's size."

Denise was worried where she was going to put the big man. Mr. Sue solved that quickly, "Tio will stay with me. Maria will stay with Suzette. I have already sent for more mattresses – and more food!" They all laughed, but the cook was relieved. Tio had already put away half of what she had prepared for the entire household.

Later that night, when Maria was asleep in the garret, Suzette talked to Denise about what she wanted for Maria. "I am going to pay to put Maria into the best girls' school in San Francisco. I gave her the money I won at Fort Union, and most of what I won betting on Mr. Sue back at Fort Wise. If she needs more or wants to go on to college, I will pay for that too. I know I am much too young to be a mother to her, but I truly feel she is my daughter, and I have felt that way ever since I found her broken and alone on the trail.

The girl deserves a chance at a good life. Lord knows she has been through more bad times than anyone deserves."

Denise said, "There is a girls' school close by here called the Rincon School. I know there are some teachers there that speak Spanish. I will take her and Uncle Tio there tomorrow. You go to school as usual. I will take care of her like she is my great-granddaughter. I guess she is just that if you are her mother. We need to make her adoption official."

Suzette hugged her grandmother. It wasn't necessary to say more; they understood each other perfectly.

The next day Suzette and Mr. Sue left the house early. They had to explain to Tio that Denise would be taking them up to the Rincon School to enroll Maria. Tio was content to wait in the kitchen until it was time to leave.

As Suzette and Mr. Sue rounded the corner onto Mission Street, they could see that there was going to be trouble. There was a gang of men waiting for them, and one of them had a pistol drawn and cocked and held it steady on Suzette. The man with the gun was the first to speak. "Well, good morning, miss. We are hoping your day will not go so well. You're out to get a friend of ours fired from the Medical College. We are here to teach you that he isn't too happy about that."

Suzette just smiled at him and said, "Big man with a gun. I would bet a hundred bucks that you are afraid to holster that peashooter and draw down on me in a fair fight." The big man didn't say anything, but the rest of the gang hooted and waited to see if their leader would answer the challenge.

He must have thought he was pretty good because he holstered the revolver and spread his feet out in the classic gun fighter's stance. Before he could draw, Mr. Sue moved so fast his staff was a blur as he swung a blow to the leader's head. Mr. Sue spun and put two more men on the ground before they even realized that the fight had started. Suzette punched another man in the stomach and then delivered a chop to the back of the neck as he bent over double. Another man tried to grab her from behind, but Suzette spun around and straight-armed him with a punch to the solar plexus that put him on the ground. Five of the eight thugs were on the ground. The other three ran away. The leader was moaning and trying to roll over to get to his feet. Suzette took his gun and put the barrel in his mouth, "If I ever see you again, I will kill you." She took the barrel out of his mouth and fired a round into the sidewalk next to his head. She was sure the muzzle blast would leave him deaf in that ear.

Suzette and Mr. Sue walked on to the college as if nothing had happened. As usual, they were early, but Bridgette was there to let them in. Some policemen from the Mission had heard the shot, and they were running up the street to investigate. Bridgette said, "I don't know if I can talk to Dr. Cooper alone. Will you help me?"

Mr. Sue said, "We will both help you. Let's sit in his office until he arrives." They left the door to Dr. Cooper's office open and sat in the chairs in front of his desk. Suzette heard the front door open and turned to see a surprised Dr. Fillmore come in. Suzette raised the revolver she took off the thug and fired a round into the woodwork next to Fillmore's head on the other side of the hall. Fillmore was no fool. Suzette had connected the dots and would be out to get him with a lot more intensity than before. He ran out of the building.

Dr. Cooper came into his office as soon as the front door of the college slammed behind Fillmore. Gunsmoke lingered in the air, and the acrid smell was offensive as cigarette smoke to Dr. Cooper. "I thought I told you, young lady, to check your weapon with Bridgette."

Suzette stood up and answered calmly, which of late was her signature voice as she closed the office door, "Bridgette needed our protection, so she came in with us. We need to talk."

Suzette related the whole story of Fillmore using the aphrodisiac on Bridgette and the ongoing abuse for the last year. Bridgette sat in silence with tears welling in her eyes, embarrassed, but glad her friend was helping get her story out in front of Dr. Cooper. The good doctor kept looking at Bridgette for confirmation and occasionally at Mr. Sue. Both would nod their heads *yes*, each time the doctor asked them a question. Suzette finished telling of the attack that morning and pushed the loaded revolver across the table to Dr. Cooper. He looked at it like it was a poisonous snake ready to strike.

While Suzette still had his attention, she started on a different tact. "Dr. Cooper, you are not blind. You knew what Fillmore was doing here, and you did nothing to stop it. Fillmore has been a constant problem and threat to the integrity of this university. You and the College should bar him from the medical profession for using his medical acumen to seduce this young woman. Now, I am not going to give you a choice about this. I want Bridgette to be admitted here for training to be a surgical nurse. I have two months to go to fill my commitment to you. I want her trained and ready to leave with me for the New Mexico Territories when I graduate. Am I clear on this? I don't care what you do with the slimeball Fillmore, but I do care that you train Bridgette as a surgical nurse."

Dr. Cooper stammered out an argument, "We – We don't have a nursing school here. You're asking me to do something I can't get done!"

"Maybe you misunderstand. You will agree to have Bridgette trained and ready to go in two months, or you will be reading everything I have told you this morning in the *Alta California* tomorrow. Now, do you understand?"

Dr. Cooper paled and was more shaken if that were possible. Suzette feared the onset of a seizure, but Dr. Cooper answered, "I will have to get the regents to approve adding a nursing program to the curriculum. That will take some time."

Suzette gave him a kind smile, "I will give you some time. You have until midnight tonight. I will be home writing up the story. Don't miss buying a paper tomorrow morning on your way into work." Suzette rose to leave, but Dr. Cooper motioned for her to take a seat.

"Bridgette, I am deeply sorry about what has happened to you here. Suzette is right. I did know what was going on. I just wanted it to go away. I will personally fire Fillmore and ask him to relinquish his credentials, or I will be the one to put his story in the newspapers. I want you to help me write his letter of dismissal, and then I want you to hire your replacement. You can start training in the surgery as soon as you finish those two tasks." Dr. Cooper sat forward in his chair to address Suzette more directly. "I should probably resign, but to tell you the truth, I don't expect to live much longer. My condition is rapidly deteriorating. Suzette, I may not be alive in two months to hand you your M.D. Please, allow me to finish my career here. It's been my life's work. I don't want my legacy to end with Fillmore's disgrace." Suzette nodded her approval, and Dr. Cooper relaxed back in his chair.

With that, the Nursing College of the University of the Pacific was born. Dr. Cooper called an emergency meeting of the Board of Regents. They argued through the afternoon, but by ten that night, Suzette received a note from the university that confirmed that the Nursing College was approved. She was thrilled. Bridgette would start training as a surgical nurse. Suzette doubted that the trouble with Fillmore was over, but if it came up again, she was prepared to handle it. She wasn't going to let the negatives of the day win over the positives. That night, Suzette fell asleep in the bed next to Maria, probably the most content young woman in San Francisco.

The next two months flew by. Every day, Uncle Tio would walk Maria to the girls' school and wait patiently on the stairs till she finished her day. He would stay there all day with no care for the weather, food, or bathroom breaks. At the end of Maria's school day, he would walk her home. News of the outbreak of the Civil War reached San Francisco, and for a while, the city was in a frenzy anticipating a Confederate attack from within. Colonel Albert Sidney Johnston, however, prevented the Confederate sympathizers from arming themselves at the Presidio. Denise was busy night and day writing editorials, cajoling the Union sympathizers to act. She knew that her grandson Jacques was working as a US Army scout. She didn't know that he was currently in the New Mexico Territory with a survey crew. She thought that Jacques would soon become disenchanted with the Army and go his own way. She didn't want any of her grandchildren in the war.

Fillmore was never again seen in San Francisco. Word had it that he went up into the Mother Lode to open his practice next to one of the big underground mines. There were plenty of accidents in the mines to keep more than a score of doctors busy. With her coursework done, Suzette poured all her time into her work with her anti-infection herbs and the surgery. She kept Bridgette by her side, helping her perfect her use of the chloroform and monitoring the patients during the surgeries. Bridgette had hired her younger sister to take care of the front desk, and Dr. Cooper promised to let her enter the nursing program as soon as she was old enough, and if she could hire and train another replacement. Suzette's biggest worry was Maria. What would she do with her when she finished her degree?

Denise solved that problem for her one night at dinner. They weren't even talking about how close Suzette was to the end of her six-month program. Denise took Maria's hand and held it firmly while she told the girl what would happen next; Suzette translated so there would be no misunderstanding, "Maria, Suzette will be a doctor very soon. She is going back to the New Mexico Territory to find her brothers and your Uncle Tio's sister. You and Tio are going to stay here with me until you finish school. That will take some years, and you are welcome to stay as long as it takes, and even longer than that if you want."

Maria looked at Suzette with tears welling up in her eyes. Suzette asked her in Spanish, "¿Lo entiendes?"

Maria got up and hugged Suzette. Tio didn't understand, but he started crying too, knowing that Maria was upset. Maria whimpered, "I don't want you to leave without me."

Suzette knew just how she felt and thought back to the day of her mother's tragic death. "I wouldn't leave if Abuela wasn't here to take care of you and Tio. My brothers might need me, and there is a war now. There will be many hurt soldiers. I have to go. I promise you will be safe here, and you will always have a home here with Abuela. You can send me a letter when you are ready to come to find me. You will always know where I am. I am your madre y siempre seré tu madre. "

Suzette held Maria until she finally raised her head and said, "I understand."

The end of Suzette's medical training came unexpectedly on her birthday, June fourth. She was fifteen. She and Bridgette just finished an appendectomy and were cleaning the surgery while the attendants moved the patient to a recovery room. They were planning on going to the Willows to celebrate Suzette's birthday.

When they had finished cleaning up, a student summoned them to the lecture hall on the third floor, where Suzette first took her oral exam to gain admittance to the college. The two women climbed the stairs wondering why the rest of the school seemed empty. When they entered the lecture hall, both were surprised. Denise and Irwin, Mr. Sue, along with Maria and Tio, sat in the front row. Bridgette's family filled the whole second row. To her surprise, she let out a small yelp when she recognized her Uncle Connor, who had been hiding behind a newspaper when she walked in. Dr. Cooper was standing behind the lectern. He had lived longer than he expected, but his hands and his voice were shaky as he directed Suzette and Bridgette to two chairs in the front of the room facing the audience. Doctors and senior students from the college filled the rest of the seats in the lecture hall. First-year students and the college non-medical staff stood in the aisles. Even the staff from the Latham mansion was there.

Dr. Cooper started to speak, with Dr. Hale in close attendance at his side. "Ladies and gentlemen, family, friends, my fellow doctors and all of the student body and college staff – I welcome you to a most prestigious event in the history of the University of the Pacific Medical College. A little less than six months ago, a most extraordinary young woman came here to learn medicine. I will be the first to tell you, we have learned as much from her as she has learned from us. We are all – We…" Dr. Hale stepped in and took over seamlessly, "…. are all enriched by her efforts here, and we are all working to higher standards because of her contributions. Our cutting-edge practices in the surgery appear in the most prestigious medical journals back east and Europe."

Denise started to cry. She could only hope that Anna and Aaden were watching from above. Dr. Hale continued, "I could talk all afternoon and into this evening about these two remarkable young women, but it is time to end their education here and send them on to their life's work. I wish they would stay, but we have no more to teach them."

"Suzette Callahan, please stand. I hereby confer on you the degree of Doctor of Medical Science with all the rights, privileges, and responsibilities pertaining thereto." Suzette was crying, and she was embarrassed to be at the most important event of her young life in her bloody surgical gown. She stepped forward, though, accepted her degree and shook Dr. Hale's hand. She then took Dr. Cooper in her arms, hugged the trembling man and kissed him fondly on the cheek.

"And now, Bridgette Ann O'Malley, please stand. Bridgette, I can only say I wish we discovered your true ambition sooner. You are the first nurse we are graduating, and your performance as a surgical nurse with Doctor Callahan has been exemplary. I confer on you the title of Surgical Nurse & Anesthesiologist, with all the rights, privileges, and responsibilities pertaining thereto. Congratulations, Nurse Bridgette, and may God go with you both."

Bridgette's family leaped to their feet and cheered wildly. Bridgette's mother was crying; she and Denise shared handkerchiefs. Irwin and Uncle Connor came forward but let Maria hug Suzette first. Irwin whispered in her ear as he hugged her, "I am so proud of you. You are the best granddaughter I ever had." Suzette pushed back and hit him in the stomach. Irwin faked being hurt and said, "Help, I need a doctor!" Everyone laughed, but Suzette took his words to heart. Irwin was truly the only grandfather she ever knew.

Dr. Hale called for quiet. "We have reserved the entire Willows Bar and Grill for a reception. Drinks and food provided by the University. Let's all move down the street." Suzette wanted to clean up, and so did Bridgette, but the revelers wouldn't hear of it. When they got out of the front door, Tio bent down and pulled the two young women to his massive shoulders and lifted Suzette and Bridgette high in the air. He carried them like that, Suzette on his right and Bridgette on his left, all the way to the Willows. He had to put them down to get through the door, or he would have carried them all the way in and set them on the bar.

Mr. Sue even came into the bar. He took Suzette aside and said, "It's been a long and dangerous journey for you. I am honored to have been your companion along the way. Where to next?"

"I am going to go find my brothers. Bridgette is going to come with me."

Connor overheard them despite the din of the celebration. He yelled over the noise, "Pack your bags, ladies; I'm taking you to Yuma in style." Suzette couldn't believe her ears. She could be in the New Mexico Territory looking for Eli, Roland, and Lia within a couple of weeks. She tried to hug her uncle, but the crowd pushed and pulled, and she couldn't get back to him; everyone wanted to shake her hand or hug her. Drinks rose high and toasted the two graduates. The evening turned into night with the students trying to out-drink the Irish, and the Irish trying to out-drink each other and the rest of the world.

It was after midnight when Suzette was finally able to leave. She told Bridgette to see her tomorrow at the college. They had to clean out their desks and lockers. Suzette and Mr. Sue finally headed for home. Suzette, still in her bloody scrubs, now smelled of beer and cigar smoke. Denise, Irwin, and Connor had quietly disappeared with Maria and Tio hours before. Age did have its privilege and a degree of wisdom. Suzette just craved a hot bath. As she and Mr. Sue left the bar, she knew Tio probably carried Maria on his shoulder all the way back to the Latham Mansion. She climbed the stairs to her room and checked on Maria sleeping quietly in her bed and then fell asleep in the warm bath. She woke hours later. Her candle was guttering, the water cold; she picked up the candle and walked naked up to her bedroom. She blew out the flame and collapsed on the bed, not even bothering to dry herself.

The next morning came late for everyone. It was eleven in the morning by the time Suzette and Mr. Sue walked down to the Medical School. Bridgette was there with several of her brothers and already had her things packed up. Suzette apologized for being so late and asked her to meet her at the mansion for dinner. They had to make some plans with her Uncle Connor for sailing around the southern tip of Baja California and up the gulf to Yuma. They needed to make a list of medical supplies, and all the items would have to be packed special to make the sea journey to arrive at their destination dry and ready to use.

It was a nostalgic time for Suzette and Mr. Sue. As they were leaving the college, Dr. Hale saw them in the hall. He came out of his office and shook Suzette's hand and wished them Godspeed again. He told Mr. Sue that he was going to miss his cooking and told him he could return anytime he wanted. There would always be a place for all three of them here at the college if they ever wanted to return.

That night Suzette and Bridgette made a long list of what they needed to take to Arizona for their first practice. The list was a little daunting to Bridgette, who could only see a lot of dollar signs attached. Medical supplies were readily available in San Francisco, but they were not cheap. It would cost thousands of dollars to get them onto Connor's schooner and out of the bay area. Suzette told her not to worry about the money. Come Monday, they would start rounding up the purchases at the supply houses. Within a few days, they would be sailing away with Mr. Sue to make a new life. Her only regret was leaving Patches with Maria. She told her daughter to take good care of her horse. Maria would need her when she came down to the desert to find her.

Connor waited down at the Embarcadero for them to get the last of the supplies crated and ready to load onto the schooner. Mr. Sue was taking care of making sure everything was accounted for and packed correctly. Suzette had heard so much about the boat that she felt at home there. Bridgette, however, was first a little frightened to step aboard. Both their families were gathered on the pier as the last crate was hoisted aboard and stowed below. Last goodbyes and Connor cast off. A steam tug towed them away from the pier. The tide was turning for the short trip out the mouth of the bay. Both women stood with Connor at the helm and looked at the city as they passed, wondering if they would ever return.

The Blessed was now an older but well-kept boat. She was still magnificent to behold as Connor ordered more sails raised as they left the last of the city behind them. The sails caught the wind, and the boat sprinted forward, rocking in the swells. Suzette knew they would both probably be seasick and had a large bottle of herbal tea provided by Mr. Sue that was guaranteed to keep nausea away. They each drank half of the bottle and stayed up forward with their eyes on the horizon. By the time they rounded the San Francisco Peninsula and turned south, they both felt like seasoned sailors.

The trip went well, but when they got south of Los Angeles, the now Confederate frigate, *Heart of the South,* saw them on the horizon and turned to give chase. Connor would have liked nothing better than to engage the frigate and put it on the bottom of the sea, but for now, he would have to settle for just out sailing the larger ship. He didn't like acting the coward at sea, but he was determined to deliver his precious cargo to Yuma in one piece. In two more days, the Confederate ship was out of sight to the rear. Connor turned *The Blessed* into the Gulf of California. He was wary and kept a sharp eye to the rear. He did not want to be caught in the narrow waters of the gulf by the far superior warship. The winds were favorable, and in two days, Connor was able to sail the schooner up the Colorado River to within five miles of Yuma before the river was too shallow for the deep keel of the schooner. He put both tenders in the water and off-loaded the crates of medical supplies with the steam winch. The smaller boats reached the ferry docks at Yuma within two hours with sails and strong backs pulling the oars.

Connor went ashore on the west bank with Suzette. Mr. Sue stayed with Bridgette on the east side. Suzette had to find wagons and mules for transport, and Major Jenkins was surprised to see visitors from the river, even more surprised to see Suzette. He had been dreaming of her ever since she left months ago. The major was eager to round up what Suzette needed for her trip into the *Interior,* as he called it.

Moses came down to the dock on the east side of the river when he heard about the arrivals. He was sure his eyes were deceiving him when a woman who looked like Suzette landed on the west bank. He crossed the river as soon as the ferry was back. He rushed up to Major Jenkins' headquarters and gathered Suzette up in his strong arms and kissed her on the forehead. Connor was amazed at the broad spectrum of Suzette's friends. She introduced Connor to Moses, and the two seafarers instantly started talking about the tenders and the bigger ship that carried them from San Francisco and up the river and Moses and the river ferry.

Suzette needed mules, wagons, and drivers. She let the two men talk while she went over her list with the major. She assured Major Jenkins that she could pay for everything she needed, but she warned Jenkins, "Don't give me any of your derelicts just because you want to get rid of them. I need good men, preferably ones that can build me a clinic when I get where I'm going."

Major Jenkins asked where she was going. She kept her answer ambiguous. She didn't want to see Jenkins again once she left Yuma. The warning written on the back of the guest room door still reminded her that Jenkins was not to be trusted. "I'm going to the Pima village on the Gila River and then turning north. My brothers are up there somewhere." She left it at that and left Major Jenkins with her list.

Moses took her down to the ferry. He was anxious to show Suzette and her uncle the improvements he had made. "Be sure to tell your brother that the ferry business is better than ever; I send money to his bank account over in Los Angeles every time the Butterfield Stage passes through."

Suzette assured him he didn't have to worry about the money. She intended to make Eli give the ferry company to Moses and his men when and if she found him. The tenders crossed the river. Connor and his men unloaded the crates of medical supplies on Moses's dock. There was a small warehouse on the bank above the ferry dock; the men carried the crates up, and Moses locked them in the warehouse.

Bridgette marveled at everything around her. Everything around her was new. The air was hot and dry. She could see empty land in every direction she looked. There were quite a few people around the fort, but very few of them were white. Brown and reddish-bronze skins were common, and only occasionally, could she catch part of a conversation in English. She was also dreading Connor leaving them there alone, but she felt reassured when Moses said he was going with them to find Eli. Connor was anxious to return to *The Blessed.* He was worried that the Confederate frigate might have followed him into the gulf. He didn't want to meet the frigate in the narrow upper end. He said his goodbyes, gave Suzette an affectionate hug, kissed Brigette's hand elegantly, then stepped aboard the nearest tender. He was down the river and out of sight in what seemed like minutes. Suzette couldn't believe she was back in the territory, just like that.

Moses took them back across the river, and they put up their things in the guest house behind the headquarters. Soldiers and civilians crowded the mess hall for dinner. There were a lot of soldiers there waiting for the Confederate invasion from the east. Jenkins was spoiling for a fight, and Major Hancock was marshaling and training more troops over in Los Angeles. The country was at war, and the Army seemed pleased that they would soon be putting the South in its place. Suzette knew differently. Over their Army fare, Suzette told Bridgette about her father and the history of the European

Civil Wars. If the fighting broke out here, they could easily be pressed into service in a field hospital. Suzette wanted to get away from Yuma as soon as possible. So did Mr. Sue. When the girls settled down for the night, he sat quietly with his back to the door of the guest house and stayed there until sunrise.

After breakfast in the mess hall the next morning, some men showed up with mules to sell. Wagons were no problem; there were more than two dozen heavy Army supply wagons abandoned at the post after delivering war material to the quartermaster. Moses was a big help, chiding some of the muleskinners trying to sell mules that were either ancient or diseased. Suzette thought those men needed a veterinarian more than a doctor. Bridgette was amazed and a little terrified by the whole process. There was even an Indian that showed up with a camel. Bridgette didn't even know what the strange animal was, but from the smell and the nasty disposition, she knew she didn't want one. By the end of the day, Suzette had purchased three wagons and twenty-six mules with the harnesses to hitch them up. There were a lot of disappointed sellers on the west side of the river. Suzette either turned down animals she didn't want or drove a hard bargain for the ones she needed. By the end of the evening, Moses had everything moved to the east bank of the Colorado.

The next day was busy with provisioning. Major Jenkins had a Quartermaster that was a tightwad. Suzette loathed having to bribe the man to get enough food and grain for the mules to make the trek up the Gila. Finally, the man gave in, and they settled on a price for everything she needed. Again, Moses and his men moved everything to the east side of the river and loaded the wagons. One of his men was checking the axles and greasing the hubs. There were several repairs required, but they were trivial.

By the morning of the third day, they set out for the Gila. Moses drove the lead wagon with Mr. Sue riding shotgun; Amos sat high on the crates behind them. The best of Moses's men drove the second wagon, and Suzette drove the third with Bridgette at her side. They stopped at the mouth of the Gila, and Moses switched the mules around to put alpha males at the head of each team. Mr. Sue took on the kitchen duties and served a lunch of ham sandwiches he had procured from the mess hall that morning.

That night Bridgette refused to sleep on the ground. She made an uncomfortable bed on top of the crates of medical supplies. Suzette, the old trail hand, spread her bedroll under her wagon and slept soundly, happy to be back on solid ground. She felt more at ease in the solitude of the desert than in the bustling streets of San Francisco. Morning found them halfway to Antelope Peak. Moses asked her if she wanted to take a short side trip up to the newly established Flap-Jack-Ranch at Aqua Caliente. Suzette declined, she was eager to find her friends in the Pima village and just wanted to keep moving east.

Moses was a good wagon master, and Mr. Sue kept them well fed. Bridgette was still uncomfortable being out in the wilds, but by the time they got to the Pima village, she was at least walking away from the wagons by herself to find the lady's room. Suzette had bought her a Navy Colt 0.44 revolver. It was big and heavy. She gave it to Brigette before they reached the Pima village and told her she would teach Brigette how to shoot and take care of the weapon when they headed up the Hassayampa River. Bridgette gratefully took the Colt but didn't strap it on like Suzette with her Lefauchaux on her hip. She did, however, start carrying it with her whenever she walked away from the wagons.

When they pulled into the Pima village, the Indians were first wary of the big black men driving the wagons. Then they recognized Mr. Sue and Suzette. Moses didn't dare move as hundreds of children swarmed the wagons. Soon they were joined by all the adults, and Moses realized that Suzette and Mr. Sue were folk heroes among the Pima. The teeming crowd surrounded the travelers and ushered them up to Deep Rivers' lodge. The old chief and his wife welcomed them with open arms, and the celebration of their return started to unfold spontaneously. Suzette would have to explain later to Moses how she and Mr. Sue ended the cholera epidemic; young mothers with new babies were already lining up for examinations.

Mr. Sue went back to the wagons and retrieved Suzette's medical bag. By the time he got back to the lodge, Bridgette was busy with triage sorting the patients, so the neediest would be first in line for treatment. Because she was with Suzette, she was instantly trusted, and most of the women wanted to touch her flaming red hair to see if it was real. Bridgette was instantly in love with the Pima children. She now could see her place in the wilderness and quietly thanked Suzette for bringing her here. Most of the children just had scrapes and bruises or mild colds. One woman, though, took Suzette by the hand when she was done with the children and led Suzette and Bridgette over to her hogan. The woman's husband suffered from a rattlesnake bite, and he was in a lot of pain. His foot and leg had swelled to the point where the skin was starting to split; the poison was starting to work on his heart, and the man was mildly cyanotic.

Bridgette was somewhat terrified. She was already deathly afraid of snakes and seeing firsthand what a rattlesnake could do didn't help belay her paranoia one bit. Suzette had the man moved down to the river and put his leg in the cool water. She gave him a stimulant to keep his heart beating and prayed she wouldn't have to amputate the leg to save the man's life. She had him breathing deeply to oxygenate his blood and sat with Bridgette at the river's edge. Each held a hand, and periodically, Bridgette would take his pulse. The man was strong; he was fighting hard and holding his own.

It took several hours for the man's condition to improve. By that time, the Pima assembled at the lodge, had prepared a mountain of food, and the drummers were gathering to beat on their drums for the dancing that would start at dark. Suzette and Bridgette wouldn't leave the man at the river's edge until they were sure he was out of danger. They had him removed from the water after the swelling started to subside. Bridgette treated the split skin with Suzette's herbal powder, and Suzette sutured up the wounds. They didn't join the festivities until they had the man settled back in his hogan. The wife thanked them in her native tongue, with tears running down her cheeks.

As they walked back to the lodge surrounded by the man's family and neighbors, Bridgette said, "I think I'm going to like it here." Suzette didn't want to dampen her enthusiasm, but she did gently tell her nurse that not everything was as peaceful and friendly as the Pima village. When they got back to the lodge, Moses and the other driver were dancing around the fire with the Indians. The beat of the drums and the rhythmic jangling of bells on the dancers' shins was intoxicating along with generous portions of mescal.

Suzette and Bridgette were famished, and all the women were carrying food to them and making them comfortable on Deep Rivers' blankets. The dancing went on and on into the night. When Bridgette started to nod off, the older women took them into the lodge and put them down on comfortable sleeping mats. Suzette didn't realize she was ready to drop. Brigette was asleep as soon as she laid down. Suzette covered her against the mild chill of the night and climbed under the blankets beside her. Both women slept soundly despite the noise of the ongoing celebration.

The next morning, Moses was feeling good, but the other driver was badly hungover from the mescal that was the backbone of the Pima alcohol industry. Lesson learned the man swore he would never partake of the evil liquid again. Mr. Sue laughed at him; he wasn't the first man who they had seen swear off drinking after a night with the Pima's firewater. It was noon by the time they started up the river. The snakebite victim improved after a night's rest. The whole village assembled to see them off as they left to head north. Suzette was hoping her old guide would take them up the Hassayampa, but he told them Eli was on the hill, and they would have no trouble finding him. He did, however, send four of his young braves with them to scout for Apaches and even help fight if Apaches attacked.

By that night, they were at the mouth of the Hassayampa, and Suzette was looking forward to seeing her brothers. Remarkably, the Hassayampa that was usually dry was a full-flowing river. It wasn't roaring, but the wet bottom still slowed their progress. It took a full week before they were at the top of the long narrow channel where they emerged onto the broad plain. The four extra Pimas were extremely useful, guarding the camp through the night and helping push the heavy wagons along when mired in the wet bottom. They were amazed, though, at how strong Mr. Sue was for a man of his age and size. All hardship was forgotten, however, when they emerged from the narrow river bottom and saw the red mountain.

Moses was glad to be out of the soft bottoms. He wasn't a hundred yards away from the river when he turned around and looked back for his Pima guides. The four Indians were already nowhere in sight. Moses knew they wouldn't want to go up on the hill, but he was surprised that even five miles was too close for their comfort. He didn't care; Suzette had driven her wagon up next to his, and the smile on her face was all the thanks Moses needed for all the hard work. They followed the small stream up from the river, and the closer they got to the hill, the hotter the water. Suzette and Bridgette were hoping there was a deep pool somewhere up ahead for a bath, but the main thing for Suzette was that she knew her brothers were here.

It took an hour to reach the base of the hill. Eli had seen the wagons coming and ran out to meet them. Moses pulled up and jumped down, and the two big men slammed together in a fierce bear hug. Eli reached up and lifted his sister down and crushed her in a fond embrace. "Doctor Callahan, I trust?" Suzette was overwhelmed and felt at home out in the middle of nowhere, held tight in her brother's strong arms.

Finally, she pushed back and said, "You have to meet my nurse and surgical assistant." She turned to Bridgette, who was on the driver's seat, still holding the reins. "This is Bridgette O'Malley. She graduated with me, and we're going to be partners in a practice. We brought all the supplies for a clinic and a modest surgery."

Eli helped Bridgette down and welcomed her to his remote corner of the world. Then he said, "Let's go over to the hill. Roland and Lia are here, and there is someone else I want you to meet." Eli got up on the wagon with Moses, and they drove the last short distance to the cabins. Roland, Lia, and Abby were waiting for them. Suzette jumped off the wagon and rushed into the arms of Roland and Lia. Abby was standing quietly to the side. Eli took Suzette's hand and pulled her away from Lia. "This is Abby; we are a lot more than just friends. I have taken Abby as my wife, even though there is no preacher around to marry us."

Suzette was surprised, but not knowing what to say as she extended her hands to Abby. Abby was pensive. Eli had told her that Suzette spoke French. It had been some time since she used the language, but she delighted Suzette asking her in French to introduce the rest of her friends. "S'il vous plaît présentez-moi au reste de vos amis."

That melted Suzette's heart. In an instant, she made the transition from stranger to sister-in-law. She pulled Abby into a hug and introduced Mr. Sue, Moses and Amos, Bridgette, and the other driver, Gardner. She looked around then and saw the two neat little cabins and the mule harnessed to the grinder. She turned to Eli and said, "There aren't many people here. How are we going to make a living with a clinic?"

Eli laughed at her, "If you want a lot of people around, I can make that happen overnight." He took Suzette by the hand and walked her over to the grinder. He was cautious that no one else followed them or were even in earshot. He opened a small wooden box next to where Abby sat when she panned. He took out a full pickle jar full of gold powder. "When would you like the gold rush to start?"

Suzette took the jar in her hands and nearly dropped it. The quart jar full of gold powder weighed at least thirty pounds. She just stood there with her mouth open; a vision of the bustling San Francisco, the Mother Lode, and the Comstock in Nevada rushed through her agile mind. Then the ramifications of a flood of people eager for gold and wealth with the attendant crime, fraud, and violence that it brought with it started to bring her back down to earth. "Eli, everyone in the west will try to take this away from you. How will you hang on to what you have here?"

"I sent a letter back to Jacques with the two men and the Indians that brought Roland and Lia here through the mountains. If he can, I want him to bring a survey party from the Army and set monuments and make a map of the area with our claims in the middle. We will set up a mining district; we'll call it the Red Mountain Mining District and send the maps and filing documents to Santa Fe just like when President Tyler and Congress put homesteading in place in 1841. Homesteading will come to the New Mexico Territories. We will have our documents and surveys to prove we were here first. Let's talk about it after Moses and his driver leave. I trust Moses, and I am going to tell him about the gold, but I don't know the other man. In the meantime, we have a clinic to build."

Moses stayed for two more days. He didn't want to go back down the river. He was sure he could find his way through the mountains to the west, and even walk if they couldn't get the mules and wagons through. Roland drew Moses a map of how they came over from the Colorado, and at dawn of the third day, Moses set out for Yuma. He had a deed signing full ownership of the ferry operation over to him, written out and signed by Eli. Moses was a happy man when he left and would soon be wealthy not having to send half of the profits to Los Angeles.

Suzette and Bridgette moved into the first cabin Eli built up on the top of the hill. The women mined gold throughout the day. Mr. Sue couldn't understand why people of incredible wealth moiled in the mud for the yellow metal. Mr. Sue was happy, though; he had a herd of oxen, numerous deer, and the occasional pig, ready at hand to keep everyone fed. Eli and Roland worked like demons hewing logs and raising the walls of a four-room structure for the clinic. There would be four rooms for the clinic and a lean-to on the back for a kitchen and living quarters for Mr. Sue.

Eli was no fool; he had the same visionary mind of his father. He knew that the gold rush would come even if he didn't make it happen. Each time he and Roland went to the Hassayampa for more logs, they took a gold pan with them. There was gold where the Hassayampa flowed out of the mountains to the northeast. There was gold in another creek bottom a few miles to the northeast of the hill. Roland wanted to stake more claims, but Eli told him it was useless. He told Roland the only land they could hold when this gold rush started would be the red hill – and that would be with a gun in their hand and around the clock vigilance.

He didn't realize just how true that would prove to be.

Red Mountain Mining

With the women occupying themselves with mining, and Mr. Sue with keeping everyone fed, the clinic building rose steadily. Abby was thrilled. She had shown Mr. Sue the drawings in the mining book that showed men assaying ores. Eli knew how to build a furnace that would make charcoal, but he was doubtful that he could make something that could reach the melting temperatures of gold. Mr. Sue had seen this done in China, and instead of trying first to build a furnace, he set out to build a set of sizeable bellows. He had already mastered using the retort for recovering gold from the mercury used in the amalgam pan. Eli and Roland extended the deer hide sluice and installed the amalgam pan behind it. That simple addition alone boosted the gold production yet again.

In the mining equipment that Roland had brought over from Hale's Mercado, there were some crucibles used for melting gold. It was unfortunate that Hale had not included some instructions for building a melting furnace. In that regard, they were on their own to learn how to do it. Mr. Sue took some time every day to sew deer hides building the bellows that would provide the air for the blast to make a high enough heat to melt the gold. It took a week for him to finish sewing the deer hides together, but when he finished, he had a bellows five feet in diameter. Eli made a crude clay pipe and fashioned a small shaft furnace where the bellows blew in the air to burn charcoal under one of the large melting crucibles. Feeding the charcoal to keep the fire white-hot was a problem, but Bridgette and Abby worked that out with a redesign of the furnace.

The furnace was truly a novelty, but everyone gave it a high chance of success because Mr. Sue tested it and proved that he could melt a piece of steel in the fire. It was hard to get Abby to give up the first pickle jar of gold for the maiden run, but she finally agreed after Suzette reassured her that the gold was noble; it would not disappear in the fire. Eli had a huge pile of charcoal manufactured out of the cottonwood limbs. It seemed that was the only purpose they could find for the fallen tree up at the hot spring. Abby carefully poured her jar of gold into the crucible, and Mr. Sue placed the crucible in the furnace. They didn't have any tools to lift it out to pour the gold into a steel mold, even though there was an iron mold in the things that Hale sent. The plan was to fire the furnace, melt the gold, and then let it all cool down in place. The process would take a while, but everyone wanted to see the results. The three women each had a steel rod fashioned to push charcoal down three flues into the combustion chamber under the crucible. Mr. Sue started the fire with a cup full of bacon fat and some kindling. Until the bacon fat burned away, the fire smelled like breakfast cooking.

For several hours the men took turns pumping the bellows, and the women stoked the furnace. The heat was intense; after the first hour, the crucible and the interior of the shaft around it turned a bright cherry red. Through the next hour, the color went from red to a dull orange, then on to a deep yellow and finally almost white. Eli's supply of charcoal was almost used up. Everyone dripped sweat. The hot desert air of middle July, aided by the heat of the furnace, had everyone on the edge of heat exhaustion. The women were better off; they had more hair to keep wet, but once Suzette singed hers leaning over the furnace to look down in the crucible. After two more hours, everyone agreed that it was time to quit.

Mr. Sue had a light meal of cold rabbit and salad greens waiting for everyone next to the cookstove. What they all would have preferred was a block of ice. As the evening cooled down, though, and the only light was given off by the cooling furnace and a small kerosene lamp, the cool meal tasted pretty good after a hard day's work. It would probably take all night and possibly the next day for the furnace to be cool enough to lift out the crucible.

Everyone turned in except Suzette and Bridgette, who took the lantern and walked up the path to the top of the hill. They undressed at the side of the spring and settled into the hot water to end the day, getting clean and soothing tired muscles in hot water. They didn't talk for a long time. Suzette was almost asleep when Bridgette asked her what had happened to Juan Pedro, the young Spaniard who came to San Francisco with her.

Suzette had never talked about him. It was a bad experience that she kept to herself – until now. For some reason, she didn't understand; she suddenly felt the need to share with Bridgette what had happened. "Juan Pedro went with his grandfather over to the east side of the bay. They had family there. I didn't see or hear from him for more than eight weeks. Then one day there was an envelope from him waiting for me at the reception desk at the college. I opened it, and there was a note telling me that Juan Pedro was in a room in the Xavier hotel, several blocks west of the Willows. I was a little mad that he didn't wait for me to finish my day at the college to see me. Mr. Sue and I walked down there to find the hotel after I finished in the surgery."

"I asked the man at the desk for his room number. It was on the third floor. Mr. Sue waited in the lobby, and I went up there alone. His door was slightly ajar. I knocked, and the door swung open. Juan Pedro was on the bed with a two-bit harlot. He didn't see me because he was busy with his face between the harlot's legs. She saw me, though, and beckoned to me to join them as if there was plenty to share. I closed the door, and I never saw him again. I ran down the stairs crying and out the front door of the hotel. Mr. Sue put his arm around me and walked me home." Suzette was sobbing anew at the painful memory. It was as if telling Bridgette made it all real again like it just happened an hour ago.

Bridgette reached over and put her hand on Suzette's shoulder. They didn't talk, but they held each other until they were ready to go back to the cabin. It took a long time for Suzette to quit crying. Being naked in each other's arms with the hot water of the spring swirling up around them was strangely erotic, but neither thought badly of the other about it. They walked naked in the lantern light and stopped at their makeshift latrine before turning in for the night. Even at night, it was too hot to sleep touching. Before Suzette fell asleep, she told her friend, thanks for listening. She didn't know if Bridgette was still awake, but she liked Bridgette holding her after she told her story. Bridgette was only a little older, but with Fillmore, she had experience enough on the dark side of sex to last a lifetime. They would have slept late into the day, but hunger was eating away at them shortly after dawn. They put on clean clothes and walked down the hill. They took the lantern with them just in case they were out after dark again.

Mr. Sue had a surprise for breakfast. Several big rattlesnakes had crawled in off the desert to the warmth of the furnace. They probably wouldn't have stayed for breakfast if they knew they were going to be the main course. Bridgette was reluctant to eat snake, but it smelled good broiling over the fire and tasted even better than it smelled. Abby kidded her, "Once you discover that snakes are good to eat, it is easier to get over your fear of them. Don't worry; you will never get over the very basic instinct to flinch every time you first see one. That reaction is important. It can save your life."

Bridgette told the story of the man they saved from snakebite down in the Pima village. Everyone liked the reassurance that Suzette and Bridgette could treat snakebite. However, Lia was the most grateful that Suzette and Bridgette were there. She was seven months pregnant and didn't want to be without expert care when her time to deliver arrived. The doctor and nurse had delivered at least a dozen babies in the surgery at the college. They assured Lia that everything would be alright. As soon as the clinic was complete, they would perform a thorough prenatal examination. Bridgette quipped, "Maybe we should have built a maternity ward instead of a surgery."

The furnace was still too hot to touch, but looking down through the top, they could see that the gold powder was now one solid chunk of metal. The women were more excited than their men. They went back to mining and milling. Eli and Roland were splitting shakes for the roof on the clinic. Mr. Sue was figuring out what to cook for dinner.

As usual, the heat of the day rose from the devil's hotbed with the sun on the desert floor. Today though, there was a little breeze, and it was easy to stay wet and cool at the mill. They didn't have a scale to weigh the big lump of gold in the crucible. Suzette suggested that the next time they had a pickle jar full to melt, that they weigh it out on the little gold scale that was in the mining stuff Hale sent over. Everyone thought that was a good idea. Mr. Sue told them that when the furnace was cold, and they could get what he called the *button* out, he would be able to weigh it. They all wondered how he was going to do that without a bigger scale, but as usual with Mr. Sue, they would have to wait and see.

The button was still too hot by lunch, but after dinner, Mr. Sue was able to put his hand down the side of the supports and lift the crucible out with his hand under the bottom. He turned the crucible upside-down, and the gold button fell out with a thunk when it hit the sand at the side of the furnace. Amazing, the gold was still warm, but it was one fantastic looking hunk of gold, the exact shape of the inside of the crucible. The crucible wasn't damaged, and Mr. Sue set it on an upper shelf in his kitchen to await the next melt.

The happy miners passed the gold around, fondling and admiring it, and praising Mr. Sue. Red Mountain Mining was a reality; they were now five equal partners with a saleable product. Roland, ever the businessman, estimated that the gold button was worth around eight to nine thousand dollars.

Mr. Sue waited until everyone was tired of holding the gold. He had set up a full bucket of water with a spout. The bucket was filled to the brim and set to overflow its spout. Mr. Sue lowered the gold into the water and caught what overflowed from the bucket in the very pickle jar where Abby stored the gold when it was gold dust. He had the gold scale from Hale's supplies set up. The heaviest weight they had was 100 grams. He had the scale balanced with the hundred-gram weight on one side, along with enough sand to offset the weight of a tin cup on the other. Painstakingly he filled the tin cup over and over again from the pickle jar till it balanced on the scale opposite the one-hundred-gram weight. He kept track of how many times he had to fill the cup to empty the jar.

At last, he had to use the smaller weights in the scale-set to weigh the last half cup of water. He had kept track of the number of cups he had taken out of the jar on an abacus he had put together from beads and wire. He slid the beads back and forth for several minutes and then announced, "Fifteen point four kilograms."

Everyone scurried for the books. They learned that gold was measured and sold in Troy Ounces. Not even Mr. Sue knew why that was so, but they found that there were 31.1 grams in a troy ounce. This time Roland worked out the math with paper and pencil. Everyone waited until he finished, and they whooped when he read off his answer, "Nine thousand, and nine-hundred three dollars." Unbelievable, and they hadn't even scratched the surface of the red hill. Now Suzette understood how Eli was going to create a city for her practice. Little did she know or care that John Gould had received Roland's letter or that Jacques had received Eli's. There were people out there in the world that would bring great change to this part of the desert wilderness. For the moment, Suzette was happier than any other time in her life, even when she got her M.D. She was with her family and her best friend. It didn't matter if anything ever changed.

The two young women bathed every night in the hot spring. A week went by, and they didn't touch each other again. It was Suzette who one night under the dark of the moon in August, that reached over and touched Bridgette. Bridgette didn't push her away. She took Suzette's hand and put it on her breast. Suzette had touched plenty of women during her training at the college, but this was entirely different. They held each other again and tentatively kissed. Then both joined in a long, deep passionate kiss that was the beginning of what they thought was a casual relationship, a way to sate each other's longings in place of desirable men to pursue.

That night despite the heat, they held each other contentedly and talked about the future. They fell asleep in the total darkness, wondering what would come next. They spent the next day taking care not to show any affection for each other. It was easy, with more excitement overtaking the camp. Eli came off the hill after his morning ritual of looking around with the spyglass. He was excited; there were soldiers out to the west. They were working their way to the hill. By noon, Jacques and thirty Calvary soldiers with two supply wagons pulled up to their sparse settlement.

After an enthusiastic reunion and introductions, Jacques explained that they were a survey platoon. He still wore the buckskins of a rugged frontier scout. Everyone wanted to talk, but the soldiers were carrying a wounded man over to the camp. He had an arrow wound in his side. From his appearance, the man had lost a lot of blood, and his fever was through the roof. The man wasn't sweating; he was already dehydrated and in shock. Not all the medical supplies were unpacked, but Bridgette had the man carried into the surgery. Suzette was already scrubbing up in a pan of hot water. Bridgette was cutting the man's shirt away and asked Jacques how long ago this had happened. Jacques told her yesterday at noon, and then Bridgette shooed everyone out of the surgery.

Bridgette scrubbed up and was taking the man's pulse, wondering if it would be safe to use chloroform on him. The man was delirious but could still feel a lot of pain. Suzette told her to go ahead and put him out, but to go easy with the chloroform. The end of a splintered wooden shaft stuck out of the wound on the lower left abdomen. It was going to be tricky getting the arrowhead out without damaging more of the intestines. It was painfully hot in the little room. Bridgette fanned Suzette and wiped the sweat from her brow as Suzette made her first incision. It took over two hours to remove the arrow and repair the intestines. Suzette went out while Bridgette closed the incision.

There was a young lieutenant there who was the platoon leader. The Indian attack had shaken him up. Yesterday had been his first armed conflict with the Apache. He also feared the soldier could be the first man he lost in combat, but given that the country was at war, it would be far from his last. Eli was going to give him a shot of rot-gut whiskey, but Suzette took the glass from his hand and walked back into the clinic. She put a teaspoon of laudanum into the rotgut and went back out and handed the glass to the lieutenant. He downed it in one painful gulp and coughed at the burn in his throat. His name was Theodore Francis Izzo from South Philadelphia. He was full of news about the war. It had started. The South had shelled and captured Fort Sumter in South Carolina. Major Hancock over in Los Angeles was promoted to Lt. Colonel and was ready to march east if the Confederates tried to come west.

A sergeant moved the soldiers off to camp at the river, where there were cool water and grass for the horses. Lt. Izzo was quite taken with Suzette even though she was a mess. Her cotton blouse soaked with sweat and blood, clung to her torso. Her hair was matted, and she was sure she smelled more like the surgery rather than just a sweaty woman. Lt. Izzo didn't care; he didn't take his eyes off her, and he wanted a full report and a lot of needless details about the wounded man's chances. Suzette was honest, "I don't expect him to live. As soon as he comes to, Bridgette – Nurse O'Malley will try to get some fluids in him. We treated the infection in his stomach, but if his fever doesn't break, he will be dead by morning." They watched as the discouraged young lieutenant rode down to the river to join his troops.

Jacques was content to stay in the camp in his bedroll and would turn in when he was done talking to his brothers. Mr. Sue warned him about the snakes and not to bed down by the hot water or the fire pit, or the rattlers would have him for breakfast instead of the other way around. Suzette and Bridgette stayed in the clinic with their patient. Somehow, they would have to get some cots for these occasions that were sure to come up in the future.

Eli, Roland, and Jacques talked long into the night about the gold in the hill, in the Hassayampa, and the creek to the northeast. Jacques said it would be no problem. In the morning, he would suggest to Lieutenant Izzo that they survey and reset the corners of the homesteads if necessary. Also, they would put survey monuments on a conical hill to the southeast and another on a prominence southwest of the hill. They already completed surveying their way up from Yuma. The survey team would put them accurately on the map and leave Eli with what he needed to survey any new claims that would be located in the ensuing gold rush. Eli showed him the fifteen-kilo button. Jacques was impressed. He said, "Wow, there really is gold in this hill. How will you protect what you have here?"

Eli had a plan. "We will build a crude building around the grinder and let the prospectors come and go around the bottom of the hill. The gold is so fine that only the most skilled and patient prospector could find it. Most of the rush will be up to the north. We will stay here even if there are better discoveries around us. I want you to send the maps over to Santa Fe, so our claims are established and recorded. If you leave me a copy of the map and a better compass or a transit if there is a spare, I can update the map from time to time, and record the mining claims of the newcomers."

Jacques had a better idea. "I will leave the map with the Army in Yuma. There are already other settlers that have staked out farms and mining claims along the Colorado River. The quartermaster is keeping the records. That is as official as a land office in Santa Fe, and if you need help with enforcement, that is going to come from Yuma anyway. With their planning done, they turned in for the night. Before he left, Jacques congratulated Eli on finding a fine-looking woman. He also wondered about the woman Suzette brought with her. With the war in full swing, though, it would be some time before he could offer any woman a reasonable life. He fell asleep, not dreaming about women or gold. The war and all its ramifications were on his mind until sleep finally overtook him.

The next morning the wounded soldier was breathing so shallowly, Suzette thought he was dead. Bridgette had been up before her when the soldier woke. She medicated him with the laudanum and the anti-infection herb and let him go back to sleep. The fever was still high; it was impossible to tell if he was any better. Lt. Izzo rode in and wanted an updated report on his soldier. Suzette gave him a report and was careful not to give him any false hope about the patient or anything else. She had Eli and Roland carry the man outside and set him with his back to a tree where the little bit of morning breeze could cool him down. He looked dead; Bridgette had to reassure Lt. Izzo that the man was only sleeping.

Jacques and Eli made their pitch to the Lieutenant. They wanted the homesteads on the hill surveyed and also several mining claims over in the river. The plan was to let all the soldiers believe that the gold came from the river to keep their attention off the hill. The lieutenant was reluctant to commit his government survey team to a private cause, which technically was against Army regulations. He agreed to do it, however, when Eli offered him two hundred dollars in gold coins. "For your activities fund," Eli told him as he counted and handed Izzo the gold. Izzo took the bribe and rode back to the river to organize his men. Eli thought, h*e who has the gold makes the rules*; the adage would be played out time and time again as the gold in the Red Mountain Mine took its place in the economy of the west.

As typical of July in the desert, dawn broke, and it was still warm from the day before. The warm morning turned into the heat of day long before lunchtime. Eli and Mr. Sue moved the soldier into the shade on a bench at the side of the clinic. Mr. Sue pulled his bellows over and propped it up so it would blow on the feverish man. He kept him wet and kept pumping the bellows all through the hot part of the day. By evening time, the man's fever broke, and he was able to keep some thin soup made from ground mesquite beans down. When Lt. Izzo came in for a report on the day's progress, Suzette upgraded her prognosis to likely-to-live. Lt. Izzo was thrilled. He didn't want to report a death back to his commanding officer. His trip to Red Mountain wasn't only his first encounter with the Apache; it was also his first patrol.

The survey of the homesteads was complete, and none of the corners had to be adjusted more than twenty feet to coincide with the survey. Eli and Abby had done an excellent job, considering the tools they had used for the first survey. The survey team didn't have a spare transit, but they did have a very high-quality compass that had sights that flipped up over the bezel ring. The sights had hooks at their ends so that the compass could hang on a string. The chief surveyor also had an extra tripod. Eli would have to fashion a small table to fit on top of it, but with the tripod and compass together, he was equipped as a surveyor. Reasonably accurate measurements of the angles to the corner monuments of new claims would be good enough to update the claims-map if he added more claims, extending the borders of the Red Mountain Mine.

The next day the lieutenant split his men into two teams. Each went to the monument locations to erect the marker monuments and shoot the angles to the corners of the homestead. Lt. Izzo stayed behind with one of his men. When the crews finished setting the monuments, Izzo's team occupied each of the south corners of the homestead claims and flashed with a mirror to the teams on the mountain tops. They kept signaling until the teams signaled back that all the measurements were completed. All that remained was to survey the monuments back to the last point in the overall survey they had completed from Yuma to their monument west of the hill. The teams finished by the next day. What was left unfinished was to close the survey by returning to Yuma via the route down the Hassayampa.

With all the soldiers away from the hill, Eli had plenty of time to formulate a plan to kick off the gold rush. Lt. Izzo and his soldiers were going to play a key part. The soldiers assembled, ready to start south. The survey team was already gone surveying a point on the Hassayampa as far south as they could go while keeping the two mountain-top monuments within in sight. The wounded man rode in one of the supply wagons, and the horse soldiers were lined up in a column of twos ready to leave.

Eli had told the lieutenant that he had a box and some letters he would like him to deliver to Moses in Yuma. Lieutenant Izzo was holding his horse, and the soldiers were formed up in a crescent around him. Eli and Roland walked up to the lieutenant and thanked him for the survey work he accomplished on their behalf. The lieutenant thanked them for saving the wounded soldier's life.

Eli made sure everyone focused on the little farewell ceremony. When he went to hand the box to Izzo, he fumbled it and dropped it onto a rock at his feet. The flimsy box had been built on purpose to break open easily, and the weight of the gold broke it open over the rock. The gold button rolled out into the plain view of all the men. The gold was brilliant in the bright morning sun; a gasp went up from the soldiers, and their eyes got big. Lia came running up with a canvas bag. Roland held it open, and Eli retrieved the gold button and dropped it into the bag. He didn't just drop it but aimed it at the toe of Roland's boot. The hunk of gold didn't hit his toe, but the canvas bag hid that fact from the soldiers. Roland yelled and went hopping off, holding his foot. Suzette rushed forward and pushed him down on the ground and pulled off his boot and looked for broken bones. Eli picked up the bag and handed it to Lt. Izzo and said, "Just go. I hope you don't have trouble along the way because the men saw the gold." He was sure to say it loud enough for all the soldiers to hear.

Lt. Izzo was just as astounded as his men. He threw the bag to the driver in the first supply wagon; he mounted his horse and gave the order, "Forward hoooo." The column set off with Lieutenant Izzo in the lead to join the survey team in the river.

As planned, the gold rush was on. As Eli and his family watched the soldiers leave, Abby quipped, "If that gold doesn't make it to Moses, you owe me ten grand." Everyone laughed. They already had another pickle jar almost full. It didn't take long, though, for the first consequence of their impromptu stage play to manifest itself. Unbeknownst to them, that night, six of Izzo's troops deserted. In two more days, one of the deserters rode into their settlement slumped in his saddle. He had a bad bullet wound in his shoulder and was asking for Suzette's help. The soldier had been wounded in a gunfight with Lt. Izzo and his loyal troops during an attempt to steal the gold shipment. Eli's foretelling that there would be a lot of business for the clinic was already coming true.

Several weeks went by, and nothing happened. It would take that long for the soldiers to reach Yuma, and then some time for the word to spread from there. What did happen, though, is John Gould arrived with a supply train of his own. He had a heavy steel arrastra (a tool for grinding rock) in one wagon and all the steel parts for a stamp mill along with a steam engine and a boiler in the other. The third wagon had another cabin kit but also pipe and fittings and a large cast-iron bathtub.

Mary hadn't seen the rest of Roland's siblings since they were infants. Introductions were in order, and Mary was beaming when she explained the tub. "I had some conditions of my own before agreeing to come on this adventure," Mary quipped, "and one of them was a bathtub."

Roland knew when he sent the letter that John would have to see the gold mine. He had no idea that John would arrive with so much equipment, but he should have expected it. The man was obsessed with gold mining. They unloaded the wagon with the cabin and tub, and the drivers set out to return to Beale's Crossing. John commented that Hale had supplied everything but the heavy mining equipment. He had sent the heavy items down from San Francisco to the L.A. Harbor, and from there to Victorville by overland freight. Everything was waiting for them at Hale's Mercado when they got there. He and Mary had crossed the Sierra Nevada Mountains on the original Donner Party Trail and worked their way down the east side of the mountains to find Hale's Mercado. As a side note, John said, "Hale is talking about a big gold strike over here in the desert. Is that you?"

Eli had to fess up, "Yep, we got the word out on purpose. I promised Suzette a whole town for her clinic; it sounds like it is going to come true."

"It will come true. Right now, there are hundreds of prospectors trying their best to get here. Los Angeles is abuzz about another gold strike, but no one is certain just where it is."

"That will change any time now. Jacques came by with a survey party. We had him survey in the Red Mountain Mining District. He has a map. The Army is supposed to keep that confidential, but you can bet Major Jenkins in Yuma is drawing maps and selling them to the prospectors as fast as he can reproduce them."

The next day the mine was ready to pour another button. This time Suzette and Abby weighed out exactly fifteen kilos of the powder, and Mr.

Sue got the furnace ready. John watched everything they were doing. When Suzette told John that it took a day to cool the crucible, John went to work. He had a supply of steel rods with him and an anvil. Using the heat on the top of the furnace as a forge, it didn't take him long to have a large set of tongs ready to lift the crucible out while it was still hot. As before, it took all day to reach the melting temperature of gold. John took it all in, and when the furnace reached the yellow-white heat, John stuck one of his steel rods down into the melt. When he pulled it out, the end was yellow hot, and sparks flew off it as it reacted with the air. No gold stuck to the rod; it was time to take the crucible out.

They only waited until the crucible cooled enough that the crucible and the gold didn't glow red, and then they turned it over. John grabbed the bottom with the thongs and finished turning it upside down. He had to thump it on the ground to get the button to release, and when he did, he broke the crucible. Mr. Sue did not approve. He only had two crucibles left. John picked the button up with the thongs and dropped it into a bucket of water. The heat from the gold boiled the water, and when it stopped boiling, the button was still too hot to pick up. John dumped it out and picked the button up again and dropped it into a second bucket of cool water. He let it soak about five minutes and then picked it out of the bucket with his bare hand. Like before, the button was beautiful. Everyone was thrilled except for Mr. Sue. He was mourning the loss of a valuable crucible for no good reason at all.

The men spent the next days planning where to put the steam plant and the milling equipment. The women worked at making more gold, but Lia, near term, tired easily and just sat and watched. Suzette and Bridgette checked on her constantly. Suzette listened to the baby's heartbeat every morning with her stethoscope and let Lia listen too. It had been a week since John and Mary arrived, and Mary already had sewn several outfits. Two were pink, and one was blue just in case.

When the first week in November rolled around, more men and some women showed up every day, ready to prospect for gold. Eli would show them the map of the mining district and then send them up the Hassayampa. There must have been gold up there because very few of the newcomers ever came back unless they were sick or hurt and needed medical attention. Every time new prospectors showed up, Eli would quiz them for news of the war. Things were not going well for the North. That worried Eli. It increased the chances that the Confederates would try to cross the desert to take California into the Confederate States of America. They learned that Jefferson Davis, a former US Senator, and military leader, was the president of the Confederacy. Of more concern, there were rumors that General Robert E. Lee was going to resign his commission in the United States Army to take command of the Army of Northern Virginia. That was the most worrisome news as the summer heat gave way to the cold nights and cool days of winter.

The good news for Red Mountain Mining was that the new gold mill was ready for operation on the east slope of the hill. John Gould proudly fired up the boiler, and the noise of the hammers falling rang out across the desert floor, signaling to all who passed that there was a gold mine in operation in the heart of the desert. Eli hired several disgruntled prospectors to do the mining. John, Eli, and Roland operated the mill. They worked twelve hours a day and were milling forty tons of ore per shift. Now all of the gold was recovered on the amalgam tables. The mercury boiled off in the retort, and the gold recovered as a porous-gold sponge. Quite pretty but not rugged enough for shipping without melting into a solid-gold button. They were careful never to let the miners see how much gold they were recovering. When John got the mill running steady, they would be making one fifteen-kilogram button every two weeks. Soon, someone would have to take the gold at least to Yuma and put it on the stage to Los Angeles. It wasn't money in the bank until it reached San Francisco.

Lia's pregnancy became their main concern. She was a little late, but because it was her first, Suzette was not concerned. They had set up the recovery room in the clinic to be the birthing room. Good thing too; no sooner had they finished that when Lia came into the clinic holding her stomach. Her labor had started. Suzette didn't expect a baby for at least a day and a half.

The men kept mining, but the women waited for the baby. Lia was strong, and she didn't even scream until the next morning. Roland was half crazy when he heard the first scream. John told him to go hunting or something; no amount of male anxiety could help a woman through childbirth. When Roland didn't seem to hear him, John tried again to set him at ease. "Stop worrying; she is with the best doctors in all of New Mexico Territory." The fact that Suzette was the only doctor within three-hundred miles didn't even register with the expectant father. It was Mary who calmed Roland down with a large tumbler of brandy.

The baby came several hours later. Lia's screams stopped, replaced with the cries of a newborn. Bridgette came out of the clinic and told Roland that he had a baby girl. He wanted to run in and see her, but Mary blocked the door. "Not yet, dad. Give us about ten more minutes." When Mary finally called Roland in, they had Lia cleaned up. The newborn was at Lia's breast, contently feeding and lapsing into sleep. Roland looked worried that the baby looked tired. Suzette could sense that and said, "Don't worry pop, getting born is hard work. Everything is perfectly normal."

"Thanks, Doctor, and you too, Nurse." Then he looked at Lia and asked, "What are we going to name her?" He realized that being busy with gold mining and house building, they had never discussed it.

Lia smiled at her husband and said, "Let's call her Anna after your mother." Suzette was sitting next to Lia on the bed. She put her arm around Lia and kissed her affectionately on her cheek. Tears had welled up in her eyes, and then she broke down and cried openly.

Roland was looking emotional, too; moments came up, reminding them of their parents, and those moments were still very difficult for them. Mary got everyone back on a happy note, "You Irish should be ashamed of yourselves. Every time a healthy baby is born, we Scots celebrate; and if we cry, it is with tears of joy, not sadness. Now give me that baby, and honey, you get some rest." Mary took to little Anna like she was her own flesh and blood. She let Roland touch her, but she didn't let him hold her. Roland wanted to, but Mary chided, "Not till you learn how to do it right." Then she walked over to the door and yelled, "**JOHN**! Build me a rocking chair. Can't you see I am finally a grandmother?" That got them all laughing, but John was no fool. He started looking for the best wood to build a rocker for his wife and the new baby. Suzette let Lia rest for an hour and then walked her over to Mary's bathtub for a long hot soak. Mary wrote in her bible that baby Anna was born on December 18th, 1861.

Christmas and the new year passed, and the mining and milling resumed its routine. Shipping the gold was discussed, and plans finalized. Roland and Lia would take the gold to San Francisco when they had one-hundred thousand dollars' worth to ship. They would shut down the mill, and Eli and the miners would guard Roland, Lia, and the baby down the Hassayampa to catch the Butterfield Stage to Los Angeles. John, Mr. Sue, and the women would guard the mill until Eli returned with the men. In Los Angeles, Roland could book passage on a steamer to San Francisco. It seemed simple enough, but in addition to getting the gold into the bank, they needed supplies. Roland and Mr. Sue had already made one trip back to Hale's Mercado for more crucibles and mercury. Roland would buy more equipment in San Francisco.

The gold rush that Eli was hoping for didn't materialize as fast as he expected. Part of the problem was the newspapers and tabloids reported that the mountains of the west were full of hostile Apache. Numerous stories of prospecting ventures gone bad appeared in the few newspapers they were able to acquire from Hale and Yuma. In evidence to the Indian violence, the Red Mountain Clinic did a constant, if not landside business treating the wounded from what was rapidly degenerating into a full-blown war with the Apache.

There were two problems. One was that the Army was busy with the Civil War and didn't have the troops to control the Apache in their remote corner of the world. The other was a symptom of the first: Individual prospectors didn't venture into the area because of the Indian danger. Larger parties fared better with the Indians. Red Mountain needed workers, but most of the people that passed through didn't want to work for wages. The majority went up the Hassayampa and didn't return unless needing supplies or medical care. What was needed was a spectacular gold strike in the area. Roland was adamant that they would not publicize the wealth of their mine. He knew from the history of the California Gold Rush and the goings-on concerning the Comstock Lode that there were at least a dozen hucksters, thieves, and thugs for every ounce of gold ever found. Mr. Sue had the best advice. Be patient, his universal cure for all that was wrong with the world

New Arrivals

The new year came with very few new miners arriving. The placer gold in the Hassayampa was plentiful, but the yield was low, and many a miner decided it wasn't worth the hard work to recover it. The Apache were also a problem. There were very few Army patrols even along the major trails, let alone the remote areas where most of the diggings were. The Apache, ever more aggrieved by the intrusion of white people into their lands, took advantage of the withdrawal of the troops, and attacks were occurring more frequently, and with more lethal force. Suzette and Bridgette were busy every week, treating the survivors of the attacks. Most of the wounds were from arrows or clubs, but the frequency of bullet wounds was increasing. Slowly, the Apache were acquiring more and more guns from ambushed pioneers or miners and learning how to use them more effectively all the time.

Life became routine again, and a few uneventful months passed as winter turned to spring. Then one afternoon, five bedraggled white men with more than a dozen Mexicans rode down from the north. They came around the west side of the mountain. When Eli saw them, he sent word over to John to shut down the mill.

The travelers arrived half-starved and on the verge of many different diseases, all related to malnutrition and poor hygiene. *Strange*, everyone thought. The mountains and deserts are full of deer and rabbits. There is no reason for a traveler to go hungry. There was more to this than met the eye.

The reason soon became clear. The leader of the party introduced himself as Pauline Weaver and his partner as Abraham Peeples. There were three more white men in the group, but the majority of the rest of the men were Mexicans. *Typical,* Roland thought, *the invisible people, not worth introducing.* Weaver's-ragged-party had found gold on the mountain to the north. They stayed up there until they ran out of food and didn't leave their diggings until hunger brought them down. There was a total of seventeen men in the party. Mr. Sue weighed up their gold. They had eleven-hundred ounces of gold nuggets, a significant find, but a total of only thirteen-hundred dollars for each man. If they all made it to Yuma with their gold, and another if -- would the white men share with the Mexicans.

Eli told Weaver and Peeples that they mined and made a little gold, but their main business was pigs and vegetables. He sold them a pig for forty dollars, and Mary put on an ample ration of potatoes, onions, and carrots to augment the pork. The Weaver Party set the pig up on the fire pit. The worst part about the men was their smell. Suzette could overhear the Mexicans insulting each other about how they smelled. One insult was particularly vulgar rolling fleas and pig farts into one long explicative involving the more intimate parts of someone's mother. She liked the easy-going way of the Mexicans. They could make light of almost any situation and enjoy ribbing and kidding one another.

Suzette and Bridgette examined the men one-by-one after each of them bathed in the hot pool up the hill. None of them were seriously ill. The Mexicans were in much better shape than the white men. They were used to meager rations and knew how to hunt and forage on the desert for food. It was cold, and their clothes were wet. They huddled around the fire pit to dry and stay warm. All of them were drooling as the pig roasted, and lard dripped off and burnt in the fire. Mary fed them what leftovers she had to hold them over until the pig was ready. It wasn't enough. As the outside of the pig cooked enough to eat, the men used their skinning knives to cut off pieces. A couple burned their hands, leaning over the fire too long, cutting on the pig. Bridgette treated them with an aloe salve and admonished them in English. Suzette was less polite, and she ordered the Mexicans away from the fire and sat them down in the ramada for a civilized meal.

Eli sat down with Weaver and Peeples at the end of the table. He asked, "Where will you go with your gold?"

Weaver boomed out his answer so everyone at the table could hear, "Tucson! Where else in this God-forsaken wilderness can a man get whiskey for a pinch of gold?"

Roland joined his brother, and like Eli, was thinking that it may be time to use this loud-ragged mountain man to start the bigger "gold rush" to their area. The focus would be on the mountain to the north and not on their mine. That would be good. Eli spread the map of the RMM mining district out on the table. He drew in the mountain, the deep drainage to its east and another mountain to the east of the creek. "This is where the Indian children found this." He plunked the ten-ounce nugget down on the map, right over the mouth of the creek below the mountain.

Weaver wasn't impressed. He took a nugget twice that size and plunked it down on top of the mountain Eli had drawn onto the map. Suzette was standing to the side and turned so they wouldn't see her giggle. *Boys are comparing their penis size,* she thought as she listened.

Roland asked, "What do you want to call your mountain? We'll draw in some claims, and when we can, they will be registered when a land office avails itself."

Weaver was loud but not very creative. Looking around the table for affirmation, "How about *Nugget Hill*?"

"Not glamorous enough, Mr. Weaver," Roland replied.

Weaver took out another nugget and plunked it down on the map. Peeples and the Mexicans produced half a dozen others ranging from two to several pounds. Mary then rolled a potato up next to the pile of nuggets. "Why don't you call the claim the *Potato Patch*?"

"That's good," Eli said. He moved the nuggets and wrote in the name on the top of the mountain where Weaver indicated the gold deposit lay with a yellowed-dirty fingernail of his right hand. "What about the mountain itself?"

Weaver was indignant. "Make it *Nugget Hill,* as I said."

"Again, not glamorous enough, Mr. Weaver. We are dealing with your legacy here. How about we name it, errr -- *Rich Hill?"*

Eli didn't wait for Weaver's approval. He wrote *Rich Hill* onto the map and named the mountain to the east Weaver Mountain. The drainage that wound its way down to the Hassayampa he named *Weaver Creek.* He showed Weaver the map and said, "You will be immortalized forever, my friend. Now I have a suggestion. Take your gold to Yuma. Put it on a stage and go with it to the mint in San Francisco. Don't spend it across some bar for a glass or two of rot-gut or a woman that will lift her skirts for a dollar. It isn't hard finding the gold. It is hard saving it as wealth to see you through the rest of your life."

Weaver wasn't in a mood to take advice from a young fool. "Son, I have been prospecting and mining longer than you have been in this world. I will go to Yuma with my gold, but the rest of what you said is pure bullshit. I don't need money in a bank in San Francisco. I need to live in this wasteland, and a man with gold in his pocket can live well."

Eli smiled at Weaver and rolled up the map. "Good luck to you then, Mr. Weaver."

Everyone noticed that Peeples hadn't said a word during the exchange. When the men were all fed, Peeples took Eli and Roland aside and asked if they could talk in private. They walked to the refinery. Peeples had a lot to say. "Weaver is a fool. He may not even make it to Yuma. Not all Mexicans are nice guys. I'm not going with them. A few of the Mexicans are going with me, and we are going to homestead the valley to the north of *Rich Hill.* My wife is behind the Confederate lines in Florida. I'll get her when the war is over. We will raise cattle. The grass up there is good; there is water, and the lands are more savanna than a hardscrabble desert."

Peeples was very impressed with the young men and Mr. Sue, who had a bullion assay in progress on one of Peeples' smaller nuggets as they talked. Peeples was impressed and said, "You young men are a lot smarter than Weaver credits you. He will be busted or tits up in a few months. I'm not going with him, and I don't intend to be broke either. Can I trade my share of the gold for Double Eagles? Would you want to buy my share of *Rich Hill*?"

Roland, the businessman, took the lead. "Yes, we could do that. My recommendation would be, though, that we would prefer a stake in the ranching operation you want to create, rather than a share of your mine."

Peeples interrupted, "What's the matter with the mine, if I may ask?"

John had joined the conversation. "It is a long way to the top of the mountain, difficult to mine for more nuggets and impossible to keep secure. I expect that when Weaver gets to Yuma, thousands of prospectors will return to *Rich Hill,* all willing to kill for a bucket of dirt."

Peeples was thoughtful, "Maybe Weaver will buy my share of the claim before he heads to Yuma."

Weaver did just that. He gave Peeples two nuggets worth about five hundred dollars each for half the claim and considered Peeples a fool. The next day, as he left for Yuma with provisions and the majority of his party, he announced, "I'll be back. Stay off my mountain if you know what is good for you."

Peeples stood at the edge of the settlement and bid his ex-partner goodbye. Eli and Roland took Peeples aside, and Roland said, "Now we are going to show you the rest of what is going on here." They went back to the refinery and had Mr. Sue open two strongboxes he used for a safe. Peeples was dumbstruck. He was looking at over a quarter-million dollars of gold buttons. Then he started to laugh, "Weaver, the great prospector. He didn't find the Mother Lode. It's right here."

Roland confided, "We knew about the gold in Weaver Creek for some time. Most of the prospectors who came into the area so far went up to the placers on the Hassayampa. Some went farther north; we haven't seen any of them for a long time. We stayed with this mine because the ore is getting richer, and the size of the gold is getting bigger the deeper we dig. Another thing, this site is secure. We watch during the day and guard it at night. For some reason, the Apache give this mountain a wide berth. They steal oxen and mules from the farms along the river, but we have no truck with them. Not so for others in the area. There is a war brewing between the whites and the Apache. We don't want to be in the middle of it, and we don't want to be the focus of a gold rush. Our friend, Pauline, is going to take care of that for us."

Eli had the miners and plant operators start up the operation again. The plant operators had three mules saddled, waiting at the portal. They rode to the top of the mountain. Eli pointed out the hot spring where Abby first discovered the fine gold. From the east side of the summit, they could look down where the men were building a trough up the mountain. Eli said, "When we get the trough run up here, we will feed the mill with ore from the bottom of the hot spring. We know the gold grade is better the deeper we dig. Also, the size of the gold is bigger. Not nuggets, but bigger than the gold dust we have been recovering so far."

When they were back under the ramada for the evening meal, Peeples said, "You boys are the real gold miners. To hell with Weaver and *Rich Hill*. Let's draw up an agreement for the ranch, and I will file it with the homesteads."

Weaver did take care of the gold rush. Within a month, there were a thousand prospectors on *Rich Hill*, more panning in Weaver Creek. The rush was on. Eli kept apologizing for his marginal operation and kept selling food to the want-a-be millionaires. Suzette charged two dollars a visit for her services at the clinic. The clinic was full every day. Shootings and stabbings were common. Venereal disease was rampant. Suzette and Bridgette treated many of the camp whores and sent all of them away with no charge and a supply of condoms.

The prospectors themselves represented every nationality, and every cut of society the earth could conjure up. There was constant racial tension among the camps, and the settlements sorted themselves out along ethnic lines. Prospectors would work hard, drink and play poker at night and head to Yuma or Tucson with a poke full of nuggets or gold dust. All successes served to bring more people to the area.

Peeples returned shortly after the first week of April. He brought good news. By an act of Congress, the massive New Mexico Territory split down the middle. Santa Fe remained the Territorial Capital of New Mexico, and Prescott was now the first Territorial Capital of the Arizona Territory. Eli gathered all the maps of the claims and the homesteads along with all the location notices and headed to Prescott with Peeples. Eli returned a week later with deeds to all the homesteads. Some of Moses's men had come up from the ferry operation and took up homesteads on the river. They looked at the deeds with their names on them with wonder. Of everyone with, they were the most pleased that there was now a government office close by that recognized them as free men, the deeded owners of the land.

One Sunday, Suzette and Bridgette walked to the top of the mountain. They stayed till dark, and from their lofty perch, they could see hundreds of fires on *Rich Hill* and in *Weaver Creek* to the north. They started back down and paused at the cabin, where their relationship first blossomed. John had turned it into a storage shed. Nothing ever stayed the same. But it was sad. Both knew that their frontier was gone forever, and nothing could return it to the raw wilderness that it was when they first arrived. Suzette missed it like she missed the solitude of the Santa Fe Trail. Their mountaintop sanctuary passed into the annals of time and would live on only in the memories of a few humans for the time they had left on the earth.

Eli was still worried about sending Roland and his family down the Hassayampa with the gold shipment. They never experienced an Apache attack close to their hill, but the Indians stealing animals from the grazing area over on the Hassayampa whenever they wanted easy meat, was troubling. Fortunately, the Apache didn't have any interest in gold, but the Apache had the company of other bad men in the area. One night after the mill was shut down and the desert was quiet, an intense gun battle broke out north of the mountain. The shots heard by the guards at the mill were faint; the battle was taking place at the mouth of the creek to the north, but in the darkness, it was impossible to see anything. There was no sleep that night; everyone was alert, standing guard around the mill and the settlement.

At daybreak, a wagon load of wounded arrived at the clinic. Among them was a pregnant woman close to term who had lost a lot of blood from a bullet wound in her leg. As usual, Bridgette did the triage, and Suzette prepared the surgery. The woman was the first to be treated, and the unconscious woman lay on the operating table in the surgery. Mary learned from the other wounded that the father died in the gunfight with two other men, and there was no other family in the area. Working fast, Suzette stanched the bleeding, but the woman was fading fast from shock and loss of blood. Bridgette was monitoring the heartbeat and yelled in alarm to Suzette when she lost it. Suzette faced a hard decision; she had to open the womb to save the baby. It proved to be the right call as the woman was dead as the first incision was made to open the womb.

Suzette had to work fast; without the mother's heart pumping oxygen to the baby, she would lose the baby within a few minutes. Regard for the mother's life no longer an issue, Suzette worked faster and with a larger incision than normal and had the baby out in less than a minute. It was a little boy, extracted from the womb, blue and oxygen starved. Bridgette was working desperately to get him to breathe. Finally, the newborn sucked in a full breath and screamed. Bridgette handed the baby to Mary and then rushed outside to get the next patient into the surgery and have the men carry away and bury the dead mother.

Eli learned that the gunfight had been over a poker game of all things with a trivial amount of gold on the table. There was enough trouble trying to stay alive with the Apache violence ramping up. It was insane for miners and settlers to fight among themselves in the face of the much greater danger. He learned that three men had died in the poker game shootout, and six others wounded along with the woman that died. He decided on the spot that there would be more security added to the workforce in the mill. He would hire enough men to be on guard duty at night and figure out how to keep everyone fed and sheltered.

Mary brought him the first problem: how were they going to feed the newborn? Lia was not built to be a wet nurse. If she fed the newborn, that would take milk away from Anna. They needed a cow. The oxen they had on the river were all castrated males, bred, and trained for the specific purpose of pulling wagons. It was Abby who solved this problem. She was careful to select dried mesquite pods from the hill that had not been attacked by insects or mold. She ground only the beans even though she said the pods were also edible. The pigs certainly didn't have any problem with them. When she had a handful of the mesquite flour, she boiled it and filtered the solution through a silk scarf to remove the hulls. She added a pinch of sugar and vanilla from their kitchen stores. With the patience that only a woman seems to possess, she fed the newborn one tiny spoonful at a time. The little boy liked the concoction. Maybe they wouldn't need a cow after all.

It was nearing the end of May. The mill had produced over four-hundred thousand dollars in gold, and it was time to make a shipment. Over at the settlement, away from the mill and the miners, John built a reinforced box that became part of the driver's seat for one of the heavy freight wagons. He also added heavy wooden sideboards and a tailgate, tall enough to shield the drivers from arrows or bullets from the sides and back.

Eli didn't like the idea of Roland taking Lia and the baby down the Hassayampa. He decided that they would go west. Moses had gone that way, and he didn't come back, so there must be a way through the mountains to the Colorado River. There was always the trail to Beale's crossing, but there wasn't stage service there. He could count on the Butterfield stage that crossed the southern desert on its way to Los Angeles.

With all preparations complete, Roland and Lia made ready for travel. Eli told them they didn't have to go and that he would take the shipment. Roland wouldn't hear of it. There was Denise, the grandmother in San Francisco, that needed to know she was a great-grandmother. He reminded his older brother that pressing banking and business arrangements needed his attention. Also, there was a wealth of supplies to purchase. John gave him a long list of more machinery to bring back. A sawmill was on the list; they desperately needed an easier way to make lumber. Also, on the list were the chemicals needed for fire assaying, fire brick, and muffles to build an assay furnace. Mr. Sue had a list of supplies for the kitchen, and Suzette and Bridgette, along with Abby, all wanted a bathtub of their own. Eli finally conceded and wrote a letter to Moses, instructing him to get together what he needed for a freight company. They were going to need it, not just for this tall order, but for sustaining the larger community Eli intended to build.

In the cover of darkness, they had secured the gold in the strongbox on the wagon and nailed it shut. There were just enough oxen left to make up the team. Eli and Roland rounded them up and herded them over to the settlement at first light. It had been a while since the oxen had been yoked and harnessed to a wagon; it took some doing to line them up ahead of the wagon. Eli and Roland would be on horseback, and two of the miners would ride in the back of the armored wagon. Lia would drive, and Abby would tend to baby Anna on the driver's seat between them. Everyone was heavily armed and ready for any trouble that would come their way.

There was nothing left to do but say their goodbyes and head west. Roland was taking them to where he had left the creek on his return trip from Beale's crossing. When they got there, there was an arrow laid out on the ground with cobblestones pointing to the southwest. Moses had marked his trail. There was a monument of piled rocks about fifty feet in front of the arrow. The message was clear. They turned left and within a mile came to another stone arrow that pointed to a high peak about thirty miles away. They found another arrow there that turned them west, and, after crossing some low mountains, they came to a valley that ran to the south that took them all the way down to the Gila River.

Marker by marker, they found their way to the Gila and the trail to Yuma. Moses had done a good job blazing and marking the trail. He was overjoyed to see them. With a big smile, he ran up from the ferry dock on the east side of the Colorado to greet them. "Good to see you, Eli. I was almost ready to set out to see what happened to you."

"We have been busy, and we have a problem." Eli looked around to see that there weren't any men within earshot and said, "We have over four-hundred grand in gold bullion in the wagon. I need to get it onto a stage to Los Angeles without anyone knowing. Roland and Lia are going to take it to the bank in San Francisco."

Moses laughed in surprise, "That's a good problem to have. Let's put the wagon in the warehouse for now. We'll figure it out from there." There was a cry from the wagon, and Moses walked over to greet the women. His eyes got big when Lia held up Anna. Moses and Lia had a special kind of friendship, having survived being swept down the Colorado together. Moses beamed his signature smile at Lia and held out his arms. "You have been busy, Señora Callahan." Lia handed Anna down to him so she and Abby could get down. Moses wouldn't hand the little girl back. He cradled her in the crook of his massive arm and walked back and forth, singing soft and low to the infant. Finally, he turned to Roland and Lia, "Did you name this kid after me?"

Incredulous, Lia set him straight, "It's a girl, Moses. Her name is Anna. Maybe the next one could be a Moses if it's a boy."

Roland was quick on the uptake, "The next one. The next one! Are you pregnant again?"

"I think so. I didn't want to tell you until I was sure."

Eli and Moses cheered and clapped Roland on the back hard, both at the same time. It nearly knocked Roland off his feet. Moses said, "Let's get you and Lia and my goddaughter over to the guest house." He took them down to the ferry and sent them across the river. He came back up the bank and said, "Let's take care of the wagon. I have a guest house of my own. You and Abby can use that one. I have a tent for your men. We all eat over at the mess hall, though." Eli asked Moses about his wife; he was supposed to have gone by now to find her in the south and bring her back to Yuma. Moses shook his head sadly and said, "We can talk about that later."

They had to manhandle the armored wagon into the warehouse. Unlike mules, Eli couldn't get the oxen to backup. Moses's men took the oxen over to a grassy field to let the animals water and graze. When the ferry returned, they crossed the river and went to Major Jenkins' headquarters. They found the man perplexed.

Jenkins welcomed them back to Yuma and then started to talk about the war. "I am stuck here in this godforsaken hole, and the war is passing me by. I should be a colonel by now in charge of a regiment on the front lines. All the regular soldiers have gone east to fight the rebels. I am marooned here with nothing but locals and ne'er-do-wells to hold off the Apaches. By the way, your brother is with General Carlton and left with the first troops to go east. My career is at a dead-end stuck here in this hell hole guarding a ferry crossing. God damn Army."

Moses had gotten to know Major Jenkins pretty well and regarded him as a friend. He was the first to reply to the tirade, "Better a dead-end than dead period. Major, I need several of your Wells Fargo strongboxes if you have some you can spare."

"I have plenty. There hasn't been any gold or silver arriving from Tucson since the rebels came over from Texas. There are some gold miners up the river at Camp Colorado that send a little gold down, but other than that, bullion shipping has been pretty slow. See the Quartermaster for strongboxes. The next stage due from the east is three days from now. The schedule isn't certain with the war going on, but if it doesn't arrive, there will be a supply train coming in from the coast in another week. You can send something back with them to Los Angeles if you have to."

The three friends picked up the strongboxes from the Quartermaster and took them over to the guest house. The door was locked, and Lia and Abby were sharing a bath. Lia called out, "Go eat without us. We will come over when we are done getting clean."

They did that, and over a hearty beef stew, Eli laid out his plan for a freight company. He wanted regular deliveries every month and would be shipping gold back on the return run. Moses said there wouldn't be any problem organizing that. Yuma, on the Arizona side of the river, had grown to be a small city of fourteen-hundred people. Wagons, drivers, and the mules were readily available. Moses would set it all up, and every month, he would come up with the wagons to see the gold shipment safely back to Yuma.

Lia and Abby came in to join them, baby Anna resting peacefully in a papoose on Abby's back. As usual, every male eye in the mess hall turned their way. Lia's hair was clean and brushed out and in a long fall down her back. Abby was equally as beautiful in clean buckskins with layers of colorful beads around her neck. Her hair was held under the beads and spread luxuriously down the left side of her bodice. There were a dozen men in the chow line, but they all made way for the two women. There was a lot of disappointment, however, when the two women sat down with their husbands at Moses' table.

There was a salesman in the mess hall that came over to the table with some poorly printed catalogs from a line of products he had available in Los Angeles. He gave one to the girls to share along with envelopes and order forms. He assured them that he had everything a pioneer homemaker could want. Lia was studying, enthralled with the catalog, but Abby asked, "Do you carry guns and ammunition?"

"Sorry," the man replied. "I can't ship guns and ammo into the territory. There are restrictions because of the Apaches stealing the guns. But I could send you anything else you might need."

Lia sent the man away but kept the catalogs. Abby reminded her that she didn't have an address – other than somewhere in the middle of Arizona Territory. Roland suggested that if she wanted something, she could have it delivered to Moses. There was going to be a freight company making regular deliveries of food and supplies to the settlement. There was a whole section in the catalog of clothes and supplies for babies. Lia borrowed a pencil and started to fill out the order form. Anna and the new infant at the settlement were going to be well dressed if the man delivered as promised.

Before they left the mess, Lia had a long list of items on the order form. Roland had added kegs of nails and hand tools and gave Lia greenbacks to pay the man for the order. Even though it was more than a hundred dollars, it was a trivial amount of money compared to what they were shipping out.

The salesman was extremely pleased and gave Roland a catalog of his own. The order would be sent out on the next stage west.

Eli sent the miners back to the settlement on horses he purchased locally. He and Abby would stay until Roland and Lia were safely away. Lia took Eli aside and gave him a gentle prod in what she thought was the right direction. She told Eli that before they left, he should do the right thing and make Abby an honest woman. It hadn't crossed his mind, and he didn't even know if Abby wanted to be married. "Eli, you have to ask a woman. She isn't going to ask you. You should ask her. The two of you are good together; you can always adopt children. There is one waiting for you back at Red Mountain." She left him to think it over and found Roland and told him what she had said to Eli. Roland agreed, it was an excellent idea. He went to find his brother to encourage Eli into doing the right thing.

Eli was in a quandary. He and Abby had settled into a loving relationship alone in the wilderness; there were no churches, preachers, or morally minded citizens to criticize their arrangement. Marriage was a white man's institution. Indians just took a wife when they could support one. With all this on his mind, he took Abby down to the river's edge to fish. They were sitting on the bank, and Eli was having a hard time bringing up the subject. Abby made it easy, "Eli, I know Lia talked to you about us getting married. I don't have any trouble with that. I love you and have already decided to stay with you forever, or for as long as you would have me. But think this over. The world is full of prejudice. Being married to an Indian might be more difficult than you think. I was married once. It doesn't always turn out for the better."

Eli sat quietly for a long time, then kissed Abby and said, "Let's go tell Major Jenkins that we want to get married as soon as possible."

Abby kissed him back and said, "As soon as possible and then forever."

They walked hand in hand back to the Headquarters Building and told Major Jenkins that they wanted to be married that evening. Jenkins raised an eyebrow and looked at Eli with an expression that was half surprise and half disbelief. He reluctantly agreed, though, to do the ceremony at six that evening. The stage from the east was due in shortly after that. Moses was waiting on the east side of the river to put the gold shipment aboard but brought the gold across the river with several of his men when he got news of the wedding. His men were heavily armed to guard the strongboxes and looked impressive in their Sunday best. They looked like a squad of black Pinkerton security officers.

As folks started to gather for the ceremony, the stage loaded onto the ferry on the east side of the river. A new team of horses would be hitched up on the west side to pull it up from the dock and take it on to Los Angeles. Major Jenkins told Roland not to worry. The stage would not leave until he sent it off with the Army dispatches; he had those safely locked in his desk in the Headquarters Building. The ceremony took place on the parade field in front of the Headquarters. There were over two-hundred people in attendance. Most of them friends of Eli and Moses, but some who just wanted to gawk at the interracial couple. It seemed like a strange set of mores. The men at the post commonly slept with Indian women, and some of the older hands even lived with them. An interracial marriage, however, was a first in the Army camp, and many of the men who even kept an Indian woman on the side did not approve.

The stage pulled up behind the Major as he recited the vows, and hand-in-hand, Eli and Abby repeated them. There was a ramshackle rifle salute from a squad of the civilian volunteers guarding the post, and it was final. As Eli held Abby in a long kiss, Jenkins turned and walked back to his office to get the mail away on the stage. Eli and Abby walked Roland and Lia over to the stage. Moses handed Anna back to Lia after she was in the carriage, and his men slid the strongboxes onto the floor between the seats. The driver released the brake, and with a crack of his whip, the stage bolted out of the camp at a dead run. Eli turned to Moses and said, "Thanks, friend." Then he asked Moses about his wife.

It wasn't easy for Moses to relate his story. He had put off going east to put the ferry back in service. He had written the constable in the town near the plantation where his wife stayed in slavery. His letter said that he would return soon, a free man, and buy his wife out of slavery. He received a letter back nearly two months later. The constable said not to bother coming. Moses's wife had attempted an escape, but slave catchers brought her back to the plantation in chains. The plantation owner had her whipped for running away. She had died on the whipping post. The three friends cried together as Moses related the tragedy. Then Moses said with resolve, "If that son-of-a-bitch plantation owner survives the war, I'm going back there to kill him. I don't care if it costs me my life."

The three made their way back down to the ferry. Moses had Eli's horse and a strong mare and a supply horse waiting for Eli and Abby at the warehouse. It was April 14th and a full moon. There was still time for Eli and Abby to get north of the Gila. Abby kissed Moses, and Eli pulled him into another bear hug. Moses was hardly ever emotional, but he pushed Eli away and said, "Get out of here. You've got a gold mine to go run." Eli and Abby mounted up, checked their weapons, and rode out of Yuma as Mr. and Mrs. Eli Callahan.

As Moses walked to his cabin, he thought that he would have to find himself another wife soon. If someone as awkward as Eli could wind up with a woman like Abby, he thought he shouldn't have any trouble finding a good woman of his own. There were a lot of black people fleeing the South and heading west to escape enslavement by the Confederacy. In the event the South won the war, there would be a lot more blacks heading west. The fear of them winning was strong, but fortunately for the North, the battles were finally turning in favor of the Union.

It took more than a week for the newlyweds to get back to Red Mountain. While Eli was in Yuma, he updated the map for the Mining District and entered the name, *Red Mountain,* for the settlement. At that moment, they were as legitimate as any other town in the American West, and the girls had a real address for their mail-order treasures. Abby gave the catalog to Mary, and it seemed like she was more thrilled with everything it offered than Eli and Abby's return as husband and wife. Suzette was beside herself with joy for her brother and his bride, and in two days, John presented the newlyweds with two hammered gold rings. He had to adjust the sizing for Abby, but with that small modification, the newlyweds donned the symbols of their love and proudly displayed their rings as they held up their hands together.

Back to the business at hand, John started the mill back up the next day. Suzette and Bridgette wanted to enlarge and deepen the pond at the top of the hill, and Eli wanted to sample the gold deeper in the hot spring. He felt there was more to it than just the fine powder Abby found in the initial discovery. Mr. Sue fashioned Suzette and Bridgette each a two-bucket shoulder pole to carry the sand from the bottom of the pool down the hill for milling. Faithfully, the women carried four buckets down each morning. In two weeks, the pile was big enough for John to test. They cleaned all the ore out of the mill and refreshed the amalgam plates. The dedicated run showed two things: The sand in the bottom of the pool was richer in gold than the ore from the side of the hill, and the size of the flower gold was somewhat larger. John immediately started extending the wooden trough to the top of the hill. Suzette and Bridgette wouldn't have to carry the ore down anymore. When the trough was complete, the miners would shovel the sand into the trough, and the hot water from the spring would carry it down to the mill.

John extended the trough up the hill as fast as the men could saw the boards. The going was slow because of the difficulty of sawing lumber. He hoped that Roland would find a sawmill in his travels. It took until the middle of summer before the first ore came down the trough to the mill. The effort proved worth it. There was twice as much gold in the ore from the top as from the side of the hill. John had his crew up at the hot spring feeding as much ore down the chute as it could handle. Within a week, the pool was extended to the base of the remaining cottonwoods and deepened to eight feet. That was as far as the men could dig without draining some of the water. Suzette and Bridgette didn't like the top of the hill changing drastically for the sake of more gold. The progress slowed, however, until the water level could be lowered, and the big trees removed from the side of the pond. John was relentless, though, in his efforts to extend the mine. It would only be a matter of time before their hilltop sanctuary-paradise would be gone forever.

Moses arrived with the first freight delivery. He brought more lumber, kegs of nails, several kegs of black powder, and a wood auger. The problem of taking down the big trees was solved. John hired more men as woodcutters, and holes were augured into the trunk of the fallen cottonwood and filled with black powder. The first time the crew tried to blow up the tree, the blasting wasn't as successful as they would have liked. The next assault, though, was more effective. The men drilled the holes deeper and filled them with more powder. Wood plugs made from limbs sealed the top of the blast holes. It took several tries to get the plugs in without breaking the fuses, but a chiseled notch down the side of the hole solved that problem. Within a week, the method was perfected, and the big cottonwood became fuel for the boiler.

The newspapers that Moses brought with him this trip all ran the headline,

LINCOLN SIGNS THE HOMESTEAD ACT.

It had taken the Republicans in the North years to get the act through Congress. With the South out of the way, the bill passed with an overwhelming majority. The North was anxious to populate the west, even though more settlers would mean more trouble with the Indians.

June 4th, Eli was thinking about his sister. He knew it was hard on her; the memories of losing their parents two years ago to the day, still weighed heavy on his mind. It weighed hardest on Suzette, who had been with them the day they perished in the tornado. Eli and Abby knew it would be hard for her, and they shut down the mill to have a day off and an outing over to the Hassayampa for a picnic and a swim if possible. Eli took the miners with them for extra guards, and they set out for where the Hassayampa flowed out of the mountains in hopes of finding a swimming hole. It was a short trip of only several miles; the Callahans rode slowly, and Bridgette drove the buckboard with the miners loaded up in the back. To their surprise, there was a prospector's camp on the river occupied by at least twenty men and a few women. There wasn't a swimming hole on the river, but there was a rock out in the middle of the stream; Suzette and Bridgette waded out to the rock and sat there watching the water flow past.

Eli, always looking for men to hire, spent the morning talking to the prospectors. The group stuck together for more firepower and safety from the Apache. The pickings were rather poor where their camp was, but it was pleasant there in the notch of the canyon walls, and cooler than out on the desert floor. The prospectors were going to move further north on the river, chasing rumors of richer placers higher in the mountains. They played the part of the all-knowing experts on gold mining and told Eli that he was wasting his time on his red hill. The gold was in the streams, not on the hills and mountains around them. Eli just smiled and told the prospectors that they were pig farmers anyway, and his gold mine just made enough to pay for their beans, provided they didn't eat too many beans. Everyone laughed; the prospectors and their women knew that phenomenon well. None of them looked well fed.

Abby noticed one of the women from the camp wading into the water, making her way quietly up behind Suzette and Bridgette sitting on the rock. The girls were quiet with their feet dangling in the water, but there was just enough ripple of the flowing water to mask the approach of the woman. Abby had her machete-like knife drawn and was keeping her eye on the woman.

Eli asked the men about the woman. One of the miners said, "Don't worry about her. That's Bible Betty, BB for short. She is a lunatic woman who talks to God all the time. The problem is God talks back to her, and she will do anything He tells her."

Betty was creeping up on the girls. She got to the boulder and leaned over right behind their heads and screamed, "**MAKE YOUR PEACE WITH THE LORD."**

The girls jumped; Suzette lost her balance and fell in the water. Eli thought Bridgette might have peed herself laughing. It was hilarious. Suzette, the hardened woman from the trail, had been done in by a religious nut. She picked herself up out of the shallow water, leaped over the rock and bowled the women over, and held her down in the water. When she let BB up for a breath of air, she said loud enough for everyone to hear, "Last time I took stock, the Lord and I were not at war." Bridgette was giggling uncontrollably. Suzette looked up at her with a look of malice, and Bridgette got the message. She jumped down from the rock and ran down the river. She got to a deeper spot, and it slowed her down. Suzette caught up with her and tackled her from behind. The pool was just deep enough that they both made quite a splash. When Bridgette sat up in the water sputtering, Suzette laughed and said, "It was your turn for baptism, Miss O'Malley."

Eli and Abby shared what food they brought with the prospectors. Eli told them that if they made their way over to the mine, he would provide them with fresh pork and mesquite flour. It was a light-hearted day, and by the time they started back for the mine, everyone had had a dip in the river. Bible Betty tried to talk to them about God and was a bit put off when told to leave them alone. She got indignant, "I am not going to apologize for trying to save your souls for the Lord. Don't you people care where you go after you die?"

As she was saddling up to leave, Abby was the only one to answer her. "Where you go and what you do when you are alive is all that matters. If I accidentally make it to your heaven after I die, I am going to ask for a guarantee at the gate that I won't have to sit next to you." With that, she rode away, leaving BB speechless standing at the river bank with the rest of the prospectors and the other women laughing at her.

Abby was the only one to notice several Indian children hiding in the brush, watching them. She rode over to them, cautious that they weren't baiting a trap with a band of braves waiting in ambush for a hapless traveler to investigate. She talked to the children in their native tongue. The children, two boys, and a girl were orphans, their fathers, and mothers killed by soldiers. Abby told them that she had food and work for them if they would follow her a few miles to the gold mine. She pointed at the red hill, and the children didn't cower at the thought of going over there. Abby assumed they were from somewhere far away, where the lore of the hill as an evil place was not well known. Perhaps the children missed that part of their education with their parents being dead for some time. They followed Abby; the promise of food was all the draw the Pied Piper needed.

Abby got them to the settlement and kept talking to them in Apache. Mary fed the children along with everyone else. The children looked to be six or seven years old. The two boys and the girl were thin, as any Indian living off the desert, but healthy. Abby told the kids that they could stay in the settlement, but they had to bathe in the hot water tub every day and work for her and Mary. Abby showed them the mesquite beans and told them that they would be her gatherers. The kids were familiar with the job; they had done that for their mother before she died at the hands of the soldiers. With their bellies full, Mr. Sue showed them where they could bathe, and Mary rounded up some sleeping pallets for them when they came back clean.

Later, when the Indian children were asleep, Abby told Eli, "We need to build an orphanage."

Eli agreed. He was cautious but answered, "We can do that, but let's see what happens over the next few weeks. These children have been on their own for some time out here in the desert. They don't have to worry about the Apache threat, but a desert is a dangerous place just the same. Also, they could walk away tomorrow."

But Eli was wrong; the children didn't walk away. The next day Abby had them gathering mesquite beans. Mary had turned Abby's old grinder into a gristmill, and John had drilled a hole down through the side of the pestle rock so the bean pods could be fed down under the heavy stone. With the children doing the gathering, Mary was producing around twenty pounds of mesquite flour a day. It wasn't like the white flour that came from wheat, but the bread she made with it was hearty with a nutty flavor and a faint taste of vanilla. It made a very good biscuit that became a favorite of the camp along with pork gravy.

In a few weeks, the children started to put on some weight. Abby reminded her husband, "We still need to build an orphanage. There are going to be a lot of Indian children to take care of when the soldiers come back from the war. Here is some work that Bible Betty would find acceptable to her God. We can teach the children how to make adobe bricks, and they can build their dormitory. We can teach the children how to read and write. Look how fast they are learning English. We can make a difference here, Eli. These children don't have to grow up as renegade Apaches. We can make them into peaceful people, one child at a time." Reluctantly, Eli built a small adobe cabin that was the first of many bigger dormitories. The Red Mountain Indian School had come of age and little did they realize just how significant it would be in the raising of Apache children to be good citizens instead of warriors.

All That Glitters

It took eight weeks for Roland and Lia to return. This time there was an entire shipload of freight that Roland sent to San Pedro from San Francisco. He had hired a freight company to take the materials to Yuma for delivery to Moses at Yuma Crossing. Roland and his family took the Butterfield Stage from Los Angeles and arrived in Yuma well ahead of the freight. Moses immediately grabbed Anna away from her mother and held the little girl, singing to her for hours before finally handing her back with a wet diaper. Moses was hoping they could buy some of the freight wagons when they arrived from Los Angeles. He didn't have enough rolling stock or pulling power to take everything to Red Mountain in one trip. Roland set him to ease on that issue, "I already bought half the wagons and the ox teams to pull them. We will have to offload and send the other half back and use your wagons to take the shipment the rest of the way. Do you think we could find a couple of milk cows to take with us?"

"No problem on the cows. Do you want a whole herd? What about a bull?" Everyone laughed but raising beef cattle on the Hassayampa grassy areas or up in Peeples Valley didn't seem like a bad idea.

Roland had a much more important question to ask now that they had dispensed with the greetings and trivialities. He asked, "Moses, did you get a report back from our banker on the first gold button we sent to San Francisco?"

"Yes, I did. It is over in the warehouse. It will go up to Eli with this shipment, but I can tell you what it said. The bank said that they had the gold tested at the mint. The mint report said it was eighty percent gold and twenty percent silver. The bank pays $19.50 for every ounce of gold on ninety percent of the delivered weight, less the silver. Then after the refinery finishes, they settle on the remaining ten percent of the value."

Roland got extremely thoughtful. "Mr. Sue knows gold pretty good, and he thought our gold was on the order of ninety-five percent gold. If that is true, our banker was looking to cut a fat pig in the ass on every shipment. I passed the shipment I brought down to him, but that may be the last one. I gave one of the buttons to the US mint myself. The assayer gave me a report that said the button was over ninety-six percent pure. I didn't have time to go back to the bank, but I will write our banker, Mr. Parish, a letter before we leave Yuma. I am sure that he is very honest, but I think he has a very dishonest deposit clerk on his staff who has an accomplice at the mint assay office."

That night, Roland composed his letter to Jim Parish. By his calculation, if the same deposit clerk who handled the first transaction handled the large shipment he just made, he would be shorted around thirty-six thousand dollars. He suggested Mr. Parish should check who the bullion assayer was that generated the erroneous report for the first shipment. He walked over to the Headquarters Building and posted the letter before turning in for the night.

It took another week for the freight to arrive from Los Angeles and a couple more days to get it all across the river and ready to go. They had an equal number of mule and ox teams and set out on a warm morning in September. With so many new teams and green handlers, Moses could see that it was going to take twice as long as normal to make the trip. There were droves of prospectors camped along the river, but none after they turned up the long valley to the north. Roland was pleased to be headed home.

It was Late in September before Moses was able to finish the trek to Red Mountain. Everyone was thrilled to see Roland, Lia, and Baby Anna return from their whirlwind trip to San Francisco. The return trip wasn't without mishap; Moses had several wounded men. One of them was in a lot of pain with a broken-arrow shaft protruding out from behind his right shoulder blade. Several other minor injuries needed Suzette's attention. However, Moses brought the man with the arrow wound directly to the clinic. Eli and John wanted to know where the attack occurred, and Moses just said they would talk about that later as he helped carry the man into the surgery.

Eli was concerned about the Indian attack, but he was also concerned with the ragtag crew Moses had put together to drive the freight wagons. None of them knew they were going to a gold mine, and upon discovering that several of them showed more than a casual interest in the operation, Eli put all the workers on alert. Mr. Sue, in particular, had a strong feeling that they were going to have some trouble before this bunch returned to Yuma. They would have to post more guards on the mill and be extra vigilant while the teamsters remained at the mine.

The men unloaded half of the wagons at the settlement. Mary smiled and hugged Roland when she saw several bathtubs come off of one of the wagons. Suzette and Bridgette had about a half wagon of supplies for the clinic. While the teamsters moved the crates of supplies into the clinic, the men started to relate tales of their trip up from Yuma. They were attacked several times by the Apache along the way; all of the attacks were at night, and seemingly were orchestrated by the same renegade band. They were about forty strong but poorly armed. Moses had his men circle the wagons every night with all the oxen and mules in the middle of the circle. Mostly the attacks were half-hearted attempts to probe the strength of the wagon train and assess the possibility of stealing some of the oxen.

The reason for the ragtag bunch of teamsters was that the good men left Yuma to go east to join the forces fighting the Civil War. Moses had to scrape the bottom of the barrel in Yuma to have two men per every wagon and an extra team of four guards. Like when Eli led his wagon train across the prairie, half the men were on guard duty through all the hours of darkness. The sorties cost the Indians dearly. Several Indians died, and at least another score was wounded in the raids. Moses didn't lose a single man on the trip, and their injuries were minimal, other than the man that was already under the care of Suzette and Bridgette in the surgery.

Eli was concerned that the Apache would even try to attack such a large and well-guarded wagon train. It still seemed safe on the hill, but the fact that the attacks were getting bolder and more frequent couldn't be discounted or ignored. A bigger worry, however, was much closer at hand. The men who unloaded the wagons at the mill were wandering around, looking at every detail of the operation. Mr. Sue stood in the door of the small adobe building they had built for the gold refinery, his fighting staff within easy reach. There was no door on the refinery, so it was easy to see in, even with Mr. Sue standing in the doorway. Several of the men hung around the refinery a little too long. Mr. Sue could see that they knew about amalgamation and the process of retorting mercury. These three knew there would be some gold to be had before long. They had a lot of questions. Mr. Sue feigned that he didn't speak English. John shrugged off the questions, deferring to the noise of the stamp mill, making it too difficult to talk.

John sent one of his men over to the settlement to fetch Eli and Roland and told him to have them come over to the mill and to make sure they came armed. Also, he wanted his messenger to put the night-time guards on alert. They were well equipped to handle the security for the gold, but never before had there been so many strangers around the mill at one time. Moses came over to the mill with Eli and Roland. All three had sidearms and Henry rifles. The teamsters and their swampers, though, were also heavily armed with revolvers and Sharps rifles. Eli took up a position by the amalgam table, and Roland joined Mr. Sue at the door of the refinery. Moses gathered up his men and sent them out to the wagons to set up for the night. Even though they were within the sanctuary of the hill, the teamsters didn't know that. Moses told them that he was still wary that there could be another Apache attack before dawn. It would be a sleepless night for Eli and Roland. They would be glad when the wagon train pulled out the next day for the return trip to Yuma.

Suzette and Bridgette were busy in the surgery, removing the arrowhead from behind the wounded man's shoulder blade. It was complicated to lay open enough of the shoulder even to see the arrowhead. Suzette cut the bindings from the point, and Bridgette carefully drew the shaft out of the wound. The man lay on his stomach, unconscious from the chloroform, but still moaned every time Suzette touched the arrowhead. Fortunately for the man, the point had not cut any tendons. It was, however, buried with both ears of the point slipped under tendons that connected the muscles of the shoulder to the back of the shoulder blade. If she pulled it out, there would be damage to the tendons. She could hold one of the tendons away to clear one of the ears, but she couldn't hold both at one time. The wound wasn't gushing blood, but it oozed enough to make seeing the tendons difficult. The surgery was stifling hot, and both women sweat until they dripped. Suzette finally got a retractor under both tendons at once and could spread them away far enough for the ears of the point to clear. Holding the shoulder blade up with one hand and the retractor with the other, she had Bridgette extract the arrowhead with a pair of forceps. The arrowhead was obsidian, and luckily, the point was complete. Obsidian arrowheads were sharp as a razor, but fragile as glass and often left broken parts of the point in the wound.

Lia and Abby pulled the women out of the surgery to cool them off. It was easy to see that both of them were on the verge of heat exhaustion. Lia said that she would close the wound, and Suzette went back in to show her two muscles that she had partially cut to get at the arrowhead. Lia would have to suture the muscles before closing the remainder of the incision. Lia could see that this man was going to hurt for a long time, even though the arrowhead removal was a total success. He wouldn't be traveling anytime soon. Suzette watched Lia work for a few minutes and then went back out, confident that Lia would close the wound correctly.

Abby's Indian children were fanning Bridgette and Suzette. Abby sat down on the bench next to them and said, "Consider that it is only the middle of June. We still have July and August to go before it cools off again. As soon as Lia finishes, we need to get that man out of there and cool him down too. I wonder if John could fashion us a fan of some sort for the surgery?"

John, however, was busy with Mr. Sue inside the refinery. They didn't have a safe, so every time Mr. Sue finished making a gold button, he buried it in the dirt floor of the refinery. Out of sight -- out of mind. That was the strategy for security. There were more than a dozen of the fifteen-kilo buttons buried in the floor. They excavated and transferred the buttons to a wheelbarrow and then covered them with dirt. After dark, they would hide the wheelbarrow over at the settlement. Mr. Sue had more deception up his sleeve; he had melted the brass barrel of a small signal cannon along with all the brass cartridge casings he could gather in the same crucible used to make the gold buttons. He had a brass button replica of the bullion buttons he produced for shipment. He left the brass decoy out on his workbench in one of the strongboxes Moses had brought him. The box had a hasp and a padlock on it, but the lock was a shabby attempt at keeping only a casual thief honest. Mr. Sue made it even easier for a would-be-thief; he left a lantern burning on the workbench and a pry bar close by so a thief wouldn't have to grope around in the dark looking for a tool to pry open the strongbox.

Darkness fell, and as Eli's night guards came on for their shift, he told them to lay back from patrolling the mill and let any visitors look around. They weren't to shoot anybody unless the teamsters and swampers attempted to damage the equipment or threaten them with physical harm. Eli pushed the wheelbarrow over to his cabin as darkness fell and left it in a toolshed that was nothing more than a lean-to on the side of the kitchen. Eli rigged up a stack of empty cans that would be pulled down from a workbench by a string if anyone tried to move the wheelbarrow. He went over and sat down with the other men to talk over the Apache problem and how they would get the next gold shipment safely down to Yuma.

Moses had a lot to say on that issue, "Shipping the gold with the likes of the teamsters who brought up this supply train is out of the question. Shipping in a lone wagon, like the last time, is also a bad idea because of the Indian attacks. I am going to send the wagon train down the Hassayampa for the return trip to Yuma. We are not going to get any help from the Army; all the troops were sent east for the war. Between here and Yuma, we are on our own with the Indian problem. My suggestion is that we draw them into a trap and wipe out the band that attacked us on the way up. They will just be replaced by more hostiles, however, so that is not a permanent solution." Roland suggested splitting the wagon train in two and sending Moses's trusted men down the Hassayampa with the gold and the ragtags down Moses's trail to Yuma. He was trusting that the Indians would attack the smaller train, and the Indian band would lose more braves. Moses couldn't go along with this. He made a good point, "If I split the train and half of it gets wiped out, I won't be able to hire another crew in Yuma ever again. Also, I don't like those men any more than you do, but it is my responsibility to get them back safely. It would be better to armor all the wagons and send them down together to meet the Indians."

The discussion went on well into the night. Lia, Mary, and Abby finally came over to claim their men. As they were ready to retire to their houses, there was shooting over at the circle of wagons. The men strapped on their sidearms and picked up their rifles. Mr. Sue checked on the wheelbarrow in the lean-to and stayed there with the women; for once, he had a rifle in his hands instead of his staff. Suzette and Bridgette were hoping for a good night's sleep after the long day in the surgery but got to work, making ready for more patients.

Eli and the others walked into the wagon circle. There was a lot of chaos and discord. One of Moses's trusted men came over to them and told them that all was peaceful, then suddenly, there was a gunfight. None of Moses's trusted men were involved. They thought there was an Indian attack and took up positions guarding the inner ring. There were two men dead and one missing. He left on foot without food or water. Eli said, "We can gather him up in the morning; he won't get far."

Mr. Sue had gone over to the refinery to check on the decoy button. He came down to the supply train and quietly said, "The decoy is gone. The thief broke into the strongbox to steal the button, and then he put another strongbox from the pile on the bench to mask the theft. The guards told me that six men were milling around in the dark. Only one went in the refinery, and they all left when that man came out carrying a gunny sack. If two men are dead and one is out on the desert, that leaves three others still here that were involved in the robbery."

Eli said, "Abby can track the missing man at sunup. I'll go with her." Just then, there were three more shots out on the desert. They sounded like they were less than a mile away. "Sounds like our thief ran into some trouble."

Moses said, "I'm still pulling out and going down the Hassayampa in the morning, but with this crew, I'm not taking any gold with me. I'll come back up the other trail with all my good men on horseback. We can hunt Indians on the way up and then take the gold down the Hassayampa again. I'll try to be back in two weeks."

At first light, Eli and Abby set out to find the missing man with the three Indian children in tow. It wasn't much of a problem tracking the thief. Already, turkey vultures were circling about a mile off to the southwest. There they found the thief, dead, laying on his back with sightless eyes staring up at the sky. The decoy button was at his side with his left hand, covering it as if for comfort. His revolver was in his right hand, and there was a bullet hole in the top of his right boot. There was a large-mature Mojave rattlesnake dead at his feet. The snake was more than four feet long and as big as a man's calf at its middle. The black skin and bright gold diamond pattern on his back identified him as what kind of a rattlesnake he was. He was big and old, the children dubbed him, *The Granddaddy of Them All*. He had a bullet hole through his head. The children pulled the snake away from the dead man, cut off its head, and started to skin him for the beautiful hide and the meat.

Abby pulled up the thief's pant leg. Just above his low boot, there were the two telltale marks of a snake bite. In a panic, the man shot at the snake and got him, however, he had also shot himself in the foot and lay quietly in the dark until he died from the snake bite. Mojave bites were always fatal. Eli didn't feel sorry for the man, but he still thought, what a waste for a piece of brass. Eli took the man's gun and gun belt and then picked up the decoy button. They would leave the man to the vultures and desert scavengers for disposal. The ants were already quite busy with the dead body. They walked back toward the settlement. The Indian children were hungry for a rattlesnake breakfast and eager to stretch out the beautiful snakeskin for drying.

Moses was ready to leave. Eli dropped the decoy on the desert before he reached the supply train. He didn't want the rest of the men to see the decoy, thinking the ruse of it might come in handy again. Eli and Moses clasped hands and then pulled into a manly hug. Moses said, "I am sorry this trip ended this way. I'll work hard on making it better next time." As he parted, he pulled a letter out of his pocket and gave it to Eli. Apologizing, he said, "I forgot to give this to you yesterday." The letter was from Jim Parish, the banker in San Francisco. Eli was anxious to read it, but it could wait until he was back at the settlement with Roland.

Mary had the patient from the surgery propped up at a table by the kitchen. The man was in excruciating pain, but he had to eat before Bridgette would dose him with laudanum again to ease the pain. He wanted to tell Eli his story but found it difficult to talk. All Eli got out of him was that he wanted to stay with the settlement. He was a carpenter and would make himself useful if he could stay. Suzette stepped in and admonished Eli for trying to have a conversation with the man. She handed her patient a dram of laudanum and told the man to eat quickly; he would be asleep soon. Eli asked Suzette to get Roland, John, and Mr. Sue. They had a letter from Jim Parish to read.

The banker reported that he had found the deposit clerk that had defrauded Eli on the first gold shipment. That man was in jail awaiting trial. The bank would make good on his lost revenues for the first shipment, and he would handle all the transactions personally in the future. He also asked if Eli wanted to incorporate the mining venture. He stated, "It doesn't appear that you will have to raise capital. However, a corporation is an excellent way to distribute ownership among your siblings and your trusted partners." Eli thought back to his father's successful formula for growth; Roland and Suzette thought it would be a good idea. Moses, Mr. Sue, and John were trusted partners and deserved to own a portion of the mine. Suzette wanted Bridgette to have a stake, as well. The family decided that Roland would return to San Francisco with the next gold shipment and take care of the details of incorporation. With that, the men got back to work; there was equipment to unpack and install in the mining operation.

There were the iron parts to add five more stamps to the mill and another arrastra. John smiled as they unpacked a small boiler and a double drum winch. There was a small clamshell for the winch and several rolls of steel cable for rigging it. John announced that they would be sinking on the hot springs before long. All they had to do was move the boiler, the heavy winch motor, and the bucket to the top of the hill. Suzette had won an argument with John; he agreed that he would not mine the hot spring pool until he finished a house for her and Bridgette. The house had to have running water, a bathroom with a flush toilet and a bathtub, two bedrooms, and a living room and kitchen. A tall order since everyone was living in one room cabins, but John agreed to the terms. The adobe walls of the house were already half complete. Wood from two supply wagons left behind in the wake of the theft, and the killings made the top mantels for the walls and the window headboards. John's only regret would be that he would have to build two houses, the second one for Mary. Eli was going to have to hire more men for a permanent construction crew.

The day was burning hot, and there was work to be done. The miners and guards started the arduous task of getting the boiler and winch to the top of the hill. Mr. Sue was busy unpacking the equipment for the refinery, and John was busy thinking about how best to expand the stamp mill. The women were busy too. They went down to the river every day to mine clay and make adobe bricks for the construction of the houses. Occasionally, they would see a prospecting party passing through or a lone Indian watching what they were doing. Abby and Lia stood guard with their babies in papooses on their backs, while Suzette, Bridgette, and Mary, along with the children, made bricks. Each day they could make around fifty bricks with the wooden molds John had made; each was one-foot square and six inches deep. Every day when Eli came with a freight wagon to take them back to the settlement, he would load a batch of finished bricks and take them back with them.

One evening when Eli returned from the river, Roland was sitting with a man under the ramada. Suzette was sitting with them and translating a sentence or two into German. Eli could see that there was a negotiation in progress. Roland introduced the man as Henry Wickenburg. Wickenburg had brought a wagon full of quartz rock that he had mined from his claim in the mountains to the southwest. He had been in the area for some time, having returned with Pauline Weaver to prospect. Wickenburg had some partners, and they settled on the Hassayampa where there was water to mill the ore. Eli asked, "Mr. Wickenburg, where is Weaver? He passed through here a while back and was angry as hell that there were thousands of people on his claim on Rich Hill and down in Weaver Creek. We haven't seen him since."

Wickenburg chuckled, "Weaver won't stay with mining when the going gets tough. He is off looking for another *Rich Hill*. I wish him luck. By the way, let's be on a first-name basis. I want you to call me Henry. I want to sell you a wagon load of good gold ore. I need money to hire some miners, and we can't mill all the ore we mine. I need a stamp mill like you have here, and

I could use some help buying the equipment and setting that up. I hope that we can work something out and be the best of friends."

Eli reassured him, "Henry, you look like a hard-working, honest miner. We are going to introduce you to John Gould, our engineer, and Mr. Sue, our gold refiner. Everything you see here is the result of these two men's expertise. We can help you with setting up a mill, and I will have Mr. Sue look over your load of ore. We can't shut down and clean out the mill to run your ore on a batch basis to get an exact weight of the gold recovered. But if you will accept Mr. Sue's estimate of value, we will buy your ore and pay with US Double Eagles, if that would be acceptable to you?"

"More than acceptable," Henry said as he extended his hand across the table to shake on the deal. Henry stayed for the night. Over the evening meal, he related the story of his leaving Austria and working his way across America. He learned to prospect in the Mother Lode country of California but wasn't very successful there. He met up with Weaver in Los Angeles and came with him to search for gold in the Arizona Territories.

It didn't seem possible, but two weeks or more passed quickly, and Moses returned with eight men and a heavy supply wagon. This time he came up the west trail, and again, they were attacked several times on the way. This time, though, each time the Indians attacked, the men would ride out with guns blazing to turn the ambush back on the attackers. They had killed many Indians in the first two daytime attacks, and after that, the Indians resorted to night-time raids. Again, all the attackers died, and after that, they were unmolested for the rest of the trek to the settlement. Moses had another letter, one from Jacques; everyone was eager for news from the wayward brother.

They sat huddled together at the table by the kitchen. Mr. Sue volunteered to read the letter aloud. It followed Jacques signing on as an Army Scout at the start of the war, and his riding east with the California Column under Colonel Carleton to drive the Confederates out of Tucson. He was more than a little disillusioned working under the fickle Pauline Weaver, who was the chief scout for the California Column. He was leaving soon for the east coast to join Colonel Hancock from Fort Moore as chief scout for his regiment.

Jacques's going east worried everyone greatly. The war was not going well for the North. As a scout, Jacques would not be involved directly in combat. However, caught up in campaigns that involved some tens of thousands of soldiers, it would be impossible at times to escape the danger. Knowing their brother, the Callahans knew Jacques wouldn't avoid danger. They all concurred that he would probably seek to be in the middle of it. From a lonely hill in the middle of Apache territory, there was little or absolutely nothing they could do about it. At the moment, they had problems of their own to keep them busy.

Getting the boiler up the hill the next day was fairly simple. Eli rigged the teams of mules from the wagons Moses had brought, while John and his miners pried the boiler up and got it on the skids for the trip up the hill. When all was ready, Eli pulled the boiler over to the bottom of the trail. Some of the men wanted to use logs as rollers under the skids to make the load easier to pull, but John nixed that idea. "We got mules working for us going up, but we have gravity working to roll it down over us if it breaks loose. Let's see how it goes." He rigged pull ropes to each of the skids, so if they had to, they could give the mules a hand. With a crack of Eli's whip, they started up the trail.

The mules were good for the first two hundred feet. Eli stopped the team to rest them. Training had the mules pulling hard against something that moved fairly easily — pulling against something that seemed immovable they fagged quickly. After a fifteen-minute rest, they started up again, this time with all the men pulling on the ropes. This round, they got another hundred feet, and both men and mules alike had to rest. Eli asked Roland to go down and roust the guards for more manpower, and also to get the women to carry up some food and water for the crew. They lay by for an hour this time, and Eli was glad that Mr. Sue remembered to bring up some oats for the mules. John was thinking that what he needed was a block and tackle, remembering Irwin Higgins pulling down the trees in Missouri. But that was quite out of reach without another trip to Los Angeles or San Francisco.

They started to move again. The miners were on one rope, and the guards, plant operators, and the women were on the other. The boiler moved up the hill another two-hundred feet. Eli was thinking ahead and asked, "How many oxen do we have left down at the river?"

Abby said, "Lia and I round them up and count them every day we go down there to make bricks. There are fourteen left. There were forty-eight from the first supply train. We ate half the difference, and the Indians have managed to steal the other half. Even if we had twice that many, I don't think you could get them to pull this thing up the hill."

"This thing," Eli replied, "we are taking to the top today. I am thinking about the winch motor. It is heavier than the boiler, and this is about all the mules and all of us together can do."

John had a suggestion. "Let's think about building a block and tackle using the wagon wheels. We have quite a few wheels and axles and about three-hundred feet of wire rope. We get this to the top, let's sit down tonight and think this out."

By the time they got to the top with the boiler, everyone was completely exhausted. The sun was beginning to set, but the heat of the day didn't yet begin to taper off. The men all took a dip in the hot spring to get wet, which would cool them walking down the hill. When the women were the only ones left, they stripped down and went for a swim. Mary was reluctant to undress. She wasn't modest or shy; she felt the young, svelte women would kid her about her older and more portly body. Lia and Abby had their babies and were already playing and splashing around. Suzette and Bridgette stayed with Mary and finally got her to get naked, telling her that she didn't smell so good after the trek up the hill with the boiler. She finally stripped down and got in the pool. All the women washed their clothes and put them back on wet for the walk down to the settlement. Suzette and Bridgette stayed behind and said they would sleep in their cabin that night. Abby gave them a knowing look and a smile and wished them a good night. Both of the girls worried that Abby somehow knew their secret; they had been so careful. How could she know?

If Abby knew, she kept it to herself. More importantly, the work at hand presented enough problems; no one needed another issue on their minds. John had everyone disassembling wagon axles and sawing planks to extend over the rims to turn a bare wheel into a pulley. The winch was pried up onto skids, and one of the pulleys was attached to the front using two wagon tongues to hold the axle for the pulley. A pulley anchored up the hill was more troublesome than mounting one on the skid. They decided to use a complete axle and dig a post hole to set it in the ground a hundred feet above the skid. This time they would use logs as rollers, and with the cable reeved through the pulley on the front of the skid and wound around the upper pulley, they would have a mechanical advantage of two. Also, the mule team would be pulling downhill. It took two days to complete the preparations, but then they were ready.

At first light on the third day, John had the steel cable rigged over the pulleys, and Eli had the mules in place to make the first leg of the assent. After the front of the skids climbed the first log, the sled moved easily up the hill. When it reached the top of the run, John had the men tie the sled to stout mesquite trees on both sides of the trail so it could remain on the rollers without losing it back down the hill. Eli backed the mules, and the men took the cable up to the next pulley. They had made four assents by noon, and then it was time to dig up the axles and pulleys from down the hill and move them up the slope. It took three days to reach the crest of the slope where the grade leveled off at the top of the hill. From there, the mules pulled the winch motor into place next to the boiler. John had some plumbing to do, but he was nearly ready to start mining the bottom of the pond.

The clamshell bucket was relatively light compared to the other two loads, and Eli opted to bring it up in a wagon. For this load, he chained up a log to drag behind the wheels in case the mules fagged, or some other unseen mishap set the wagon to rolling backward down the hill. It wasn't necessary; the mules made it to the top with only one rest stop. With all the equipment on the hilltop, John set the miners to work setting the boiler and winch to where the clamshell could be traversed back and forth over the pond and dig straight down. The mill men extended the feed trough from the mill to a bin where the clamshell dumped. The rigging was rather ingenious, and it took another week to get everything working just right, but they were soon on their way down. The present set up would allow them to reach a depth of at least one-hundred feet.

With the mine ready, the men turned their attention to expanding the mill. They knew the gold particles would get bigger as they deepened the mine, so John had the men building a sluice box uphill from where the feed would split to feed the old stamps and the new extension. This work was going to take much longer than setting up the mine at the top of the hill. Roland had included a steam-powered drag saw in his shipment, so at least sawing the beams and planks needed for the new works was still laborious, but much easier than the first time around. Eli asked Roland why he didn't buy a real sawmill. "Simple, brother, we don't have a forest to feed one. We scrounge every one of our sawlogs from the river. That takes more time than sawing the beams. I know you are thinking about the sawmill back home. I wonder what will be left there after the war. I sent letters to Rufus in Independence to get an update on what was left of *The Complex*, if anything."

Mr. Sue was working on improving the refinery. Roland had brought him a bullion roll. It was more often called a jeweler's roll, used for flattening gold and silver buttons into flat plate or wire for manufacture into jewelry. It could also roll the long thin ribbons needed for bullion assays or refining larger quantities of metal. There was a new-model button balance that could weigh up to a gram with a precision of a hundredth of a milligram. The new button balance needed a solid base, but that was a trivial job compared to the accuracy it would bring into the operation.

There were two other items added to Mr. Sue's treasures. One was a huge double beam platform balance with weights that allowed weighing up to twenty-five kilograms at a time. The other item was a coin press. The coin press was an item usually found at a mint or an assay lab authorized by the mint to strike coins for circulation. Roland had bought a brand new one on the recommendation of the chief assayer at the San Francisco Mint. The mint had bought it to make smaller denomination gold and silver coins, such as half and quarter eagles, but set it aside in favor of power coin presses needed to feed the gold-greedy commerce in California. Roland's press was hand-operated, but it would be adequate for making the coinage they would make for their weekly payroll. He paid dearly for the dies to stamp R*ed Mountain - 999 fine*, ten, and five-dollar gold pieces. Roland paid a fortune to have the dies ready by the time he left San Francisco. The die maker at the mint worked night and day to have them finished by the time Roland and Lia departed.

The press itself was massive, and it performed the four steps to make a coin that precisely weighed one-half or a quarter ounce. First, a gold button was rolled through the bullion roll into a ribbon just a little thicker than the finishing roll of the coin press. The finishing roll was an adjustable precision set of rolls that could make a flat slab of gold up to six inches wide. A punch was the next operation that cut a round-blank piece out of the slab. There was a balance scale on the side of the press for weighing each blank before the next step of the process. Blanks that were too light, recycled to the melting furnace. Those that were overweight were filed down to make them correct. When everything was working perfectly, very few blanks were rejected or adjusted for the next step, which was a set of grooved wheels that turned a blank into a *planchet*. A planchet was still a blank, but one with a raised, grooved edge. The planchet was the piece of metal that went between the dies that stamped the front and back of the planchet with the images that made it into a unique coin with markings of its value, purity, and the mint of manufacture.

There wasn't enough room on a ten or five-dollar coin to spell out Red Mountain, so Roland had the die maker cut the image of their round hill with a river running past its toe on one side; the values $10 or $5 on the back with 999 for the purity. The hand-operated coin press was obsolete for the mint but was perfect for the young, isolated mining company. The die maker in San Francisco told Roland to make coins using only 999 fine gold. The mint made coins that were ninety percent gold and ten percent silver. It was a harder alloy, more durable for circulation, but requiring annealing between each step of the coining process to soften the metal for the dies. 999 gold was malleable and soft and didn't work-harden, so it would be easy on the dies. The die maker guaranteed that each set of dies would make at least one-thousand coins before showing signs of wear.

The trick was to have clean metal to feed the process. Mr. Sue was using the salt refining process to extract the silver from a portion of their bullion for the coins. Roland brought him alumina crucibles used for that process along with an ample supply of salt. He intended to be in the coin minting business for a long time. He also brought Mr. Sue an iron door for his refinery and a safe for storing the bullion. He joked that one day, Mr. Sue would bury a button and not be able to find it. Mr. Sue gave him an incredulous look and shook his head, *no*. One problem, though, was having a trustworthy crew to help in the refinery to make the coins. Roland said, "Train the women to do it. They are trustworthy, and I am sure they will be able to do the refining as well as run the press."

Mr. Sue laughed and said, "I won't get the women for a crew until they finish the bricks for their houses. Besides, I still have to learn how to do it myself. That should give the girls and John time to finish the houses."

Roland asked, "Did you know that the man Suzette and Bridgette patched up with the arrow wound was a carpenter? I'm going to make him an offer to stay on as our housebuilder."

"That would be good. Maybe the carpenter could build me a bedroom and office onto the side of the refinery. We need a bigger room for the coin operation anyway. There you have it. A bigger assay lab, a refinery, and an apartment for the eminent Mr. Sue, Red Mountain Refinery Manager, and Chief Minter."

"I have a better name for you, Mr. Sue. How about *One Damn Fine Man*?" They both laughed. Mr. Sue was glad to see Roland laugh. He thought his young friend was very good at what he did, but he approached everything way too seriously. The Chinese had a word for this affliction, but it didn't translate into English. In Chinese, it was a word used to describe a man who was obsessed with his work and went after it night and day in a much too serious manner. English would have to catch up with his ancient language.

It took over a month to complete all the work. The mine, mill, and refinery were complete, and the houses for the womenfolk and their families were also nearly complete. The carpenter recovered but was still not up to hard labor. He was an excellent foreman, however, and the Callahans and Goulds were no longer living in shacks. As soon as they finished the houses, the carpenter turned his building skills to a new and bigger kitchen and mess hall. Slowly a new complex was being carved out of the desert wilderness. Moses was transporting gold every two weeks, and now with the mill expansion, the shipments were approaching two-hundred grand a month.

As predicted, the size of the gold was getting larger as the clamshell dug deeper and deeper into the pool. John was working on a plan to drain the mine; a tunnel would be driven in from the side of the hill to drain off the water. He needed more miners but couldn't find men he could trust; the war had taken all the unemployed from the Arizona Territory. One piece of good news came with the newspapers Moses brought with each supply run, Abraham Lincoln signed into law the Homestead Act of 1862.

The Republicans wrote the act in the 1850s. However, it was impossible to pass in Congress until the southern states seceded from the Union. The South resisted the development of the west out of the fear that more abolitionist states would tip the balance in the US Senate, and that would negatively affect the slave culture and economy of the South. With the Union divided and the southern representatives established in their capital in Richmond, the Republican North made the Homestead Act one of their important agendas. Eli got busy immediately with surveying homesteads for all the rest of Moses' free blacks. They were going to own all the farmable land along the hot spring drainage down to the Hassayampa and all the tillable land along the river. The only catch would be convincing the ferry operators to take up residence for six months to validate the filings.

It wasn't as difficult as he first thought. There was a ferry company that was going to arrive in Yuma with two steam-powered ferries. The Army was already looking at Moses and his men for the US Army, expecting Congress to pass a Conscription Act. The men jumped at the chance to abandon the ferry company and come work at the gold mine. There wouldn't be any critical witnesses to claim that they didn't live in residences on the land for the required six months to un-validate the filings. Each filing would have a water well and an adobe dwelling as evidence of occupancy. Moses would continue to enlarge the freight company and give up the ferry operation on the river. All would still go well along the lines of some unwritten plan that all tied back to the success of the Dragon Tooth Gold Mine. Eli just needed to avoid the hazards and pitfalls. There was nothing ahead he could see as a problem.

It was Abby who brought a big concern to his attention. The mill stood idled for over a month, and the stream from the hot spring had kept winding its way down through the tailings from the stamp mill. John had built a diversion dam so the new tails would cover the desert floor in a different direction. It was the old channel that posed a problem. Abby told Eli they needed to take a walk one morning and look at the tailings from the mill. With the mill shut down, the stream kept washing the tailings down toward the river and was still taking the water bypassed by the mill.

The stream had washed a pathway through the tailings, and the sand and gravel of the desert floor were acting as a natural riffle. In the pools and eddies of the streambed, there was a fine gray powder. Her herd of sheep had been drinking from the stream ever since the water had cleared up. Abby pointed up to a flock of turkey buzzards soaring overhead and led Eli a hundred yards to the north of the stream where there was a grassy knoll where the sheep liked to graze. The entire herd lay dead. It was obvious to Eli; the gray powder in the stream bottom was mercury lost from the amalgam table in the mill. It was a deadly poison. There was only one conclusion to be drawn. They had to build a tailings dam before the mercury moved downstream and poisoned the Hassayampa. He would shut down the mill if necessary until the tailings dam was complete. That night they would have a meeting after dinner. He had more items he wanted to discuss with everyone besides the errant mercury.

Perry's Payback

The rest of the summer slid by into the welcome cool nights of the fall. With the daytime temperatures back to reasonable levels by the third week of October, Red Mountain wasn't surprised to see a stagecoach with a supply wagon and a squad of cavalry approaching from the Hassayampa route. What was a bigger surprise was who was inside? Jim Parish was the first one to step down, followed by a dandy who dressed like he was on his way to a nightclub on San Francisco's Market Street. The biggest surprise was the last person to come down the coach stairs, assisted by the dandy. It was Denise Higgins. Suzette gasped, then ran up and pulled her grandmother into a loving hug. When she pulled back, both their eyes were streaming tears, but Suzette's also showed deep concern. Something was wrong; Irwin was not with her grandmother.

Denise introduced the dandy. He was John Perry, Jr., president of the newly formed San Francisco Stock and Bond Exchanged. Mr. Parish went on to elaborate on Perry's background. "Mr. Perry came west with the 49's. He tried gold mining in the Mother Lode but turned his hand to securities some years ago. He worked on the New York and Boston Stock Exchanges and has spent ten years building up the San Francisco Stock and Exchange Board, and now is striking out on his own. I hope you will listen to what he has to say. I have told him some of the details of your operation here. He thinks you could be a world-class stock offering if you are interested in incorporating."

Mary could see that this was developing into a business meeting way too fast and took Jim Parish, by the arm and invited everyone into her home for some tea and something to eat. She well knew what a week or two from Los Angeles to Red Mountain via stage and chuckwagon could do to a sophisticated city dweller's stomach. She fed them cold roast pork, mesquite bread, and cold-sweet tea. Their idea of life on the frontier just took an upbeat with the accommodations in Red Mountain. Suzette introduced Abby and sent the children to fetch the men from the mill. Then Suzette asked, "Grandmother, where is Irwin?"

"I am sorry, Suzette, he passed away from a stroke. Too much shellfish and red wine, the doctors said." Suzette was deeply saddened and started crying but thought that might explain the presence of Perry a little more thoroughly than his interest in the mine. Bridgette walked up behind her and put her hands on Suzette's shoulders to comfort her. The room quieted down as the travelers finished their meal.

The men came in from the mill. Eli and Roland hugged their grandmother. It seemed like decades since they last saw her, but it was two years for Eli and only months for Roland and Lia. By that time, Denise had Anna on one arm and Abby's adopted baby on the other. "What's this one's name?" she asked.

Abby smiled and answered, "Kitchi Mac. In Algonquin, Kitchi means Brave. We call him Kit; his full name is Kitchi Mac Callahan – the brave son of Callahan if you extract all the meanings. Have Roland and Lia told you that I could not bear children? Kit is our adopted baby, along with the Indian children you see running around outside. I want to build a bigger orphanage. There are going to be a lot of Indian orphans when the soldiers come back from the war. With any luck, I will be ready for them."

Denise truly looked like a matriarch. The damp air, moistened by the fogs that embraced San Francisco almost every day of the year, had been kind to her skin. Her silver hair and kind smile reflected ageless wisdom. She smiled at Abby, "You don't need luck, my dear. I will give you everything you need to build the largest orphanage you want. You have to agree also to build a school and teach Indian children to be good people and good citizens."

Just then, the three Indian children came running into Mary's house. The oldest, Henry, had found a large gold nugget in the sluice in front of the stamp mill and was very excited about it. They were jabbering to Abby in Apache. She stopped them short with a raise of her hand and said, "Children, say hello to Mrs. Higgins."

The three children lined up next to Denise and as one, said in perfect English, "Hello, Mrs. Higgins." The girl curtsied as she spoke the words, and the boys did a polite bow with one hand behind their back and the other on their stomach.

Denise was overwhelmed. With tears welling up in her eyes, she said to Abby, "You're going to do fine, child." With that, she cried openly. Her daughter had been dead for over three years, but the recent loss of her second husband and the memories of leaving Anna in the lone grave in Independence was as fresh as the day Suzette left the alabaster knight in her mother's coffin. Lia and Abby retrieved their babies, and Suzette held her grandmother for a long time until she stopped crying. Denise could be a tough businesswoman, but when it came to her family, she was just another human being. Eli and Roland took the men over for a tour of the mill to give the women some privacy.

As they stepped out of Mary's house, another squad of soldiers with two more supply wagons reined to a stop in front of the settlement. In their lead was Major Jenkins. Eli was surprised to see him. "What are you doing here?" he asked.

"I came to look you up and see how you were doing out here on your own. Also, I wanted to see if your sister and her nurse would sign on as a team to run a hospital at Fort Yuma. Where are they anyway?"

Eli answered, "Inside with our grandmother. We are going on a tour of the mill. Want to come along? There is something I want to talk to you about anyway."

Major Jenkins ordered his men to set up a camp and then joined Eli for the tour. On the way over to the mill, Jenkins had more questions about Suzette. "How old is she now? Is she still packing that Lefauchaux revolver? How about her nurse? Aren't these girls ready for husbands?"

Eli always knew that Jenkins had an unhealthy fixation on Suzette, but it was Roland who sobered the conversation. "How's your wife, Major?" Jenkins had little to say other than his wife told him she wanted a divorce at the end of her last visit out to Yuma. Jenkins shrugged off the question telling Eli and Roland that she was a Confederate sympathizer. The brothers knew this was probably a fabrication, but they let it pass.

Jim Parish and the stockbroker Perry were very impressed with the mill. Mr. Sue was making $10 gold pieces. The coins were beautiful, dazzling when he gave each of them several out in the sun at the door of the refinery. Perry took exception to the mint operation. "You can't make your own money! You need authorization from the mint. I am pretty sure it is against federal laws."

Mr. Sue said, "With all due respect Mr. Perry, it doesn't say that it is a US coin. It just says it is worth $10 and that it is three nines fine. Don't you like the impression of the mountain and the river? I think it is very nice."

Jim Parish didn't let the Major or Perry speak again. "It is a beautiful coin, Mr. Sue. Could I buy a bag of them and take them to your sister? She asks me about you all the time."

"Now you can tell her where we live. She can come to visit anytime. She can even bring her children if she can find them." They all laughed; the contrast between Mr. Sue and his sister had become a legend during his stay with Suzette during her time at the Medical College.

The operation was humming along, processing eighty tons a day coming down the flume from the mine at the top of the mountain. The gold nuggets from the sluice box were getting progressively bigger and weighed more than the gold produced by the stamps and the arrastras. Parish looked out over the growing tailings dam. There was an oxen team pulling a box scraper, making a circle pulling sand and gravel off the desert floor, and depositing it on top of the dam. Eli waved a greeting to the operator, and he waved back. Tirelessly, making figure eights with the scraper, the man had raised the tailings dam five feet high in front of the advancing tailings. "Why are you doing that?" Parish asked.

Eli answered, "That's a containment dam for the tailings. There is a slight loss of mercury from the amalgam tables. We don't want it to reach the river."

"Good thinking," said Parish. "There are tons of tailings washing down the rivers in California from the hydraulic operations. They are going to fill the north end of the bay over the years to come. There should be laws against mining that way. All Congress can think about is the war, and the government needs the gold so they can print more paper money to pay for everything. Do you keep up with the war out here?"

"Best, we can. We get newspapers with every supply run Moses makes from Yuma. Last we heard Hancock was promoted to Brigadier General and was involved in the Virginia Peninsula Campaign. Jacques is with him."

Jim Parish was becoming a Civil War historian, and he had a lot to say. "A lot has happened since Hancock distinguished himself on the peninsula. Lincoln is moving to free the slaves, North and South. He thinks that freed slaves will make excellent soldiers. From the looks of your workers here, I think he may be right. By the way, you need to post a war chest to pay off the waiver fee for your men in the event of a draft. I hear it will be three hundred dollars per man. The North is turning the war into a rich man's war, but as usual, it's a poor man's fight. I think it has been that way since man invented the first club."

"You have got that right. My father was a history professor. He said there was never a short civil war, and they tended to go on until all the poor people were dead or the rich people were broke. Antietam was an excellent example of that, and neither the North or the South gained anything from the battle."

"The coming year is going to be a lot different. Lincoln is pressuring his good generals to advance and relieving all the generals too timid to fight. He knows the South can't replace its losses in personnel and treasure. He wants a general that will use the arithmetic of attrition to crush the rebellion. It will work in the long run. The only hope for the South is foreign intervention, and no nation on earth wants a war with the North. It's not going to happen."

"Let's talk about what comes after the war tonight. Roland tells me to expect depression, economic upheaval, and financial chaos. I don't know what gold will do through those times, but I expect to have plenty in the bank by the time Jeff Davis is vanquished." The men finished the tour of the mill, and Eli led them to the top of the hill on two mules he had trained as saddle mounts. Sure-footed and with a smooth-gentle gate, the mule was the transportation of choice in the rough country. Jim Parish was comfortable, but Perry couldn't wait to finish the ride. It was all very amusing to Eli and Roland.

The mine was more impressive than before. John had constructed a walkway around the pit with a handrail so the men could work safely guiding the clamshell to where they wanted it to land on the bottom. Parish wanted to know how deep they could go with the present setup. Eli explained, "We have enough cable to sink one-hundred more feet of the shaft. The winch could dig it down to below five-hundred feet, but we would have to tunnel in from the side of the mountain to drain the water. If we go below five-hundred feet, we will have to replace the water feed to the settlement and the mill. Right now, the water runs down there by gravity."

Perry was busy taking notes and lining up more questions. "How deep is the pit? How much gold have you recovered from there to date? When will you start the tunnel? I financed Sutro to drive a tunnel under the Comstock Load, and that was a disaster for everyone. He never broke through to the water. The Comstock will stop mining when they reach the limit of the pumps, and they have the best pumps available on today's market."

John had just arrived and joined in, "They will never reach the limit of the pumps. They will keep building bigger pumps until they run out of ore."

Perry commented, "They will never run out of ore. The vein runs down into the middle of the earth."

John was patient, "Every mine ever discovered will eventually run out of ore. The Comstock and this mountain aren't exceptions to the rule. The trick is not to spend all of the money you make mining the ore before it dries up for good."

Perry asked, "How deep do you think this mine goes?"

"I'm a realist, Mr. Perry. I don't speculate on things like that. I start at the top and quit when I get to the bottom. And I reiterate, there is always a bottom, whether you can see it from here or not."

Perry huffed up. "I don't like your attitude. It is bad for promotion."

Roland stepped in, "We are not asking you to promote anything. Is that what you have in mind?"

"Let me guarantee you, *son*. I can make more money promoting a good mine than you will make mining all the ore. I have some agreements in my bag down below. I would be happy to let you read them over."

Roland said, "Let's head down and get started. If I like what I see, you might leave here with a deal." Mr. Perry didn't realize it, but Roland had slipped into attack mode for having been called *son*. One thing you did not do to a Callahan, was to belittle them for their age. Roland was confident that collectively, they had more business acumen than Salmon Portland Chase, Lincoln's Secretary of the Treasury, who was taking in and spending every dime he could in support of the war. Mr. Perry was going to be in for quite a ride.

Roland spent the rest of the afternoon reading the agreement offered by Perry. Occasionally, he would make a note in the margin; and if Perry saw him do it, he would display a nervous tic, blinking his right eye more tightly than the left. Mostly Perry watched Suzette and Bridgette as they came and went to Mary's house. The women busied themselves with preparing a proper frontier dinner for their guests. Perry was obsessed with Bridgette, and it was all too obvious that Major Jenkins still fixated on Suzette.

It was easy to see why. Jenkins had an obsession and fantasized about Suzette since the first time he saw her when she was just fourteen and fresh off the Santa Fe Trail. She still looked much the same, but her bearing was that of an accomplished young woman. He couldn't get over her getting her M.D. at only age fifteen. As far as he was concerned, it just enhanced her appeal.

Perry spruced up his dandy self to maintain his appearance, trying to impress Bridgette. He knew her history with Fillmore and figured that she should fall for a guy like him. While Suzette was a deep brown from the desert sun, Bridgette was still lily-white. She freckled badly in the sun and kept herself covered at all times and wore her flaming red hair over her shoulders to protect her neck and shoulders from the sun. A wide-brimmed straw hat, long sleeves, and light gloves took care of the rest. Major Jenkins and Perry would make ridiculous, futile conversations with them every chance they could get. It was beginning to annoy the girls. Major Jenkins got particularly annoyed when they turned his offer of making them the post medical team down flatly.

By dinner, Roland had completed his review of the stock agreement. He had a few guidelines for Perry and said he would write them up as an amendment to the agreement offered. Perry would incorporate Red Mountain Mining and issue a million shares for ten dollars a share. Roland specified that seventy percent of the shares would assign to the four Callahans, John Gould, Mr. Sue, and Moses in equal numbers of shares. Thirty percent was designated for fifteen minority shareholders, to be named by the RMM board of directors. The only one Roland named in his edits so far was Bridgette. The remaining twenty percent was assigned to be sold by the Bond and Stock Exchange of San Francisco; Perry designated as the agent. Perry would join the board of RMM, and Roland would take a seat on the board of Perry's company.

It all seemed simple enough. A corporation would be established and managed along with the business model of Callahan Meadows, but Roland had some tough questions of his own. "Is your company a public company? Who are the largest shareholders? What is your stock selling for on today's market?" Perry was getting a little wary. The Callahans were a financial force unto themselves, and Denise Higgins was one of the richest and shrewdest women in America. She now controlled most of the newspapers from Los Angeles to Seattle. Was what he was planning to do with his twenty percent of RMM worth the risk of reprisal. They could hurt him badly if they wanted to, and he knew it.

Then Roland led Perry through the changes to his agreement that would be necessary before he signed. The first clause to go was way in the back, guaranteed to be missed by a hasty or tired reader. It allowed Perry to issue more stock as he felt fit. Roland didn't pull any punches. He asked Perry, "Is this how you gained ownership of a good deal of the Comstock?"

It was getting dark, and in the light of several kerosene lanterns, Roland could see that Perry flustered and displayed impatience with whom he probably considered to be a young and inexperienced adversary. "It is a standard clause, and all my management agreements have it. I won't do a deal without it."

Roland pushed the agreement across the table and just stated flatly, "We don't want what you are selling here. I suggest you travel a little farther up the Hassayampa and incorporate the prospectors up there. Goodnight, Mr. Perry, and thanks for coming all this way to see us."

Jim Parish could see that Perry had met his match but probably didn't know it yet. Perry had won his share of a good deal of the mines he represented by diluting the stock after the initial offering was bought up by the greedy marketplace. The new shares created would be sold to friends who gave him control by proxy or voted as per his wishes. Roland would have none of that. "Wait," Perry yelled as Roland was walking away from the table. "We can strike that clause. What else is there that you can't live with?"

Roland sat back down at the table; siblings, wives, miners, guards, and the new men, Moses' men, had nothing to say. Other than a welcome breeze and the rise of a spectacular full moon, all was quiet as a church during a funeral while Roland led him through the rest of his edits. Finally, in desperation, Perry took out a fancy pen for the signing. The pen was a variation on an invention that had been around since the turn of the century. It had a steel point like any other ink pen, but it came with a cap that covered the point of the pen. The cap held a sponge that held a little ink, perfect for a deal maker on the road. You couldn't write a letter with it, but it held enough ink for at least several signatures.

Roland chuckled as he saw there were ink stains on the pocket of the dandy's shirt. Perry may have paid a lot for the new-fangled pen, but it had a leaky cap. No doubt, the rough ride up the mountain jostled some ink out of the cap and stained his shirt. Perry didn't notice the stains; he was pushing the pen at Roland, but Roland stopped him. "I am not signing tonight. My wife and I and our baby girl will be returning to San Francisco with my grandmother. We will take the next gold shipment with us under the guard of Major Jenkins and his men. Mr. Parish, I trust you can take charge of this document and generate a clean copy for my signature at your desk by the first of November?"

Denise winked at the banker and smiled. Parish picked up the document and said, "I will be more than happy to." How much gold will be in the next shipment?"

"Twenty thousand, four hundred and eighty-two ounces," said Mr. Sue from the shadows. Perry brightened up. He could still make a fortune selling half of the twenty percent at a good commission to his friends. He would buy the other half with that money and drive up the price of the shares as news of the fabulous gold mine opened the wallets of the San Francisco greedy rich. Little did he know that Roland had a plan of his own.

The next two days were spent getting an armored wagon ready for the gold shipment. Mr. Sue had gold buttons everywhere. In the safe at the refinery, in the wheelbarrow in the tool shed, under the bed in Mary's bedroom and several others buried here and there. They would load the strongboxes and put them on the wagon in the morning. This night everyone wanted to party, especially Mr. Perry and Major Jenkins. Abby thought it would be a good occasion to introduce the city slickers to the mescal, the strong local drink of the American southwest. Perry and the Major got pretty liquored up. Everyone familiar with the strong drink knew they would be suffering greatly by the sendoff tomorrow morning.

Everyone retired for the night. It was well after midnight, and the full moon lit the desert bright enough to read a newspaper. Suzette and Bridgette walked over to their house joking that Perry and the Major were going to need some medical attention in the morning. They stripped down, bathed together, and then fell asleep in each other's arms. Not everyone was asleep in the camp, especially the two men who were obsessed with them. Perry stood guard while the Major quietly snuck into the clinic. He emerged in a few moments with two gauze pads and the bottle of chloroform the girls used for the anesthetic. They looked around, and stealthy as Indian thieves, they walked over and entered the girls' house.

A lantern burned low on the kitchen table. Perry checked the first bedroom on the left; it was empty. Jenkins opened the door to the second room and saw the two women lying together naked on the bed. "No wonder they always say no to the men," he whispered to Perry. Their time had come. With Perry holding the lantern, Jenkins stole quietly over to the bed. He pulled the stopper on the chloroform bottle and poured a generous amount on the pillow between their two noses. Both girls startled awake but were then quickly unconscious, drawing in a deep breath of the chemical in alarmed surprise.

Jenkins was on Suzette in an instant. He rolled her over on her back and pushed his throbbing erection into her. Perry took Bridgette, where she lay.

Brutal, unlubricated sex. Rape in all its ugly manifestations. When they finished, Jenkins rolled them back together and then made a wick from a piece of cloth and ran it from the bottle to the pillow an inch from each of their noses. He hogtied both of them and gagged them good with different articles of their undergarments and clothing, just for good measure. "Sleep well, lesbian bitches. Until we meet next time." Then he slapped Suzette on the ass hard enough to leave a deep bruise. She didn't even moan. They left the house as they found it, save for the bottle of chloroform. It would be first light in an hour, and they would be long gone with the shipment before the two rape victims started to stir.

As was their design, the two drunks joined the effort to break camp and load the wagons. The only one to notice that Perry and the Major didn't walk over from the camp, but from the settlement, was Mr. Sue. He thought nothing of it for the moment. He had a lot of gold to load onto the armored wagon. In less than an hour, Jim Parish signed for the gold and left with the soldiers to head down the Hassayampa. Perry and Jim Parish rode in the armored wagon with the gold and two guards. Major Jenkins rode in the lead with his color bearer. It was several hours before the rest of the camp was up for the day.

Mr. Sue had a special breakfast ready by the time the rest of the partygoers were ready to join the living. He figured that Denise and the girls were sleeping late. That was the case for Denise; the girls were still deeply unconscious while the last of the chloroform was evaporating from the wick. It was after breakfast that Mr. Sue got concerned. He went over to the girls' house and quietly knocked on the door -- no answer, no cheerful greeting. He went inside; when he saw the two girls hogtied on the bed, he covered them with a sheet and then sounded the alarm. Yelling from the front door, he got Roland and Eli and their wives to run over. They were appalled at what they found.

Both girls had been bruised badly and had bled after the rape. Bright red blood stained the sheets. Both girls were moaning awake, and Abby gently cut the bonds from each of them. It was just in the nick of time. The hogtie was cruel, and their feet were pulled up tight with the sashes of their robes around their necks. The cramping had set in, and in another hour, both of them would have been dead by strangulation.

Eli and Roland were ready to saddle up and go after the wagon train. Mary brought them around to their senses. "Boys, listen to me. I know you think you know who did this, but ask yourselves, do you have proof? Jenkins has a dozen loyal soldiers with him. If you go riding in there with guns blazing, you won't be coming back. Let's take care of the damage for now. There will be other ways to get at Jenkins and Perry, but not today."

Roland was the first to agree. "You're right. I'm not going to kill Jenkins; that would be too kind. I am going to destroy Perry at his own game. I'll leave Jenkins to Suzette. He will be lucky he survives with his manhood or his life. Abby and Lia had the girls cleaned up and dressed. They came out and sat down at the table. Mary, Denise, and Mr. Sue joined them at the table. They said very little, and when they discussed the rape, it was done so in hushed voices and whispers. Denise had been listening to the report of the rape and was deeply concerned for the girls. Her rape aboard *The Blessed* had nearly cost her life. She was particularly concerned for Suzette; Denise sensed that her granddaughter was still a virgin. What a terrible way to be introduced to something that was meant to be pleasurable between a man and a woman.

Eli and Roland went into the girls' house to inspect the bed where the rape took place. They found a major's oak-leaf epaulet on the floor by Suzette's side of the bed. There were several drops of blue ink on the sheets where Bridgette had laid tied. The brothers agreed; they had all the proof they needed. They could see two dead men in the very near future. They left the house but decided to leave the group at the table alone. There was still a lot of quiet discussion going on. As Eli walked by the table, he dropped the Major's gold maple leaf into the middle of the group.

He could hear Denise asking, "Why were you sleeping together?" Denise wasn't happy with the answer. As Suzette explained, Denise saw dream after dream for her granddaughter's marriage and babies to come, fade into the haze of a homosexual relationship.

Suzette was crying, "We have been lovers for quite some time now." Eli and Roland had more information than they could assimilate. They didn't discuss it on the way to the mill. John, oblivious to the happenings back at the settlement, had the miners and operators busy with steam building in the boiler; making gold would go on as usual.

Back at the settlement, Mr. Sue was explaining that homosexuality was older than the millenniums. "It is only the Christian West, Eastern Europe, and the countries of Islam that deny the institution. In China, more than half the aristocracy is homosexual at one time or another during their lives. There is nothing to be ashamed of here. If the two of you love one another, it is up to the rest of us to leave it at that."

It was hard for Denise to accept the reality of homosexuality affecting her granddaughter. She was looking forward to more grandchildren, but more so, she wanted Suzette to settle into a relationship with a loving man like Anna had done with Aaden. She held Suzette tight as the young woman continued to weep. Bridgette held Suzette's hand. She had the comfort of being out in the open without any family incriminations or concerns to worry over.

When Roland came back to the settlement, Denise took him aside, and they went in and sat down at Mary's table to have a private conversation. Denise asked, "Are you sure it was the Major and Mr. Perry?" Denise was feeling some guilt for bringing Perry to Red Mountain.

Roland said, "Someone could have planted the Major's insignia to frame him, but I doubt it. It was still pretty dark when he left; I didn't notice if one of his insignias was missing. There are blue drops of ink on the bed. No one else has a leaky pen around here. It was Perry for sure. With him there, I think it is conclusive that the Major and he did this together. I can't believe that they thought they could get away with it. I'm going to destroy Perry; Suzette will take care of Jenkins on her own."

Denise knew all about hostile takeovers. She built her newspaper conglomerate successfully applying the techniques several times since destroying Halverson, the owner/publisher in Jefferson City. They formed their plan; they would work together. Perry would be history in another three to four months. Denise turned the conversation to sorrow for her granddaughter. "The only sex the child has experienced has been a brutal rape and a lesbian relationship. It doesn't seem fair. She is so beautiful; you would think that the best men in the world would be standing in line for her."

Roland was compassionate. "She is still young, and she knows how to love deeply. Give her some time; everything will work out for the best. Think of Mr. Sue's favorite adage; *every day breathes its own breath*. This one is no exception, but it is only one day. We will give her revenge, and she will heal."

Denise would stay another week. Roland and Lia and the baby Anna would return with her to her home in San Francisco. They would be there at least a week before the November 1st signing of the corporation papers. She was already writing the articles that would fan the fires of their devious plan to wreck Perry. She was proud of Roland. He had formulated the plot just by being called *son*. Now he had a mature deadly purpose that she would help him see through to the end.

Like clockwork, a stage with four armed guards arrived two days later to pick them up. They were in Yuma in three days. *The Blessed* was anchored in the middle of the river, waiting to take them to San Francisco. Roland asked his uncle about the Confederate warship. Connor didn't answer. He just said that it wasn't around anymore to cause trouble. They were back in San Francisco by the 18th of October. They had two weeks to fan the fires of Perry's damnation.

The first article Denise ran, splashed the headline across the top of the front page:

RED MOUNTAIN MINING INCORPORATES.

The article went on to spell out the details of the mine and the gold production. The Dragon Tooth Mine was the only company asset, but it was a rich mine, expected to rival the richest mines of the Mother Lode.

The next day the front page of the *Alta California* related the saga of the Callahan children crossing the prairie and making the fabulous discovery of the Dragon Tooth Mine. The story circulated to Denise's papers up and down the coast. Investors were beating down Perry's door purchasing warrants for one-hundred share lots and paying up to fifty-dollars per share for them. The marketplace was paying five-thousand dollars a warrant. Perry was sitting with a million dollars in his account and hadn't even signed the agreement as of yet.

Denise arranged for Roland to speak at the San Francisco Stock Exchange. He played the part of the wealthy child millionaire well. With his beautiful woman on his arm, he walked into the ballroom of the Palace Hotel five minutes late. He wore an impeccable charcoal gray silk suit with a ruffled shirt. A five-dollar fake diamond ring adorned his middle finger, next to his wedding band. He had his long blond hair slicked back, and his sideburns trimmed. Lia wore her hair brushed out in the long fall behind her back. She had on riding pants, a flawless silk blouse showing ample cleavage, and wore the dragon tooth amulet around her neck. The house fell silent as she walked in with her hand on her husband's arm. Denise followed with Anna held tightly to her bosom. If this went as they planned, the bubble they were building would inflate beyond the five-thousand-dollar warrants that Perry had already sold.

Roland was eloquent and spoke of his family's history. His immigrant parents, the operations in Missouri, and the untimely death of his father and mother. Many of the women in the audience were weeping, and the men sat at rapt attention. Roland went on to tell of their crossing on the Santa Fe trail, the battles with the renegades, and the Indian tribes. He told of the map they found on the Peralta party, Suzette's becoming an M.D. right here in San Francisco, and Eli's return to the desert to search out the Spanish Cross on the map. It didn't matter that the map was either a hoax or as of yet they had not discovered the Spanish lode. This crowd only wanted to hear about the mine and plan how to sate their greed. The Spanish cross on the map fed the fire of their greedy imaginations.

Roland finished up his speech with a dramatic ending. He had the large nugget the Indian children had brought in from the creek to the north of their hill. He said the mine was getting richer at depth, and the gold nuggets were getting bigger. He dropped the nugget on the table in front of the husband and wife owners of the Palace, who were seated to his left. It made a resounding thump hitting the table. "I trust this will pay for the rental on the ballroom. Send the bill to me for drinks and dinner for everyone kind enough to come to hear me speak today."

With that, he picked Anna up from Denise's arms and with Lia in tow, made his way to the door and left the ballroom. Questions hurled at him from every direction. Roland closed the door behind him and returned his family to the Presidential Suite on the top floor of the hotel. Denise stayed behind and socialized with the women in the ballroom. There was an orchestra, and tables and chairs were set up for the guests. The results of the trading even exceeded Denise's wildest expectations right there during the gala that followed.

The warrants were trading among the wheelers and dealers in the audience. All around her, she heard offers of up to a hundred dollars a share. Their plan was going to work better than even Roland thought possible. Perry was the most pleased man in the place. The grin from ear to ear lasted all night. He had bought the rights to the twenty percent of the stock for ten dollars a share. He sold the warrants for one-hundred dollars a share and was looking at ninety-dollar per-share profits on half of the shares he had left uncommitted. He would have a million and a half in his pocket before he even signed the agreement. He was more than content; this was the best deal he ever made.

Only one man stayed behind in the ballroom until all the guests were gone. He was a professor from the Jesuit College near the Presidio. He made his way up to the Presidential Suite and knocked quietly on the door. Roland and Lia were enjoying a fine bottle of wine and a cold plate of Dungeness Crab legs with French bread. Roland opened the door and invited the man into the suite. The baby was asleep, suckling at Lia's breast. The man respectfully paid no attention and introduced himself as Doctor Laity. "I am a paleontologist from the university. I wanted to talk to you about your *dragon tooth*. I don't believe it is a tooth at all. It is a raptor claw. A fossil from the dinosaur era." Lia slipped the amulet off over her head and handed it to him for a closer inspection. "Yes, from the weight of this, it is definitely a fossil. The bone of a tooth would be much lighter. You have a rare item here. This claw is one of the best specimens I have ever seen. Could I buy it for the university museum?"

"Sorry," Lia said, reaching for the amulet. "It doesn't belong to me. My sister-in-law found it in the hot spring at the top of our mountain. That is where she first discovered the gold. She is rather attached to it. I have to give it back. We only borrowed it for the presentation today."

"Well, if she ever wants to loan or donate it to a museum, please keep us in mind. I am greatly pleased to meet you both. But be careful. The desert is a dry wasteland, but it's going to be full of sharks after today's extravaganza."

That is what Roland wanted. A desert full of sharks, dead sharks, with the Great White himself, Perry, rotting in the sun. He was going to see that Professor Laity got a sizable endowment to support him, his museum, and his students. The Professor was probably the only honest man in the hotel that day, besides himself; and with what he and his grandmother were contemplating, he had to question his honesty, but he didn't let that thought bother him for long.

Denise snuck up to the suite and congratulated Roland on his performance. "You couldn't have done better. When I broke away from the women, the warrants were trading back and forth at higher and higher prices. I expect they will be over a hundred-fifty-dollars a share by the end of tomorrow. She was right; Roland's plan was working better than she expected.

Denise kept pumping the hype with more articles about the family and the gold mine. She even re-printed the story Anna had written just before the twins were born, *The Christmas Horse*, how the time had flown. She was lonely for Irwin. He would have enjoyed this undertaking immensely. She had a strange thought for a moment. She wished Roland was perpetrating his Perry disaster on her first husband, Mercier. She stayed on that thought only a moment and then turned sad at the memory of her daughter, Anna, and her husband, Aaden. She brightened at the thought of the babies, the new orphanage she was going to build, and the school for the Indian children that would grow up there. She went to bed that night with pleasant thoughts. She wanted to live on for enough years to see how it would all turn out.

By the time of the signing, Perry was badgered to sell warrants for the rest of the stock he would soon receive. The morning of the signing, James McClatchy of the *Sacramento Bee* approached him and offered him two-hundred and fifty dollars a share for his remaining ten percent. Perry agreed to sell half of what he would get that morning, but he was going to speculate on the rest. They would discuss it over lunch at the San Francisco Men's Club and finalize payment for the deal after the signing.

There was a crowd waiting for Roland in front of The Bank of San Francisco. The bank president, Jim Parish, and four men from the US San Francisco Mint met Roland inside the door. They were Lewis A. Birdsall (superintendent), John Hewston Jr. (Chief Assayer & Refiner), J.A. Snyder (Treasurer), and Agoston Haraszthy (independent bullion assayer). They were all eager to turn the RMM gold into coinage. Jim Parish let them make their pitch and then led Roland into his office. Perry was there waiting for him. There were two copies of the agreement on Mr. Parish's desk. Roland greeted Perry with a perfunctory nod, sat down, and started reading.

Perry was indignant. "Are you going to read every word again? There are a lot of important people outside waiting on your signature."

"Right now, Mr. Perry, I and my family are the only important people in San Francisco. I am going to read every word. Why don't you leave for a couple of hours? Your impatience does nothing to help me read and concentrate." Jim Parish smiled; his boy was living up to his expectations. Out on the street, Denise had planted some of her staff to spread the rumor that Roland might not sign. After three hours, Mr. Parish summoned his chief secretary. Perry was sitting outside the Bank President's door. He was hopeful when Mr. Parish summoned his secretary, but she emerged with a page in her hand and said, "Sorry, investiture is misspelled on page twenty-three. I'll fix it." She went to her desk to retype the page.

"Holy Mother of God," Perry moaned as he collapsed back into the easy chair next to the President's door.

Inside his office, Jim Parish was enjoying the show to the fullest. He had been through these kinds of signing ordeals many times in his life. Roland was cool and collected, fully in control of the event. He told Roland, "By now I expect Perry stinks of fear and stress. You must have a reason for putting him through this, right?"

"I do, and I will tell you all about it in a month or two. Right now, I would like some cold lemonade. How about you?"

Parish summoned a different aide with a different button under his desk. His steward magically appeared and then hurried out for the lemonade. He was proud of a new ice maker that was chugging away in the back of the kitchen. Lemonade with ice, he couldn't wait to surprise Roland with real ice.

The secretary returned with the retyped page. Roland read it again word-for-word, then slipped it into the document where it belonged. He wanted Perry to come in and loan him his pen for the signing. Jim Parish got up and brought in the broker. He was right; Perry did stink of fear and stress, and he was angry. "God damn it, son. Don't you realize that I have a lot riding on this deal? You have spent all morning on one misspelled word! What do you want now for Christ's sake?"

Roland wasn't taken aback by the man's blasphemous outburst; he was once more offended by being called *son* again by a man he loathed. "I need to borrow your pen, *old man*." Perry handed him a new-silver pen snapped into its ink holder, and he didn't have any ink stains on his shirt. Roland commented, "I see you got a new one. Your last one leaked. You left some stains in a most unfortunate spot back at the settlement."

Perry turned ashen, and his stink of fear got worse. *Did Roland know he was one of the rapists?* Perry had wild thoughts running through his mind. He relaxed, though, when Roland signed the document. He signed his name to the agreement and went to slide it off the table. Roland stopped him with his hand firmly on top of the document. "This is going directly to the recorder's office at the exchange. Mr. Parish, would you do me the honor of taking it there for me?"

Mr. Parish got up from behind his large mahogany desk and said. "Let's go there together. It's just a couple of blocks away on California Street. Why don't you go home and take a bath, Perry? You stink. I am going to have them air out my office while I am down at the exchange."

When they walked out of the front door of the bank, Jim Parish held up the agreement and told the crowd it was signed. A wave of relief swept the crowd like a warm wind on a cold winter day. Reporters rushed off to get the news out for the evening papers. As they walked down Market Street in the cool San Francisco air, Mr. Parish asked, "Are you going to confide in me as to what is going on here?"

Roland nodded his head, *yes*. He trusted the banker. "You remember the Major who brought you up to Red Mountain? He and the smelly Mr. Perry back there raped my sister and Bridgette the morning you left. I hope you don't have any money wrapped up in this because I'm going to destroy him. If you lose anything, I will make it up out of my funds. Please keep that to yourself. I need another month or so to make this work."

"I am your banker, Roland, and I am an honest man. In some ways, that makes me more responsible than your confessor if you have one. I don't have a dime in Perry's warrants. I do want some stock, though. I am thinking you are going to precipitate a storm and buy all the outstanding shares for pennies on the dollar. Am I right?"

"Yes, the stock will recover, but my real objective is Perry's company itself. I am going to issue a short sell on his outstanding shares. If it takes every penny we have in your bank, I am going to own the son-of-a-bitch. If that doesn't work, I'll have to kill him."

"Roland, don't kill him. You have a bright-brilliant future out ahead of you and a wonderful family to protect. They won't have that if you are sitting in jail somewhere or swinging from the end of a rope. I'll help you with the hostile takeover. I know all his shareholders and the fifty original investors. We will make this work together. By the way, where were the ink stains you mentioned? I thought that comment was going to stop his heart."

"They were on the sheets on my sister's bed. They raped the two girls side-by-side after they knocked them out with chloroform from the clinic. They did it just before you left that morning with the gold. We didn't find the girls till later. Mary talked Eli and me out of going after them right there on the spot. Jenkins had his cavalry with him. Mary was sure we wouldn't live through it if we attacked them. She probably saved our lives."

As promised, Jim Parish let the bubble run-up unmolested. As reliable as the tide in the bay, the gold shipments arrived on time every two weeks.

Denise started running a report column weekly on the production of the mine. She was saving Professor Laity's identification of the dragon tooth for the killing blow. Six weeks passed. The share price of a single share of RMM, Inc. stock topped three-hundred dollars. Every night Roland calculated how much money it would take to cover his short sell if his scam didn't work. It was nowhere close to the family fortune, but it was pushing the limits of his account. Every morning at breakfast, he would share the calculations with Denise. She kept reassuring him. "Roland, I have been through this more times than I can remember. It takes nerves of steel and in your case, *brass balls*. No, in your case, make that *gold balls*. Don't worry about the money. The world is full of money, and so is the Dragon Tooth Mine. We will be fine no matter how this turns out. I watched my first husband destroy himself with arrogance and self-confidence. And his worst traits would pale compared to the new rich of San Francisco. The greater the greed, the easier it is to accomplish what you are trying to do. My bet is, you'll walk away from this quite a lot wealthier than when you started it. Let's drop the bomb tomorrow. I can't wait any longer for the fun to begin."

Later that morning, Roland issued an offer for all the outstanding shares of RMM, Inc. for five dollars a share. He also shorted Perry's company even more cruelly at twenty-five cents. Everyone thought the young man was out of his mind. The next evening edition of the *Alta California*, and all the papers in Denise's conglomerate ran the headline:

THE DRAGON TOOTH IS AS DEAD AS THE DINOSAUR THAT LEFT IT

The gold is exhausted; it is the end of the line for the rich little gold mine. The Callahans are not available for comment.

No one wanted to believe it. But when the gold shipment didn't show up the next day or again in two weeks, emergency meetings were held all over the city. Greed and fear seemed to originate from the same part of the human brain. The avalanche sell-off only took four days to hit rock bottom. Roland bought up all the outstanding shares of RMM, Inc. for one dollar a share and delivered them into the hands of the people who took him to be crazy. He cleared over eighty thousand dollars on the move. But the return on shorting Perry was astounding. He bought the promised shares for the short sell for a measly two cents a share. His take on that was over three and a half million. Denise didn't care a wit about the new rich of San Francisco. However, she ran an article in all her papers that she would cover the losses of the small investors. That only cost her a little over fifty thousand dollars, but it greatly lessened the public outcry and animosity toward her family, especially toward her grandson.

When all the shares for the short sale were delivered, Connor deposited two million dollars in gold from *The Blessed* with Jim Parish at the bank. With that complete, *The Blessed* raised her sails and spirited Roland and his family away from San Francisco for their safe return to Yuma. As they cleared the mouth of the bay and turned south, Roland couldn't help but think back more than twenty years when he spirited Aaden and Anna out of New York. It was the only marriage at sea he ever performed. Connor wasn't one to dwell on remorse, but he took the same pride in Roland that his father would have, had he been alive to watch his son.

Denise never broke the story about why Roland destroyed Perry. She left that to Jim Parish, who just had to drop one comment to the lady's guild that backed the men's club. In a few days, Perry went missing. Some fishermen found him hanging from his neck under a pier at Fisherman's Wharf on the north end of the peninsula. The Italians who ran the fishing fleet had lost some money. Denise included that in her reparations, but the Italian Catholics didn't abide by rape either.

In another month, RMM, Inc. stock was back up to twenty dollars. The investors that bought the first offering at ten did well. They balanced the losers, and in a couple of more months, most had forgotten about the incident except for one powerful man. James McClatchy didn't care about his losses. He resented Denise and her skillful manipulation of the press. She was a dangerous woman, and he had political agendas of his own to pursue that were opposed to hers. Life would be easier if she were out of the picture. He turned his agile mind to a hostile takeover. He planned to make payback hell for the rich widow from New York.

The Ultimate Revenge

Connor told Roland he was going to take him and his family on a sightseeing excursion of the Mexican coast, but Roland knew he was hunting for Confederate warships. The trip was relaxing, however. They rode the trade winds down the west coast of Mexico until they reached the southern tropical shores, and then turned back north to the Gulf of Baja California. Connor had modified the keel of *The Blessed* so he could navigate shallow rivers. Yuma was now one of his regular stops, hunting Confederates and transporting gold. This trip, though, he was going to take a break from captaining the schooner. He decided to travel to the gold mine with Roland and Lia and left his old friend and first mate, Santiago, in command. Santiago was starting to show his age but was displaying his years well as an elegant Castilian gentleman.

Returning to Red Mountain, Roland and Lia, the baby Anna with her great-uncle Connor in tow, arrived by stage with a contingent of cavalry as their escort. Eli looked over the troops. A young lieutenant led the column of troops to the settlement — no Major Jenkins for lesser peoples than the eminent banker and the rapist stockbroker. Jenkins was probably not going to show his face in this part of the territory ever again. Everyone was thrilled that the family was reunited, and they were anxious to hear how Roland's dealings with Perry turned out.

Roland had heavier news, however. He took a bundle of newspapers with numerous issues that only reported on the war out of the stagecoach and carried it to the table next to the kitchen. General Hancock had distinguished himself at Antietam. It was the bloodiest battle of the war to date. Casualties stood at 22,717 dead or missing in battle, North and South combined. Jacques had left from the California Column to join General Hancock as a US Army Scout at the start of Hancock's Peninsula Campaign. They hadn't heard from him since he arrived in Virginia. The papers were full of gory blow-by-blow descriptions of the battle. Most of the papers Roland brought with him were Unionist Rags. Some were even famous for misreporting facts about major battles. However, one Washington correspondent that was close to Lincoln, Lawrence A. Gobright, who worked for the Associated Press Conglomerate, was noted for his accuracy and total lack of bias to either the Republicans or Democrats.

He had published a complete list of the Union casualties from the battle of Antietam about a month after the battle. Roland had the issue and had gone through it once looking for the name of his brother. He hadn't found it, but it would have been easy to miss among the 12,400 Union dead. The dead were listed as the names came in from the battlefield and the many field hospitals that treated the wounded. It wasn't in alphabetical order or any other order based on Army Division or Unit. It must have been agonizing for tens of thousands of parents, wives, siblings, friends, and relatives to comb through the list looking for the name of a loved one. Roland divided up the papers, and the grim family set to work searching the names again. After two times through the list, they finally concluded that Jacques had survived the battle.

Relieved that Jacques was still alive, the family wanted to know all about Roland's exploit in San Francisco. Among the luggage was a traveling trunk, and from it, Roland produced another bundle of newspapers. Most all were from the *Alta California*, but he had other papers that carried accounts of Perry's demise. Roland led them through each of the published articles in order. When it got to the signing, he relished the telling of how he made Perry squirm for three hours. Bridgette enjoyed hearing about his discomfiture and was wide-eyed but happy when Roland told about mentioning the ink drops on the bed. He was an excellent storyteller. As he progressed through the news releases promoting the Dragon Tooth Mine, his family's excitement flowed and crested just as the greedy San Franciscans who had danced to the tune of Denise's manipulative editorials.

Gathered around a table as the sun went down with a magnificent red sky, Roland kept the story alive with every detail leaving his family craving for more. They were just as excited as Roland and Denise were the morning they decided to drop the bomb. With a flourish, Lia unfolded the edition that carried the headline about the dead dinosaur and the tooth it left behind. Suzette and Bridgette loved that one. Roland told them about the short sales he issued and how that worked. Then he showed them the clippings of the daily stock quotes on RMM, Inc. and Perry's company. Eli could see that they hadn't made that much on the RMM short sale, so he asked about the Stock and Bond Exchange. Roland looked very contented and said, "It wasn't completely certain by the time we left, but Mr. Parish said that ninety percent of the short sales filled and the profits stood at three-point-two million. But that wasn't the best part. When I took control of Perry's company, he had seven-point-five million in the bank from selling his warrants and half of his stock. I transferred six of that to our accounts at the Bank of San Francisco and left the fifty founders of Perry's company with a million in working capital and gave them back the company."

There were over twenty articles with various theories about Perry's demise and several lithographs of him hanging by his neck under the pier. Bridgette got up from the table and hugged Roland. She kissed him like a brother and thanked him. She said, "For more than a month, I thought I was pregnant from the rape. Suzette kept telling me that I was late because of anxiety and nothing else. Mary had worked out the cycles for both of us and convinced us both that we couldn't have conceived a child at that time; she was right."

Suzette had a determined look on her face and said, "We have to go after Jenkins next." Mr. Sue admonished her with a look of disapproval. Roland sensed that she had discussed this with Mr. Sue and had some evil plots in the making to pay back Jenkins. He would have to learn through Lia just what his sister was planning.

John ended the reunion, "It's late boys and girls, and tomorrow is a workday. This old man needs some rest." Roland put all the papers but one back in the trunk. He kept Eli, Abby, and the two girls there to show him the editorial that McClatchy had printed about Denise in the *Sacramento Bee*. The newspaper magnate didn't have anything good to say about their grandmother. While there were no laws against how she manipulated the media to guarantee the success of Roland's hostile takeover, McClatchy was calling for sanctions against Denise by the newspaper community in general and the California Governor's office.

Even though Denise made all the small investors well with her own money, there were handfuls of death threats in the mail every day. Some were nothing more than empty threats, but some were sincere and much viler. Suzette was a bit terrified, "She could be killed!"

Roland said, "Rest assured, an assassin would have to kill all the Pinkertons in San Francisco to get at her. She is living with Jim Parish and his wife, Susan, up on Nob Hill. There are guards on the newspapers day and night, and she is on the attack on the McClatchy front accusing him of trying to do to her the same as she did to him and his cronies. McClatchy was already giving in by the time we left. He is a busy man, and he held on to his RMM, Inc. stock. He'll do fine, the price per share was up to twelve-fifty when I left. The corporation is all in place. When RMM, Inc. hit three-hundred dollars, you were all filthy rich for about one day. Don't worry, if the mine holds out or gets better, we'll get there again. I am the only one that can issue more shares. If McClatchy wants to play, I will dilute him out just like Perry set out to do us." Almost as an afterthought, Roland asked, "By the way, how did the mine do while we were away?"

Eli smiled and reached into his pocket and pulled out a half-dozen nuggets that ranged from a quarter inch to more than an inch. "It just got a lot more interesting this week." From the other pocket, he took out a handful of RMM gold pieces. Even though it was dark, the pure gold coins were beautiful in the lantern light. Roland was impressed, but Eli went on. "Wait until you see them in the sunlight." Mr. Sue was pleased with Roland's reaction. He felt deeply for this young family; it pleased him greatly every time he could do something for them that made them happy.

The soldiers were going to stay for a week and then return Connor to Yuma. They made at least one sortie every day, searching for hostile Apache and getting a feel for the area. One day they returned with two casualties. One was the lieutenant with an arrow embedded in the bone in his right arm. The other was a private who was suffering a serious reaction to a scorpion bite. The boy was an Easterner and had a poor opinion of the desert. He raved with fever, "Everything out here wants to stick, bite or eat you, and we have to go out and hunt savages that want to kill us for the fun of it! Take care of the lieutenant; I'll survive."

Abby wet the boy down and had the Indian children fanning him even though the day was cold. The lieutenant dismounted and walked into the surgery without help. The pain was intense, but the wound itself was far from fatal. Bridgette asked, "Do you want anesthetic or just some painkiller? We'll have that out of there in a minute, but you're going to feel it."

Suzette tried to wiggle the arrow. It was buried in the bone and solidly held. "Doctor's call," she said. "Give him the chloroform."

The lieutenant was a good-looking young man. As Bridgette applied the gauze to his mouth and nose, she said, "Goodnight, sweetheart." The last thing the handsome lad remembered before waking up without an arrow in his arm, was the redhead with the green eyes hovering over him. It made a lasting impression, one that he intended to follow up on pending his involvement in the war and what was becoming known as the "Indian Troubles" in the area. His name was Russell Edgar. His father was a wealthy

New England factory owner. That somewhat explained why he was in the territories rather than on the front lines fighting the rebels face to face.

The carpenter that was still convalescing was finishing a large ramada outside of the kitchen/dining room that he had built for the settlement. Suzette was there with a cup of hot coffee after removing the arrowhead from the lieutenant's humerus. Her mood was dark and lugubrious. Mr. Sue and Connor joined her, and both men sensed her mood. Connor thought he could brighten her day and asked, "Dè as fheàrr a tha an cùis?" (What is the matter pretty one?)

Suzette stumbled for a moment on the language. She hadn't spoken Gaelic since her father died. It surprised her as the translation and the implications it implied seeped to the forefront of her consciousness. Not wanting to talk about Bridgette's attraction to the young lieutenant, she brought up the bigger problem that troubled her many times a day ever since the rape. "I have a problem, and it is a serious one. I took an oath to do no harm. I want to kill my rapist, Major Jenkins. I worked hard to be a good doctor, and here is my problem: am I going to set aside my oath and kill him, or am I to live the rest of my life in this quandary?"

Both men were quiet for several minutes. Finally, Mr. Sue, seeing that Suzette's uncle wasn't going to step in with advice as the senior family member, put his arm around Suzette and pulled her close to his side. With his arm still around her, he had a lot to say. "My child doctor, we have been together now for quite some time. I think I know you as a daughter. You could kill Jenkins, and he deserves it, and it would make you feel better for the moment. But then you will have to live the rest of your life with the guilt of breaking your oath. Being a good doctor is who you are. Breaking your oath will dishonor the very essence of that. It won't happen until the elation of killing Jenkins ebbs over time. But then the guilt will be what is left forever. Like a single cabbageworm, it will eventually eat the whole plant. Some years from now, you won't be Dr. Suzette Callahan anymore. You will be a person living in constant duplicity. It won't end until it is time for you to leave this earth. I can't tell you what to do. I can only help you see the two paths that lead from where you are now, to where you will be in the future you make for yourself. Take some time to make your decision. As always, I will help you with whichever path you choose."

The sadness was deep. A lot of thoughts were all in her head at one time. Suzette wept quietly thinking of her father and mother, and the principles they lived by, the principles that made them great people. She had killed a lot of men; was that without principle? It was self-preservation. Indians, renegades, Chico de Diablo – the only one that she ever regretted was the Apache scout she shot in the back on the San Pedro. It was a regret. There was Mr. Sue's cabbageworm. She regretted killing the Apache every time she thought of him. She didn't need to live with another regret. Her decision rose out of a morass of unreconciled possibilities; she resolved not to kill Jenkins. She would live with it taking comfort in the fact that he lived because she allowed it.

Suzette put her head down on Mr. Sue's shoulder and said, "Thank you." She still wept for a long time as Mr. Sue held her. Connor felt as if his role as the family patriarch had been upstaged by this strange Chinese man. But he also had the iron will of a Callahan, and he had not taken an oath. He also had killed hundreds of men: The Argentine frigate in self-defense; the *Heart of the South* – that would be first-degree murder when he found them; and a score of Confederate ships of war and innocent merchants since the war started. Jenkins would never know, but he just gained a most formidable and committed enemy, one that would end his miserable life or at least leave him emasculated for the rest of his life.

The Indian children came running down the hill, excited with a sighting that took the threesome at the table under the ramada in a different direction. There was a small and strange looking wagon train approaching from the south. It took an hour for the newcomers to pull within sight of the hill. It was a band of gypsies. When they pulled to a stop in front of the settlement, Suzette could see that it was the same troop they encountered where the San Pedro met the Gila. The woman that led the troop, Katarina, recognized Suzette immediately, and the happy reunion lifted Suzette's heart.

Suzette ran out to greet her as she climbed down from the wagon. The troop had gained more travelers since they met on the San Pedro. There were several more gypsy wagons, and at the end of the train, there was a large freight wagon that had the tools of the trade of an assayer hanging on the side. She didn't pay much attention to it, but there was a small assay furnace mounted on a platform at the back of the wagon along with other equipment she did not recognize. Returning to the gypsy woman, Suzette said, "We need another performance."

The gypsy woman sniffed the air and said, "You have pork cooking and a warm fire. We will sing for our supper." She pulled Suzette into a very smelly hug. Suzette thought, *I also have a bathtub, and you are going in it.*

The woman wasn't offended by the offer. It had probably been years since she had anything but a cold dip in a stream or a river. A whore's bath was always welcome on the prairie or the desert, but it was nothing compared to a soothing soak in a tub. Mary washed all the woman's clothes while she bathed. The men and boys of the troop used the outside pool that was for the Indian children. The young women and girls came in, and one-by-one washed up in Suzette's bath. Suzette and Bridgette knew there would be a thorough house cleaning in order before the cleansing of the troop was complete; for the moment, they were pleased that the troop smelled better and would also be well fed.

The men had one of Horatio's grandchildren roasting whole on the spit over the fire pit. Mary had a large pot full of potatoes and another full of wild onions from their gardens down on the river. The gypsies were uncomfortable when the black men came over from the mill with the miners and operators to eat, but there was nothing like a good meal to break down racial biases.

Eli and Mr. Sue had locked up the refinery when the gypsies arrived and had spent the afternoon conversing with the man who owned the assay wagon. He was a German immigrant and went by only one name – Otto. He joked that there wasn't enough room on the form on Ellis Island to write down his full name. He was just Otto, and he was content to be known only by that.

Otto claimed he had a unique process and could extract gold and silver out of ores that didn't yield to conventional assay procedures. All through the evening meal, he spouted off about complicated chemistry, all of which was his justification as to why only his process could find the hidden gold and silver. The gypsies were oblivious to the fact that the settlement was operating a gold mine; the workings, however, were obvious to Otto. He offered to demonstrate his process the next day. He would extract gold and silver from the mill tails. Mr. Sue said, "I'll have samples ready for you in the morning."

While the mill was extracting a good deal of gold from the red ore from the mine, there was still a consistent two dollars per ton of gold tied up in the tails. That was another reason to build the tailings dam. The tailings still contained considerable revenue; it was just waiting for a process to make extraction possible. Otto kept plying his sales pitch all through dinner. Eli and Mr. Sue were looking for an opportunity to get away from Otto by the time the feast was over.

The evening progressed, first into the puppet show and then into the concert. As before, the music was beautiful. It made Suzette wonder where Paul Hayman was these days. For the finale, the gypsy woman took the stage with her balalaika and sang her traditional songs. Her operatic voice filled the settlement and wafted out over the desert in the night air. Then with a look of amusement, she shifted moods and played Stephen Foster's *Camptown Races.* "Gwine to run all night, gwine to run all day," had everyone slapping time on their knees. The soldiers got up their courage and asked the gypsy girls to dance. The negros particularly liked the rhythmic music and danced with the older women. Mary broke out what mescal that they had, and more magically appeared from the soldiers' saddlebags.

For a lonely spot in the remote desert southwest, it turned into one hell of a party. Even the serious Mr. Sue was stepping around and gyrating a little in time to the music. It was well after two in the morning before the settlement settled back down in the desert night. When the concert was over, one of the older gypsy men that was a luthier, presented Suzette with a guitar. It was a fine instrument made of rosewood and cedar with catgut strings. Perfect for the beginner. The man wouldn't take any money for the guitar, but Roland slipped ten RMM $5-dollar gold pieces into his pocket when he wasn't looking.

Eli and Roland and their wives did not turn in for the night. They knew the settlement was vulnerable to Indian attack when hostiles could take advantage of the drunken soldiers. It was about five hours before dawn would arrive. The four Callahans patrolled around the settlement, both on horseback and on foot. Roland joked, "Maybe if we become known as a party spot, we'll get a lot more visitors."

Dawn came with the late fall morning of the season. The settlement was slow to come alive. The soldiers were up cooking bacon and biscuits for breakfast. Eli saw his uncle Connor climbing down from the back of the gypsy woman's wagon. He looked content and *good for him,* Eli thought, as Connor made his way to the ramada for a cup of coffee. His uncle Connor probably helped Mr. Sue maintain his celibacy. The gypsy woman had her eye on their Chinese friend all through the party. Like all single frontier women, though, she probably decided to take what she could get, rather than what she wanted. The gypsies would leave in a couple of days; it didn't matter.

Mr. Sue brought Otto two samples. Both appeared to be RMM tailings. However, one was red dirt from the southwest monument butte for the mining district. He had the Indian children gather the red dirt for him the previous day. Through the night, he had ground it by hand in a large steel mortar and pestle, his latest addition to the equipment in the refinery. Mr. Sue had the best assay lab in the territory, and he had become an expert at fluxing and firing. The RMM tails ran consistently around two dollars in gold and very little silver. He never assayed the red dirt from the monument butte, but it was red volcanic rock, very unlikely to contain gold of its own. Otto set to work, and Eli and Mr. Sue watched his progress and made mental notes.

Otto's process consisted of digestion of the ore with salt, hydrochloric acid, and bleaching powder. While the ore was cooking in beakers in the small assay furnace, he had one ounce of silver digesting in nitric acid over to the side. The red fumes were noxious, and he warned his audience not to breathe them. When the digestions quit boiling off their noxious gas, Otto separated the solutions from the residues by pouring them off and washing the residues several times with clean water. Otto combined all the washings with the leach solutions. It all looked very professional and was meant to impress. He carefully split the silver solution he made into two equal portions and added half to each of the solutions from the digestions. A gob of curds precipitated, which Otto called his *cottage cheese*. He carefully separated the white precipitates and wrapped them in lead foil.

It was time to fire the furnace and reduce the white precipitate to metal. Otto had a hand-operated blower that raised the coals in the firebox of the furnace to a yellow heat. Eli said, "Let Mr. Sue crank the blower. I want to talk to you about the process and maybe offer you a job. Let's get a cup of coffee. I didn't see you eat any breakfast."

While they were gone, Mr. Sue filled a small bottle from his pocket with the acid Otto had used to dissolve the silver. He also took a sample of the hydrochloric acid and had small paper sample bags for all the dry chemicals Otto had used in his process. By the time Eli and Otto returned, the lead had burned down on the cupels, and there was a silver bead left on each cupel that looked much larger than the half ounce that went to precipitate the leach solutions. They had to wait for the beads to cool, and when they weighed them, the one from the RMM tails weighed five grams more than the half-ounce of silver used in making the *cottage cheese.* The one from the red dirt weighed just a tenth of a gram less than five grams. Otto was triumphant. He had extracted a good deal of silver from where there was very little silver found to date. He still had more to tell, "You have to add silver to get the silver from the ore to come out. The process is called *Inquarting*. The gold is still in the wash solution. I will now precipitate it and make it into a bead. You will see the rest of the riches in your tailings."

Eli and Mr. Sue excused themselves with business needing their attention. Eli saddled up and rode down to the river. Mr. Sue disappeared into his refinery and locked the door behind him. He spent the rest of the day there and didn't emerge until dark. He took Eli aside and said, "The extra silver was in the nitric acid; also, there is gold in the salt he added. We weren't supposed to notice. Otto either put it in there himself, which would make him dishonest, or he doesn't know it is in there, which would make him delusional. He hasn't got anything special."

"No problem," said Eli. "I will deal with him."

After a quieter dinner that night, Eli asked Abby to send the Indian children down to fetch Otto up for some dessert and coffee. Otto came up anxious to hear what Eli had to say, which wasn't much. "Otto, I see you can extract quite a lot of silver out of the tailings. However, I don't see how that process could be economical way out here in the desert. We aren't parked next to a railroad, and the amount of chemical you used in your test would require a boxcar or more a month to treat just a fraction of our total tails. I appreciate what you pointed out to us. Here is a hundred dollars for your time and supplies." Eli took five-double eagles out of his vest pocket and handed them to Otto.

Otto was either shocked speechless or formulating sentences in German and translating in his mind to speak them out loud to Eli. Eli took advantage of the break in the conversation to get up and walk away from the table. He crossed to his house, went in, and closed the door. He had paid Otto in US gold coins because he didn't want the man to know they were minting gold coins there on the mine. That would be an unnecessary display of the extraordinary wealth of the RMM operation, a fact that he kept suppressing as much as possible around the few local folks that knew about the mine.

In the morning, the gypsies left heading north, and Otto went with them. From the top of the stamp mill, Eli could see them moving to go upriver on the Hassayampa. He didn't care if the German was dishonest and trying to scam him, or if he had purchased his large vat of nitric acid from a gold refiner in San Francisco who had used it to part gold and silver. That would explain the large quantity of silver that reported to his assays. He may have been blissfully finding silver in everything he assayed, not realizing his mistake.

Connor started looking in on Lieutenant Edgar and asking Suzette when the lad would be able to travel. "As soon as he can stand the pain," was the only answer she could give him, but he kept asking every day. Connor finally caught on that the young man didn't want to leave. He was obsessed with Bridgette and wanted to stay at the settlement as long as possible. In a few days, though, Connor himself wasn't ready to leave; he had a problem of his own. He knew he had contracted gonorrhea from the gypsy woman, and he was embarrassed to talk to Suzette about it. The first day he just put up with the discomfort. The second day he was having trouble sitting still, and the third was downright painful, and he couldn't urinate. It was time he talked to the doctor.

Connor took Suzette aside and asked her to sit with him in the ramada. Suzette could see that he was uncomfortable, but she had no idea as to what was wrong. Suzette waited in silence. After hemming and hawing around, Connor blurted out, "I caught something from the gypsy woman."

"You mean Katarina? She didn't even have a cold! What are you talking about?"

Connor turned red, "I think it is gonorrhea. I've been with a lot of women in every seaport in the world. I have never caught one of these diseases before."

Suzette tried her best not to look or sound judgmental. "I can treat you for that." Then she started to chuckle and covered her face with her hands, and then she couldn't control her laughter. When she was back in control, she said, "Welcome to the frontier uncle. Come with me. How long have you known?"

"Since several days after she left."

"That's good. I can cure that. Syphilis takes longer to gestate. You should have told me right away. I am not a child, you know. I am a real doctor, and I have either treated or arranged treatment of your ailment for many, many men coming over on the trail." She didn't tell him that Mr. Sue was her chief assistant in the treatment of venereal disease. The wicked side of her nature wanted to punish her uncle personally for his indiscretion.

Suzette took her uncle into the surgery and had him strip down. Luckily, there wasn't anyone close by to hear his scream when she injected the silver nitrate solution up his penis. "I'll have a gallon of the astragalus tea ready for you in an hour. I want you to drink as much as you can each day until it is gone. No whiskey until you finish the tea. And here."

Connor blushed again when he accepted several condoms from his niece. Then he asked again, "When can the lieutenant leave?"

"He can leave anytime, but he probably won't go until he convinces Bridgette to have sex with him, or she turns him down." Suzette wasn't surprised that thinking of Bridgette with a man didn't bother her as much as she thought it would. She needed to talk to Bridgette about it. She wouldn't have minded if the handsome lieutenant wanted her instead of her redheaded friend.

The two young women had their talk, and they decided to have sex with the lieutenant, the three of them together, a ménage à trois. It would be a sexual adventure, and it wouldn't pose the problem of unfaithfulness between them. The lieutenant left the settlement three days later. He considered himself the luckiest man alive and promised to come back. He went back to Yuma on the Hassayampa route and took Connor with him. The girls kissed him goodbye and bid him to be careful and to stay out of the war if he could. The young man took the lead of his column of soldiers and rode off to the south. Bridgette took Suzette's hand, and they stood upon the hill watching him go. Both wondered if they would see the young man again; Lieutenant Edgar wondered the same as he rode away from the hill. Hand-in-hand, Suzette and Bridgette walked to the refinery. Back to work making coins, there was a payday coming up, and they were way short of meeting it with the distraction of the gypsies, the party, and the wounded lieutenant taking up their time.

Then there was her uncle, Connor. He hadn't said anything to Suzette after he listened in to the conversation she had with Mr. Sue about the rape. It would take a week for the troops to return to Yuma. Suzette felt that Connor was anxious to get back for more reason than hunting Confederates. She knew intuitively; he was going to go after Jenkins. So be it, she didn't want to hear that her uncle was in jail in Yuma or hung for murder. She didn't worry long. He was a clever man and had survived smuggling and war at sea for even longer than his involvement with the Union.

Suzette was right. Connor had a lot more on his mind than hunting Confederates when he got to Yuma. He left the lieutenant behind at the Pima village riding sorties against a band of Apache that was harassing the Pima. He rode alone to Yuma on a fine black gelding; Eli wanted him to give the gelding to Moses. Connor found Moses and gave him the horse. Moses accepted the gift with a big gracious smile. He was busy, though, assembling a freight delivery to RMM that was mostly lumber and more mining supplies. Connor rode the steam ferry across the river alone and walked unannounced into Major Jenkins' headquarters.

The major was glad to see him. He had a New York Tribune that ran a bold headline,

CONFEDERATES LAUNCH SCREW POWERED WARSHIP.

The follow-up article said the *Alabama's* sister ship was rounding Cape Horn and heading to the west coast of the Union to make war on commerce along the coast of California. It gave Connor a perfect excuse for leaving immediately. He shook Jenkins' hand and said, "I'll have my sails up and be down the river in an hour. I don't want to get caught in the gulf with a powered frigate hunting me." With that, he turned and walked down to the ferry dock for a ride over to *The Blessed.*

As promised, he left within the hour. But not everyone from *The Blessed* left with him. He put Santiago ashore in a rowboat several miles down the river. Santiago was feeling his age as he scaled the bank and walked back up the river. Connor told the Spaniard to be careful and that he would heave-to and wait for him further down the river where his sails would be out of sight from Yuma. He also thanked his friend for undertaking the emasculation of Jenkins. Santiago assured his captain, "Don't worry, when I finish with him, he will die as a woman."

Santiago waited until dark and then walked back up the river to Yuma. Jenkins was still in his office when he got there. Santiago knocked on the door politely. The major called for him to come in. Jenkins didn't remember him; at least it was obvious he didn't recognize him. He stood up behind his desk and extended his hand to shake with the stranger, a simple cordial hello. Santiago took his hand, then jerked Jenkins across the desk and knocked him out with a smashing blow with his left hand. He turned and locked the front door of the headquarters building and then checked the back.

Santiago completed his work in less than ten minutes. Jenkins was naked, suspended from the rafters hanging facedown with his wrists held in two loose slip knots on the end of a short rope thrown over a rafter. His ankles were tied up more firmly so that if-and-when the major got his hands loose; he would fall and be left hanging upside down. That wasn't all; Santiago had tied a noose of fine wire around the major's genitals and pulled it tight over the rafter above him. Last he gagged the major and tied the gag in place with a leather strap.

There was only one safe way for a man to get himself out of this Castilian punishment for sex offenders and child abusers. Jenkins would have to raise himself by the ropes on his wrists until he was standing in the ropes on his legs. Only then could he free himself from the wire and get himself down without emasculation. In the mountains where Santiago grew up, a rape victim's family would kill the rapist. The cruel punishment that Santiago served to Jenkins was levied against offenders that had families to support or were valuable to their community in some other way. Jenkins would wake up. He would struggle and finally exhausted, he would free his wrists and fall. Suzette's rape would be avenged and in a way that would leave Jenkins in hell for the rest of his life if he survived.

Santiago took a moment to see that he left nothing behind that would identify the crew of *The Blessed.* The rope was common; he had stolen it from the ferry dock. The leather strap was from scraps behind the furrier's shop. The only thing from *The Blessed* was the fine castration wire he brought with him. Satisfied all was in order, Santiago blew out the lantern; and quiet as a panther in a jungle stalking prey, he made his way back down to the rowboat.

The Major's orderly found him the next morning, and the news of how he was found spread like wildfire through both sides of the river. He hadn't bled to death; when emasculated and hung upside down, most men didn't bleed out. He was unconscious and still had the gag in his mouth. The post doctor figured he passed out when the wire cut him. His genitals were a bloody mess on the floor behind him. The doctor cauterized the wound and did his best to make the Major comfortable. He dosed him with laudanum and kept him in a coma for two days before he let him wake up and discover that he wasn't a man anymore.

Reunion and Departure

John had put it off until they had the advantage of the cold winter air; now it was time to tunnel into the mountain and drain the hot spring water from the top of the mine. Starting the tunnel wasn't easy. They started digging into the mountain next to the trough that brought the ore and water down from the top. The problem was that the rock on the surface was soft, more like topsoil than the harder rock of the mountain. Every morning, when they came back to the start of the portal, there was material that had slumped down from the face of the mountain, covering the start of the adit they mined out the previous day. If they were going to get safely into the mountain, a headwall would be required. John and the miners were spending a lot of time thinking about what they had on hand to construct a headwall.

Some discussions yielded adobe brick as the best option. Sawing mine timbers out of their limited supply of sawlogs was not an option. Adobe was labor-intensive, but there was an endless supply available in the event they would have to shore up the tunnel once they started into the mountain. The effort shifted from digging to brick making. John knew how long it took the women to make the adobe bricks for their hoses and the clinic. He suggested that they shut down the mill and put all the men to the work of mining the clay at the river and making brick. The women could supervise, but the men would do the bulk of the labor. It was still slow, but the headwall was finally up and solid. The miners started into the mountain. The progress was slower than expected; the digging was easy in the soft rock but shoring up the adit with an arched brick structure took time. Not bad, though, for pick and shovel handwork. In a good week, the men would advance the tunnel twenty feet or more. The rate of producing the bricks governed the forward rate of progress.

It was the day before Christmas. Eli had the men knock off early, and everyone gathered in the settlement for a good meal and a Christmas Eve party. Abby's Indian children, who had become the lookouts watching the desert for signs of trouble, came running down from their perch above the ramada yelling, "There's a wagon train coming!" They were excited because Moses always brought a bag of horehound candy with him and other treats for the kids. He also brought Amos on every trip to the delight of Abby's children. The four of them had become close friends.

Suzette and Bridgette came out of the clinic. Suzette's mouth dropped. Even from a half-mile away, she recognized her horse. It just couldn't be. She drew in a deep breath and let out the ear-piercing whistle. Patches walked free, trotting along next to Moses by the lead wagon without the restraint of a halter. She had leather leggings to protect her forelegs from desert thorns and a bridle. She heard her mistress call and broke away from the wagon train. She ran to Suzette and slid to a stop next to the corral. Suzette pulled her head down and hugged her laying her head on the horse's cheek, letting the mare nuzzle her with its soft nose. The owner and pet held the embrace for a long time. Suzette finally turned Patches free and introduced her to Bridgette like the horse was a human. At Suzette's gesture, Patches extended her right leg and presented Bridgette with an elegant curtsy. That did it for Bridgette; she wanted a horse of her own.

Moses brought the wagon train up to the settlement. Patches wasn't his only surprise. This time he also had an Indian woman next to him on the driver's seat — not a North American Indian woman, an East Asian-Indian woman complete with a bright blue sari and a dot on her forehead. More curious, there were two stagecoaches behind his lead wagon.

When Moses pulled up, Eli was thinking, *Oh no! Not more bankers.* His worries, however, vanished like steam from his engines on a hot day. Denise stepped down from the first stage, followed by their old trail friend, Paul Hayman. A bigger surprise, though, was the last two people to come down. They were Ben and Lily grinning broadly, watching the Callahan's hugging their grandmother and pumping Hayman's hand.

The travelers in the second stage were even more of a surprise. The legs and back end of an enormous man appeared, who was levering himself out of the stage door through a door much too narrow for his bulk. He had to turn sideways to get his shoulders through the narrow door. Even then, he fell on his ass on the dusty ground instead of emerging gracefully to land on his feet. The man was more than seven-feet tall when he got himself up. Lia screamed, "Tio!" and ran to her brother, throwing herself into the gentle giant's arms. Maria stepped down from the coach, embarrassed and shy. Now it was Suzette's turn to scream, "Maria!" She ran to welcome her adopted daughter into their rugged, remote settlement with a big hug and a kiss. Suzette hugged her daughter longer than she had hugged her horse, and tears were streaming down both the women's faces.

Except for Paul, it seemed that everyone aged since they had last seen each other. He was still a young musician with an easy-going nature. Denise, though, didn't look well. Suzette and Bridgette could see there was something wrong. Ben and Lily were in their forties now and looked and held themselves as the accomplished scholars and educators they were. Loving hugs, kisses for the babies, and lots of handshakes for the men were the order of the day. Maria was shy, and she clung to Suzette and Denise. Suzette wondered about the Germans; they were the only ones missing from this reunion.

Moses was holding hands with the East Indian woman. He introduced her as Ragini, his friend, and companion. He said her name in Sanskrit meant something like a melody or music. She had to be a good woman; she had her arm around Amos, who she clutched close to her side. Amos was antsy; he wanted to be off with his Indian friends to see what was new on the mountain. When Ragini met Lia, they both smiled at one another. Ragini was the only woman their family had ever seen that could even start to match Lia's long luxurious hair.

When Lily hugged Suzette, she said, "We need to talk."

Suzette answered, "I can see that. How long has grandma been like this?"

"We found her this way in San Francisco two months ago. We went there from Independence by the Overland Stage. Travel down the rivers is impossible because of the war. *The Complex* lays in waste, destroyed by the Confederate bush-whacker, Bill Quantrill. He came to Independence through the forest from the south. When he found the end of the railroad, he destroyed the locomotive, burned all the homesteads, and killed everyone that he could find. The men tried to fight back but didn't have time to organize. Anyway, there were too few of them left after the tornado. When they got to *The Complex*, the raiders destroyed that too. There is nothing left there but the empty field and the piles of stones that were the warehouses. The Union has marked Quantrill as a war criminal. He doesn't wear a uniform, and the Confederates don't even claim him as a soldier. I'm sorry to bring such sad news."

"What about your mother and father? What about Jessica and her family?" Suzette asked.

"Mom and dad are elderly and were left alone. The Union moved Jessica to Washington, D.C. some time ago. She is running a field hospital for the Army of the Potomac. No one has heard from them since the Army took them. I have a hard time being around the war. Everywhere I look, I see young men who I know will be dead soon. Sometimes, when I am near one of the battlefields, I can feel the killing and hear the sounds of the dying. The Union Army wanted to use me to see the future of their movements and battles. When I got word of that through some friends of yours up in Leavenworth, Ben and I got on the stage and didn't stop running until we found Denise in San Francisco. I can *see* that she is dying. I can't *see* why."

Suzette gathered up Bridgette, and they led Denise to the surgery hand-in-hand between them. The doctor, nurse, and patient were in the surgery for hours. When they came out, Denise was pale and holding her side. Lily didn't have to ask; she knew the news was not good. Suzette had Bridgette take Denise over to their house, and then she told her family. "Her time is very short. She is full of cancer; there is nothing I can do. It probably started in her ovaries or her uterus. It has spread to all her major organs. Her Christmas here will be her last. I'll talk to her. I want her to live out her last days or hours with us as comfortable as possible."

Suzette did just that. Having her family around her when she died was exactly why Denise had made the arduous journey in her condition; to end her days with the only family she had left, and also to return Maria to her mother. She had Suzette call Eli and Roland. She had some things she needed to tell them while she was still able. The young men came into Suzette's bedroom, and Bridgette excused herself, knowing the family needed privacy.

Denise spoke for a long time. "All my affairs are in order. I have already put all my assets in the hands of Jim Parish. He will hold the funds in trust for you and yours. Mostly I want the money to go to my great-grandchildren. That includes Abby's children. I sold the *Alta California* to McClatchy. He was a bit miffed I was going to publish my findings on the safety of the mining operations in the Comstock. The house on Nob Hill will always be there for you when you are in San Francisco. Jim will pay the staff to keep it up. Maybe you will all go there one day when you finish mining and wandering around in the wilderness. Maybe you will have to leave the country if the South wins the war. Too many maybes for a dying woman to consider even for a minute of the time I have left. I want you to go about your lives as normal. When I am gone, I'll just be gone; no big funeral, no fanfare. Don't forget; death comes around for all of us. When you see Jacques again, tell him what I said. I want to talk to Mr. Sue now." It was a perfect way to end the sad get-together — Denise in control, as always.

The family went out, and in a heavy mood, made ready for Christmas Eve. Mr. Sue spent an hour with Denise. When he came out to the ramada, he told Suzette that she was sleeping. "What did she want?" Suzette asked.

"When the pain gets too great, she asked if I would help her kill herself."

Suzette stood there for a long time, not knowing what to say. Finally, she asked, "Could you do that?"

"No. I am sorry. We can make Denise comfortable, but neither of us could kill a patient, no matter how hard the pain. You, especially." Suzette started to cry. Mr. Sue took her into his arms and held her for a long moment. Together, they walked over to join the Christmas Eve festivities. Paul Haman was playing and singing carols; what a comfort it was to have him back. He was playing and teaching Abby's children to sing *Silent Night.* Denise's last Christmas; it was hard for anyone to comprehend. The Callahans tried their best not dampen the festivities; it was hard with their grandmother nearby, wrapped in a painful blanket of death, waiting to start her last journey.

Paul was amazing. He was much more than the musician they traveled with on the trail. He had a whole stable full of clever songs that started seriously and ended with an antidote that had everyone laughing and slapping their knees. San Francisco had been good for him. He was already an excellent musician when he arrived there; now, he was an expert storyteller, a raconteur with amazing talent. He had all the children dancing around the large fire pit next to the ramada. Tio danced with them, and they danced until they were exhausted. It was time to drink the Christmas Eve toast and give thanks for another year and the togetherness of the occasion.

Denise shambled out of Suzette's house. She had a sheaf of yellowed papers in her hand, and everyone quieted down as she walked into the circle of firelight. She gave the papers to Suzette and said, "This is the original copy of your mother's Christmas story. She was reading it when she went into labor with the twins. I want you to read it." She led Suzette under one of the lanterns that hung from the eves of the ramada and handed her the manuscript. Denise sat and patted the bench next to her for Suzette to sit; Bridgette came from their house with a blanket and wrapped Denise tightly to protect from the chill of the night air.

Suzette held the manuscript to her breast and said, "I..... I don't know if I can."

Paul stepped in and said, "I can help." He sat in the background with a fine guitar and quietly played a beautiful rendition of *Shebegga Shemora*, one of Turlough O'Carolan's most beautiful Irish ballads. The music itself drew the Callahans back to Independence and the memories of their happy childhood and formative years at *The Complex.* But mostly, the music and the story together seemed to transform Suzette into the perfect image of Anna, her mother.

Several times, Suzette choked up and couldn't go on. She knew the story by heart, they had read it every Christmas Eve, ever since she could remember. Bridgette was by her side and would seamlessly take over reading the story each time Suzette paused to dry her tears. When they finished standing side by side with an arm around each other's waist, there wasn't a dry eye in the entire settlement, and every child wanted a Christmas pony, and Bridgette wanted a horse of her own, more than ever.

Gifts were meager. Lia and Abby had been busy through most of the evening sewing, crafting something out of one of the beautiful Black Mojave snake skins Abby's children were fond of collecting. They finished just before the storytelling finished. In the quiet that followed, Abby and Lia presented Paul with a strap for his guitar. It was a piece of soft leather that they had wrapped with the snakeskin. It was stitched together on the back of the strap, and there were two brightly colored beaded buttons where the snakeskin ended, and the leather thongs for tying the guitar began. Paul held the strap in his hands with a look of reverence. "Thank you," he said, and promptly took off the plain leather strap from his guitar and put on the new one. With that, he started to play again, and as he ramped up the tempo, the dancing and gaiety swept back into the party like a summer sandstorm. Eli secretly slipped ten RMM gold coins into Paul's pocket.

His music focused on Suzette. He played *Annie of the Veil,* the J. R. Thomas ballad he played the night she killed Whitey, their third night on the Santa Fe Trail. Bridgette noticed Paul's attention to Suzette. Bridgette quietly told her partner, "If you want to have sex with this one alone, I will understand."

Suzette answered, "It would be to no end. No one will ever hold Paul; he is married to his music and will never be happy playing to one woman. Let's see what happens." Together, they took Denise back to their house. Suzette put the manuscript in a cedar chest where she kept her most precious things. There was a small stack of medical papers she had written and her degree from the medical college in the top tray. The scent of cedar was strong when she opened the chest, and it took her back to Independence and her bedroom in her parent's mansion in the forest. She put the manuscript on the top of the pile. It would always be on the top of the pile. She felt close to her mother when she closed the chest. She wanted to feel close again every time she opened it.

Bridgette stayed with Denise and doctored her with a small dose of laudanum to help her sleep. Suzette walked back to the party. She didn't know what was so funny, but Tio and the children were laughing, rolling on the ground, laughing so hard they were gasping for breath. She learned that Moses tried to imitate a belly dance that Ragini was performing in the firelight. While he was trying to keep up with the gyrations, his pants had fallen. He didn't wear underwear. At first, everyone was shocked, but then the laughter gripped the crowd and fed on itself like a fire on kerosene.

Suzette walked over to the corral. It was three days past the dark of the moon, and the night was lit only by starlight and a dim glow from the firepit. She whistled, and Patches came over to the rail and put her head down and nuzzled Suzette as she held the horse's head to her chest. She murmured to her horse, "We'll go for a long ride tomorrow; I promise."

Paul joined her at the rail. He had waited for his opportunity to talk to Suzette alone. He spoke only a few words but had a lot to say. "It seems like a long time since we crossed the prairie, a lot has changed. I guess you know, there were a lot of women in San Francisco. I am somewhat of a weak man in that regard." Then unexpectedly, he asked, "Are you still a virgin?"

"No, Paul. I hope that wasn't your expectation. I have a partner."

"Lucky man," was all Paul could manage.

"It's not a man. It's Bridgette. We are a couple, and we take care of each other's needs."

Paul was a bit taken aback and then felt a bit of regret. "I've dreamt about being with you almost every night. It is an obsession I guess I will have to get over."

Suzette smiled, "Not necessarily. How long will you be here?"

"I'll go back with Moses. He said three days."

"Let's see what happens. Bridgette and I don't want sex outside of our relationship. There is a simple solution to that problem. When we see a man that we are attracted to, we do him together, a ménage à trois." She kissed Paul goodnight, half-sister like and half passionately. She left him amazed and speechless, standing there in the dark. As he walked over to the wagon train to sleep in one of the stagecoaches, he couldn't help but think he wasn't the only one who changed since they were on the trail. Suzette was a remarkable woman, her brothers and their wives, and the children; it was all a lot for him to put into perspective. What did Suzette intend? The kiss was far more than a peck on the cheek. Was she serious about a ménage à trois? Was he destined to be the luckiest man in the Territory? He had a difficult time falling asleep thinking about the two beautiful young women.

Suzette walked back to her house. Tio was asleep on the ground at the door, wrapped in two blankets with a towel-covered rock for a pillow. Denise was sleeping easily in Bridgette's room with her arm around Maria; Bridgette was in the bathroom getting out of the tub. Suzette dried her back and then ran her hands over Bridgette's breasts; the touch was their familiar invitation for a sexual encounter. Suzette bathed, and Bridgette washed her back. They slept well that night, cuddled in each other's arms. Before they drifted off to sleep, they talked about Paul and tacitly agreed that he would be the second young man they'd make incredibly happy before he left them.

The next day there were some hangovers but not many; liquor was scarce. Moses and Eli were the worst of the lot. Moses had a gallon of red wine he had made; his new enterprise – a vineyard in the rich Yuma soil. The wine wasn't half bad; luckily, it was a little weak, or the hangovers would have been devastating. After a dose of strong coffee, they settled into a bundle of newspapers from Moses's wagon. All the papers reported that Lincoln won his second term in the White House in the November election. Union Major General Ambrose Burnside was making ready to attack Fredericksburg. Slowly, maybe too slowly, the war seemed to be turning in favor of the North. With no idea where Jacques was and no clues from the papers, they finished reading and set the papers aside.

Lily joined them. She said, "Jacques is safe. I don't know where he is, but as of yet, he is uninjured. I do see some hard times for him, though, when the war is over. Most men who escape unscathed, suffer from insurmountable guilt over the loss of their friends or family. This war is terrible, father against son, brother against brother. America will never be the same again, and the rest of the world is looking at us like we are insane. Nothing makes sense anymore."

Eli took her by the hand and stood up. "Let me show you and Ben something that does make sense." They walked to the mill and the tunnel. No one was working; it was Christmas Day. The children were standing in the portal of the tunnel and yelling absurdities that amplified and echoed back from the heart of the mountain. Eli shooed the children away and took Lily and Ben inside the mountain. Lily was in awe. Eli had pushed the drift forward almost two-hundred-fifty feet. They still had a long way to go before they reached the ore shoot they were mining from the top. The heat inside the mountain was intense, and hot water drained from the walls and ran down the slope of the drift to the portal. The last hundred feet of the tunnel were unsupported. The rock was still soft enough to dig by hand, but the rock was strong enough to support the walls of the arched-shaped drift without the brick.

As they walked farther into the mountain, Eli could see that Lily was experiencing something that only she could feel. Lily filled with a feeling of great wonder that grew stronger with each step as she went deeper into the mountain. Eli was trying to explain how they were driving the tunnel to intercept the hot spring and drain the top of the mountain. He was also trying to explain how the gold in the hot spring was too small to see, and how it got bigger the deeper they dug. He was excited and animated, trying to explain that he expected a bonanza when they reached the middle of the mountain.

They were standing at the end of the drift; Lily didn't seem to be listening, but then she said, "I don't know what it is, but there is a lot more than a bonanza of gold in there. I think it is going to make you all famous. There is a man; he has been here before. He's going to help you. He might be a teacher. Do you know who I mean?"

"The only teacher that has made the journey out here is a Professor Laity from the Jesuit College in San Francisco. He is a paleontologist and came because of Abby's dragon tooth. I'll have her show it to you back at the house." The rest of the tour included the mill and the refinery. Mr. Sue was in his element. He was refining gold and operated the coin press and made some $5 and $10-dollar gold pieces for them as they watched. Ben watched in awe, "You can make your own money!"

Mr. Sue smiled, "It's not that hard. The trick is to make something other people think is money. We happened to have the gold. If we didn't, we would print paper money." Lily held the coins like they were the most precious thing she ever possessed. She couldn't get over the feeling she had inside the tunnel. She was anxious to see Abby's dragon tooth and asked about it as soon as they returned from the tour.

Abby was glad to show it to her. She hadn't worn it for a while and explained to Lily that it wasn't a tooth at all, but a raptor claw from long-extinct reptiles that roamed the earth before man was even a twinkling in the eye of the universe. Abby held the claw for a long time. Finally, she said, "There is a history here. I can't see it with any degree of clarity. You are not the first one to wear this. Where did you find it?"

"At the bottom of the pool at the top of the mountain. Even before we discovered the gold."

"There's more," Lily said. "But it is deeper than the tunnel, and I can't see why, but it's going to make your Dragon Tooth Mine a very famous mine indeed. Eli, you have to keep digging, even if the gold runs out."

Eli didn't intend to quit digging, and he didn't expect to run out of gold. The next day they were back to running the mill and driving the tunnel. Moses was getting ready to leave. Tio and Maria were staying behind. With Denise close to death, San Francisco would soon no longer be a home for them. Suzette and Abby would take over teaching Maria. It seemed that the girl couldn't be filled with knowledge fast enough. She reminded Suzette of herself when she was in her mother's school in Independence and at the hospital with Jessica. Suzette noticed two things when Moses started south on his trail. First, it took a long time for Maria to say goodbye to Amos. *Good for her,* Suzette thought, maybe *her psyche is wired normally*. Second, Paul Hayman was asleep on the seat of one of the wagons with a smile on his face. Suzette smiled too, recalling how she and Bridgette undressed the nervous musician and pushed him onto the bed in Suzette's bedroom the previous evening. Her relationship with Bridgette was as sound as ever, but Suzette was discovering that she liked having sex with men, the right men. Thinking about Paul and Lieutenant Edgar, she was surprised to find herself aroused and chided herself as she walked back to her house to check on Denise.

Death came for Denise before the new year. She never left the house after Christmas Eve. Suzette and Bridgette moved her to their hospital room in the clinic. Denise knew the end was near. Mr. Sue, Suzette, and Bridgette kept watching and waiting. One of them was with her all the time. When her color turned to pale yellow, Suzette summoned her brothers. "Her liver has failed, and she is very weak. It will be a matter of hours now." Denise tried to talk to her family, but all she could manage was a fleeting smile and a squeeze of a hand. Lia was on the side of her deathbed with Anna sleeping on the pillow next to her great grandmother's head. Denise turned her head to the baby, and with her hand on Anna's stomach and a look of peace and contentment, she slid into the next world. The look of peace and the small smile on her lips said everything about the woman's life that could be said. She had lived it to the fullest.

Suzette was holding Denise's other hand when she passed. Everyone knew she was gone, but still looked to Suzette for a final confirmation, "She's gone," Suzette said.

The family sat quietly for a time, and then the stoic Mr. Sue said, "I'll prepare a grave." They buried Denise at sunset wrapped in a blanket at the foot of the mountain on the west side. Roland delivered the eulogy and spoke of her life from France to the frontier. He spoke of Denise, a woman that changed the world in which she lived. Everyone had walked in a slow procession out to the gravesite with the boys, Mr. Sue, and John carrying the body. Now they walked back in silence, each with their thoughts and quiet tears. Eli drew in a cemetery on his map of the Red Mountain Mining District. He made it an acre square and marked an area in the northwest corner as the Callahan Family Plot.

Life in Red Mountain settled back to normal. Lily and Ben left with the third cycle of the Moses supply trains heading to the house in San Francisco. The settlement mined and milled gold; they drove the tunnel deeper into the mountain. Life is for the living, and it continued, but a little lonelier without Denise there to share the world the Callahans were building.

Eliza's Secret Room

Connor returned to Red Mountain in early March. He stepped down from the stage behind the lead supply wagon. Eli greeted him and could see that he was troubled. Two identical twins stepped down next dressed the same: black, coal-black, from Stenson to the silver tips of their toes. *Fancy boots and hats, but no horses*, Eli thought as he looked them over. Pearl handled Colts in quick draw holsters – gunfighters Eli thought again. The last man off appeared overdressed for a trip to the frontier. *I knew it, Banker or stockbroker*, Eli thought before the introductions started.

Connor didn't need or offer introductions. He walked to the ramada with a bundle of newspapers under one arm and a set of leather-bound books under the other. Eli glanced at the titles as his uncle walked by, Nineteenth-Century Naval Warfare. Eli couldn't tell if Connor was troubled over the gunfighters or some situation involving *The Blessed*, but his not even offering his hand to Eli put him on high alert. Eli was right about the overdressed man. He introduced himself as Mr. Hobbs of Hobbs, Colburn, and Hayes, a brokerage house in New York City. The two gunfighters were left nameless. "My assistants," was all Hobbs offered. Eli led them over to the ramada. Connor got up and went into the clinic. He took one newspaper and the book set with him.

Eli was wary, "What brings you here, Mr. Hobbs?"

"I would like a tour of the operation, and then I have some business to discuss with you, some corporate business."

Eli seated them on one side of the table with Hobbs between his two assistants in the ramada and asked Mary to bring some coffee and cold water. Eli didn't like showing the mill and refinery to strangers, especially a stranger with armed men. He told more than asked, "A tour can come after you have washed the dust of the trail down. What exactly do you mean by corporate business?"

Hobbs was coy, "I've come to take possession of my share of the mine." He opened his satchel and took out a very formal contract and a set of stock certificates.

"Really!" Eli replied. "Let's see what you got?" He was more than skeptical; he was bracing for a confrontation with armed men. Under the table, he made a gesture, and Abby's oldest boy, Henry, was off to the mill to raise the alarm. Roland came out of the clinic and joined the conversation at the table. Suzette and Connor also came out of the clinic. They didn't sit; they stood at the edge of the ramada behind Eli. They were opposite the gunfighters with a clear field of fire; their attention focused on the chests of the two men in black; Suzette with her Lefauchaux on her hip, Connor with a Henry rifle. The gunfighters had already made their first mistake; they were sitting at the table, hands around warm coffee cups. They should have been standing up on either side of Hobbs. The situation was still calm. Eli was stalling for time. Abby came over from her house and quietly and without notice, walked up behind the gunfighter on Hobbs' left.

Eli was thumbing through the contract. He was a good actor when he needed to be. He asked, "I see you have issued and sold shares for RMM on the New York Stock Exchange; exactly on whose authority?"

Hobbs reached into his satchel again and pulled out a letter. "This is a letter from Jim Parish, Bank of San Francisco. He authorized me to generate an issue, a majority issue. It sold out; I have several million dollars to move into your coffers. I need some signatures." He pulled a stack of proxies out of the satchel and pushed them across the table to Eli. The proxies, along with his shares, gave him a majority position.

Roland spoke up, the businessman of the family, putting Hobbs in his place. "Mr. Hobbs, by our Articles of Incorporation, I am the CEO of Red Mountain Mining and the only person in the corporation that can issue stock. Could I see that letter from Jim Parish?" Hobbs had retrieved it from Eli. He handed it to Roland. The look on his face wasn't as confident as when he first sat down.

Roland didn't read the letter. He looked at the paper it was written on and at the signature. "You should have taken a little more time with this. The signature is wrong. It is not Jim's, and even if it were, he doesn't have the authority to authorize the sale of more stock. That would take a majority vote of the shareholders. The majority of the shareholders are right here. No board meeting. No vote to issue. This letter is a forgery and not a very good one at that." Tension ratcheted up a degree higher; the gunfighters still held their cups, but they leaned slightly to their left to favor their gun hands. Suzette was ready; feet spread, knees bent a little, leaning forward, ready to draw. It was months since she fired a shot in anger, but she was still fast as lightning; teaching Bridgette to draw and shoot had kept her sharp as a cholla cactus thorn.

Roland took a paper from the inside pocket of his vest and unfolded a letter from Jim Parish, written on The Bank of San Francisco stationery. The paper was heavier than Hobbs' letter. Roland pointed out that the real stationery had the name of the bank embossed in gold at the top of the page. There also was a watermark with the bank's name diagonally across the middle with an intricate border lining all four edges. He showed the letter to Hobbs but didn't hand it over. With amused ease and politeness, Roland said, "Mr. Hobbs, I suggest that you and your assistants leave immediately. Go back to New York and return the money you bilked from your clients with your bogus authorization. Leave now. Get back in the stage and wait south of the corral till we unload a couple of wagons to accompany you back to Yuma. And you, gentlemen, he glanced first at the gunfighter on Hobbs' left, then the right, leave your guns here on the table."

Who would ever know what went through the gunfighters' minds in the tense milliseconds before they stood to draw? Perhaps they thought they would have Eli and Roland covered with their quick draw, held hostage for Hobbs' convenience. Perhaps they intended to shoot. It didn't matter what they thought as Suzette's bullet ripped through the right shoulder of the man to Hobbs' right. The gun flew out of his hand across the table by its momentum. Eli caught it and pointed it at Hobbs.

Abby had a death grip with both hands on the other gunfighter's forearm. He pulled the trigger. His shot went through the seat of the bench close enough to Hobbs' leg that splinters from the wood drew blood. Abby gave the forearm a vicious twist. The man went down. She fell on the forearm with her knee. The bone snapped, and as she stood, she delivered a kick under the armpit, dislocating his shoulder. They were still twin assistants, but they would never be twin gunfighters again unless they learned the trade left-handed. Mr. Sue gave Abby a thumbs up from the sidelines.

Eli jumped up on the table. He jammed the barrel of the ivory-handled revolver into Hobbs' opened mouth and pushed until Hobbs fell off the bench backward. Eli followed him down and said, "Stand up." His voice was cold and cruel. He walked Hobbs backward with the barrel of the gun in his mouth back to the stagecoach. John and his operators from the mill loaded the gunfighters into the stage with Hobbs. The driver's seat was empty. Eli unclipped a whip from the side of the boot box. He tied it with a loop to the top of the collar loop of the lead horse and another loop around the top of the loin strap. The end of the whip would play on the lead horse's hindquarters when he ran. Eli slapped the lead horse on the rump and fired all five shots from the Colt in the air next to the rest of the six-horse team as they ran past him. The stage rocked and swayed wild on the road down to the Hassayampa. It would run until the horses fagged. Moses' men could pick it up on the way down the next day.

The stagecoach driver stood openmouthed and watched his stage disappear down the road to the Hassayampa. Then he smiled and turned to Eli, "I didn't like those assholes the minute I saw them in Yuma. They treated everyone like low-life hired help. *Deep Rivers* down at the Pima village called them something derogatory in his language. I didn't understand what he meant, but his meaning was clear when he spat on the ground. He warned us there was to be trouble and to watch the two men with the guns carefully."

Eli walked back to the ramada. He put his arm around Suzette. "I am glad you haven't lost your touch." He kissed his sister on the cheek. Then he kissed Abby and said, "You are one hell of a woman." His children hugged his legs.

Roland gathered up Hobbs' papers and threw them on top of the coals in the fire pit. He kept the satchel and the two Colts. Someday, he decided, there would be a museum or maybe a less ostentatious display in the atrium of Jim Parish's bank. They were gathering more items from the scams all the time, and every item would have a story. It made him think of his grandmother.

The next morning Connor was reading one of the volumes on naval warfare. He had his index finger pointing to something in the book, and his hand spread across a newspaper from the bundle. Connor slid the newspaper to his nephew. Connor was more serious than Eli had ever seen the happy-go-lucky Irishman. Connor spoke with a heavy Irish accent, "There be trouble, mate. The bloody British have built a steam-powered sloop-of-war for the Confederates. She's a big one and can make 14 knots without a sail. She's got the big guns too — one, 110-pounder that can shoot accurate over three miles. I have to work hard to shoot something three miles away. We have done it, but hitting something at that distance is always more luck than marksmanship."

Eli asked, "You are thinking of taking it on?"

"No, it's going to stay in the Atlantic. Here is what troubles me." No accent this time; he pointed to the last sentence in the article about the sloop. He put his finger down on the line and read it. "Another sloop is under construction and will be launched to cause havoc to Union shipping on the California coast."

To Eli's raised eyebrows, Connor answered without being asked, "Yes. I'm trying to figure out how to fight it."

"Maybe, you should just leave it alone."

Connor shook his head, "There is a bounty on both ships. A million dollars each. Another thing, you can't ship gold on *The Blessed* until this menace is on the bottom."

Roland had joined them and had overheard most of the conversation. He offered, "I'll give you two million dollars if you stay here and leave the Confederates alone for the rest of the war."

Connor looked at Roland like he was the devil who just made a pitch for his soul. "I'm sorry, boys. My father said there would always be one last fight for every Callahan that took to the seas. He was right. This one might be mine, or it might not. I don't want the million dollars. I want the British to remember me as the captain of the Irish schooner that put the bloody British contribution to the Confederate cause on the bottom."

Eli was thoughtful for a moment, "You could lose *The Blessed* and wind up dead. What about your crew?"

"They, to a man, all voted to fight. Santiago has *The Blessed* tucked into the mouth of the Gila. He is stripping her down to the bare minimum. In a good wind, she'll make just over fifteen knots. I can out sail her if we get in the first shot and damage her boiler. I have a base camp in the cove on the southern tip of Catalina Island. We will go there. I'll lay in wait. I'll pick the time and place for the battle. The wind, the tide, everything will have to be just right. And maybe *Badb Catha* will be in a good mood that day."

"Who?" Both boys asked in unison.

"Badb Catha, in Irish mythology, is a war goddess who takes the form of a crow. For us sailors, she is the Battle Crow. We don't have a crow, but we do have Santiago's myna bird, Grog. The only thing Grog can say is, sink the bastard. Let's hope we can."

Roland had read the article about the Confederate ship while they were talking. "Look, unc; this warship has two guns that can hit you more than three miles away. If you miss the boiler, she'll overtake you and sink you. Against a schooner, she only needs to hit you once. You'll die. Don't expect them to pick up survivors. You won't be coming back."

Connor nodded his head, "You're right. It's dangerous, but you proved to me yesterday that it is dangerous sitting at this table. I would rather die at sea fighting for a good cause than die safely on land waiting for old age to overtake me–or having a stray bullet find me in one of your gunfights. The crew of *The Blessed* isn't young anymore. None of us are looking to retire peaceful and safe on land. Another thing, the Irish were born to fight. Our history proves it. When we don't have an enemy to make war with, we fight among ourselves. It makes us look as dumb as most men think we are."

Suzette and Bridgette were standing behind Connor by then. Suzette put her arms around Connor and said, "I know you will go, but we love you and don't want you killed." Then she murmured an old Irish adage for smugglers to Connor in Gaelic, then translated for her brothers, "Sail with a vengeance, but let God bring you home."

Connor reached up and put his hand on Suzette's cheek. His touch was as soft as his voice. "You know, child; you are the only daughter I ever had."

"That you know about," Suzette said. Everyone laughed.

Suzette held him for a long moment. Uncle and niece shared what could be their last farewell. The boys got up. There was work to organize. There was a tunnel to drive. A mill to run. Wagons to unload and a heavy shipment of gold to send on to San Francisco. The supply train would leave in three days; Connor was leaving with them.

The next day the wagons were unloaded, and the supplies stored away. Late in the day, the miners driving the tunnel came out. They were excited to find Eli. They had broken through to what they called a cave near the center of the mountain. Eli and John went in to see it. It wasn't a cave, only a narrow channel too small for a man. Eli lit a candle and tossed it as far as he could into the darkness of the void. Beyond the light of the candle, the cave seemed endless.

Abby's girl had followed the men into the tunnel. She had picked the name Eliza for herself out of Mary's Bible studies. She was small; Eli didn't know she had followed him into the tunnel. Eliza slipped into the cleft of the void and stepped out of Eli's reach. She went over on the rough bottom and picked up the candle. The passageway was wide enough for her, but Eli didn't want her to go any farther. He asked, then pleaded, then shouted at her to come back as she disappeared around a bend in the passage a hundred feet or more away from the tunnel. He was trying his best to be a good father to the Indian children, but it was hard for them to warm up to a white man.

Eliza made a strong statement when she wouldn't come back to him. Her Apache still ran deep, deeper than the friendship that was only in its infancy toward her adopted father. Eli wasn't the father he wanted to be, not yet. Parenthood was a challenge; one he couldn't master by brute force or firepower. It was his greatest frustration.

Eliza didn't return for an hour. All through that time, Eli called to her at the entrance to the passageway. Abby's boys had gotten her from the refinery, and after Eli's voice turned hoarse, Abby sat on the tunnel floor, calling Eliza's name and imploring her to come out. The smaller of the two boys offered to go after his sister. Eli wouldn't let him. He didn't need two kids stuck in the depths of the mountain. Abby was starting to dread the outcome and imagining all the things that could befall the young girl alone inside the mountain.

Time drug on as slowly as the sun crossing the desert sky. Then, a dim glow appeared beyond the darkness at the end of the passage, and Eliza emerged from the bend, her face aglow behind the light of the candle. Abby would never forget the image of the girl walking toward her out of the darkness, her face lit in the halo of candlelight. The candle almost burnt to nothing. Eliza had stuck the base of what was left of it onto a rock with its own melted wax from the wick. Abby, Eli, and the miners let out a collective sigh of relief. Eliza was smiling. Abby took her in her arms and held her. She didn't admonish the girl, and Eli followed that lead. He asked, "What's back there?"

"A big room, and there are a lot of bones." She took a long tooth out of her pocket and handed it to Eli.

He turned it over and over in the lantern light, then said, "You scared us, Eliza. You could have gotten stuck."

"The tunnel gets wider after the turn. Can I have that room for my secret place?"

"Yes, but not till we can make the passage bigger. I don't want you back there alone until we can look it over and make sure it is safe. Promise me you won't go back in till then."

Eliza was a bright child, and she knew that she had caused Eli considerable worry. She looked down and said, "I promise," in a small voice. She knew she had done something wrong, something very wrong that scared her parents. With the same small voice, she asked, "Can I have my fang back?"

Eli handed it to Abby first, and then Abby handed it back to Eliza. Eli said, "Let's go back to the ramada. We need to write a letter to Dr. Laity, and I want you to tell me everything about your secret room so I can write it into the letter."

They did just that. Eli and Abby sat with Eliza as she talked about her secret room in great detail. There was another passage leading beyond the room, but it was too small for her to get through. She said, though, that the ground there was cold. Unusual for the inside of the hot spring's mountain. When she found the fang, she got scared thinking there had to be a really big snake in the cave. That was when she started back. It was easy to find the passage back; she followed her mother's calling voice. Abby traced the outline of the fang on the back of the letter. Eli would give the letter to Connor to post when he left the next morning.

Mary was sitting at the table by the time Eliza finished her story. When everyone finished talking, Mary put her arm around Eliza and said, "I want to talk to you about something." She looked at Eli and Abby; the look said it all, Eli and Abby left Eliza with Mary, but they hovered close where they could hear. Mary kept her arm around the girl. "Eliza, you heard your mother's voice and followed it back to safety. There was another voice calling before that, though, your father's voice. He called until he couldn't call anymore. Do you remember the Decalogue, Eliza? Do you remember God's fifth commandment?"

In a small voice, Eliza answered, "Honor thy father and mother." She put her head against Mary's breast and started to weep.

"I didn't want to make you sad, child. I just wanted you to realize that it was wrong to run away from your father. Obeying your father is what honor means in the fifth commandment. It is what God meant when he gave the commandments to Moses on Mount Sinai. Eli loves you, Eliza. Give him a chance. Love him back and remember, we wouldn't even know what God said if Moses didn't honor Him."

Eliza got up and ran to her parents. They gathered her to them, and Eliza held onto Eli's neck as he raised her in his arms. Eliza said, "I am sorry. I won't do it again." Abby's eyes glistened, and Eli's might have too. This moment was the most he had ever gotten from the girl. He looked at Mary with profound gratitude. Being a parent wasn't so hard, after all. Not when you had the help of your friends, especially a friend like Mary.

By that evening, a rider returned from the river. They found Hobb's stage several miles south of the mouth of the canyon. The banker and the two gunfighters were dead, scalped, and staked out on an anthill on a low bench above the Hassayampa. The Indians took the horses along with all the harness leather. Frontier justice was harsh and freely served with cruelly once again. Hobbs, Colburn & Hayes needed to find a new partner and change their shingle. The gold mine Hobbs came to steal was still shipping gold west instead of east, while Hobbs' and his assistant's bodies baked in the sun, a long and satisfying feast for the ants.

The rider was going to stay until the next supply train returned. He took the risk to ride alone back to Red Mountain, but he wouldn't take the risk of two days on the road by himself to catch up to Connor's wagons. As for Connor, his thoughts were all on risk. He wanted to take the Moses Trail back to Yuma. It was two days shorter. He wanted to get back on *The Blessed*. He needed to get her out of the river. He needed to get prepared. He needed to train his crew for what could be their last mission. His relief was palpable when the masts of *The Blessed* loomed into view. Santiago had been busy. *The Blessed* was completely gray again from its topgallant to the waterline. Waves of heat and thin smoke were rising from the boiler as Connor stepped onto the tender waiting for him. The men at the oars welcomed him home as Connor handed Eli's letter for the professor to the wagon driver. "Please post this for me on the next stage out of Yuma." He took a $10 RMM gold coin out of his pocket and handed it to the driver who snapped to attention with a salute and said, "Si Captain! Via con Dios, Capitán." Odd, Connor thought, a black man that speaks perfect Spanish.

Santiago was raising the anchor as Connor climbed up and vaulted over the gunnels to take command of his schooner. There were men in the rigging. The topsails, the foresails, and the aft mizzen moved *The Blessed* out of the mouth of the Gila. Santiago turned *The Blessed* into the current of the Colorado, and they made their way down the river. They didn't stop in Yuma. Santiago slowed *The Blessed* to pick up a crew member, their watcher. The watcher abandoned his rowboat in the middle of the river as he climbed the side of the schooner. Connor left Santiago at the con and went down to his cabin. It was stripped down to nothing but a hammock. Connor slid into the hammock and was instantly fast asleep. As he had ordered his crew to discard their belongings to lighten the ship, he would discard the rest of his belongings tomorrow when they were back at sea.

At the first smell of the saltwater marsh, Santiago sent the second mate to wake the captain. While Mexico was a neutral nation in the Civil War, the Sea of Cortez was not safe waters. The Confederates had several small bases in the Gulf, and small, agile sloops armed with four-pound cannons plied the waters looking for easy Union targets. Connor didn't want to engage them. He was after a bigger prize. His first destination was a cove on the south end of Isla Angel de la Guarda. They would beach *The Blessed* and change out to the deep-water keel. That operation in itself only took one day. But they would spend more time than that painting *The Blessed* below the waterline gray so the black tarred hull would not show when the schooner was heeled over to raise the big-rifled guns to their maximum range.

Connor and crew worked night and day to get *The Blessed* ready for sea. Beached, she was vulnerable. Connor had the cove guarded with all the swivel guns mounted on the rocky points of the cove. No match for a bigger warship, but protection enough from the small Confederate navy trying to control the gulf.

As the tide came in on the third morning, Connor eased the schooner off the beach into the deeper water of the cove where she could roll up straight with her keel down. He could have left the shallow-water keel behind, but that seemed like a fatalistic gesture. They took the time to pull it up the beach with the cable from the steam winch looped around a dead-man pulley above the high tide line on the beach. They blocked it up and gave it a new coat of tar. Connor didn't know if it helped the men, but he wanted them to believe that the shallow-water keel would be needed again.

There was a strong westerly wind blowing as *The Blessed*, painted and primed for battle, sailed out of the cove. Connor wanted to get to his supply base on Santa Catalina Island, but first, he wanted to make a name for *The Blessed*. He sailed north, his large-green Irish flag flying from his topgallant and a smaller one on the short-jack staff at the stern.

The Sea of Cortez was choppy but empty of warships. He sailed into the bay below Cabo Tepoca. There was a Confederate sloop lying at anchor. Most of its crew was on the beach swimming and enjoying a day off, a most unlucky day off for them. There was one man on watch on the deck. Connor hailed him and told him to abandon ship. He didn't waste a shell on the sloop. He brought *The Blessed* alongside and fired the sloop with several gallons of kerosene, lit by a flare rocket as he pulled away. The helpless crew on the beach was left to watch their ship burn to the waterline.

Connor turned *The Blessed* down the narrow channel between Isla Tiburon and the mainland. He had been here before. He threaded *The Blessed* through the blue water channel off Punta Arenas, his target – a Confederate warehouse at Punta Chueca, twelve miles to the south. He issued his first battle command for the big guns down in his hold. "Santiago, an incendiary round in the port gun, por favor." Santiago shouted the order down the speaking tube to the gun deck. The gun crew opened the breach on the port rifle and changed out the round to incendiary.

It wasn't a real battle. It was a sail-by turkey shoot. Connor put *The Blessed* close into the docks. The swivel guns barked, reloaded, and barked again. The decks of two sloops were swept clean of sailors scrambling to arm the cannons. Abreast of the warehouse, he rang two bells for the port gun, and at point-blank range, the incendiary exploded under the warehouse dock. There was a frigate at anchor in the deep water a mile south of the warehouse; it looked familiar. It looked to be a proud ship. Connor wasn't expecting that. The alarm was up; there would be no surprise. Connor's second order, "Santiago, an incendiary in the starboard gun, por favor." The order relayed to the gun deck.

The Captain of the frigate thought *The Blessed* was going to sail into his broadside; he was ready. The wily Irishman was no fool; the Captain realized too late. Connor turned *The Blessed* to bear on his starboard quarter. His forward guns on the forecastle of the frigate could not swing far enough to bear on the schooner. The starboard gun roared, again at point-blank range. The incendiary pierced the hull of the gundeck. The shell exploded, killing all of the crews on the forward guns. As *The Blessed* turned to catch the wind, the swivels opened up on the main deck. As *The Blessed* passed, they turned their fire onto the aft gun ports. It wasn't necessary. The gun crews were scrambling, trying to save themselves. Powder in open buckets ignited and caught many of them before they could scramble up the ladder or dive out of a gun-port on the dockside of their dying ship.

The Captain of the dying frigate drew a revolver and took a shot at Connor. The bullet whizzed by the con, and Santiago threw the Confederate the Spanish salute – his right hand clutching his left bicep, his left fist thrust up into the air. He shouted the obscenity in Spanish. The Confederate officer raised his revolver to take another shot but dove for cover when Connor's aft swivel gun turned to rake the stern. The ship's name was under the stars and bars hanging from the jack-staff. *The Heart of the South* was losing heart fast. Out of the two-hundred forty crew, less than fifty got off alive.

The Blessed sailed away unscathed; the outcome better than Connor expected. Ireland was at war with the Confederates as far as the survivors of Connor's attack were concerned. *The Blessed* was miles away when the powder magazine on the *Heart* blew up. The boom rolled over the Sea of Cortez, and when all eyes turned north, a mushroom cloud rose over the bay next to Punta Chueca. It was sad; Connor knew the Age of Sail was coming to an end. Soon all the gallant wooden ships of all the nations of the world would be obsolete, the proud warships replaced by steam-powered iron ships. It was the second time Connor had that thought. The first time was when he heaved his volumes of naval warfare overboard at the mouth of the Colorado. He was out to end his Age-of-Sail in a blaze of glory.

Everyone relaxed as they rounded the tip of Baja California and sailed into the open Pacific. *The Blessed* measured one-hundred thirty feet on the waterline. The math said she should be able to make just over fifteen knots. It was time to see if the old girl could still do it and how much wind it would take to push her up to the maximum in her stripped-down condition. He spent a week far offshore putting *The Blessed* through her paces in all kinds of seas and winds from every point of the compass.

With the sailing practice complete, Connor sailed to a point on the Baja coast for calibrating the big guns. There was a black outcrop of rock exactly three and a quarter mile inland from the beach. The desert there was nearly flat leading down to the ocean, so the elevation of the rock wouldn't play a role in calibrating the guns. The wind was never right. In the westerlies, he couldn't heel *The Blessed* far enough over even to try to reach the rock. They sailed up and down the coast, waiting for a wind from the east. It came with a storm blowing across from the Gulf of Mexico. It was a strong wind, coming off the tail of a hurricane, everyone thought.

Connor planned to fire each of the guns only once. Survey crews were put ashore in the tender, and Connor waited for signals that the two teams were in place. They were north and south of the black outcrop, ready to triangulate the hits. It was time for the final gun run. Santiago put *The Blessed* a hundred yards offshore and heeled her over to the max. For this type of elevated artillery fire, the gun crews could not see their target. Connor had improved the aiming system as more tools and telescopes became available. The war was pushing the technology. It wasn't available commercially, but his connections in England provided a set of the newest aiming equipment for *The Blessed*. The guns were locked in their midship positions, elevated to their max. So was Connor's aiming telescope, locked perpendicular to the line of the keel. The telescope floated in a gimble, its crosshairs tracking to the north. Santiago was reading the degrees of the list on the inverted bubble protractor that circled the top of the pulpit in front of the helm. The crosshairs moved to the south edge of the rock. Connor pulled the signal bell. The gun fired. The two surveyors marked the bearing to the ship with the edge of the alidades on their plane tables. They swung inland to mark the bearing of the hit. The shell exploded well behind the outcrop! And that was firing into the wind!

Out at sea, Santiago sailed north a mile then turned *The Blessed* to the south for the second run. Connor had Santiago hold four fewer degrees on the bubble. It was more difficult to hold the course, but Connor pulled two bells, and the port gun fired. Santiago was righting the ship when the shell hit the rock. A cheer went up from all hands. The outcrop was smaller than the *Alabama's* sister ship. Connor smiled, knowing he could hit it while sailing out of range of all but the biggest gun of his enemy: the 110-pound cannon. He needed to have a look at this ship, and he still needed to think about how to disable her steam engines. They retrieved the surveyors and headed to their base on Santa Catalina Island.

On the way, Connor put into the San Pedro harbor. He wanted news, any news about the newly launched Confederate warships. *God bless the free press of England and the United States*, he thought as he sat in the back of the Golden Mermaid bar. There was not only an article about the Alabama; there was a full cutaway drawing of the hull and the power plant that drove her. On an inset of the drawing, there was a full listing of the ship's weight, dimensions, armaments, and crew. In the details of the article, every gun appeared, illustrated in detail with specifications. The weight of the shot, the range of each smooth-bore cannon, even details to include the guns the marines carried. With a smile on his face, he pushed the drawing across the table to Santiago. He couldn't believe that the arrogant British published every fact about the armored frigate that should have been kept secret. Connor smiled at Santiago and said, "Pride cometh before a fall." The old Spaniard smiled back. They both knew how this had to unfold. They had to get close enough to the big ship to destroy the boiler with the first shot or disable the steam plant some other way.

Deception and guile; no one excelled better at cunning than the Irishman and the Spaniard. They were whistling the Star-Spangled Banner when they walked up the street to Madam Wong's brothel. There was a coalition of cheetahs on the boardwalk; each dressed and dolled up to perfection; each decorated in the way of the trade for seduction. They needed to hire a few women for as long as it would take to find the Confederate ship and bring it to its knees. When Connor asked, "How would you ladies like a fulltime job for a few months at twice the pay you make working for Madam Wong?"

It always bothered Connor that women always went for his tall, elegant friend first. Three girls encircled Santiago, two holding him by the neck from his sides and one pressed to his front, looking longingly up into his dark eyes. He didn't brush them off. They were starting to argue among themselves as to which would get the privilege of the first shtupping.

Two more girls came out to pay some attention to Connor. Then Madam Wong came out of the swinging doors of her palace of young men's dreams and took Connor's hand. She spoke softly with a smile on her face. "Welcome back, sailor. What have you got on your mind this time?" Her voice and look were more seductive than all five girls together. Connor led Madam Wong back inside the brothel to negotiate the deal. Later, much later, the two sailors made their way back to the harbor. Five young Asian women dressed in breeches joined them to go to sea. The game was on.

The Second Paradigm

Suzette and Bridgette were leaning on the rails of the corral, enjoying a warm winter day. They were watching a flock of large birds soaring on a large thermal current south of the mountain. There were hundreds of huge-majestic birds. The black edges of their wings contrasted with their offwhite breasts and brown backs. Long necks and long legs, they had to be cranes. Mr. Sue joined them on the rail. "What are you doing?" he asked.

"Watching the flock of cranes. I haven't seen so many of them in one place since we passed that spot on the Rio Grande."

"Hmmm. It is not right to call the cranes a flock, like a flock of pigeons or a flock of blackbirds. Cranes would be a siege, a serge, a herd, or just a flock if you didn't know a better name. I prefer serge because the Sandhill crane always migrates in a group, like the one you see here. *Surging* out, looking for a marsh to winter on. They might stop at a pool on the Hassayampa but will probably go down to the marshes on the Gila."

As usual, Suzette was amazed at Mr. Sue's encyclopedic knowledge. "How do you know all this stuff?"

Mr. Sue replied easily, "It's all hidden in books. When I was mastering English, I read a lot. I still read everything we can get here, but it would be nice to have a library close. When you were in medical school, I was reading in the library, whenever I wasn't cooking."

"Look," he cried, pointing at a speck in the sky. "Now, they are feeding the eagle." Suzette didn't know how Mr. Sue even knew the tiny dot was an eagle, but it was. The eagle was diving on prey, swooping down on the unsuspecting cranes. He swept through the column of cranes, hit one with his talons while still in his dive. A cloud of feathers marked the spot; then, the eagle spread its wings to fly away with dinner.

"How did you know that was an eagle when we could hardly see him?"

"He wasn't a speck until he folded his wings for the killing plunge. A mature golden can reach speeds of 150 miles per hour. That was an immature specimen. He probably only hit 120 or so this time. He will get bigger, heavier, and more experienced. If you watch for them, you will see them. I see them all the time. Eagles can carry about half their body weight. They will kill much larger animals than that, though, hitting with their talons at the end of a plunge. I saw one carry away a small javelina down at the river a while back. There is a brood of eagles up the Peeples wagon road. I'll take you up there if you want to see the aerie."

Mr. Sue might have thought it was a trivial conversation, but Suzette and Bridgette took it to heart. Yes, they would go with Mr. Sue to see the eagle nest. For the moment, however, they had something to talk about with the rest of the women. Suzette gathered them under the ramada. The five women talked for a while, then wrote a letter to Jim Parish. They wanted him to find a library to buy and ship to Red Mountain. The women were tired of reading newspapers. They were tired of reading and re-reading about war and politics. The pages in the mail-order catalog were dog-eared and worn out. They wanted Jane Eyre and Charles Dickens. They wanted love stories and poetry. They wanted what women read and enjoyed. They wrote it all into their letter to Parish. Maybe it was an odd request to send to a banker, maybe not. They would wait and see what might show up. They wouldn't have to wait long to send the letter. The children were running down from their mountain lookout. They were excited; it had to be Moses with the supply train. He always arrived on schedule as expected.

Something wasn't right with the armored wagon. Instead of six armed men in the gun box, there were only two. Moses had some contraption in there covered with an oiled canvas instead of a squad of armed men. He took off the canvas, and as he climbed down a smile spread across Moses's face as powerful as the Gatling gun, he sported on top of the wagon. He got down, shook Eli's hand, and said his hellos all around. Eliza and her oldest brother, who had taken the name Henry after the rifle, and the younger boy that still went by his Apache name, Bimisi, ganged up on Moses for their usual bag of candy.

Eli, Roland, and John climbed up with Moses to look at the Gatling gun. The gun had six barrels and shot 0.30 caliber ammunition; two-hundred rounds of the deadly bullets a minute. Moses swiveled the gun out towards the desert and fired a full magazine into the cacti and greasewood. One big saguaro fell under the hail of bullets. More magazines stood in racks on both sides of the gun enclosure. In all, Eli estimated that Moses had more than three-hundred rounds at his fingertips. Moses put on his big grin, "No more fooling around with the Indians. This gun is some serious firepower. You want to shoot it?"

John didn't want to shoot it. He wanted to study it. Eli opted to shoot. He turned the crank one revolution; the gun fired three times. "Impressive," he said. "Deadly if you were firing into a crowd, but how about at one Indian?"

"When they chase you, they are never alone, and they line up behind the wagon. It won't take long to teach the hostiles it isn't smart to do that anymore."

Eli still wasn't completely convinced, "At Bowie, we had Suzette in the rear wagon with Marie reloading. I don't know how many they killed, but I bet it took more than a week for the buzzards to pick the corpses down to the bones. It only took one bullet per Indian. Your gun that fires with the turn of a crank looks like it is going to take a lot more. There isn't even a sight on the gun. What say we set up some targets at three-hundred yards and have a contest? John's Sharps against the Gatling gun."

Moses chuckled, "Set up about a dozen in two rows: one for John and one for me. We'll see who can knock them all down the fastest. A moving target would be a real test. But I'm not putting an animal out there."

John said, "Maybe we could rig something up. Give me a little time. What say we do this shootout at about two, tomorrow. Is there going to be some betting? That would make it a real shooting contest."

The men were non-committal. The best Moses could get out of them was a collective, "We'll see."

Moses was anxious to show off one more new invention. It was a breakaway harness that allowed a dead mule to fall out of the harness without stopping the rest of the team. With the breakaway harness, the Indians or renegades would have to kill more than a half dozen of the team before they could stop the wagon. He had a dozen mules pulling the armored wagon, twice as many as needed. Steel plate lined the sides of the wagon, making it heavy. "Not bulletproof, just fireproof," Moses said as he thumped the side of the wagon to show how thin the metal was. "Next-generation, we go for bulletproof."

Eli stayed with Moses while he put the cover back over his prize possession. Eli was curious, "How did you get ahold of this? There is a war going on. Didn't the Army want it? Another thing, how much did it cost?"

They talked on their way up to the tunnel. Eli had sparked his partner's interest with the discovery of the passageway. He had the miners enlarging the passageway to Eliza's secret room; he knew Moses would enjoy seeing it; imagining the mysteries it held.

Eli got all his answers to the rest of his questions on the way to the mine. Moses was chatty, a rare mood for the big man-of-few-words. Moses talked on the way to the entrance of the tunnel. "The gun was a prototype. The Army sent it to Leavenworth for evaluation. From there, it went to Yuma. Don't ask me why. There is a new quartermaster in Yuma. He didn't want the gun. It burns too much ammo to suit him. I bought the gun and several thousand rounds of ammunition for two-grand. I made sure that everyone in Yuma and on the Indian Reservation knows that I have it. By reputation alone, we won't be seeing the renegades around Yuma out looking for a gold shipment. If they do, I will be putting them down hard."

Eli led Moses into the tunnel. Eli couldn't explain it, but every time he came into the mine, he felt an ambiance of well being and home like he was walking up the steps of his parent's chateau in the woods. They lit kerosene lanterns and walked into the tunnel. They went to the entrance of the passageway and walked as far as the bend. The miners were already mining out around the turn. "There is a big room back there, and it is full of bones. Eliza found what we all think is a big fang, but there is a lot more. We wrote to Professor Laity. I bet he will be coming down soon. I hope he brings his wife this time."

Moses asked, "What will you do with them?"

"Who?"

"The bones, Eli; the bones."

"I'll leave that up to the professor. Let's go look at the end of the tunnel."

Back at the end of the mine rails, Moses asked, "How close are you to the middle of the mountain?"

"About another hundred feet, we'll be right under the hot spring." There was a lot of hot water running down the ditch on the side of the rails. The walls of the tunnel were hot. Too hot to lean on. The men were down to working ten minutes out of every hour. Five relief crews were playing cards at the mouth of the tunnel, not an ounce of fat on any of them. Sweat dripped from the men working at the face. They had a few minutes to go till their break. The relief crew was walking in as Eli and Moses walked out.

Moses asked, "What do you expect to find under the hot spring?"

"More gold, but there is something else. Lily couldn't tell what it is, but she said it's going to change everything."

Moses gave a shutter despite the heat. "Lily. There is some deep juju. The woman scares me. I think she can read my mind. I don't like it. It isn't natural. Sometimes what's on my mind ain't for female viewing."

Now it was Eli's turn to chuckle. "Juju? You need to listen to more of Lily's teachings. She isn't going to hurt you. She's discrete. She is like Suzette. She will do you no harm."

Moses listened to but didn't address Eli's comments. Instead, he asked, "You know what you need?"

Before Eli could answer, Moses told him. "You need a big fan. One that could blow cold air into the back of the tunnel."

"I think John was looking for a fan that would do just that. He hasn't ordered one as of yet, but he did get a smaller one that he put on the coin-room of the refinery. Another one is coming for the clinic."

There was a group of men waiting for Eli when they came out of the tunnel. Eli recognized one of them, a placer miner named Banes from up on Weaver Creek.

Banes was excited and appeared to be the spokesman for the other three men. They looked on with reverence as Banes showed Eli some silver beads. Banes had a lot to say, "Eli, I can't believe our luck. We have four claims on the creek, and they all have silver on them. A lot of silver. These are the beads from the assays."

Eli wasn't too interested in silver, but he said, "Let's go over to the refinery and have Mr. Sue weigh them up. I didn't know you had an assay lab up there."

Banes said, "We don't. The German, Otto, he did the assays."

"Otto was here some time ago. He got silver out of our ore, too, but I have to stay focused on the gold. I would be cautious, Mr. Banes. We didn't think Otto's work was accurate, maybe even dishonest. Did you have to pay him to do the assays?"

"He did the first one for free; the rest of these boys had to pay five dollars in gold for theirs."

"So, if I may ask, how many assays has Otto done?"

"He is still up there running assays. Everyone is paying for the work, but so far, we have the richest claims."

Eli was diplomatic, but Moses was quick on the uptake, "Mr. Banes, sir. You have been taken for a ride. This Otto you speak of, he is mining the miners."

Eli wanted to soften up the revelation. "Did you bring down some of the silver ore. I'll have Mr. Sue run it through our fire assay. You'll get an accurate and honest report from Mr. Sue."

Banes sent a man back to their mules for the ore samples, but he remained argumentative. "Otto says the silver in our ore is not recoverable by fire assay. His process gets all the silver, even the part that the fire can't find."

Eli didn't respond to that. He introduced Banes and his friends to Mr. Sue. The fellow that went back to the mules returned with the samples and laid them out on the table. Four of them were red dirt, typical of the gold deposits in Weaver. The fifth was a heavy silver-colored mineral. Mr. Sue took a book down from the shelf behind his desk and thumbed through the pages until he found what he was looking for – "Galena, lead sulfide. Where did this one come from?" Mr. Sue asked.

"Up on the mountain across to the east from Rich Hill."

Mr. Sue had some good advice, "When you go back up the creek, I want you to stake claims everywhere on the mountain you can find this mineral. Eli will pay you to stake the claims, and we will record them on the RMM district map as 50/50 ownership. You four men will have half, and RMM, Inc. will own the other half."

Banes didn't know what to say. A big man, one of the other three, named Daryl, said, "You haven't even run the assays yet."

Eli wanted the foursome out of the refinery. "Why don't you fellows put your mules in the corral over at the settlement? Mary will fix you a meal. Mr. Sue will need several hours for the assays. The deal for the claims is still on, regardless of what Mr. Sue's assays show." He winked at Mr. Sue as the men left the refinery. As far as Otto was concerned, Eli and Mr. Sue knew the German had hoodwinked an entire mining camp into paying him for his expensive assays. He helped his victims discover a lead mine, though; Eli thought that was the only good outcome of Otto's buffoonery. Delusional or dishonest, that was still a question to be answered. Mr. Sue was firing up the assay furnace as Eli left with the Banes party. These days, the assay furnace fired with kerosene. It heated up fast. He would have answers in a few hours.

Over at the settlement, Roland joined his brother at the table. Eli spread out the master copy of the RMM mining district. Banes told Eli that there was a man named Stanton up on the creek nosing around that was trying to organize the miners into the Weaver Mining District. Stanton wasn't having much luck with that; nobody trusted him. Eli had all the claims in Weaver

Creek and Rich Hill drawn on his map. Banes pointed out their claims; then, he put his finger down where they found the galena sample.

Eli reaffirmed his offer. "Mr. Banes, gentlemen. I will grubstake you and pay you $50 per each claim you stake. I want it done right with location notices, samples from the outcrops, and monuments on the corners. Roland will come up in a week and survey in the claims, and we will put them on the map. What say you?"

Banes looked around the table. His partners were nodding their heads, yes.

Eli went on, "I want you to stake claims everywhere you can find the galena. If you happen to find a big quartz vein with a lot of gold in it, you can stake that too. I don't care how many you stake. I'll cover the cost."

Banes was a bit incredulous, "Why are you doing this? You haven't even seen Mr. Sue's assay results."

"Mr. Sue has had our backs for some years now. We have trusted him with our lives more than once. He is a lot more than he appears to be. He is the best assayer in these parts. Look, what do you have to lose? I will grubstake you and pay you in advance for the first two claims." Eli took out five $10 RMM gold pieces from his vest pocket. Roland put a leather poke on the table and took out five more. There was a lot more in the poke.

"You don't know us from Adam. You ....."

Eli cut him off, "I know who you are. You're the men who discovered the lead mine on Weaver Mountain. Now I want you to be exploration geologists. Go back up there and find all the galena that is sticking out of the ground."

It was obvious Eli could make good on his word. Banes swept the coins into his left hand, then he offered his right and said, "Deal. I need some of your $5 gold coins so we can split this money four ways right now."

Eli was comfortable with this man. He liked his sense of fairness. Roland was magnanimous; the twenty dollars in $5-dollar coins were trivial. He took four coins out of his vest pocket and gave them to Banes. Banes dropped two $10's on the table and pushed them across to Roland. Roland pushed them back, "Keep them; I'll see you on the mountain in a week. One more thing, don't tell anyone up there that you are looking for galena. One gold rush in this area at a time is all we can put up with."

By evening, Mr. Sue had the assay results. "The red dirt runs about 0.3 grams of gold per metric ton and a trace of silver. However, the galena is over eighty-six percent lead. It runs forty ounces of silver per ton. Banes and his men had already accepted Eli's offer. The news about the silver made them even more enthusiastic. They left that night anxious to get back with provisions, three pigs, and $120 in RMM gold coins. As they left, Eli turned to Mr. Sue, "You have rolled the dice for us, my friend."

"Not a problem, Eli. I rolled sevens, and our *partners* are going to roll some more." Mr. Sue pushed a book about lead-zinc mining across the table. "There are five chapters on lead with silver in here. Goodnight, my friend, and good reading."

Eli called a day off the next morning. The men needed a rest anyway, and Moses was going to provide the entertainment for a feast in the afternoon. There was a pig on the firepit by sunup. Mary had the rest of the food all planned. She would get the kitchen going around noon. Abby cooked up bacon and biscuits for breakfast. They ate mesquite bread and ham for lunch and then started to gather in anticipation of the shoot-out.

The miners were putting up rows of targets out in the desert south of the corral. John had rigged up a wagon with a man-sized target made from gunny sacks full of red tailings from the mill. The miners tied the gunny-sack man to a chair in the bed of the wagon. Then the miners clamped the old cable from the clamshell on top of the mountain to the tongue of the wagon, and there was a team of horses on the far end of the cable, ready to pull the target-wagon across the range.

Moses removed the cover from the Gatling gun. His gunner's mate loaded a magazine onto the gun, getting ready for the shoot. "Wait a minute," commanded John. "Are there going to be two of you? If so, I should be allowed another shooter on my team."

Eli, the grandmaster of the event, agreed. John chose Suzette. Roland brought an 1859 - .52 Caliber Sharps carbine out from his house. The rifle was brand new, the same as John's. Both guns were whistle clean, oiled, and ready for action. Roland opened the breach of the carbine to see it was empty. He closed the breach on an empty chamber, cocked the rifle and pulled the trigger. The primer fired; he was sure the cap roll was loaded correctly and functioning properly. Roland handed the carbine to Suzette and said, "Go get'um, Sis."

The shooters were ready. Eli had one more rule to impose. He announced, "This shouldn't be a race, or that wouldn't be a contest at all. Here is how we'll score today's competition. I'll award two points for each hit. I'll penalize each miss, minus one-quarter point. We need to count your rounds. How many you got up there, Moses?"

"Four magazines, one-hundred-twenty rounds," Moses sang out.

"Ten rounds each," shouted Suzette.

"The moving target wagon target will not move until each team has all their targets down. The moving target is worth twenty points." Eli drew his Colt. "Ready?"

"Wait!" Mr. Sue yelled. "I want to make a bet!"

Moses laughed, "I don't want to take your money, old man."

Now that irked Mr. Sue. His real objective was to put Moses off his mark a bit and – he wasn't that old. "Five-hundred dollars on the rifle team."

Moses laughed harder, "You have to be kidding?"

Mr. Sue didn't laugh; he was deadly serious, and it resonated in his most authoritative voice. "You got the name Mr. Moses Callahan, but you haven't got the blood." Then even louder, "Two-to-one odds on the rifle team."

Eli called out, "Anyone else?"

Brigette stepped forward with a double eagle, "Even money on the rifles."

Eliza stepped up with the most precious thing she had. "I want to bet my fang on Aunt Suzette and Uncle John."

Now everyone wanted to bet. Eli called upon Roland to keep track of the pot. Most of the miners bet on the Gatling gun. It took some time to get all the bets placed and written down. Lia was the scribe. Finally, Eli raised the Colt in the air and yelled, "Ready?" This time he pulled the trigger.

At three hundred yards, the gunny-sack targets exploded in clouds of dust. The Gatling gun magazine was empty in eight seconds. There were still three targets left untouched on that side of the range. John and Suzette were shooting from the prone position. They both had a technique of pulling the cocking lever down and flipping the rifle to the left to eject the spent shell; their fresh rounds stood at the ready in a wood strip on the ground to their right. Their rate of fire wasn't anywhere near the Gatling gun, but it was methodical and deadly accurate. They had half their targets down while the gunner's mate was loading the second magazine onto the top of Moses' gun.

The second magazine was empty, and there was still one target left un-hit on Moses' side of the line. Suzette fired her seventh round, and Moses' last target exploded. The wagon lurched out from behind a big mesquite to the right of the gunny-sack line. Moses opened up. There was a lot of dust, and then he found the range. The Gatling rounds cut the wheels out from under the target. The wheel-less wagon was careening back and forth; the mate fumbled the fourth magazine. John and Suzette both fired at the same time. No one could tell which one of them hit it, but the man-sized target exploded in a cloud of red dust just as the wagon was tipping over from having hit a boulder.

The spectators were jumping up and down, cheering out of control. Moses looked down at the rifle team from the side of the gun box. He didn't have much to say; he knew he had lost. It wasn't really necessary to tally the score. But Eli, a stickler for the rules, said, "Gunners, count your bullets." Then he gathered the tally and did a quick calculation. "Rifles – forty-six points. Gatling – **Minus! MINUS zero point five!**"

The crowd cheered again, and this time, they danced. The miners who bet on Moses were walking away from their money. The winners were waiting under the ramada for their winnings. Moses got down from the gun box, unlocked the armored wagon, and took his moneybox over to the table. He paid off the small losses, and then he got to Mr. Sue. He started to count out the money. Mr. Sue said, "That won't be necessary, but you have to pay Eliza. She bet everything she had in the world on her family. I'll let you figure out what that is worth."

Moses summoned the child over to the table and put his arm around the girl. "What do you want, child?"

"I want to go to Yuma with you. I want to ride on a boat. I want you to take me to see the ocean." Eliza opened a book; she showed Moses a picture of a lighthouse with a hundred seagulls in flight around it. "I want to see one of these."

Moses looked at Abby. Abby nodded her head, *yes*. "Okay, little lady, you won this fair and square. You and I are going to see the ocean. Can Amos go with us?"

"Amos can go, but not my brothers." Eliza sensed that she could get anything she wanted from the big man at that moment. She pressed her advantage, "I want to take Maria with us, and I want candy, every day." With the last demand, she put her hands on her hips to emphasize her last demand.

Abby had to step in. "Maria's going will be up to Suzette. Some candy, okay, but not every day. I want you to come back with all your teeth."

Moses said, "Don't worry, Abby, I will take good care of her."

As John and Moses walked out to look at the shattered wagon, Eli said, "I will never understand the Apache mind."

Abby smiled at him. "That's not Apache, husband-of-mine. That is a woman getting what she wants and using everything she has to work with to get it. You are just a mere man; you are not supposed to understand. A man who understands a woman is as rare as unicorns on the South Pole."

Eli looked at Abby with a look that said he didn't understand. "See," was all Abby said, and she left him alone at the table. There was a lot of women's work to do to be ready for dinner.

The next day a woman walked into the settlement with a herd of goats. Mary saw her coming and was standing at the corral to greet her. The woman wasn't Mexican; she wasn't Spanish. She could have had some Indian blood in her. Mary gave up trying to figure her out. The woman was all three. She wasn't pretty, but she wasn't ugly either. She was weathered and rugged. Dressed in buckskins and strong. She had on high boots and leather leggings above those. There was a 0.54 caliber Hawken slung over her shoulder and a long knife in a scabbard on the side of her boot. This woman spent a lot of time in the desert.

"I'm Josefa Alvarez. They call me *The Goat Herder Woman.* I thought you might be getting tired of pork and mutton. I've brought you some goats. They make excellent stew and jerky, and there are two females you can milk to feed the infants." She held out her hand. Mary took it and pulled her into a welcoming embrace.

Mary was amazed; a single woman walking in off the desert seemed impossible. She asked, "Where do you live? What do you do?" Although her name tended to say everything about the stranger, Mary wanted to know more.

"Anywhere I want and anything I want," Alvarez replied to the two questions.

"What do you want for the goats," Mary asked.

"Nothing for the moment. Business is good on the creek, but I need to see your doctor."

They put the goats into the corral, but it didn't seem likely they would stay there; the rails of a corral didn't make a very good goat pen. Mary put in a bucket of oats. The little herd would stay there, at least until the oats were gone. Mary took her new friend into the clinic. She introduced her to Suzette and Bridgette. She left her there and went back to her kitchen. Whatever the woman needed from the doctor, was none of Mary's business.

That night Eli told Eliza that the passageway was clear to her secret room. He talked to her as an adult. "The miners went in to make sure it was safe, but they didn't disturb anything. The room is close to the surface. They want to break through to open the passage up as a ventilation tunnel. I wouldn't let them do that unless it was okay with you. It would still be your secret room, and you would have a way in from right up there." Eli pointed up the side of the mountain to where he thought the new tunnel would daylight. "We'll go into your secret room in the morning. I want you to make a drawing of everything on the floor: the bones and anything else you can find. You shouldn't move anything until the Professor gets here. I'm worried, though, that something might get disturbed or stolen."

The next day Eli and Eliza took several lanterns and went through the passageway into the cavern. It was amazing. Eliza set up a small folding table Eli carried in, and she unrolled a clean sheet of paper, like the surveyors used, and took out her pencils. She started with an outline of the cavern and then marked the number one and drew a circle around it where she had found the fang. Eli walked around, and each time he found another bone, Eliza marked it on her drawing. Eli was close to the opening of the cleft that must have led to the surface in some ancient time. *Oh. Oh,* he thought as the distinct rattle signaled there was a rattlesnake beyond the opening of the cleft. "Eliza," he called. "We have to leave now. There is a snake in your secret room. I can hear him."

Eliza came over and nodded her head. Her eyes got big. There was more than one rattler buzzing now. They backed away from the opening. Eliza picked up her drawing but left everything else. They walked out of the tunnel and went into the refinery. Mr. Sue was busy weighing out a gold shipment and filling out the manifest for Moses. He had been holding back, worried about security on the trail. Moses showed up with more security than he could imagine. He was cleaning out the safe. He had more than a half-million dollars in gold bullion to ship.

Eli told him about hearing snakes in the cleft at the far side of the cavern. Mr. Sue said, "It must be a nest."

Eliza asked, "Why weren't they in my secret room the first time I went in there?"

As usual, Mr. Sue shared his knowledge. "There is no food in your secret room. Rattlers have to eat once or twice a year so they will hibernate close to the surface. They only come out to hunt in the spring and the fall. The big ones will look for mates or a bigger place to hibernate for the next winter. If you start enlarging the opening to the surface from the inside, it will drive them out. You might have a whole army of rattlers coming down the hill into the settlement."

"What should we do?" Eli asked.

"Catch them and eat the big ones," Mr. Sue said as he laughed. "I'll make a smoke bomb and set it off in the cleft in Eliza's cavern. It'll drive them to the surface. You'll have to be ready to catch and kill. There could be many of them in a nest: big ones, small ones, militants, and some pacifists. But don't trust any of them. Eventually, they will all be mad about having to leave a comfortable home."

Eli chuckled at the anthropomorphism. "I'll have the shop make us about twenty snake catchers. The surveyors can go in now and survey their way to the cleft that leads to the surface. We'll have them plot the cavern and where the nest is on the mine map. They should be able to tell us where the cavern would daylight on the mountain. We will be there ready for the snakes. When will you have the smoke bomb ready?"

"In five minutes if you want. Let's get everything ready along with the snake catchers and the crew. Tomorrow we catch snakes, and we will eat well at supper."

By evening, the survey crew was done mapping the passageway and the cavern. The chief surveyor took Eli and Mr. Sue up the hill and drove a stake where the opening to the den should be. Eli couldn't see an opening, but that meant little. Even for what they thought was likely to be a large den, the rattlers only needed a gopher hole for access. All was ready; the rattlesnake roundup would start the next day after breakfast.

The winter sunrise was magnificent. Everyone was up early waiting for the first rays to warm the desert floor. Mary and the girls served biscuits and gravy for breakfast. Everyone ate quickly, anxious to see how many snakes would come out of the den. Eli nodded to Mr. Sue, and he left to go set off the smoke bomb inside the cavern -- sulfur and saltpeter. It would fill the cleft, the cavern, and the tunnel with sulfur dioxide for days. Mr. Sue was going to cover the passageway leading out of the cavern with an ox hide and set the bomb off in the cleft. The surveyors left with him to assist.

Eli gave them some time to walk around to the tunnel, and then he moved his platoon of snake catchers up the hill into position to receive the charge of the rattlesnake brigade. He had twenty men; each had a six-foot pole with a rope noose at the end. Below that line, there were seven women: four from the settlement and three from the workers camp. The women all had hoes and wore boots and leggings. Mr. Sue returned from the tunnel, built up the fire down by the ramada, and set the table up with an oilcloth cover and fillet knives. Eliza and the boys were ready to harvest a plethora of snake skins.

There was a yell from up the hill. A fair-sized rattler crawled out from under a tangle of mesquite about ten feet above the marker. He wasn't alone; there were hundreds more behind him; the charge of the Western Diamondbacks was on. The catching and killing started in earnest. Soon the women were chopping up the survivors that made it through the front lines.

It was just like a Civil War battle, Eli thought as he watched for anything that got past the women. There were bushel baskets full of big snakes. Eli went up and got one and took it down to his kids, waiting at the table. Mr. Sue said, "Too soon. You have to wait for another hour. They can still strike even though they are dead." He wasn't worried about the females being full of baby snakes. They hatched their young in the spring.

The battle reached a crescendo, Eli had his revolver full of snake-shot. He was on his third cylinder full. Then it was over. Dead snakes covered the hill, and there were bushel baskets full under the ramada waiting for skinning. Mr. Sue gutted the snakes, on the watch for out of season hatchlings. The children skinned them and rolled the skins up with salt. Abby cut the filets off the sides of the bony skeletons and put them into a big pot of vinegar marinade with shredded jalapenos. Mr. Sue kept the venomous heads in a bucket. "We will bury them when we finish. Don't worry about the snakes on the hill. The pigs will find them."

It was a grand feast with grilled and skewered rattlesnake. Josefa Alvarez stayed for supper and then walked back to Weaver Creek in the dark. The children were stretching snakeskins for curing. They were going to be wealthy. They had no idea that they already were. It would be several days before the miners could get back into the tunnel. Mr. Sue's effort with the oxhide worked well on the snake den, and it didn't take much of the acid gas to make the air uncomfortable and unsafe inside the mountain.

Abby and Suzette had their girls packed for their adventure with Moses. They were standing with Lia and Mary as Moses cracked the whip over the heads of his massive mule team and started back to Yuma. Suzette was comfortable having Maria go with Moses. It was the first time for Abby, though, and her eyes were full of tears as she watched her daughter go. Mary put her arm around Abby and with wisdom, said, "Get used to it, Abby. It is what children do. It's never easy, even after they are adults."

The four women turned and walked back under the ramada. Uncle Tio sat down by the corral, just as he did when he waited for Maria outside her school in San Francisco. Lia knew the big man would be distressed all the time his niece was away. She went to him and got him up and kept him with her through the rest of the day. She would have to find something to keep him busy while Maria was gone. Lia didn't fault Eliza for not taking Tio with them. It was even hard for grownups to understand that Tio was emotionally about the same age as Eliza. As she led Tio back to the ramada by the hand, she wished she could understand it herself.

The Blessed and the Damned

It was a clear spring day, and Connor could see a hundred miles in every direction from the top of *Mount Orizaba*, the highest point on Santa Catalina Island. He had been waiting for what he called *The Rebel*, for want of a better name, for a month. Even if the Confederate frigate went to Mexico as its first port of call, it was sure to make a call on the secessionist groups in Los Angeles for provisions, moral support, and crew. The Army kept the secessionists suppressed in the Los Angeles basin, but the sympathizers' efforts to interrupt the flow of California gold and recruits for the Union cause was always boiling under the calm surface of what looked like a benign society.

As long as the westerlies blew strong, Connor and the crew of *The Blessed* wouldn't give up hope. It was the first week of April when Connor spied the frigate anchored off the Los Angeles beaches. The crew of *The Blessed* packed their gear and made their way back to the cove on the southern tip of the island. It was time to put their plan into action. Under the cover of darkness, *The Blessed* slipped out to sea.

The next morning Connor was sailing up the beaches from San Pedro to the Confederate ship. He was in one of the tenders from *The Blessed* with the five women and a boatswain at the tiller. Connor wore the clothes of a gambler; the women had on their best uniforms; there was no mistaking their tradecraft. Connor could see the armored frigate was named the *Jefferson Davis*. He hailed the Captain, who was watching him from the poop deck. The Captain of the big warship wasn't concerned; a small cutter full of a fat dandy and a bunch of whores was of no concern to him.

"Captain, we would like to come aboard your fair ship." Connor still looked elegant, but he also appeared like he had put on fifty pounds.

The captain replied, "No. Standoff until tonight. We are waiting for supplies from our support inland."

"Perfect," Connor shouted back. "I have several kegs of whiskey for you. We will be back this evening."

The boatswain put the cutter back into the wind and sailed a mile up the beach. Connor took note of the lax appearance of the ship. Sailors were going about their duties: swabbing decks, repairing rigging, and mostly wasting time against the inevitable boredom of sitting still. There was a lookout in the highest crow's nest, but all-in-all, the ship wasn't worried about

Union warships. What few warships the Union had that could engage the armored frigate, were anchored in San Francisco Bay or docked at Benicia, the military command post of the California militias.

Connor had them put into the beach a mile north of the *Davis*. They disappeared into the dunes for several hours; then, the women came out buck naked to swim in the surf. Connor was watching through a spyglass. The sailors on the frigate were typical of sailors who had spent a month at sea. They were more than interested in Connor's entourage, lining the bulwarks and peering at the women. Connor had shed the heavy coat. The sleeves and breastworks of the coat were full of sand. There were tubes tucked up into the sleeves, all part of the plan to disable the power plant that gave the *Davis* its advantage of speed without the wind. The boatswain swam naked with the women (tough duty), but Connor kept watch through the day. As the sun started to dip in the west, they sailed back to the frigate.

This time the Captain let them come aboard and sent a detail to unload the whiskey casks. The crew swarmed around the women; the young Asian girls had plenty of takers. It was obvious that this was a newly commissioned ship without a battle-hardened commander or crew. The Captain was a new breed of a sailor, a steamship commander whose training consisted of more engineering than sea-craft. He wore the uniform of a Confederate Commodore; his name was Lucas Beau Hutchinson, and he was more southern than the *Southern Cross*. He let all his men drink as if he lay-to in friendly waters. Connor was hoping three casks of good Irish whiskey would be enough. The last cask to come aboard, and with luck, the last cast that the sailors would drink carried a trace of laudanum just in case. He took a deck of cards from his inside pocket and fanned them elaborately and asked, "Any gamblers aboard?"

The sailors jumped to the task of bringing a table up from the ship's mess, and chairs were carried out from the officers' cabins. A green felt matt was stretched out over the tabletop. Connor produced a bundle of Confederate money. He spread the cards in a row on the table as he sat down and then flipped them over from end-to-end, back-and-forth. The Captain sat down to play. The evening was unfolding better than he expected. The Captain was probably there to make sure the card-shark pimp didn't cheat his men. That wasn't a problem. Connor didn't want to win; he wanted to keep them playing – and drinking. No one paid any attention to the boatswain. He was the youngest member of the crew, still in his early thirties. He spoke with a southern drawl and had been working with Connor for months to perfect the accent. Indeed, Connor spoke with a southern drawl like he just stepped off a riverboat in New Orleans, and he played poker with a fistful of Confederate money. No one questioned his legitimacy.

Connor got the Commodore/Captain talking about the ship. The Commodore boasted, "It is brand new, the best of the best. She and her sister ship are the heaviest armed frigates on the sea, and also the fastest." The Commodore was full of boasts, "The *Davis* can make twenty knots with a good wind and a full head of steam." On and on, about every detail of the ship. The guns, the crew, even the support groups of secessionists ashore. The only thing not mentioned were tales about combat experience. There were none. Other than target practice, the crew had yet to fire their first shot in anger, or as Connor was planning, in self-defense.

Connor lost as many hands as he could; he even folded on four kings once to keep up the charade. The boatswain watched the game but kept his eye on the ship, especially the marine guarding the entrance to the boiler room. At the end of the second dog-watch, the marine was relieved by one who came on duty drunk. If what the boatswain was watching for was going to happen, it would have to happen soon. It didn't take long. The marine was asleep halfway through his watch. The boatswain sat next to him and kept up a conversation. Everyone would assume that the marine was still awake. Connor excused himself and asked directions to the head. He disappeared into the darkness. Most of the crew were passed out or asleep after their turn with the ladies. It was late, four bells into the first watch. Other than the men still interested in poker, the decks were clear.

Connor didn't go to the head even though he needed to. He went down into the engine room. He pulled the oil cap off the port engine, pulled the tube down from his sleeve, and emptied the sand down the oil-fill tube. He walked over to the starboard engine and did the same with his other sleeve. The rest of the sand from his coat went into the reserve oil tank. Finished, he blew out the lantern before he went up the ladder to find the head. He was gone longer than it would have taken for him to relieve himself, but no one noticed. His stack of bills was almost gone. Maybe there were a few less there than when he left for the head. He didn't care. His mission was complete. He wanted to lose the rest of the money, so his leaving the ship wouldn't appear premature or suspicious. Another hour passed before the money was gone. By then, the girls were all gathered around the table watching. The whiskey was all drunk; the men sated in every way imaginable; it was time to say their goodbyes. Now, only one more stroke of luck was needed. The wind had to blow and blow hard at sunrise for *The Blessed* to do her best.

Connor sailed down the beach and around the Palos Verdes Peninsula. It was a good night for sailing. He dropped the ladies off on the San Pedro pier, paid them for their service with a bonus, and then set the cutter on a course to take them back to the cove on Santa Catalina. The sea was choppy, but the little tender handled it well. By sunrise, he was at the helm of *The Blessed* sailing large for the mainland. The *Jefferson Davis* was still asleep when Connor fired on the Confederate frigate from the maximum range of his guns. He didn't hit the big ship, but his gun run served its purpose. As he watched through the sighting telescope, sailors scrambled up the mainstays to let down the sails. The anchor raised, and the Commodore tacked northwest to get the big ship off the shore. Within minutes the rebel boiler was stoked, and black smoke was pouring from its stack.

Connor turned to the southwest. With steam up, the *Jefferson Davis* turned on a course to run him down. That is what he needed, but he still wanted to give the rebel captain a reason to hurry. He turned sharply to port and let the sails sag. At more than fifteen knots, *The Blessed* heeled to starboard, nearly reaching the maximum bubble. Connor fired the port gun, a long shot at best. Luck of the Irish is never something to discount. His shell hit the forecastle deck, killing the gun crew and disabling the 65-pound gun. The crew of the *Davis* weren't green anymore; in fact, quite a few of them were gray with fear. Not Hutchinson; he tacked to starboard to bring the big gun to bear. Connor saw the move and turned *The Blessed* back on course to make his profile as small as possible. The smoke from the big gun told him the rebel got off a shot.

Connor waited for the heavy round to arrive. It was wide and more than a hundred yards aft; the splash it made was spectacular. Connor tacked northwest. Now it was a race until his sabotage had time to cease the engines on the frigate. The *Jefferson Davis* was closing fast; then it seemed to hold even; then it started to fall behind. A huge cloud of steam blew off from the boiler. At first, everyone on *The Blessed,* including Connor, thought that they had fired another round with the big gun. In a moment, they could see it wasn't so. The white cloud of steam blew away, and a constant stream of white steam could be seen blowing off through the boiler stack. The *Jefferson*

Davis was a proud steamer when she slid down the ways in England, but now she was just another sailboat. All be it, still a powerful frigate, but a sailboat none the less.

Connor was soon out of range. The agile schooner was sailing for the southern tip of Santa Catalina. Connor had his chart spread on the table behind the con. He was triangulating with the sighting scope between the frigate and the cove. He stayed on course for ten more minutes and then triangulated again. The frigate could only make seven knots, and she couldn't hold the angle into the wind that Conner could with the schooner. The frigate was going to be four miles behind by the time Connor would round the southern tip of the island and turn north. At fifteen knots, he would be up the west coast and around the north point of the island in another ninety minutes.

The *Jefferson Davis* didn't try to hug the coast. The captain sailed out to the west of the island. By the time he turned to tack back to the northeast, Connor was in one of the tenders watching him, laying off the north point of the island. Connor had *The Blessed* anchored around the point, out of sight. It only took one look at the big ship, and Connor knew he wouldn't make it far enough north to clear the point with its first tack. The frigate not clearing the point was a bad misjudgment on the part of the Commodore. Connor chalked up another point for the luck of the Irish. Bad seamanship on his opponent's part was an extra and welcome bonus. Hutchinson was comfortable at sea in a steamer, but he was no sailor.

Connor returned to *The Blessed.* He had both of the rifles changed out to incendiary rounds. They were useless against the heavy armor of the frigate. He was hoping to get an incendiary round inside the gun deck. If he did, that would be the end of the battle. Santiago rigged *The Blessed* for speed. A large spinnaker was furled on the forecastle, ready for when he needed it. Connor could see the top gallants of the frigate approaching the other side of the point. He was ready to retreat at the first sign that the frigate might clear the point. Connor had his topsails down. He doubted that the rebel would see him or recognize his bare masts for what they were. He was ready, however, to turn *The Blessed* to the south and run for distance if the frigate cleared the point. At the last minute, the rebel tacked to the northwest; *careful in unfamiliar waters,* Connor thought as he gave Santiago a one-word command in Spanish. "Ataque."

With a motion of his hand, the topsails went up, and Santiago turned *The Blessed* into the wind to fill the sails. In less than a minute, they cleared the point. With the wind on his port beam, Santiago could heel *The Blessed* over and hold the course. The range was less than two miles; the port gunner hit the *Jefferson Davis* five out of six shots with the incendiaries. The one that fell short, Connor aimed at a gun port on the stern of the big ship. They didn't get a single round inside the *Davis*, but chaos and panic ruled the day. There were fires in the sails and on the ratlines. Sailors were diving off the ship to douse their burning clothes. The rebel captain turned the big ship and fired a broadside at *The Blessed* with his 32-pound cannons. There were only six on each side of his ship, three forward of the engine room, and three aft. A lot of gun deck area was sacrificed in place of space for the boiler and engine room. The broadside fell short and well behind *The Blessed.* It was obvious the gunners on the 32-pounders had never shot at a moving target before.

Connor spun the schooner around like a top in the water. The starboard gun hit the rebel four more times with armor-piercing rounds before the schooner slipped south of the point. Too bad, the boiler wasn't up to pressure. Connor was sure one of the shells pierced the hull right next to the boiler. What he needed was an armor-piercing shell with a delayed fuse, a shell that could pierce the hull and explode inside the ship. If he survived this battle, he would return to Ireland and set the engineers to develop perfecting that.

Enough for one attack. Santiago turned into the wind and raised the spinnaker; in a minute, they were out of range of the big gun. Connor sailed large toward the mainland with the strong wind behind him. Another deception. After dark, he was sailing to anchor on the north side of Santa Cruz Island. Another seascape perfect for an ambush. *The Blessed* survived the first round of the battle without a mark.

The *Jefferson Davis*, however, was in serious trouble, and the Commodore knew it. As impossible as it seemed, the Irishman had sabotaged his engines, outsailed him, and outgunned him. His big-forward gun was out of commission, and he had lost fourteen men and his third mate. If he wasn't careful, his proud ship was going to wind up on the bottom of the Pacific. The hopes of the Confederacy would go down with it. He didn't give chase; he turned south to lick his wounds.

By the time Connor dropped anchor, he had been up for forty-eight hours. Santiago and the crew rested in shifts, but there was work to be done. The two rifles had to be cleaned and made ready for the next battle. The galley was busy feeding the men. Connor slept in his hammock till first light. He awoke to his ship teeming with activity and ready for the next battle. Sunrise was a vulnerable moment. If the *Davis* was looking for him, it could round either side of the island at any moment and catch him at anchor.

As the morning brightened and the first rays of sun touched the mountain in the middle of the island, a mirrored signal from the peak flashed the all-clear. The wind that was the lifeblood of the schooner had died down to a soft breeze. With only a light wind, it was not a good day to go to war. Connor would rest his men. Check and recheck his aiming mechanism. He inspected the rifles. He wanted to make sure that the guns were locked in the middle of their traverse. They would stay that way until he gave the order to fire-at-will. The *Davis* was still far too dangerous to take on at close quarters. The next battle would be the same as the first, at the maximum range of the rifles. He needed a lucky shot. If he could stay afloat, he knew he would eventually get it.

Two days passed without a sign of the *Davis*. If it didn't show itself soon, *The Blessed* would have to turn hunter. The afternoon of the third day, the signal flashed from the top of the mountain. The *Davis* was heading north, working its way up the coast looking for targets. Connor didn't know if Hutchinson was looking for him or trying to get north for easier and richer pickings. There was no hurry. The wind was light. Within an hour, one of the tenders returned the lookout to *The Blessed*. Connor hoisted anchor and sailed northwest. He wanted to standoff with his gray hull backdropped by the vast Pacific behind him. He would wait until dark. A waning moon would rise after midnight. If the rebel stayed his course, Connor would sail to intercept him and wait until the rising moon backlit the frigate. Connor and Santiago were both up in the crow's nest, watching for the frigate and talking over the strategy. They needed to hurt the *Davis* again. Maybe it would be the last time; maybe not. Connor still had high hopes for a lucky shot.

Several hours passed, and with the sighting telescope, they could see the frigate still hugging the coast east of Santa Cruz Island. It was the first dog watch. Connor went down the ratline of the mainmast and got busy with his chart and calculations. He didn't want to hoist sails until dark. He didn't want to let Hutchinson know that he was still in the neighborhood. The wind wouldn't give him the maximum knots, but it would put him off the point of

Santa Barbara by midnight. With any luck at all, the *Davis* wouldn't know he was there.

It was a little over forty miles to where the coast turned north. Connor estimated that the *Davis* would arrive halfway into the middle watch. *There are a lot of ifs,* Connor thought: if she stayed on course, if she could make good time on the westerly course; if she didn't turn around to return to the safer waters off Los Angeles. Connor had *The Blessed* in place by midnight, six miles off the point. All hands were watching for the moon to rise. Connor and Santiago were watching the sea to the southwest. They didn't expect Hutchinson to cut across and arrive out on the ocean to their west and spring the very trap they were planning for him, but Connor was wary. The sky lightened in the east. There wasn't a cloud in the sky. The moon rose over the inland mountains, and there was the *Davis*, right where she needed to be.

A tense moment came and went as two clipper ships passed just west of *The Blessed*. If the *Davis* saw them, it didn't alter course. Connor hoisted the mainsail and the foresails. He would keep pace with the *Davis* until it was turned full abeam to his guns. He didn't have to wait long; the frigate picked up speed as she turned north. *The Blessed* was invisible, a ghost in the night. The schooner couldn't heel over in the light wind. Connor would have to close to within two miles to hit the frigate. Tension in the crew was palpable as he edged the schooner closer to the frigate. The gunners had the rifles elevated to their max, locked perpendicular to the keel, and ready to fire. The first rounds would be incendiary. Connor would sail ahead then turn south to let the port rifle rake the frigate with high explosive rounds as he ran for the cover of San Miguel Island, the farthest west of the island chain that stretched into the Pacific from Santa Cruz Island.

Every shot hit the unsuspecting frigate. Connor was well into his second pass by the time the *Davis* got off her first salvo. It was harmless. The *Davis* was shooting where *The Blessed* used to be. Four high-explosive rounds hit the Davis. Three hit the armored side of the frigate. They didn't damage the ship, but the concussion of the blasts killed more of the crew. The last shell fired, hit the base of the mizzen mast. In the light of burning sails, the crew of *The Blessed* cheered when they saw the mizzen topple over. The big gun on the *Davis* was firing blind. *The Blessed* needed to end this attack; without the light of the rounds fired to mark her position, the schooner was invisible again. The rifles had to cool. As much as Connor wanted to press the attack, he couldn't risk damaging one of his guns.

He wanted the *Davis* to follow him down to the islands. That wasn't going to happen. The *Davis* was busy fighting fires and taking care of her dead and wounded. The mizzen mast had to be cut loose and jettisoned before she could maneuver effectively again. Connor knew he could win now. He had reduced the *Davis* almost down to a barge. She could still fly a lot of canvas, but it would take a long time to turn her without the mizzen to help bring her around. If the *Davis* followed him down to the islands, Connor would end it tomorrow in the light of day. The gunners were cleaning the rifles and oiling the breach blocks. The cook was feeding the crew. More ammunition was made ready. Santiago turned to his Captain. He had known Connor all the younger Irishman's life. He said, "Mañana, sólo habrá una nave después de la batalla."

Connor agreed with him. There would only be one ship left if they fought the next day. What else could Hutchinson do? He had to fight. If he ran north, Connor would attack him again in the darkness. His best chance was in the daylight, where he had the advantage of the range where he could bring his 110-pounder to bear with some degree of accuracy. Connor wouldn't let the rebels catch him close to the islands. He wanted the next fight out on the open sea where he could easily out-sail the crippled frigate.

Connor positioned *The Blessed* six miles southwest of San Miguel Island. He hove to in the open ocean and waited for sunrise. The westerlies promised to build up. There was a fair amount of chop, and *The Blessed* pitched in the waves. Less seasoned seamen would have complained, but Connor's crew walked the decks and climbed the rigging like a troop of monkeys at home in a tall jungle tree. Connor did not attempt to hide. The large Irish flag streamed proudly from the topgallant screaming: *I'm here. Come and get me.*

The wind from the west got stronger at sunrise. Connor loved this part of the ocean. The weather was always predictable, and so was the Commodore. The *Davis* was sailing south, three miles off the western tip of San Miguel. At least Hutchinson had learned to be wary of the islands. Santiago gave the order to raise all the sails. Connor turned *The Blessed* to the northwest. The *Davis* kept coming. *Maybe this guy can't learn, after all,* he thought as he started plotting courses and calculating again. He would tease the rebel; he wanted more sea room behind the frigate so he could turn in behind it with the wind to his back. Upon Santiago's suggestion, they were going to attempt to disable the rudder on the *Davis*. Connor was holding *The Blessed* into the wind. If his calculations were right, the frigate would pass on his starboard side just out of range. It took an hour; then, they saw the smoke of the big gun's first shot. The shell didn't hit the water; it exploded in the air a thousand feet short. The noise was deafening. The *Davis* fired again; the result was the same, but shell exploded farther away yet.

Connor was expecting the *Davis* to turn towards him. The big ship stayed on its course due south. Connor needed a couple more miles. He got them, and he nodded at Santiago. The Spaniard spun the wheel. *The Blessed* handled like a gazelle putting the wind to its back. Like a runner starting a race, she was making fifteen knots in an instant. The *Davis* could only get off one more shot with the big gun before it was blinded by the mainmast. Why Hutchinson didn't turn her into the wind, or with the wind so he could keep firing, is one of those mysteries of naval warfare that time would never answer. Connor swooped in to take advantage of the other man's blunder.

He closed to within two miles. He sent the signal to fire at will. The starboard gun opened up on the back of the ship. Six hits with high explosive rounds. When Connor felt he was too far east, he spun *The Blessed* around, and the crew rigged for sailing against the wind. The port gun kept up the barrage. The *Davis* didn't turn. Santiago yelled down the speaking tube, "Incendiary." They were going for the kill. The *Davis* was on fire again. Hutchinson couldn't turn the big ship to bear for a broadside. They must have disabled the rudder. With what was left of his crew fighting the fires, Hutchinson lowered the Stars and Bars and ran up a white flag.

The *Jefferson Davis*, defeated and without a rudder, was at the mercy of the wind and the tide. Its foresails brought her around with the wind to its back. The topsails were still intact. The westerly wind was blowing the frigate towards the islands. Connor figured Hutchinson wanted to get close to land to give his mangled crew the best chance to get off the doomed ship. Connor held *The Blessed* against the wind, his guns still at the ready. The wind would deliver the *Davis* to the south side of Santa Cruz Island – unless it shifted, then the frigate would be driven ashore on the beaches west of Los Angeles.

Connor waited on course until the *Davis* passed well out of range to the northeast. Even though Hutchinson had surrendered, Connor had no intention of leaving the frigate afloat. It was still a powerful, enemy ship. It belonged on the bottom, and he wasn't quitting the battle until he put it there. Safe, well out of range, Santiago turned *The Blessed* to follow the *Davis* to her final resting place.

It took several hours, but Hutchinson managed to get the *Davis* close enough to a beach on the south side of Santa Cruz Island to drop anchor. He only had one lifeboat left after the last attack. Connor furled the sails and stood off, watching the lifeboat take the last of the survivors and the wounded to the beach. Had the crew left the *Davis* adrift, Connor would have left her to die on the rocks. At anchor off the small beach, the crew could board and work to put her back in fighting shape as soon as he was gone. That could not be allowed.

Connor had let *The Blessed* drift in to within a mile of the abandoned frigate. Maybe he was distracted by a pod of California gray whales that passed between him and the frigate. Maybe he wanted to be close enough to see the look on Hutchinson's face when he fired his ship. It didn't matter. Later on, he would remember that it was blind-stupid and unlucky. Santiago advised him to back off to fire the last incendiary and then set sail for Ireland. His instinct was true and correct, and his advice sound. Connor regretted not taking the advice as soon as the incendiary went through the *Davis's* aft gun port and exploded inside the ship. The gun ports lit up as bright as the sun. The 32-pounders had been abandoned but waited charged and primed for a gun crew to fire them. All fourteen cannons cooked off in the inferno. *The Blessed* was directly in the line of fire from the broadside.

The first round was low and skipped across the water and thudded harmlessly against the side of *The Blessed.* The second flew high over the topgallant. Santiago rolled the schooner into a turn to starboard. *The Blessed* was rocked up, heeled into the turn. The third-round hit and pierced the hull just below the deck line. The round was mostly spent but still deflected down off the center deck beam. It broke through the floor of the whiskey hold and opened a seam in the plank cladding of the hull, well under the waterline. If that were all it did, *The Blessed* would have survived. But that wasn't all. The whiskey hold filled with steam. The cannonball had broken the steam line that ran back to the bilge pump. They still had the manual pump, but the crew couldn't keep up with the water gushing in through the split seam. Santiago came up out of the whiskey hold and shook his head *no* at Connor. Connor ordered the cutters lowered into the water. Unlike the lifeboat on the Davis, the cutters comfortably fit all of the crew.

Santiago was yelling from the forecastle, "Turn her toward the shallows!" He was pointing to the east end of the island. Then he was shouting an order to the crew, "Man the pump, man the pump. Keep her afloat till we reach the shallows." Half the crew was already in the tenders; they scrambled back aboard. Six men went to the manual pump and worked the rocker arm handles like demons trying to douse the fires of hell. The rest of the crew started bailing from the bottom of the whiskey hold with whatever they could find. Connor needed more sail. He tied off the helm and ran forward to raise the mainsail. It had been years since they used the capstan; he was inserting the handles into the turning head when the crew saw what he was doing and jumped to assist. It took a minute to raise the mainsail then the crew raised the foresails by hand while the rest of the men rigged the mizzen to the capstan. With the mizzen raised, the crew returned to bailing. It was several miles east to the shallows on the south side of the island. A mountain range that cut across the island to the north marked the spot Santiago wanted to reach. *The Blessed* was riding heavy, taking on water faster than the men could pump or bail. It would be a race now to make it to the shallows to embrace the inevitable end.

Santiago looked up at the sails; then, he was scrambling up the rigging. Connor knew he was going to the crow's nest. When he got there, he unfurled the topsail and then raised it using its ratline to repel back down to the deck. The older Spaniard was as agile as a gazelle; he ran back to the con, and Connor yelled, "What are you doing?"

Santiago yelled back, "I want to leave her where we can come back and retrieve the guns."

Connor hadn't thought about that. He lost himself in the emotional fray of having made a disastrous mistake that cost him his beloved ship. But maybe they did have a chance. The water was shallow farther down the south side of the island. There was a place around the point called Smugglers Cove, but he knew they wouldn't make it that far. If he could beach *The Blessed* before it went down maybe, just maybe, they could patch her up and save her. Santiago had one more command for his captain, "I will be the last man off. If we don't can't beach her, I want to drop the anchor before she goes down to hold her on the bottom against the currents. It was going to be close. The water was already two feet deep on the floor of the whiskey hold. When the water reached the gun ports, the battle to save *The Blessed* would be over in less than a minute. They were still a half-mile away from the beach

Connor wanted to reach, but the water color was changing to the lighter blue of the shallows. Connor yelled his last command to the crew, "Watch the gun ports; release the tenders before she floods. Don't let her drag them down."

Connor looked back at the rebel ship. The *Davis* was fully ablaze; she would soon join *The Blessed* on the bottom. Santiago was back on the forecastle; he could see the bottom now, the water was only six fathoms deep, but the battle was lost. As Connor turned to make the last leg to the beach, the gun port on the port side went below the waterline. The crew was up and over the gunwales and pushing off from *The Blessed.* Santiago released the anchor and then dove into the water and swam to the tender. Connor walked forward on the top of the gunwale as the whiskey schooner settled deeper in the water. She was turning in the breeze held by the anchor. The crew in the closest tender let *The Blessed* come alongside, and Connor stepped onto the tender as his ship slipped under the surface.

The two tenders lay in the choppy sea side by side. Grief overtook Connor, but he joked, "Well men, I promised you a return trip home, but it looks like we are in for a stay in San Pedro. Maybe Madam Wong will have some extra beds ready for us." They hoisted the sails and struck a course for the base on Santa Catalina. The men still had possessions there. The only thing Connor took off *The Blessed* before she went down was his father's sextant and the logbook. There would be only one more entry and never another. There would never be another *Blessed by the Wind.* The long-lived Irish schooner was on the bottom, sunk by a bad decision and a cruel, unlucky twist of fate.

Lighthouse Quest

Winter ebbed, but it wasn't yet spring. It was just a beautiful day on the California coast. Moses had Eliza by the hand. Amos and Maria walked ahead. They were a little older than Eliza and more confident. They were walking down Main Street in San Pedro, on their way to Point Fermin. Mr. Phineas Banning had sent an invitation to their hotel to meet with him. Banning would be waiting for them on the land his Lighthouse Society bought to preserve for the beacon that would show the way into the harbor. The group of San Pedro businessmen had been trying to get the Federal Government to build a lighthouse there since 1854. The inquiries Moses made around San Pedro for the whereabouts of a lighthouse brought the invitation to meet Banning down at the park that morning. Moses knew he was there; an elaborate carriage was on the road just north of the park. Mr. Banning was sitting on a bench in the shade of a tall cypress tree. The children ignored him and ran to the rail to look over the cliff.

Moses introduced himself and offered his hand to Mr. Banning. Banning took it and said, "You need no introduction, Moses. I know who you are, and I want to talk to you about the freight business." Banning ran the stage line between his new city of Wilmington and Yuma. He started in business a freight man, just like Moses. "You are shipping the gold out of Red Mountain, and I want to talk to you and Eli Callahan if you could arrange it. First, I want to ask you about the children. You have a red one, a brown one, and a black one. You're missing a yellow one. Are you here to adopt another youngster?"

Moses laughed; he liked the man right off. Not everyone accepted race casually enough to joke about it. He also knew who Banning was before he accepted the invitation to meet him in the park. He sat down on the bench with Banning and told Eliza's story. "Only the *black one* is mine. I adopted him. The *red one* was an Apache orphan. Eli and his Algonquin wife adopted her. The *brown one* is Suzette's girl. She found her orphaned on the Santa Fe Trail. You're right; I do need a *yellow one* for racial balance."

Banning said, "Maybe one of Madam Wong's girls has an accident she would like to place in a good home."

Laughing, Moses called the children over to meet Mr. Banning. Banning signaled his driver, and the man carried a large picnic basket over to the bench. There was a picnic table over by another cypress. The driver unpacked a fine spread. No sandwiches. Fried chicken, French fries, cookies and chocolate, and a fine bottle of white wine for the men. The children drank cold lemonade. "Wow!" the children said as one and dug in.

Moses put his hand on Eliza's shoulder. "This one won a bet. I was the prize, and I have to take her to see a lighthouse. I hope we don't have to travel to the east coast. I won't go back there until the war is over."

Banning saw a great opportunity to solidify his friendship with Moses. "You won't have to. There is one in San Francisco Bay on Alcatraz Island. When it's safe, I can take you and the children there on one of my clippers."

"What do you mean when it's safe?"

Banning's driver answered, "There was a Confederate frigate anchored off the beach west of Los Angeles. Sympathizers were packing it full of provisions. Some little boat took a shot at it the other day, and the warship chased it out into the Pacific. We haven't seen her since."

Moses was curious, "A *little boat*. Were there any more details?"

"No, but it was all gray from top to waterline, and it flew a large, green flag. Someone said it was Irish."

"Connor Callahan, the Callahan family uncle. He couldn't wait to put to sea. We left him at his schooner in the mouth of the Gila River weeks ago. He was down the river by the time we got to Yuma. He knew about the armored frigate. He carried the newspaper with an article about the launching of the frigate around with him everywhere; all he did while we were up at Red Mountain was study books on naval warfare. Do you say he only fired one shot? That doesn't ring true." The driver went back to the carriage to fetch a newspaper that carried the report of the one-shot sortie.

Banning renewed his offer to take Moses and the children to San Francisco. "I have to go to Benicia. The Army of the Pacific is going to make me an honorary Brigadier General. It's amazing what donating some acreage for a base here in Wilmington will do for a man's stature in the eyes of the Union. They are building an Army base. It will be called the Drum Barracks. By the way, that last gold shipment went to the San Francisco Mint on a heavily guarded freight wagon. I'm not sending any clippers north until the Navy deals with that frigate. I'm not going to leave until the sea route is safe."

"We'll see," Moses said. "That *little boat* is a heavily armed schooner. Connor Callahan is an experienced smuggler and somewhat of a pirate himself; another thing, he is one hell of a sailor. He had the bit in his teeth when he lit out of the Gila. One of the ships will be on the bottom before he finishes with this. I wouldn't bet on the *Rebel*."

"Nonetheless, I'm not risking a ship until it's certain the sea lanes are safe. How would you like to stay on the clipper until we leave? It alone would be a real adventure for the kids. It's my flagship; fit for a king and his entourage."

Moses looked at the kids. They were all shaking their heads *yes*, hoping he would say the same. "Sounds a lot better than a trip to Alcatraz in a dusty stagecoach. We'll take you up on that offer."

Maria shook her head and gave Moses her best young woman look of patience with the mere man. "Alcatraz is an island, Uncle Moses. You can't get there in a stagecoach."

Banning said, "You're a smart girl. What's your name?"

"I'm Maria Callahan. I went to school in San Francisco while my mother was in the medical college."

Banning was even more impressed than before he spoke to the children. He had more to offer. "My driver will take us back to town. You can pick up your things from wherever you're staying, and we'll go out to the Banning House for the rest of the day. The driver will get you out to the clipper after supper."

The children played and watched the sea lions from the top of the cliff. Moses and Banning talked about freight companies, shipping gold, and security. Banning couldn't believe that Moses owned a Gatling gun. They were still talking by the time the children were bored with the park. When they passed through San Pedro, the streets were noisy with rumors of a battle out on the ocean. The rumors said that one of the ships had burned, but no one knew which one. Moses knew it was hard to burn an ironclad. It had to be the wooden schooner. He dreaded the worst.

That evening Banning's driver took them down to the clipper – *The Banning of San Pedro, CA*. It was luxurious. A grand old clipper, one of a handful left not converted to steam. Moses and the three children each had a cabin of their own. Eliza asked if she could stay with Maria. She wanted to stay with Moses, but she didn't want to let on that she was afraid to stay in the strange surroundings alone. The children hardly slept that night. They were up with the watches, ringing the bells, and learning how to tell time on the ship.

The first mate was a seasoned sailor. He told the kids, "No climbing until I can rig some safety lines." The first mate told them his name was Johnson Johnson from Johnson, Tennessee. He blamed it on uncreative parents. During the first evening, he became the children's best friend on the ship.

Like many career sailors, he didn't have a home or a family of his own. Books lined every wall in his cabin that told about everywhere he had been in the world. It seemed to Eliza that he must have been everywhere there was to go.

The cook let the children sleep in, and then he had breakfast waiting for them in the officer's mess. Moses was sitting at the table with a large map of every shipping and receiving point west of the Mississippi. He was estimating how many wagons, men, waystations, and how much pulling stock it would take to connect all the dots with armored freight wagons. Maria asked, "What are you doing?"

"An estimate for Mr. Banning. He is trying to take over the world, and he asked me to help him."

Amos asked, "Wasn't there a guy named Napoleon who tried that?"

Moses answered honestly, "I have no idea."

Eliza answered for him. "He was a French emperor that took over most of Europe in the first part of this century. He must have been an asshole."

Moses jumped on her. "Where did you learn that word?"

Eliza stood her ground, "The miners say it all the time."

"Well, we are not digging gold, and I don't want to hear it again while we are on our trip. You can use it on your brothers when we get home. Think of another way to say someone isn't a very good person."

Eliza smiled and said okay to appease Moses. Moses knew she would obey him, but he also worried that showing an Apache a way to get his goat was a bad idea. He needed to end this admonition on a positive note. "Eliza, I never want you to call me one of those, even when you are mad at me and talking to yourself."

Eliza went around the table and put her arms around Moses' neck. "You never act that way. Henry and Bimisi, now there is a much different story." Moses was surprised; Eliza was growing up faster than most people thought.

It was time for fun and games on the boat. Johnson Johnson came into the mess to collect the children. "Time for climbing lessons; all swabbies on deck–NOW." His voice boomed through the mess. The children scrambled out onto the deck. The first mate smiled at Moses as he turned and walked out of the companionway. Moses smiled back. He wanted to finish his work. He loved parenting the children, but he also appreciated breaks in the twenty-four-seven routine.

There were three light safety lines rigged through a pulley on the mainmast above the crow's nest. Johnson Johnson told the children always to keep three points connected fast to the ratlines while they climbed. "Move one foot or one hand at a time. If you fall, we will have you by the lanyard tied to the belt around your waist. You could still get hurt, though, swinging into the rigging or hitting the mast. Best not to fall at all. There is only room for two of you in the crow's nest. The first two up there can stay as long as they want. The other one will have to come down and wait a turn. **ON YOUR MARKS!**"

When the three climbers heard the word **GO**, they realized it was a race. They scrambled to the ratlines. Eliza was the lightest and the agilest. Halfway up the one-hundred fifty-foot climb, she was clearly in the lead. On the ratline on the other side of the ship, Amos was vying for a lead against Maria. He wanted to be ahead when the ratline narrowed at the topmast; only one person would fit on the last leg to the top. Amos knew he had to climb faster if he was going to get there first. He made a major mistake; he started to run up the ratline; he had seen the sailors do it, and he figured he could too. He passed Maria, and he shouldn't have looked back down at her. His handhold was slippery, and he lost his grip. He fell. Maria laughed when she saw he lost the race because of seagull poop on the ratline.

From the crow's nest, the two girls could see far out into the Pacific. They talked about going to all the places Johnson Johnson had pictures of in his cabin. They wanted Mr. Sue to tell them about the Great Wall. They wanted to see the emperor's palace in Tokyo, the Forbidden City in Shanghai. Nothing was beyond their imagination. They were going to hold their prize until they got hungry for lunch. There were still a lot of places they were talking about visiting as the morning wore on.

Amos grew more and more annoyed that one of the girls didn't come down so he could go up. The deckhands tied off the two safety lines for the girls and took Amos up to the bowsprit. They hitched up the safety line again, and then one agile youth said, "Watch this." He grabbed a rope that Amos could see was the line that would hoist signal flags up to the top of the mainsail. The sailor ran down the gunwale and flung himself off where it curved back into the bow of the ship. He swung way out past the hull. In a long arc, he swung around the front of the foresail rigging and then down the other side of the ship back to the poop deck. He was running back with the rope when Johnson Johnson told Amos he would be next.

Amos got his last instructions, "You have to run down the gunwale as fast as you can. If you don't run as fast as you can, you won't make it around the foresail rigging. If you don't swing out far enough, you won't make it to the poop deck. If you don't run as fast as you can, you might wind up swinging down into the ocean. Ready?"

Amos' first try was a good one; he didn't make it to the poop deck, but he lifted his feet when he skimmed the water. He grasped the gunwale, twenty feet forward of the poop deck, and then scrambled up. He didn't have to get down on the deck to walk back to the bowsprit. He walked back to the bow on the gunwale. The deckhand was waiting there with a pair of rubber-soled deck shoes. "I know you can run faster than that. I saw you slip a step, trying for more speed. Here, put these on, and on your next run, run like *Hermes*."

Amos didn't know who *Hermes* was, but he knew he had to run like hell. He put falling into the water out of his mind even though the mate had unhitched the safety line. The mate handed him a rolled-up piece of oiled paper. "Hermes was the Greek Messenger God. We use this swing to deliver messages to the helm. Warships use it all the time when they are sailing in the dark, sneaking up on an enemy. Calling out from bowsprit to stern wouldn't exactly be like sneaking through the dark. Pretend you are under the guns of Fort Sumter trying to sneak into the Charleston Harbor."

Amos knew about Fort Sumter and the Charleston Harbor. He knew everything the newspapers knew about the war. He ran like hell with the oiled paper clenched in his teeth. He was delivering a message to his Captain, telling him to turn to port. They were past the guns of the fort. He swung way out past the gunwale with the rubber soles and the drag of the safety line gone. He swung down the other side of the ship and around the ropes that held the back of the mizzenmast. He landed on the deck next to the con. The sailors all cheered. Johnson Johnson was waiting at the wheel. "One of the finest swings *Hermes* ever made, mate." Amos beamed as everyone shook his hand and clapped him on the back.

The girls were shouting down from the crow's nest. Amos thought they were yelling their congrats, but then all eyes swept to the south where they were pointing. Maria recognized the cutters from *The Blessed* sailing into the bay. Connor recognized Maria and tuned in to moor on the side of the clipper. Moses and Johnson Johnson met him at the rail. Moses introduced Connor as the Captain of *The Blessed*, the Irish schooner. "Welcome aboard, skipper. I be the first mate. Let's get your crew aboard."

Moses counted the men as they came over the gunwale. No one was missing. Moses asked, "Where's *The Blessed*?"

"On the bottom with the *Jefferson Davis*." Connor was still berating himself up for what he considered a needless, stupid loss of the schooner.

Santiago put his arm around his Captain and said, "It was better than a draw. Half of the rebel crew is dining with Davy Jones for the rest of eternity. We left the rest stranded on Santa Cruz Island. We need to send someone up there to pick them up before they starve to death."

Johnson Johnson dispatched a messenger to spread the good news in San Pedro and to tell Mr. Banning that it was time to set sail for San Francisco. The second mate went ashore and took Amos with him. Connor asked, "Where's the Captain?"

"Ashore in the hospital in Wilmington. I don't think he will be back aboard to make this voyage. He was banged up pretty bad in a fall down the ladder to the rudder hold in a typhoon north of the Galapagos."

The girls were yelling down from the crow's nest. They were ready to come down. The deckhands untied their safety lines. Both girls looked down to make sure the hands below were on their lines and then jumped off the crow's nest, flinging themselves as far out into space as they could. Arms spread wide like angels; they swan-dived down to the deck. Maria ran to her uncle's outspread arms. Eliza was more reserved and came over and shook his hand. Connor smiled to himself. He was starting to understand Eli's feelings.

Banning arrived three hours later with a sea trunk. The crew of the clipper had pulled *The Banning* over to an empty spot on the Wilmington pier so he could walk aboard. With the sea safe again, the clippers that moored there were already on their way to all points of the compass. Banning acknowledged Johnson Johnson's two-fingered tip to his seaman's cap and then extended his hand to Connor. "Connor Callahan, soon to be the most famous sea captain in the world." He took a newspaper out from under his arm; the headline read,

THE BLESSED SINKS THE DAMNED.

The paper seemed moist, like the ink was still wet.

"I lost my boat, Mr. Banning. I don't deserve any fame."

"Well, Captain, you're going to get it anyway. I will buy you two schooners if you want, but I have a better offer than that for you." He turned to Johnson, "First Mate Johnson, here is your commission to Captain. You will take command of the *Far West*. She is due in tomorrow. You'll take her to New Delhi as soon as she is ready. Captain Connor, it would be my pleasure if you would sail us up to San Francisco. The bay is full of abandoned ships of all sizes. You can have your pick. Consider a new ship prize money for sinking the *Jefferson Davis.*"

Connor said, "It would be good if we could go back to Ireland in something bigger than a schooner since I lost *The Blessed.*" A smile spread clear across the deck. Every crew member of *The Blessed* hoped they would be retiring in some seaside cottage on the lee shore of Ireland.

Banning could see that the Irish crew was delighted. He said, "I think I have just the ship for you, but you might need a bit more crew." The two men shook hands. "Captain Johnson, clear out your cabin. Where's Harlow? I need to promote him to first mate."

Harlow stepped forward and received his promotion with great pride. He acknowledged Connor with the seaman's salute and gave orders for the crew to pack up and clear Johnson's cabin. Crates appeared, a lot of crates for Johnson's library. Before the packing started, Johnson took a tome off his shelf. He gave it to the girls. It was handwritten; the title was elegant gold leaf, and the binding was leather. As he handed the book over, he said, "Finish this for me." The title read *My Ports of Call by Johnson Johnson, Able Seaman*.

Eliza took the book, but Maria said, "We can't accept this, sir. It looks like your life's work."

Johnson smiled, "I'm not much of a writer. I need an editor and someone more literate than me to make it understandable. I can't think of anyone better I know than two young girls with imaginations as big as the seven seas I am sure you will roam." He hugged both of them. The crew all cheered him as he left the ship for the last time. It wasn't long. His crates of books and his other few possessions waited for him on the pier. It would take a freight wagon to get him to the Seaman's Hotel in San Pedro.

Connor was ready to cast off, but Banning asked him to wait for one more passenger. He would arrive at any moment. Connor was getting to know the first mate better and also met more of the crew. His men were put up in the forecastle, going to sea as passengers for the first time in their lives. Banning was at the table in the mess with Moses, going over the map and the estimate. A carriage arrived on the pier, and Professor Laity got out and walked up the gangplank. A seaman's chest followed him aboard, and he carried a satchel.

Moses remembered the Professor and asked, "What are you doing here?"

The Professor was happy to explain. "I have been at the La Brea Tar Pits recovering bones. Mr. Banning is funding the dig. I got the letter your women wrote to Jim Parish asking for a library; my wife sent it down to me. She is a retired librarian. Your banker friend asked her to take over the library project. I am hitching a ride with Mr. Banning to San Francisco to pick her up. We might need another boat to get the library she is collecting back to Red Mountain." Moses smiled and pointed at the two girls. They were reading Johnson's saga. Professor Laity walked over to say hello to the two girls; they were sitting on a roll of heavy hawser, but they popped to their feet as the Professor approached. Amos was off somewhere with the crew learning to tie knots.

The tide was beginning to ebb. Connor gave the command to cast off but let his First Mate Harlow take the con. He didn't want to embarrass himself, trying to get the clipper out of the narrow harbor. He would learn how to sail it when they were well out in the open ocean. Eliza and Maria never put their reading down until the clipper started to roll back and forth in heavier seas. The girls were getting a little seasick with their noses tucked into the book. So far, they had followed Johnson Johnson from cabin boy to midshipman and halfway around the Horn of Africa on his first trip to China for tea. The deckhands got them up to the forecastle deck, where they could keep their eyes on the horizon out in front of them and rock back and forth with the ship. It wouldn't take long to get their sea legs. Amos was still busy trying to master a *monkey fist*; he could already tie *bowlines* and *square knots* in his sleep.

Connor took the helm and sailed them past Santa Cruz Island. The rebel crew of *Jefferson Davis* had made driftwood shelters. Several cook fires were burning, and the men that were standing around them were waving enthusiastically for rescue. Ignoring the *Law of the Sea*, Connor ignored their plea for help. The crew of the clipper also ignored them, but Santiago threw the sailors on the beach the Spanish salute again. Santiago wanted to let the Confederates know that the crew responsible for sinking them, was safe aboard the clipper. The crew of *The Blessed* were lined up on the starboard gunnel; as one, they followed Santiago's lead and threw the salute and shouted, "Remember *The Blessed*." The men on the beach quit waving when they recognized the big Spaniard and his men.

The sailing was good when Connor turned the clipper north off the point of Santa Barbara. There were ground swells, though, rolling in from some storm far out to the west. Nothing like the legendary swells of the Cape of Good Hope or the straights of Magellan, but heavy enough to put the clipper into a gentle roll back and forth as it made its way across the swells. By the beginning of the first dog watch, the girls were back to reading their saga. Amos was at the con steering the clipper and waiting for orders from the first mate.

Connor was down in the officers' mess with Moses and Banning. The two shipping magnates were figuring out how to build a better-armored wagon and where they would get it built. Banning was writing up a patent application for the breakaway harness. Moses was working on a drawing of the next generation wagon. Not all of the armored wagons would carry a Gatling gun, only the wagons that would transport bullion from the troubled areas like Bannack, Montana, and Nevada City, California. Connor felt like he was intruding on a secret meeting of war. He sat quietly and listened until the cook and his mates came to clear the table for the evening meal.

The next day the ground swells were living up to their name. Now the *Hermes Run* took on a new and dangerous form. Instead of just swinging along one side of the ship, the runners ran forward, and with the assistance of a rollover the top of a swell, they were hurled forward and around the foresails and down the other side of the clipper. The ground swells were rolling in from the west. From crest to bottom, the swell was more than fifteen feet. The timing of a run had to be perfect. Start too soon, and one wouldn't clear the foresail. Run too late, and a sailor was going to take a plunge through the swell that just passed before being hauled back aboard. Letting go of the rope in the heavy sea was deadly. In these seas, the *Hermes Run* wasn't a game to be taken lightly even though a crew was standing by to launch a lifeboat if someone lost his grip on the signal line.

Moses and Connor watched man after man make the run. They were standing on the main deck, watching the sailors swing by the starboard side of the ship. Both their hearts stopped beating when they saw Amos making the run. Amos didn't just reach the poop deck. He held on and waited for the roll of the ship to swing him in next to the con. Harlow was at the wheel.

By the time Connor and Amos got back to the poop deck, Harlow was showing Amos how to nudge the ship into the next swell.

Moses and Connor walked to the con, not knowing how to handle the boy risking his life. Harlow was explaining, "If you don't steer a little into each wave, the ocean will be moving you a little bit with every wave. In a day, you will be quite a way from where you think you are. The part of the sea where the swells build is called a *fetch*: the bigger the fetch and the stronger the wind, the stronger the swells. Sometimes swells are coming from two directions. When they are perpendicular to each other, it makes for quite a ride." Harlow handed the con over to Amos. Moses had learned something about parenting, after all. He didn't want to rob Amos of the glory of his moment. Connor stayed with Harlow and Amos at the con, Moses went below to find the girls.

Two more days at sea and the *Banning* was abeam of San Benito as the sun settled into the Pacific. The sea was relatively calm, Harlow was at the con with Amos. The girls were in the crow's nest on the mainmast. Eliza wanted to see a lighthouse; Connor had the *Banning* arriving off the mouth of San Francisco Bay at night so she could discover one. The Banning was ten miles off the coast, and the night turned inky black. No moon and a light cloud cover obscured the stars. Two hours after dark, Eliza's voice rang down from the crow's nest. "Lighthouse, **HO**! Off the starboard beam."

Harlow had Amos hold the course due north until the lighthouse was exactly at a bearing of seventy-six degrees on the compass; at Connor's command, Amos steered the clipper onto the bearing and sailed into San Francisco Bay. They anchored on the east side of Alcatraz, well out of the shipping lanes. Amos was sad that the sailing was over. The sadness was gone in an instant, though, when Connor told the boy he would teach him how to navigate on the way back to Los Angeles.

Moses spent the entire trip with Mr. Banning. Banning's cabin was reminiscent of a fine hotel room. The planning for an armored stage line was complete. A carriage works by the racetrack south of Mission Bay would be commissioned to build the prototype. Moses wasn't surprised that Mr. Banning owned the carriage works and a goodly share of the racetrack too. Banning would go to Benicia in the morning. Moses would go to the carriage works and take Amos with him. Connor would take the girls to the mansion on Nob Hill. Lily would know they were coming to visit. Connor still marveled that with Lily, you never had to send word ahead. Professor Laity had his steamer trunk and books ready to leave the ship.

Moses and Banning weren't the only ones planning. Connor and Santiago were deep in discussions with the crew about retrieving the guns from *The Blessed.* One of the younger men hailed from Kalymnos island in the Aegean Sea. His father was a sponge diver, and as a boy, Xander Tavoularis learned the trade from his father. At age fourteen, Xander was kidnapped and pressed into service in the British Navy. Connor had picked him up in the middle of the English Channel after the young man dove off of a British man-of-war to escape a whipping with the cat o' nine tails. He was swimming toward France, but it wouldn't have mattered which direction he went; he didn't speak either English or French. Xander could have swum to the French shore, but he credited Connor for saving his life because the water was cold, and he knew he could cramp up and drown. Xander was the youngest man in the crew and had unconditional love and loyalty for Connor and Santiago.

Besides a diver, they would need other equipment, namely a way to raise the guns. Raising *The Blessed* itself didn't seem reasonable; it would take a heavy salvage barge to pick her off the bottom and take her to a drydock for repair. What they needed was a ship with a boom strong enough to lift the guns. Each gun weighed around four tons, more weight than most cargo booms were designed to handle. It had to be the right ship, not just a clipper like Banning wanted to buy for him. San Francisco Bay was full of ships. There had to be one that could fill their needs.

For the children, it took more than a week for the excitement of the city to wear off. The youngsters got a tour they would remember the rest of their lives. Mr. Parish took them to his bank and then to the San Francisco Mint. They went with General Banning, as he now liked to be called, to the carriage works and then the racetrack. Moses took them on a tour of the Mission San Francisco de Asís. Maria showed them the Willows, the infamous bar on Mission Street, but they didn't go inside; they just looked through the door. They toured the University of the Pacific Medical School, where her mother became a doctor and walked to 3rd Street to see the mansion on Rincon Hill, where she had lived. They spent one whole day on Alcatraz. Eliza wanted to stay till dark so she could help light the beam that they followed in from the open ocean the night they arrived.

No trip to San Francisco would be complete without theaters and restaurants. Lily and Ben took the children to the theaters several times. Fancy restaurants were too numerous to count, and a walk down the main street of Chinatown left them in wonder. At Fisherman's Wharf, they ate Dungeness crab until they could eat no more.

The last day belonged to Professor Laity. He picked the children up early and took them to his office and museum at the St. Ignatius College. The Jesuits were a tough bunch and didn't completely approve of Professor Laity's version of paleontology. They humored and tolerated him, even though he believed in evolution. The Jesuits taught their students that bones were all created in place; at the same time God created the earth. On that basis, they shared a comfortable working relationship with the Professor. The Professor's wife, Adrianna, was waiting for them in the Professor's office. Eliza's eyes got big when she saw several fangs in a display case tucked between floor-to-ceiling bookcases that covered every wall of the office.

But there was a high point on the tour yet to come. With reverence, Professor Laity led them into the Paleontology Museum. Jaws dropped when the kids saw complete skeletons of dinosaurs and cases full of bones, teeth, and claws that lined every wall. There was a huge skylight over the center of the large museum room, and the sun shone through on a *mastodon* skeleton that workers were mounting for display. Professor Laity explained, "Most of these more recent creatures came from the La Brea Tar Pits. I expect we are going to find something much more interesting deep in the Dragon Tooth Mine."

They spent the rest of the morning in the paleontology workshop and then had lunch with the students in the cafeteria. The food was quite good, but it wasn't like a restaurant down on the wharves. After lunch, they rode in a carriage over to the bay. Four freight wagons followed. Adrianna had assembled quite a library; it filled two of the wagons. The other two carried tools and packing materials for the *finds* expected inside Red Mountain.

They didn't ride the *Banning* back to Los Angeles. They didn't ride in one of the cast-off clipper ships either. Connor had selected a heavy three three-mast ship that had been used to transport heavy mining machinery from the east coast to San Francisco for the hard rock phase of the California gold rush. Banning had argued that Conner should have a more elegant ship but agreed to buy it for him after Connor confided his plans. The ship was much larger than *The Blessed* but smaller than the *Banning*. It had the same lines as the schooner but was more than twice the size. It also had a cargo crane that could lift ten tons out of the hold and swing it over onto a dock, or so the agent for the owner claimed. At the expense of the owner, Banning had the old ship hauled up on the dry dock in Mission Bay for inspection and cleaning of the hull before he would pay for it.

With Banning's clout, the old transport was at a pier east of Fisherman's Wharf in three days. Tons of supplies including sails, rigging, steel cable for the cargo hoist, food for the galley, and amenities for the passengers were arriving by the hour. One load of supplies raised more than a few eyebrows as kegs of gunpowder, two barrels of cleaning solvent, a keg of grease, and a barrel of gun oil was loaded into the hold. Banning had over a hundred men working on the ship. Everything was cleaned and painted anew. Within a week, the old workhorse that looked like a garbage scow emerged from the deadly clutches of despair to take her place as a proud ship of the sea.

The crew from *The Blessed* was aloft replacing sails and repairing rigging that had deteriorated over years of sitting idle in Mission Bay when the entourage from the college arrived at the pier. Connor welcomed them aboard. When Professor Laity introduced his wife, Connor said, "Mrs. Laity, your name reminds me of my deceased brother, Aaden, and his wife, Anna. Do you mind if I borrow it and paint it on the stern? I didn't like the name of this boat when I bought it; *Hardrock Sea Dog* didn't appeal to me. I painted it out. Would you mind going to Los Angeles in a boat named *Adrianna*?"

The Professor beamed with pride as his wife answered, "Captain Connor, you could take me there in a rowboat named *Ugly*. It will be an honor to go there on a ship named *Adrianna*. Special too, with the most famous Irish Captain and crew in the entire world."

Santiago had a man in a boatswain's chair hanging from the mizzenmast. Connor wrote out the name and made sure the spelling was correct. Santiago smiled when he remembered Aaden and Anna's marriage on *The Blessed* and the crew waiting for Aaden to do his duty. "What port of registration are we going to paint below *Adrianna*?" Santiago asked as he handed the name to the sailor with the black paint.

"Donaghadee," Connor answered, his voice deep and sincere, reflecting the reverence the crew felt for their homeland. There was no need to spell it out for the sailor. Everyone in the crew knew how to spell it. They were going home. They would leave as soon as the paint was dry.

The Tail of the Dragon

The voyage back to San Pedro was uneventful as far as Confederates and calamities were concerned. It was, however, spectacular for viewing the gray whale migration. Connor knew that there were tens of thousands of these cetaceans in the sea, and from time to time, it seemed that the majority of the herd was swimming south with the *Adrianna*. Connor pointed out to the children that gray whales had two blowholes on the top of their heads. Occasionally they could see a perfect heart-shaped blow. A close look was fine but a sea full of whales that ate tons of krill a day, made for a lingering, unpleasant odor on the surface; krill-breath didn't do the stench justice.

On the second day down the coast, a large humpback breached the surface less than a hundred feet off the port beam. Luck-of-the-Irish, Connor had all the kids up next to the helm learning how to use the sextant, and the humpback breached right in front of them. Any closer and they would have gotten wet when the huge mammal crashed back under the waves. Maria wanted to see it again, but Connor told her and the other children that the humpback could stay down for more than an hour. They would have to watch for another one.

Even more spectacular, on the third day, when they were off Santa Catalina Island getting ready to make the turn into San Pedro, the lookout in the crow's nest spotted a blue whale. Connor turned toward the big animal and hoped it would stay on the surface so the kids could see it. It was rare to see one, and rarer still to see one in the winter off the California coast. The blue whale was the largest living thing in the sea or on land. "There!" yelled Santiago. The largest tail fluke they had ever seen rose out of the water as the blue got ready to dive. Connor steered to where the blue dove and had the sails furled to drift with the currents to wait for the giant mammal to come back to the surface. They waited for an hour, and it was time well spent. The blue breached within a half-mile of the *Adrianna*. He almost got his whole body out of the water, and his huge maw gaped open like a trout going after a fly over a mountain lake.

There was a second blue whale that broke the surface and blew another perfect heart-shaped plume, a mate that could have swum in for the male from a thousand miles away. They wouldn't stay off the California coast long.

Connor thought the blues would head to the Antarctic, where they would mate. Maybe the female would return some years later with a calf.

Many sailors spent a lifetime at sea and never saw a blue whale. Here they had seen two in less than two hours. Amazing. Maria had been keeping a log of their sightings. The gray whales were too numerous to count, but she entered all the heart-shaped blows they spotted in the log. The two blues and the humpback were the pride of her growing log. Of the three children, Maria was the one most interested in sea life. Amos spent all his spare time studying navigation, and Eliza spent all her time with the Laity's learning more about paleontology. They were just children when they left Red Mountain; in a few short weeks, they were returning as students: Amos the midshipman; Maria, interested in marine biology; and Eliza, a paleontologist understudy. Connor hoped these new directions were agreeable to their parents. Amos, in particular, Connor was going to talk to Moses about him when the time was right.

Whale watching complete and as good as it ever gets, Connor set sail for the Gulf of California. He wouldn't be able to take the *Adrianna* up the river, but he had the two tenders from *The Blessed* and some lifeboats that came with the ship. The gulf would be safe. With the North's total blockade of the southern ports and no more warships expected in from England, he could sail to the mouth of the Colorado River without worry.

When they dropped anchor and were transferring the crates and their traveler's luggage to the tenders, Connor took Moses aside and asked, "What would you think about Amos going to Ireland with me? He is a natural-born sailor, and he has gotten a taste of the salt on this journey. I have seen this before. When he is older, I will bet that he will run away to the sea. It would be better for him to learn the trade with me where his color won't hold him back. After the war, I will either send him back or bring him myself. You have some time to think about it." Moses had never thought of the boy leaving him. He had a lot on his mind, presented with a direction for Amos wasn't something he was expecting.

The next day as they were unloading the first of the freight in Yuma, Moses had a question for Connor. "If I let Amos go, would you be willing to take Ragini to New Delhi to see her parents? I'll give her more than enough money to find her way back on her own."

"No problem to get her home. I will take her there. I owe it to my men to return them to Ireland. Most will stay there, but Santiago and I will go back to the sea with some green hands. The truth is, I want to retire with my family at Red Mountain or wherever else they may roam. I know you are planning on expanding the freight business with Banning. Maybe I could be part of that?"

"You would be welcome. I agreed to give Eli the first right of refusal on anything new that came up. Banning is a good opportunity, but Eli might say no to the deal because he is busy mining gold. It wouldn't matter. Banning would be thrilled to have you fill out the armored freight service with secure ocean transport. I need to talk to Amos, and I need to talk to Ragini."

Moses and Amos walked over to their home, and Connor stayed with the Professor and his wife in the guesthouses over at the fort. Yuma was growing into a half-passable city. It would take two more trips with the tenders to get all the freight from the *Adrianna* to Yuma. Connor watched Amos walk away with his father; he already walked with the swagger and sway of a man who had been at sea for years.

Connor chuckled at the possibility of a black-Irish sea captain. His whole family in the old country were considered *Black-Irish.* His brother, Aaden, was the only one who didn't make his living *smuggling*. Could be, he thought, *I could turn White with my nephew.* Connor spent the evening thinking of a fleet of fast ships with trusted crews for the sole purpose of transporting bullion, money, or other precious items like diamonds or diplomats. He was already planning a new generation of armored schooners with bigger, more versatile guns. He was also thinking long after dark of an armored piercing round that could put a steel ship on the bottom with one shot. He kept retrieving the guns from the sunken *Blessed,* a closely held secret between Santiago and the crew. The last thing they needed was unwanted attention while they worked to free the big guns from *The Blessed.*

Connor didn't have to wait long for his answers. The next day when he crossed the Colorado on the ferry, Ragini was waiting for him with a steamer trunk. Amos was by her side with a suitcase and saluted Connor when he stepped onto the dock. "Reporting for duty, Captain." The smile on Amos' face spread from ear to ear, and his eyes were on fire with adventure. Moses stood resolved with his hands in his pockets, ready to say goodbye to his son. He knew it was the best for Amos. He was thinking of the story of Irwin Higgins letting Ben go with Connor years ago on the dock in New Orleans. Deep down, he knew it was best for the boy. He was also sad to see Ragini leave, but that was different; he knew she would come back. The tenders finished unloading the cargo; it was time for farewells. Everyone on the dock hoped that this farewell would not be their last. Connor would wait for the last load of cargo to come up from the *Adrianna*. He stood as the tenders hoisted their sails, turned into the current, and disappeared down the river with Ragini and Amos aboard.

Connor knew Moses needed something to do right then. He turned to the big man and said, "Let's go get a drink. I have some ideas I want to run past you and also some drawings for you to look at." Friends, partners, associates; they didn't know exactly which as of yet, but they were working together, and that meant a lot to both of them.

The next day Connor left for Ireland, a voyage halfway around the world starting with a modest ride down the Colorado in a lifeboat, or so he let everyone think. Moses had a proposal that he needed to post to Banning. Eli hadn't seen the proposal for the armored freight line, and already Banning was being asked to expand the armored freight business to cover the seven seas. It was good for Moses; this would be the first trip he made to Red Mountain without his son. His men loaded the last of the crates of boxes and tools onto the wagons for the trip north. Moses could see the Professor and his wife with the girls waiting for him at the ferry dock, anxious to leave. His last task as he posted the letter to Banning was to collect a large bundle of newspapers from the post headquarters. The headline on the latest newspaper on the top of the bound bundle read

REBEL SIEGE OF CHATTANOOGA ENDS.

That is good, Moses thought; *the South is ready for a total defeat*.

Moses crossed the river with his small entourage. The girls ran to the carriage, but Professor Laity and his wife walked. Moses went to the end of the waiting wagon train. There were three of the heavy wagons there in line loaded with the parts of a bigger mine hoist for the top of Red Mountain. The last wagon was the armored transport with its double complement of mules and the Gatling gun; a second armored wagon trailed, hitched to the back of the first. The second wagon was going to remain at the RMM refinery.

Moses looked over every wagon on the train as he walked to the lead wagon. The girls were up with the driver on the stagecoach and yelled at Moses, "Let's go! Let's go!" Moses just nodded at them as he climbed up on the lead wagon. There was a driver so he could relax. As the driver released the brake and snapped the reins, Moses split the bindings on the bundle of newspapers. He would read every one by the time they reached Red Mountain. The pain of leaving Yuma without Amos grew softer as he read Lincoln's *Gettysburg Address. "Four score and seven years ago ....."* He read it over and over. By the time they reached Antelope Hill, he had memorized every word. He wished Amos was with him; he would have him memorize it too. One more week and he would have the girls reciting it under the ramada at Red Mountain.

By the time that week passed, Lia and Tio had excavated a tunnel back into the mountain. They were beyond the small cavern that had been the rattlesnake den. The floor of the small cavern was piled deep with dry-shed snakeskins. Tio worked like a madman on his tunnel every day since Maria had left. The miners were working their way out from Eliza's Secret Room; Tio could hear them through the cleft in the wall. Lia was leaving Tio's tunnel with a wheelbarrow full of diggings. She was building a switchback path down the mountainside with the cast-off rock Tio was mining. When she turned to the southeast at the turn of the path, she saw the supply train. She emptied the wheelbarrow and ran back to get Tio. When he saw the wagons, he ran straight down the mountain and sat down by the corral in the same spot where he was when Maria left.

It was almost an hour before Moses pulled to a stop with the lead wagon. By that time, everyone from the mine and mill had gathered to welcome the girls back. Roland was the first to notice that Amos was not at Moses' side. Moses walked to the ramada with the bundle of newspapers under his arm. To Red Mountain, the newspapers were like gold. They wanted more news about Gettysburg and Vicksburg. Moses waited until all the hugs and hellos finished, and then he said, "I have a surprise for you." He summoned Eliza and Maria over to him and announced in a commanding voice worthy of any ringmaster, "Lincoln's Gettysburg Address." The two girls recited the two-minute speech word-for-word.

Abby and Suzette were proud of their two girls. Tears welled in their eyes as they hugged their daughters, and they both sensed that their girls would never be the same after their trip to San Francisco. Suzette was not the first to wonder, but the first to ask, "Where is Amos?"

Maria answered with a tone of sadness in her voice. "He is on his way to Ireland with Uncle Connor. He wants to learn to be a sailor!" It seemed that Maria was more angry than sad when she finished her statement.

Lia hugged her niece and said, "Don't worry; he will come back." Maria shook her head, *no*. She didn't believe her.

Lia didn't want this to turn into a sad moment that lingered on and on. She said, "Tio and I have something to show you. Her path wasn't complete, but she led the girls up to the end of it, and they walked the rest of the way into Tio's tunnel. Eliza was thrilled; she knew that they were making a way into her secret room. She ran to the end of the short tunnel and then came out disappointed. Lia said, "Go back in and listen at the end of the tunnel."

Eliza and Maria went back in, and both come out with wide eyes and excited. "I can hear the miners in there. I called them, and they answered me. It can't be much farther. If I was still small, I could probably slip through the hole into my secret room."

"You're not to try that. Understand? Why don't you take Professor Laity around to the main tunnel on the other side? You can show him your secret room and also show him the end of the big tunnel where the miners found this bone." Lia took a fossil out of her pocket and handed it to Eliza. Eliza took it with wonder, a new find, and it looked like bones she saw in the museum at the Jesuit College. The girls ran down to get the Professor and his wife. When Lia walked down to the ramada, she sat with the rest of their family at the table and started reading the newspapers with them. The papers had graphic accounts of the battle of Gettysburg but stopped publishing the lists of the dead. It was bad for recruitment efforts. Lincoln's Gettysburg Address dominated the latest news. The armies of both sides were asleep for the winter; everyone knew, though, that Lincoln would have to turn the Army of the Potomac south and march on Richmond as soon as the weather broke.

Abby and Marie had Mrs. Laity between them, each holding a hand. First, they walked to the refinery and introduced Mrs. Laity to Mr. Sue. Mrs. Laity said, "Please call me Adrianna or Lila. My mother's name was also Adrianna, so I grew up being called Lila. My middle name is Lilian, but my sisters dubbed me, Lila. All my close friends call me that."

Abby said, "We are going to take them into the tunnel."

Mr. Sue said, "There is something new; let me show you." They walked up to the portal. It was noisy with the stamp mill hammering away and the rest of the machinery busy sorting out the gold from the ore. There was a steam-driven blower off to the side of the portal howling away as it blew air into a canvas tube that ran into the adit. There was a large board with a little roof over it just outside the mouth of the tunnel.

Mr. Sue had to shout over the noise to be heard, "This is a *tag-in-and-out* pegboard. It is for keeping track of who is underground. Everyone has a piece of brass with their name on it. All these men on the right side of the board are not underground; their brass is on hanging on the **OUT** side of the board. When you go in the mine, you move your brass to the underground-side of the board." He took his brass off from its hook on the right side and moved it to the left and hung it on a hook right under the word **UNDERGROUND**. "Now, I am tagged in." He turned and walked into the mine, taking the Professor and Lila with him. There were almost forty brass pieces on the board between the two sides. Abby and Maria were pleased to find they had brass pieces and moved them to indicate they were underground. There was another hanger board shaped like a mountain that was labeled **TOP**. Between the three boards, everyone who worked on the mine was accounted for, and a glance at the board told where everyone was located in the case of an emergency.

Inside the tunnel where it was quiet, Mr. Sue had more to say. "Tomorrow, I will have brass tags for you, Professor, and also one for you, Lila. Don't forget to move your token when you go out. If something happens like a cave-in, we will know who we have to rescue. If your token is in your pocket down at the settlement, lots of precious time will be wasted looking for you." The girls both nodded their understanding and then ran ahead anxious to show their visitors Eliza's Secret Room.

Mr. Sue went on as they walked into the mountain, "We stopped driving the tunnel when we found several more bones. We left them in place and started mining around both sides of what I think will be a complete skeleton. They walked on; kerosene lamps spaced every twenty feet lit the way. With a blower providing fresh air from outside the portal, there was no worry of fumes from the lanterns. The air supply wasn't enough to cool the inside of the mountain, but it was enough to provide the men working at the end of the tunnel a degree of relief. It swept enough heat and kerosene fumes out of the mountain to make the workspaces comfortable.

The girls were waiting at the drift that led to the cavern. It was also well lit. As they left the tracks of the main tunnel and started toward the cavern, Mr. Sue pointed out that there was a warm breeze to their backs. "The blower puts cold air into the end of the tunnel. It's a long way out to where we entered, so some of the air from the end of the tunnel comes this way. The cavern opens to the outside of the mountain. Tio is digging his way in from there. The air escapes out through the old opening. Did the girls tell you about the rattlesnake den?"

Lila got concerned, "Rattlesnakes! Are there still some here?"

"No, we killed all the small ones and ate all the big ones."

"You ate all the big ones?" The look on Lila's face was incredulous.

"Did," said Mr. Sue, "they taste good marinated with vinegar and oil laced with jalapenos."

They caught up with the girls in the cavern. Like the tunnel, it was well lit; there was only a trace of kerosene fume in the air. The Professor was impressed. There was a wooden-duck-board path around the edge of the cavern to where the miners were working on the opening to the outside. The floor of the cavern was undisturbed. The little table where Eliza was taking notes and making her drawings was still just as she had left it. Eliza showed the Professor where she found the large fang. The imprint of the fang remained undisturbed in the soft dirt of the floor.

"Remarkable," said the Professor. "We'll excavate the whole cavern down an inch at a time after the miners finish. These discoveries will not be as ancient as the skeleton in the main tunnel, but they will still be interesting and important in the overall cataloging of the site. Eliza, you and Maria will be in charge of this part of the dig. I am going to focus on the skeleton. If it is all there, it will be one of the first complete ones found in North America."

They went back to the main tunnel. The heat was still intense but not as bad with the cool air from the blower blowing into the room the miners were creating. The miners had completed an oval drift from the tailbone, extending twenty feet around where the rest of the skeleton must lay. They had started to mine out the roof so the area of the oval could be removed a layer at a time. The Professor took down one of the lanterns and knelt to inspect four more sections of tail bones. He turned slowly, craning his neck around to address Mr. Sue, "This is very good, very good indeed. I think you are right, Mr. Sue. Chances are very good that the remains of the entire animal are preserved here. We might have a complete and perfect fossil. I want to go out and have my tools brought in here and get started."

And so it began. The professor began work on the more important site, and Eliza and Maria started the excavation of the cavern; Tio continued working his way into the cavern from the rattlesnake den, and the miners did the heavy lifting of carrying out the rock removed in the excavation of the *digs*. The miners sifted everything removed from the mountain for small bones, and then all the rock went into the gold mill when the professor was satisfied that it was clean. The location of every bone the girls found was measured from three monument markers John had driven into the walls of the cavern. Eliza and Maria would enter the measurements in a logbook, and if it were a large bone, they would draw it onto a map for that layer of the cavern, label, and save it. The girls drew a map for every one-inch layer. Lila oversaw the girls' work, but it was rare that she ever had to help or correct errors.

Every day the girls would finish up with a visit to the dig at the end of the main tunnel. Every night *Cliff*, as the Professor now wanted to be called, would go over every find the girls posted on their map. Abby and Suzette would look on with great pride at their young paleontologists; even Tio had a map of his tunnel, and every day, he would mark his progress. He was close to connecting with the miners working their way out from the cavern. He could shake hands with them through the narrow opening to the cavern. He had made only one trip into the cavern from the main tunnel; one time was more than enough. He was too big to stand in the miners' tunnels. He had to crawl most of the way in, all the way in from the portal at the mill. It was an exhausting trip for him; Lia and Suzette stayed with him all the way, worried that he would get stuck. Everyone was relieved when Tio came back out of the passageway to the cavern. John met them at the tracks with a flat mine car and wheeled Tio to the portal. Tio thought it was great fun; everyone thought the big man would ease off for the rest of the day, but he returned to his tunnel with more enthusiasm than ever. Maria was inside the mountain every day, and he wanted to be able to spend his days with her.

Everyone kept digging. As Eliza and Maria worked their way down, they soon discovered that the floor of the cavern was shaped like a dish or more like a soup bowl. It wouldn't be long before they were to the bottom of it. The Professor had excavated the entire tail of a large dinosaur. Every time he found a bigger piece of the tail, he upped his speculation as to just what they would have when it was all uncovered. John, Eli, and Roland just kept digging for gold. Mr. Sue was in the lead business. He had built a small reverberatory furnace next to the refinery using a hearth that Moses shipped in from San Francisco. He wasn't producing lead metal; he was using the hearth furnace to make lead oxide out of the galena ore from Weaver Mountain. The lead oxide was the red litharge used in fire assaying.

Tio had completed the tunnel into the cavern and spent all his time in there with Maria and Eliza. The excavation of the floor was complete. The girls had found hundreds of shattered bones but no complete skeletons. The saber-toothed tigers that lived there had done a good job of crushing the bones to get at the marrow. The girls did find one more fang, but it wasn't as large as the first. Professor Laity, *Cliff*, was a bit disappointed but not surprised. Most of the bone fragments were from small mammals. He said that what the mature tigers didn't eat, the cubs would gnaw on, spending their days in the den until they were big enough to hunt on their own. As Cliff excavated more of the skeleton in the main tunnel, the girls were assembling it piece by piece under Lila's watchful eye. They had completed the tail, hindquarters, and rear feet of the skeleton. Tio watched with reverence and helped make the wood supports for every bone. He stayed with the girls every day until they left the cavern to check on the main dig. Then he would come out of his portal and heckle Mary in the kitchen for some food. More than ever, the giant man was hungry after a hard day's work.

There were a lot more people arriving in the Arizona Territory, and a good deal of them would come to Wickenburg looking for work in the mines. It was hard not to notice that a lot of the newcomers were southerners. Some still wore pieces of tattered gray uniforms. Some were better dressed and better equipped but were still easy to identify from their deep-southern drawls. It was easy to figure out. The rugged, lean men still wearing parts of, or complete rebel uniforms were deserters. The better dressed and equipped men were paroled prisoners-of-war. Some of these men returned to frontline units and rejoined the battles. Some of them returned home and stayed with their families. Some of them were disgusted with the losing cause and came west to start a new life. The deserters were dangerous. The parolees were honorable men, honoring their pledge to never again bear arms against the United States of America. These men were welcome. The deserters usually moved on, but of the ones that stayed, most wound up in Weaver Creek, falling in with the likes of Bill Stanton.

One beautiful spring morning would become the most memorable in RMM history. Three soldiers came riding up to the clinic. They were riding close abreast, and the outside two were supporting the rider in the middle. They pulled up at the corral and got the man down from his saddle and held him up as they walked him into the clinic. Suzette and Bridgette met them at the door. The settlement, it was now called a townsite, was empty other than the doctor and her nurse. Mary was over in the kitchen with the toddlers. Suzette had the sick man put on the gurney in the examination room in the front of the clinic. He didn't have any external wounds. She asked, "How long has he been in this condition."

One of the men answered, "Just since this morning." The other man, who had corporal stripes on his sleeves, left the clinic, making the excuse that he was going to put their horses in the corral. Bridgette could see the man through the door, and he didn't go to the corral. He was looking around the houses and making sure nobody else was in the townsite. All the men were working in the mine, Lia and Abby were in the refinery making coins; only Mary was there, over in the kitchen with the youngsters. Bridgette was wary; her streetwise sixth sense was telling her that something was wrong. She could see that the revolver in the Corporal's holster was not an Army issue revolver. Another detail, the boots on the sick man were not right.

When the third man returned, he reported to the Corporal in a telltale southern drawl, "All clear, we're the only ones here except for a woman and some kids over in the kitchen."

The realization came too late for Bridgette to act. The man on the gurney pulled his revolver and pressed it up under Suzette's chin. The Corporal grabbed Bridgette and put a knife to her throat. These men were deserters posing as Union soldiers. The sick man got up and pressed Suzette back against the wall with the revolver still under her chin. The Corporal spoke, "Now, girls, we are all going to wait here for a little while. Just stay calm, and no one will get hurt."

Over at the mine, more than twenty men had left their horses at the miners' camp and walked to the mill through the camp. They left a half-dozen men there to guard the camp. The rest of the troop walked to the mill and gathered up the operators and held them hostage. Four men went to the refinery. One was Chinese, dressed as a gunslinger. At the door, the gunslinger drew his revolver. The rest of his band had all types of rifles and revolvers, mixed remnants from the war. They pulled their revolvers; cocked their rifles. These men did not attempt to disguise their identity. The gunslinger walked into the refinery, and the three other men followed him in.

Mr. Sue was in front of his assay furnace, extracting a white-hot crucible from the furnace. The Chinese gunslinger walked up behind him and said,

"Lǎo Dragon. Remember me?" He pressed the barrel of his revolver to the base of Mr. Sue's skull.

Mr. Sue put down the crucible and closed the furnace door. He turned slowly, craning his neck around to see who was behind him. "Xiǎo Wang Wei!" Then he continued in Chinese, *"Hello, nephew. I see you are not honoring the name my sister gave you."* Mr. Sue looked through the door to the coin room. Two men were guarding him with guns drawn. The third man was handcuffing Lia and Abby to the heavy wheel of the coin press.

"Open the safe, old man, or I will kill the women."

"You, nephew, are dishonoring your family and signing your death warrant. Don't hurt anybody here, and you might be spared. I'll open the safe. There is around three-hundred thousand in gold in there." With the gun still at the back of his skull, Mr. Sue knelt on one knee to work the combination and then opened the safe.

As soon as Wang Wei saw the gold, he used the barrel of his gun to land a vicious blow to the top of his uncle's head. The tough Mr. Sue went down, unconscious. "Sleep well, Dragon. I will see you again in hell."

The three men loaded the gold into two strongboxes and carried it out to a packhorse that had been brought up to the door of the refinery. They tied the two strongboxes together and slung them over the back of the packhorse, one on each side. The band of robbers brought their mounts around from the back of the mountain, saddled up, and waited at the refinery. All the rest of the outlaw troops were now mounted and ready to ride. They made sure the operators were not armed and that the miners' camp was still quiet. Wang Wei fired a shot into the air and waited until the three Union soldiers rode over from the townsite. They rode to the south in a column of twos, just like a company of soldiers would. Had they gone to the north and around the hill, they might have gotten away clean.

Lia and Abby came running out of the refinery. Lia's wrist was bleeding bad; she had cut herself when she slipped the handcuff. Abby still had her half of the handcuffs around her left wrist. They climbed Moses's armored wagon that had been left there for the sole purpose of strengthening the security of the refinery. The gun was on a hinged mount, laid down in its traveling cradle. The two women were struggling to lift the heavy Gatling gun and lock the mount into its firing position. Between the two of them, they couldn't quite get it high enough to lock the mount in place. Lia started yelling, "**TIO. TIO. TIO, help me!**" The big man was in the machine shop all through the robbery, working on a piece of metal for the dinosaur mount. The outlaw that guarded him through the robbery was gone. He came running to Lia's call.

He didn't know what was wrong, but he saw the two women struggling with the gun. He rocked the heavy wagon as he climbed the ladder. He lifted the Gatling gun and the mount up into the firing position with one hand. No sooner than they heard the mount mechanism slap home, Abby was loading a magazine into the hopper on top of the gun. Lia was on the handles swiveling the gun at the escaping column. Tio knew how the gun worked; without being told, he started turning the handle.

The column was at least three-hundred yards away and was lined up at a slight angle to the gun. The outlaws were riding down the road to the Hassayampa. Lia had swiveled the gun to aim at the lead horse before the first round left the barrel. After the first few rounds, the gun smoke was so thick she couldn't see the column. Abby kept loading, and Tio kept up the steady hail of death, turning the handle. By the time the gun overheated and jammed, the ground around the armored wagon was littered with empty magazines, and the floor of the gun box was covered with empty shell casings. The smoke cleared; there were five riders left in their saddles. The packhorse was down along with all the rest of the mounts that didn't run away after their riders fell under the hail of lead.

The five men turned back for the gold but gave up that idea when one dropped from the saddle with a rifle shot from the townsite. It was Mary firing from a prone position on top of the table under the ramada. John had taught her how to shoot, and she was shooting like a true markswoman. Suzette and Bridgette were firing with their revolvers. It would be a miracle if they hit anyone at that distance, but the noise made it sound like there was a much bigger force over at the settlement. Mary fired again and shot the horse out from under Wang Wei. That was enough for the young hoodlum. He swung up behind another rider, and they rode away to save their lives. The renegades didn't know there was a Gatling gun at the refinery when they started the raid. They turned toward the river and pushed the horses as fast as they would go. If the Gatling gun opened up on them again, they wouldn't survive.

No one inside the mountain had a clue as to what was happening. The miners camp was awake now, and all the men at the mill were gunned-up and ready if the robbers dared to return. That was doubtful; they had suffered massive casualties and knew defeat well. The women at the townsite were breathing a sigh of relief. Other than the one shot that signaled their three gunmen to join up with the main force, the robbers fired no other shots before the Gatling gun opened up. The relief didn't last long. Tio was carrying Mr. Sue in his arms and running to the clinic. Tears were running down the giant's face, and he couldn't talk. He carried Mr. Sue into the clinic and laid him down on the examining table. Suzette and Bridgette got to work as Tio pointed to the massive knot on the top of Mr. Sue's head. Bridgette soothed the big man who was still crying. "You did well, Tio. You are a hero. Mr. Sue will be fine. Suzette will take care of him. You'll see; he will be fine."

Lia had run into the mine to alert Eli and Roland. Roland knew when he saw his wife's bloody wrist that something bad had happened. Roland bandaged Lia's wrist with a clean bandana, and the three of them came running out of Tio's tunnel. Eli and Roland ran to the corral and started to saddle their horses. Abby was at the door of the clinic, out of breath. Lia had lost a lot of blood. She sank to her knees, and Abby gathered her up and took her into Suzette. She stayed there to help Bridgette staunch the bleeding. Suzette was still working on Mr. Sue. She had the knot, and the area around it shaved. She was preparing a surgical drill to drill a hole into his skull and relieve the pressure inside. Mary was back in the kitchen with the children. Eliza and Maria joined her; the children were scared and wanted to know what had happened.

Over at the mill, the operators were hitching mule teams to wagons and going out to retrieve their gold and pick up any wounded. By the time they got out to the scene of the carnage, it wasn't necessary. Eli and Roland had shot several wounded in cold blood and then put the wounded horses out of their misery. The men had to roll the packhorse off one of the strongboxes and then loaded both on a wagon. They policed all the weapons so the Apache wouldn't find them when they moved in to scavenge the bodies. The gold and the operators went back to the mill. Eli and Roland rode over to the clinic. They wanted to track down the rest of the renegades and kill them, but they needed Abby to track them. Lia had told them about the Chinese gunslinger, Wang Wei, Mr. Sue's nephew. He wouldn't get far riding double.

Eli said, "Wang Wei. What does that mean in English?"

Roland knew it wasn't a moment for levity, but he couldn't resist the irony. "*Wang Wee* – Little Dick, of course."

Everyone laughed but sobered in an instant when Abby walked out of her house in buckskins, her machete on her back, a revolver on her hip, and a Henry rifle over her shoulder. "Let's go get them," she said. Eli already had her horse saddled. John and Mary were tying trail packs and saddlebags with three days of provisions on the backs of the saddles. Eli and Roland wanted to check with Suzette and Bridgette on Mr. Sue before they left. Suzette was still concentrating on the hole needed to relieve the pressure. She looked up at her brothers and shook her head *no*. Mr. Sue was still unconscious. She wouldn't know if he would recover without brain damage or even die. The injury was as severe as it could be, but the skull was not fractured as Wang Wei must have intended.

The three of them rode down to the carnage and then picked up the trail to the south. The renegades didn't ride down the river. They turned and took the road into Wickenburg. The horse with the double rider was easy to track with the deep print it left in the soft dirt. One of the other horses had broken a shoe. Their riders might just as well have stayed in plain sight. Abby didn't even have to slow down to follow the trail. It led past Wickenburg's stamp mill and right into the heart of town. There in front of the *Rainbow's End* bar, the deep prints changed to a single rider and headed down the river road to the south. There was another bar on the other side of the street named *The Pot of Gold*. There were several old-timers there rocked back in chairs under the veranda; all three pointed at the bar across the street. Eli and Roland tied off on the hitching posts, checked their weapons, and walked into the bar. Abby followed but stayed at the door with her eye on the street, her Henry at the ready.

There were only a handful of men that frequented the *Rainbow's End* that time of the morning. Only one had a look of fear about him as the drinkers turned to look over the newcomers. The man with the fear had fresh blood splattered on his shirt. His hand went to his gun. Two Henry rifles tore his chest open. Eli and Roland walked out of the bar without saying a word. The Undertaker was running over from his shop next door to the *Pot of* Gold; he was hoping that whoever they shot had money for a proper burial. Eli flipped the undertaker a ten-dollar Red Mountain gold coin. The threesome mounted up and rode down to the river to pick up the trail. There Abby spotted a telltale drop of blood. "One of them is wounded. We have to be careful down in the canyon. They might be holed up in the brush nursing wounds."

There was no need to follow at a gallop. The trail was easy to follow. Eli thought back to the first time he came up the river bottom. Now there was a real road up on the side of the river. They had an advantage. *Little Dick* had never seen them at the mine. They, however, knew who they were after. A Chinaman couldn't hide in the middle of the Arizona Territory, and a wounded man would need care. There was a settlement at the mouth of the Hassayampa, but the trail didn't stop there. "This is good," Abby said. "Two are walking their horses; one is still in the saddle. Unless they have canteens, they will have to stay on the river for water."

Unhurried, they kept moving down the river. True to its name, the water disappeared into the sand as soon as they were out of the canyon. Roland and Eli rode to the top of every prominence, trying to spot the outlaws out ahead. Abby was crossing the river bottom and tracking to the west. Eli and Roland rode down to join up with her. "They are heading to Vulture City," Abby said as she knelt at the top of the west bank, examining another drop of blood. "This drop of blood is maybe ten minutes old. We are catching up with them. All three are riding again. Two are riding fast, the one that is bleeding didn't rest his horse. He will be falling behind, or maybe they will leave him in Vulture City. There's a sawbones there that takes care of the miners. I bet he will have a patient with a gunshot wound in a little while."

They covered the ten miles to the Vulture Gold Mine at a gallop. Vulture City was in an uproar when they rode into the town. Men gathered at the livery stable, and they were in a heated argument. Eli got down into the middle of them and asked, "What's going on?"

A man dressed in the leather apron of a blacksmith with massive forearms from a life at the forge must have thought Eli and Roland were lawmen. The blacksmith was raving mad, "A Chinaman and his partners rode in here and stole two horses. They took my best ones; all saddled up with trail packs and everything. They left those two behind along with the one that the third man rode up to the doctor's office. He fell off his horse right at Doc's doorstep. I want you to catch those two who got away. I want my horses and gear back."

Roland spoke first, "We are not lawmen, but if you have some good horses to trade for these, we will go after them."

"Sorry, buddy. Those are good horses; I can see that. I don't have anything left here but hags and plugs. You would do better resting your horses and then go track them down. They went south on the road back to the Hassayampa. East or west at the Gila is the only choice unless they go south over the desert to Mexico. The Indians will know which way they went."

Roland thanked the man, and they left all three of their mounts with him for some feed and water. The man broke into a big grin when Eli gave him an RMM $10 gold piece for his trouble. He led the horses into the stable. They took their rifles out of their scabbards and walked up Main Street to the doctor's office. The crowd at the livery dispersed. Everyone above ground at a gold mine had a job to go to on the day shift. Off-shift miners would be asleep, just as the miners at RMM had been when the outlaws showed up. The surface crew would be sawing timber, repairing tools, or loading wagons with ore for shipment over to Wickenburg for milling. Main Street was quiet behind them when they reached the Doc.

He indeed looked and acted like a sawbones. Scruffy-unkempt clothing, a drinker's red nose, and the potbelly to go with it; he not only reeked of whiskey but swayed when he walked to block his doorway. He spoke with the raspy voice of years of alcohol and cigarettes, "You can't take him, he is unconscious. I stopped the bleeding, but his shoulder is busted up bad. He needs a lot more care than I can give him, and even if that were available, he would probably still wind up crippled."

Eli didn't want to let the man out of their sight, and Abby was quick to ensure that that wouldn't happen. "Can I stay with him? I am his wife."

The drunk sawbones stepped aside and let Abby into his office. The wounded man was passed out on a table in the second room of the two-room shack. Abby poured some water into a basin and started to clean him up. His arm was bloody from the shoulder to the end of his fingers. It was a convincing act, exactly what a concerned wife would do finding her husband badly wounded. The sawbones settled down with a bottle in the front room. Eli and Roland walked over to Wickenburg's mine office to gather what information the mining town had to offer on their Chinese friend.

Wickenburg jumped up from behind his desk as Eli and Roland entered. "Eli! Roland! What brings you here to the second-best gold mine in Arizona? Hope you aren't involved in the trouble over at the stable?"

"We are. There was an attempted robbery this morning up at our refinery. Around twenty men led by a Chinaman who, as incredible as it may seem, is Mr. Sue's nephew. You ever see him before?"

"Gunslinger, right? All dressed in black? Two ivory-handled Colts?" Eli and Roland were nodding their affirmation to all the questions. "He has been hanging around here for several weeks. He wanted a job guarding the ore shipments from here to the mill. Also, he wanted to guard the gold shipments down to Yuma, but Moses takes care of that just fine with his armored freighters. I sent him away. He didn't look trustworthy to me."

Roland said, "Good call, he seriously wounded Mr. Sue, his uncle. If I find him, Henry, I'm going to kill him."

"I expect you won't find him. They rode out of here hard, and both the little chink and his partner had the best horses in town; one of them was mine. The horses have full packs for the trail with provisions, ammo, bedrolls, everything for a week on the desert. If he is Mr. Sue's nephew, I would look for him to show up in Chinatown up in San Francisco. They will try to make it look like they headed for Yuma, but this time of year, they will probably split up and make their way up the east side of the Sierras. It's easy to hide out as a Chinaman over in the Mother Lode country."

Eli invited Wickenburg to come up again and see the dinosaur dig and the new equipment he and John had for the mine. Wickenburg said, "I would like to see the dinosaur, but I am losing my interest in mining. I want to sell this place. There is a group from back east that's going to come by and look at the mine. If they make me an offer, I'm going to take it. How about you fellows? Would you be interested in buying it?"

Eli answered. "We have our hands full right now, and our ore is still getting richer as we mine deeper, and the nuggets we are finding are getting bigger. As soon as the dinosaur is out of the way, we will continue sinking the shaft. The shaft is going to connect to the end of the tunnel. No use going down any farther until we can pump water and get more air into the mine." Eli shook Wickenburg's hand, and they walked back to the Doc's office.

There was a new bar in Vulture City; it was called *The Rancid Bird*. The brothers always had a beer together whenever they came to town. The doctor's office was within easy view from the bar. The visit to the bar was productive. Roland bought a round for the house (there were only three patrons and a bar girl dressed for action), and he learned the name of the man who escaped with *Little Dick*. Robby Galveston was one lucky bandit, but along with *Little Dick*, he was now a marked man.

Roland said, "Let's gather up Abby and go home. We won't catch them with tired horses and the head start they got. Another thing, if they split up, you and I are not going separate. We would have to turn around and come back. If Mr. Sue lives, he will kill his nephew. Galveston is a different story.

He could hide anywhere, but if he doesn't change his name, a guy named after a famous port in the Union blockade will be easy to track by word-of-mouth."

Abby was leaving the doctor's office as they crossed the street. Eli asked, "What about your *husband*?"

"He's dying of infection. I want to go home."

"Infection?" Eli was incredulous. "He only had a broken shoulder and a small opened wound. He wouldn't even show infection for a day or so if he even had one!"

"Trust me, he has one," was all Abby had to say as they turned toward the livery.

Resurrection

Ragini was an experienced world traveler. When Connor rounded the tip of Baja California and turned north, she knew that she wasn't going directly home. Amos was standing with her on the forecastle looking across the vast Pacific, searching for the pods of Grey Whales they saw on the way down. Ragini knew they were sailing up the coast and wondering what Connor was up to, she turned Amos aft with her hand on his shoulder and said, "Let's go see your captain.

The second mate was at the con and told them that Connor and Santiago were below in the Captain's quarters. They walked down the port ladder to the main deck so Amos could continue his watch for the whales. He didn't want to go below, so Ragini left him at the gunwale, his eyes sweeping the sea intent as any New England Whaler. Ragini walked through the officer's mess and entered the companionway that led to the Captain's quarters. Respectfully, she knocked on the door and called, "Captain, I want to talk to you."

Santiago opened the door and stood aside so she could enter. Connor was sitting at his chart table, working on a drawing. There wasn't a chart visible anywhere except rolled up in the cubbyholes behind the table. Laid out on the table was a large sheet of paper, and the two men had drawn a detailed sketch of a sailboat. Ragini raised an eyebrow looking at the drawing, and Connor said, "It's *The Blessed*; we're going back for the guns. Maybe we will try to raise the whole boat if it is possible.

Ragini marveled at the cabin. Mr. Banning spared no expense when he refurbished the *Adrianna.* Dark teakwood lined the walls. Polished-brass hurricane lanterns hung over the chart table for working at night. Sunlight streamed down from a skylight over the chart table and lit not only the chart table but the whole cabin. A set of ship's clocks and an elegant compass adorned the sideboard of the table. The windows at the back of the cabin were heavy-tinted glass and shaded by the transom behind the helm. The bed under the windows rivaled the finest found in hotels around the world. The cabin even had a privy behind a door fashioned to look like a closet. Ragini swayed back and forth with the roll of the ship and finally remembered why she came to talk to Connor.

Ragini smiled, "I knew we were not on a course for India as soon as we turned up the coast. Where are we going?"

Connor could see no harm in telling her. Every sailor on the ship knew. Ragini and Amos were the only ones still in the dark. "*The Blessed* went down in the shallows off the south shore of Santa Cruz Island. I apologize for not telling you sooner, but this part of our voyage was kept a secret while we were in San Francisco. I didn't want anyone to know that I might have the guns back, and I didn't want to have to compete with a salvage company for the privilege of raising my father's ship. The guns are incredibly valuable. We had to keep the location a complete secret."

Ragini wasn't upset. She said, "You have a good and loyal crew. Not a single man ever mentioned or implied that we were not going directly to India. How long do you think it will take?'

"Hopefully, not more than a week. She has been on the bottom for more than a month. We won't know until we get there and get started."

"Do you have a diver?"

"Yes, we do. Young Xander grew up diving for sponges with his father off the coast of Greece. You have probably seen him training, holding his breath, and running up the mainstays until he is ready to drop."

Ragini wasn't sure she wanted to volunteer, but she finally offered, "Sponges aren't the only things people dive for; I grew up diving for pearls. Maybe I could help?"

Santiago asked, "How long has it been since you dived for pearls?"

"More than ten years," Ragini answered.

Connor asked, "How long can you stay down?"

"Several minutes. Mabey longer if I start training."

Now, Connor came to the last problem. "Xander will probably dive naked. We can't have you doing that. Santiago and I will talk this over. You might want to find something to wear that won't get the crew overly excited while you dive."

"I can sew. I will make myself a diving suit out of sailcloth. How deep is the sunken ship?"

"Less than forty feet," Santiago answered. "It would be good to have a rescue diver ready if Xander should become tangled or trapped in the wreck. There may also be some heavy lifting you could help with on the bottom. There will be some danger. I can't let you get hurt. Moses would kill us both if something happened to you. You should train and get your diving suit together. Xander will still be the lead, and you are to follow his orders all the time you are down. We will work out some way for him to signal us if he is in trouble."

Connor asked, "Are you sure you want to do this?"

Ragini rolled her head and gave Connor a look all women used to put a mere man in his place. "Of course, I want to help. I don't want to sit around and watch."

"Okay. It will take almost a week to get to the wreck. This cargo ship is no racing schooner. You will have plenty of time to get ready. We won't start until you are ready."

Ragini turned and had one more look around the cabin. She said as she walked to the door, "Thanks, Connor, or Captain Connor. I won't let you down, and I won't hold you up." She walked the few steps along the companionway to the first mate's cabin. Santiago had vacated it for her and moved all the rest of the mates one more cabin down the line. Her cabin was by no means shabby, but nowhere close to the luxury of the Captain's cabin. It was infinitely better than the third-class passage she had on her first trip to America.

Ragini went through her luggage. She had a corset with whalebone ribs. She didn't wear a corset regularly, only for fancy occasions. She found the corset at the bottom of her footlocker, under her evening gowns. She set to work stripping out the ribs. Next, she needed a sailor's needle, heavy thread or light rope, and sailcloth. A diving suit would be easy, but she needed some light deck shoes or a pair of Chinese slippers for the other item she had in mind. When she finished stripping the whalebone ribs, she went looking for the sailmaker in the crew.

Connor was right. A trip that they could have made in a few days in the schooner was going to take a week in the freighter. Ragini couldn't find a pair of shoes or slippers that would serve her designs. She asked Connor if he could put in at San Pedro so that she could do some shopping for her diving gear. Santiago thought that it would be a good idea. Not just for shopping but to give the crew some shore time to have their ashes hauled. He and Connor wouldn't mind a visit to Madam Wong's brothel. It had been a long time for them and the crew. It would be good to give them all something to think about and remember instead of lusting after Ragini in whatever she created for a diving suit.

San Pedro was warm and inviting as usual. Banning turned into the bay ahead of them in his flagship clipper. Connor admired the sleek ship and its broad expanse of sail. He would own one of those soon. For now, he was going to talk to Banning about his plans for *The Blessed*.

Connor docked *Adrianna* at the pier, and he and Santiago rowed over to *The Banning*, which dropped anchor in the center of the bay. They took Amos with them; he was learning to row a small lifeboat that they chose to make the short-haul over to *The Banning*. The rest of the men drew lots to see who would stay on watch at the ship. Two sailors with the short straws moaned, "Don't stay too long," as the crew headed down the gangplank, escorting Ragini to the shops on Main Street. Ragini didn't find what she wanted until she reached the shoemaker on the backstreet. The crew found what they wanted as fast as Madam Wong's girls could service them. Madam Wong herself was waiting for the Captain and the tall-dark First Mate.

Ragini returned to the *Adrianna,* and she told one of the crew members left behind that she would take his watch. The sailor was reluctant at first but agreed when he saw that Ragini was armed. She only had to show the butt of her Navy Colt under her dress to convince the sailor she was capable of guard duty. She was sitting in the shade of the mainmast with her sewing project when Connor and Santiago returned from Banning's clipper with Amos pulling at the oars of the lifeboat like a seasoned sailor. When Connor climbed over the gunwale of the *Adrianna,* he saw Ragini sitting with her back to the mainmast, working with the sailmaker's tools.

Connor asked, "What are you doing?"

"Well, first, I am on watch. I let one of the crew go into town, and I took his place. I hope you don't mind?" She could see that both men were looking at her assortment of sailcloth, whalebone ribs, and the pair of shoes she bought in town. "Second, I am building a swim tail. Divers in my village back home use them for deep diving. Western sailors call it a mermaid's tail. Mabey it is what started the myth. I'm having trouble making the holes in the bottoms of these slippers how I want. I might have to go back to the shoemaker."

Connor didn't address the man who left his post. He would have a chat with him later. He sat down next to Ragini and asked, "I would like to know more about your pearl diving. We are going to be at sea for quite a while. I would like to know more about your village and your father, your family, where you grew up. I will have to know how to find you when you are ready to return to Yuma."

Ragini looked at Connor with the saddest eyes he ever saw. It was if a cloud shadowed the sun, and the temperature dropped ten degrees. "Connor, it is easy for me to talk about India, not so easy to talk about my father. He was killed diving for pearls. The pearl beds offshore from my village are about fifteen kilometers out in the ocean. The depth there was about twenty-five meters deep. A shark bit my father. He made it to the surface but bled to death before they could get him to shore. My mother went insane, and one morning she was gone. We never saw her again. Our village was old, Chenna Patnam, just a slum now in the port of Madras. My brothers and sisters may not be there anymore. Ten years ago, before my mother left, she gave me a large pearl, very valuable. I bought passage to Los Angeles with it and been in America ever since."

Connor put his hand on Ragini's shoulder, "I didn't want to make you sad, and now I am worried about leaving you in Madras while I go back to Ireland. What if I don't make it back?"

Ragini put her hand over Connor's and said sincerely, "You don't have to worry about me. Moses gave me more than enough gold to ensure I could buy my passage back to America. I will be fine. One of the millions of Shudras, invisible in a sea of humanity."

"What is a Shudra?" Connor asked.

"You have much to learn about India, my friend. The British called the Shudras – *Untouchables.* Not a very becoming name, but most of the people in India are in that caste. They do the work of growing the food, keeping the streets clean, hauling out the night waste. That is where the nickname probably started. My village was *Paravars*, seafarers, fishermen, pearl divers; Paravar is a subclass of the Shudra caste. It's complicated, too complicated for a Western mind. The British couldn't comprehend three-thousand separate castes. They boiled it down to just four. We were on the bottom."

"Maybe I will stay there with you and let Santiago take the Adriana back to Ireland."

Ragini turned thoughtful, "I don't think you would enjoy it very much. You should go to nice places. Go to Delhi, see the Taj Mahal, shop for diamonds and rubies, find a guru or a doctor. There is no place for you to stay in Chenna Patnam. For all I know, it wouldn't be safe now for a foreigner."

Connor made a suggestion, "There must be a hotel in Madras. We could stay there and look for your family on short trips to your village. When you are ready, we both could ride a clipper back to the states. Think about it; you don't have to decide now."

Two men were returning to take the watch. Connor met them at the gangplank. Connor called Santiago to join him; it was time for the two men to walk into town. Amos was anxious to go with them. Santiago had been talking to the boy. Connor looked the boy over. He wasn't a boy anymore. Amos was seventeen; it didn't seem possible. Connor agreed to let him come along. They weren't in a hurry, but neither of them wanted to leave San Pedro, perhaps for the last time, without seeing Madam Wong. They also wanted to initiate Amos into one of the time-honored ways of the sea. Connor was sure the young man would never forget Madam Wong's establishment.

San Pedro had a lot to offer a lonely sailor. It was two days before Connor had the *Adrianna* sailing up the coast for Santa Cruz Island. The weather was clear, and Amos was at the con. As they neared the Island, Santiago was on the bowsprit, looking for the wreck on the bottom. He didn't see it on the first pass because it was more than half covered with sand. Connor took the con and tacked over to where *The Blessed* fired its last shot. He furled most of the sail and then slowly traversed back over the track they took struggling to get *The Blessed* into the shallow water. The tactic worked; Santiago signaled to drop anchor when he spotted the wreck.

Connor joined Santiago on the bowsprit, and Xander was ready to dive. Ragini called in alarm from midships, "Wait!" She was pointing to a small beach on the island where hundreds of seals were scrambling to get out of the water. Then she went over to the gunwale and peered into the depths. There was nothing at first, but then hundreds of hammerhead sharks swam by in a huge school. Most of them were nearly twenty feet long. If it were only the hammerheads, neither Xander nor Ragini would have been too concerned. But the rookery of seals had to be afraid of other predators. There was blood in the water a short way off the beach, and a large fin of a shark could be seen before the shark dove to rejoin the cover of the school of hammerheads.

When the school of hammerheads was gone, Ragini nodded at Xander, and he dove on the wreck. While the men were watching Xander on the bottom, Ragini dropped her robe and picked up her swim fin. Xander wasn't the main attraction when she climbed the gunwale and slipped her feet into the slippers on the swim fin. The sailcloth suit she made for herself was modest, but there was still a lot to catch everyone's attention. Her brown legs were muscular, and the suit perfectly outlined her ample body. The men feasted their eyes as she bent over to fasten the straps on the fin, and Ragini was grateful that Connor allowed them two days to languish around Madam Wong's, the Mermaid Bar, and the Seaman's Hotel. Without hesitation, she dove into the water and swam like a dolphin down to the wreck.

Both divers were down for what seemed like four minutes. Santiago had the men lower a hinged shelf that he had built at the water line to serve as a diving platform. Xander bobbed to the surface and hauled himself up onto the deck, deftly turning in the air before he fell back onto his butt. Ragini burst from the surface, almost completely out of the water, turned in the air, and landed on her butt next to Xander. Everyone was astonished, especially Xander; there was still a lot he had to learn about diving and swimming. No one believed in mermaids, but all agreed that they had finally seen one.

The men had set up a table on the forecastle and pinned the drawing of *The Blessed* down, so it was safe from the wind. Santiago had the anchor raised so they could drift to a better position over the wreck. Connor and Santiago sat in the chairs brought up from the officer's mess, and Xander and Ragini joined them at the table. Ragini had her swim fin under her arm. Connor looked at her and said, "That was the most amazing thing I have ever seen and believe me; I have been watching women swim all over the world."

Ragini was modest and a little shy with all the men still looking at her. She responded, "It is nothing, swim fins are common along the coast of India and Ceylon. Even the children make them. Let's talk about what you want us to do next."

Connor took charge of the impromptu meeting. "I want the guns, of course, but I also want the aiming telescopes from the pulpit. That's going to be hard. It appears they are under the sand. We have some small mines for opening the hull to get the guns. I hope that the gundeck isn't full of sand. We can free the gun mounts with the explosives, but they have to be placed right next to the bolts to break the timbers under the gun carriages. You'll have your work cut out for you. Ragini, I only want Xander to handle the mines. It is dangerous work, and he has been training to do it ever since we left San Francisco. You will be mostly standby if he should become tangled in the wreck, especially when he is placing the mines. You can dive and help with all the other work. We have a float that Xander can release if he is in trouble. If it hits the surface, I know that you can dive and reach him in seconds. Tell me about the sharks; you seem to know enough to be wary of them.

"Ragini answered, "The hammerheads are harmless in the daytime. They hunt at night and swim in schools during the day. They don't eat seals and have not been known to attack humans. It is the bigger sharks that are the most dangerous. You saw the blood in the water and the fin. I think that was a great white, worst of the hunter-killers. Attacks aren't very common, but they are deadly when they occur. I think any big sharks in the area will be well fed by the seal population. Not much to worry about unless they are hungry and think we are a seal."

Santiago disappeared into the forecastle and returned with a trident. The points were razor-sharp, and the handle was a light wood, perfectly balancing the steel trident, so it was at neutral buoyancy in the water. Santiago said, "They dive off the coast of Spain too, and there is always one diver on guard armed with one of these." He handed the trident to Ragini, and his mind flashed back to teaching Lily how to throw the pirate's knife after they left Pamlico Sound many years ago. A different ocean, a woman of a different color, but so much that time had not changed. He would teach Ragini how to throw the trident like a harpoon and also had a knife for her to wear on her back when she dove. He would teach her how to throw that too.

On the next dive, Xander would bail sand down to the first aiming telescope, and Ragini would stand guard with the spear. They would trade places on the next dive and work until they recovered at least one scope. It only took one more dive, and Xander was able to release the first telescope. There weren't any sharks, but there was a curious school of barracuda that came around on the second dive to look over the divers.

Connor wanted Xander and Ragini to rest and breathe deep for a while before they started excavating for the second scope. He had marked the drawing of the wreck to indicate to Xander where he wanted the first mines placed to remove the hull from the side of the gun deck. Connor tried diving on the wreck himself but could only get about fifteen feet deep before the pressure in his ears was killing him. He did get deep enough, however, to see exactly where the ends of the boards that made up the hull fell where they covered the gun deck. He was going over where to place the first round of explosives with Xander when Ragini dived off the bowsprit with the trident held with both hands, poised for a deadly thrust. She came up with a large tuna speared exactly through the middle of its body and heaved it up onto the diving platform. The crew was glad to have it. They carried the big fish up to the galley in expectation of a good dinner.

The divers were ready to go down after the second scope. Santiago had a suggestion, "Instead of trying to bail all that sand, what say we hook up the cargo hoist to the pulpit and see if we could pull it up off the deck?" Everyone agreed that it would be worth a try. Santiago had the men start a fire to bring the boiler for the wench motor up to steam. It took an hour for them to be ready, and then they lowered the hook down to the seabed. Xander walked the hook across the sandy bottom and hooked it under the piece that held the curved bubble level in front of the helm. Both divers came back up and sat on the diving platform while Santiago took up the slack in the winch cable. The cable tightened, and the Adrianna was pulled over until the cable was exactly vertical. The big ship was listing about ten degrees as the powerful wench pulled on the pulpit, and then there was a boom that resounded up out of the depths, and they couldn't see the pulpit through the swirling sand and the silt down below.

Ragini dove down and could see that the cable had come unhooked when the pulpit came loose from the deck. The armored enclosure was lying on the side from where they already removed the first scope. It was easy to unlatch the second scope from the other side and return to the surface. The first mission was complete. The sun was setting behind Isle San Miguel, and Conner called an end to the operation for the day. The Cook had a fine meal of tuna steaks, with abalone and crab, fresh-baked bread, and wine for everyone.

The next day was cooler, and the sea was choppy at dawn. A pod of dolphins was the only one enjoying the choppy sea along with the dinner scraps from the night before. The divers wanted to wait till it calmed down before they started placing the mines. After a couple of hours, the air was warmer, and they could see the bottom as clear as the day before. The mines were small black powder hand grenades, fitted with percussion cap detonators sealed with wax that would work underwater. There was a safety plate that was kept in place to prevent a spring-loaded hammer from striking the cap while the hammer was cocked and set against a seer. The seer operated with a pull string. For the work on the hull, they would detonate the mines after the divers were safely on the surface. It was still dangerous. For testing the system, Xander would start with only one mine at a time.

While Ragini stood ready to dive from the bowsprit if Xander got into trouble, the young Greek set the first mine. He released a small float that carried the detonator cord to the surface. Then he checked that there was no tension on the cord, cocked the hammer on the mine, and set a hook on the end of the cord into the ring that operated the seer. Last, he slid aside the protective plate, backed away, and swam upwards, careful not to tangle in the cord on the way up. Standing on the back of the diving platform, Santiago pulled the float over with a boathook. He checked that Ragini was still on the bowsprit, called "fire-in-the-hole" and pulled the cord. A dull thump resounded below, and a huge bubble broke the surface. Sand and silt again made it impossible to see.

When the cloud settled, and the silt drifted off in the current, a hole about two feet in diameter in the side of the hull was visible from the surface. Xander didn't want to set more than one mine at a time. Connor agreed, there was no reason to go fast. It took all morning, but by midday, the entire side of the gun deck was demolished. Next, Connor wanted to remove the remaining ammunition. It wouldn't be safe to blast deeper in the gun deck with the live rounds still in their racks in the wall. Removing wasn't particularly dangerous, but one of the divers had to be down inside the hull to retrieve the rounds. Diving into a dark space is always intimidating. Ragini was the first one to enter, but there weren't any denizens of the deep waiting for her trident.

It took the rest of the day to remove thirty-three rounds from the racks. It was difficult with the ship lying on its side. Usually, gravity would drop the next shell to the bottom of the rack. Connor and Santiago knew the exact inventory, along with both gunners. They wouldn't let the divers rest until every round was up on the main deck of the *Adrianna*. That night, both divers were exhausted. Because the artillery rounds were hoisted to the surface a few at a time in a basket, removing them from the wall racks proved to be the hardest part of the operation.

The next morning Connor let all the crew sleep late. The cook laid out the breakfast at the start of the forenoon watch. Connor and Santiago were going over the plan to raise the guns when the watch called from the main deck. The school of hammerheads was making its round of the islands again. This time, about half the seals were on the beach; the others had to be in the ocean feeding. That was a good sign that there were no large predators in the neighborhood. The big hammerheads looked almost languid as they cruised by uninterested in the wreck or the Adrianna. Connor noted the time in the ship's log just the same.

Xander was still reluctant to set more than one mine at a time. There were six mounting bolts in each of the gun carriages holding the carriage to the timbers that crossed below the gun deck. The best plan was to blast all six at one time while holding the gun up with the hoist. Xander would place the charges but reiterated that arming six mines at once was dangerous. Ragini volunteered, "It is delicate work. I can do it if I don't wear the fin."

Connor was concerned and spent some time on the decision, "Ragini, are you sure? I can't afford for anyone to die for something that is only one of my wants, not necessarily a need. Especially you."

"Trust me, Connor, I can do it, and I can do it safely."

Santiago looked at Connor and gave him an almost imperceptible nod of his head. Connor finally answered. "Okay, Ragini. But tell me how you are going to do this. I want to hear every detail." It took till early in the noon watch before the divers were ready. Xander rode the hook down with a heavy chain to wrap around the gun carriage. While he struggled to loop the heavy chain through the carriage, Ragini tied the mines to the bottom of the gun carriage, where the six bolts went through the deck. Both divers returned to the surface to breathe and rest.

Ten minutes and Ragini was ready to go down and arm the mines. She dove without the fin; she would need all the dexterity afforded by her bare feet and also wanted to be able to feel if she tangled in a string. She had six detonator cords threaded through an eye on the end of a spike that she would drive into the wooden hull outside of the gun deck. Connor was tense as he watched from the surface and kept track of the time. Three minutes elapsed, and then he could see Ragini outside of the hull. He knew what she was doing; she was very gently pulling the slack out of each detonator cord. When she had all six tight, she would tie them together and then release the float for the pull cord. Three and a half minutes, and she was still working on the cords. Four minutes and the float with the pull cord broke the surface. Ragini started up and gasped for air as she heaved herself up on the diving platform. Everyone was on their second or third breath, holding each breath as long as they could while Ragini worked on the bottom. Xander was the only one that made it with one breath. Santiago retrieved the float with the pull cord but let Ragini have the honor of setting off the charge.

Connor was on the controls of the hoist and gently pulled tension on the hoist cable. When he had the ship on a ten-degree list, he signaled to Ragini to set off the charge. This time, everyone felt the thump of the blast through the hull of the *Adrianna.* Water was blown up from the blast and drenched the crew. The ship rocked up, and Connor pulled on the winch lever that raised the cable. He knew he had the first gun because the ship still listed to port from the weight of the gun. The crew cheered when the heavy gun broke the surface. Xander swam over and attached a lanyard so that they could swing the gun over onto the main deck. As Connor lowered the gun gently to the deck, he thought, *what a strange way to go fishing.*

Ragini wanted to go after the second gun, but Connor put a stop to that. "One gun a day is enough. You were down a long time; I know you had to push yourself to finish in one dive. The other gun will still be there tomorrow. I want you fully rested before we do this again." Ragini donned her robe and walked to her cabin to dry off and get dressed. The gunners were already busy cleaning the gun, inspecting the rifling, and disassembling the breach and firing mechanism. A month in the ocean demanded a complete turnaround on the gun. Every part had to be cleaned, scrubbed free of rust, inspected and oiled before re-assembling the piece. Others in the crew were in the mess hall, disassembling the artillery rounds. Most were found to be watertight; however, dry powder and primers were replacing wet components.

Xander talked to Connor. He could retrieve two of the swivel guns easily. The one on the stern was only under a foot of sand; he could get that one too. The swivel guns were easy to unlatch from their spindles. Three, maybe four dives depending on the stern gun; Connor let the young diver get back to work. Before the day was over, the gun crews were cleaning three swivel guns and ten rounds of ammunition. The only ammunition that Xander could recover was in the day lockers on the gunwales. Connor was glad to add the swivel guns to the ship's defense, even if the ammunition was limited.

The morning of the last day, Connor hoped to be diving on the wreck, was dead calm. He didn't trust that the weather would stay that way. He woke the divers before daybreak and had them diving to place the charges before the sun broke the horizon. His intuition paid off. By the time Ragini was ready to go down and arm the mines, a dark squall line was forming to the west. He figured that they had about an hour before the storm was over them. Ragini still needed to rest before her long arming dive. Santiago watched

Xander on the bottom hooking up the hoist cable to the second gun. Xander was having trouble. The heavy chain slipped through the iron beams of the gun carriage and pulled the young Greek down into the darkness of the gun deck. Santiago summoned Ragini and told her to dive to see what was wrong.

Ragini slipped her feet into the shoes on the swim fin and pulled the straps tight. She fastened one while Connor fastened the other to save time. She dove off the gunwale and was down to the wreck in seconds. Xander was still down in the darkness. Rajini disappeared into the darkness. She was down a long time, too long, then she shot up to the surface and gasped for air. She yelled up to the crew, "I need a bar, quick as you can. I gave Xander my air, but I can't do that again, and it won't last him long. Lower the bar on the lanyard. I'm going back down."

This time she went directly to Xander and blew her full breath into his mouth and returned as fast as she could to the surface. Connor, Santiago, and a dozen other men were in the water as deep as they could dive. Santiago moved the crowbar over to the edge of the hull, and Ragini grabbed it and headed back down into the darkness. It took a minute, but she emerged with Xander. He was unconscious, and he was gushing blood from a wound on his leg. Ragini was kicking like a dolphin raising him to the surface. Santiago was a strong swimmer, he helped Ragini to the surface, and strong hands hauled Xander onto the diving platform.

Connor was the last man out of the water and just in the nick of time. The fins of several tiger sharks broke the surface as Connor pulled himself up on the diving platform. The sharks were looking for the source of the blood, an easy meal for them if a wounded seal was still in the water. Santiago had Xander up on the deck. He had him on his stomach doing artificial respiration. Xander wasn't responding. Ragini rolled the young man over and blew into his mouth while holding his nose. Santiago thumped him firmly on the chest and then pushed his chest down to empty his lungs. Ragini was going to inflate his lungs again when Xander coughed up more seawater and drew a deep breath on his own. The cook had stopped the bleeding and was sewing up the gash on his leg. Xander wasn't going back down again anytime soon. Everyone considered him lucky to be alive.

Connor had forgotten about the storm. When he looked up from the effort to save Xander's life, the squall line was only a quarter of a mile away, and the sea was no longer calm. The wind rocked the *Adrianna* when it hit, and from the jerking every time the ship rose on a wave, Connor knew that they were dragging the anchor. It wasn't likely that this storm would last very long, but after it passed, they wouldn't be over the wreck. They would have to find it again if they were to retrieve the second gun. All of the day's events seemed less bleak over a hot cup of coffee while sitting around the table in the mess. Xander looked much better eating some hot chicken soup while trying to apologize profusely for having let the chain fall in the first place. Ragini felt the worst; she had cut Xander's leg on a shard of broken glass from a hurricane lamp she hadn't seen when she pried up a piece of iron to free Xander and pulled him out of the gun deck.

Now Ragini brought up a different problem. She told Connor and Santiago that the chain that almost cost Xander his life fell and tangled in the wreckage at the bottom of the gun deck. There was no way she would be able to free it by herself. "Why couldn't we use a length of rope looped over the gun carriage several times. A rope almost floats in the water; it would be easy to loop it around the carriage."

Santiago looked at Connor, and both men said at once, "Why didn't we think of that?"

Ragini only smiled at them with wisdom beyond their understanding. She had heard Lia and Abby answer that question several times with; *you're only a mere man.* She stayed silent, though, she still wanted to get to India and didn't know Connor well enough to kid him. The mood of the conversation was too serious for a glib answer. There would only be one diver when they went after the second gun.

It was easy to find the wreck after the storm had passed. The wind shifted, and Connor sailed the ship back up the path that the anchor made dragging along the bottom. By the middle of the noon watch, the *Adrianna* was back in position over the wreck. Everything was ready to go; however, Connor thought it would be good to wait another day, rest up and go over the plan for raising the second gun. Ragini was practicing with the hawser Santiago had made for raising the gun. There was an eye spliced at both ends. One end would hang on the hook, and the other end would be threaded through the gun carriage six times to equal the pulling weight of the chain. The other eye would be looped over the hook. In theory, it would be much more work, but much lighter work for Ragini. She was anxious to get started. So was the rest of the crew. Connor agreed that they could get the hawser rigged up to the gun carriage, but he still would have them wait for the next day to arm the charges and free the gun. Ragini knew it was a good decision. She was exhausted after the three dives it took to weave the heavy rope through the carriage.

The sea was calm again the next morning. Ragini had her cords and hooks ready to arm the mines. Connor cautioned her, "You don't have a backup diver. If you get stuck down there, you will drown. How about I tie you off with a light line? At least I could pull you up if you are late."

Ragini didn't want a safety line. It would be one more thing that could tangle with one of the detonation cords. She did agree to tie off a safety line on the wreck. She was pretty sure Santiago could reach her if he had the line to pull himself down. All was ready; Ragini would dive with the swim fin, tie off the safety line, and then inspect the gun deck to make sure the mines were still attached where she left them. She was only down a little over a minute. All was well; she was ready to arm the mines.

Ragini thought that with luck, this would be the last dive. The water was a little colder after the storm stirred it up, but the bottom was the same temperature as always. She slipped into the gun deck but sensed that she wasn't alone. A huge grouper rose out of the darkness and fled. Ragini laughed to herself, the grouper was lucky she didn't have the trident, or he would have been their dinner. Yet, she didn't welcome the faster heartbeat; she needed every bit of oxygen she had to arm all the mines in one dive. By the time she got to tying off all the cords, she knew that she was pushing it again. She finished the task, though, and swam to the surface.

Connor took up the tension on the hoist cable, and Santiago let Amos detonate the charge. This time, however, the ship did not raise. The gun wasn't free. Connor let the cable back out to right the ship. They would have to wait until the debris and silt cleared from the gun deck below, and then Ragini could make another inspection. Connor had her wait an hour. After all, there was still a live mine down there. It didn't seem prudent to rush things; they didn't have anything to do with the time they saved going faster.

Ragini dove with her swim fin and was back up in a minute. One of the mines in the middle of the carriage didn't go off. It was probably waterlogged, soaked from a seep during its longer stay below water. Santiago went into the forecastle to retrieve another mine. Ragini rigged up another cord and dove again to place the mine. Connor thought she was getting better at this because she was up again in less than a minute. Santiago retrieved the float, and this time he had Regina ready to pull the cord. Connor drew the tension on the hoist cable and signaled Ragini. She pulled the cord, and this time the ship rocked up. The bubble from the blast broke the surface along with the grouper; he would be providing dinner after all.

The crew swung the second gun onto the main deck, and then Santiago sent them over to the capstan to raise the anchor. Connor went to the con and ordered all the sails raised. There was a weak breeze, enough to turn the ship due west. He wasn't concerned about the slow progress; they would have a good look at the islands where the sea battle that put the *Alabama* on the bottom took place. Connor gave the con over to Amos and went down to his chart table. He started writing a full account of the battle, the trip to San Francisco and back, and the retrieval of the guns. He was one happy Irishman. Amos was happy too. He caught the trade winds and was on his way across the Pacific. Ragini was the only one with a regret. She wished Moses was here to see them raise the guns. She wished he was here to make love to her, hold her and make her feel safe. There was a score of unknowns in India, too many for her to contemplate at one time. She stripped off her wet suit, crawled under the comforter on her bunk, and let the gentle roll of the ship rock her to sleep.

Usenbestia

Eli, Abby, and Roland filled with trepidation as they rode back to Red Mountain. When they neared the townsite, they could see the scavengers picking the remains of the gang of robbers. Now there was an additional worry; the scavengers weren't Apache. They were white men with some women — failed prospectors or settlers who had grown tired of trying to eke out an existence on the harsh desert.

Roland was the first to speak. "I don't recognize any of those people. They are welcome to the saddles and the dead men's boots and clothes. If people weren't afraid of us before, they certainly would be now. What a hard way for the locals to learn we aren't an easy mark."

Arriving back at Red Mountain, they went into the clinic to see if Mr. Sue was still alive. Abby pointed Roland to the recovery room. Lia was asleep, and Roland kissed her on the forehead and left her to talk to Suzette. Suzette was deep into one of her medical books. Bridgette was at Mr. Sue's side, bathing his forehead with a damp cloth. Suzette was all doctor, "I have relieved the pressure on his brain, but the concussion is severe. We don't know if we relieved the pressure soon enough or if there is brain damage. We have to wait until he regains consciousness before we will know. "

Bridgette asked, "Did you catch them?"

Abby answered, "We shot one in a bar in Wickenburg. We caught up with another one in Vulture City. He had a busted-up shoulder and was with Sawbones, the drunk." Abby didn't relate what she did to ensure that the man would die of infection, but she finished up with, "He won't survive. The *Baby Dragon* and a man named Randy Galveston stole horses from the livery there and escaped before we got there. One of the horses was Henry's. The horses were ready for the trail with bedrolls and provisions. They had a head start with fresh horses, the last ones at the livery, so we came back."

Suzette said, "They won't be coming back. They have had quite a day with robbery and horse thieving; they will have to stay ahead of the news of the robbery, the massacre, and their horse thieving. Where do you think they will go?"

Roland said, "If they are smart, they will go up the east side of the Sierras and hide out in the gold camps. Abby, why did you call Mr. Sue's nephew, the *Little Dragon*?"

"Mr. Sue told me some time ago. In the province where he came from, he was heir to one of the largest armies in China. His ancestors were a long line of generals that earned the title of *Dragon* by defeating all challengers in hand-to-hand combat. The title has been in his family for three centuries. I know he never told the story of why he left China. I don't know that either, but he does speak of a great war. I found some history in Lila's library. About ten years ago, armies of more than a million men each clashed for control of the country. I don't know if Mr. Sue was a winner or a loser, but something in the outcome of the war was his reason for immigrating to America. His nephew wants to be the next *Dragon*. He could become that by killing Mr. Sue in combat: either with an army or in a one-on-one fight to the death."

Suzette said, "Explains the blow to the head. He did mean to kill him. Had he fractured his skull, Mr. Sue would be dead. Wang Wei is a coward. I expect he was planning to go back to San Francisco and proclaim himself the victor in a fair fight. He might still do that. Who would know that Mr. Sue died of anything other than his nephew's cowardly act?"

The conversation would have gone on until Mr. Sue woke up. However, it was interrupted by two men that arrived and presented themselves as Federal Marshals, the only law in the Arizona Territory other than a handful of weak local sheriffs. Marshals John Sanders and Larry Pope. They wanted all the details about the robbery and any other information that Red Mountain could provide. Suzette and Bridgette stayed in the clinic, but everyone else went out to the ramada. Mary had coffee and a newly baked apple pie. The lawmen didn't encounter such good hospitality in most of their investigations.

When Marshal Sanders heard the name Randy Galveston, he had a lot to say. Sanders had a wanted poster in his saddlebag that posted a five-hundred-dollar reward for Galveston – dead or alive – for two murders: one in El Paso and the other in Tucson. Marshal Pope said, "I expect that there are more wanted criminals out there among the dead. We need an official complaint, and then we can have Wang Wei posted as wanted for attempted robbery and assault. Would you want to offer a reward?"

Roland, ever the businessman, spoke, "Yes, let's make it an even one hundred thousand dollars."

Marshal Sanders said, "With all due respect, Mr. Callahan, that will get a lot of innocent people killed. I suggest you start with something that would be of interest to honest lawmen and bounty hunters, but not worth the risk to common citizens. I would recommend two thousand dollars at the most. At that level, every newspaper that receives the notice will print it and distribute it."

Roland agreed with that recommendation and would go up to Prescott and post the reward with the Territorial Office. He had another thought, however, to run by the Marshals. "How about we post a bigger reward among the Chinese community in San Francisco. Let's post the reward for the cowardly killing of *The Dragon.* Something big enough to ensure betrayal by his closest friends or even his mother, Mr. Sue's sister, in Chinatown. Say a half million in gold?"

Marshal Pope answered, "If that is a private matter in the Chinese community, the Federals wouldn't be involved. You would have to arrange that on your own, but I like the idea. If Wang Wei believes his uncle is dead, he won't have any fear of operating in the open. Besides wanting your gold, he wants the fame of being the last *Dragon*."

Bridgette came running out of the clinic, "He's awake! He's awake!"

The Marshals wanted to talk to him, but Suzette put a stop to that. "He is awake but hasn't talked yet. We have to give him some time. There may be brain damage. Why don't you at least stay the night? If he is going to be able to talk, we may hear from him in the morning."

The two Marshals were glad to stay. They wanted to see the mine and mill, and especially the refinery where the assault took place. Mary's cooking may have had something to do with their wanting to stay; at dinner, they ate like ravished animals. Abby and Lia showed them where the third man handcuffed them at the beginning of the robbery. One thing the Marshals didn't understand was why Wang Wei let them live. Why didn't he shoot everyone?

John knew the answer, "He had to make it look like a ritual killing; a bashed-in skull is what you would expect if they fought with the traditional staffs. There would be no honor to claim if three were dead with bullet holes in them. That would look like murder."

The next morning another unexpected visitor showed up. It was Edward Sigler, the newspaperman that had made Suzette famous. He took up station under the ramada and started interviewing everyone that would talk to him and write his account of the robbery. He was going to add another chapter to the Callahan's fame.

Suzette and Bridgette were sitting with Mr. Sue. They had him moved to the recovery room. Mid-morning, Mr. Sue turned to Suzette and said, "Hello, Doctor."

With tears filling her eyes, Suzette answered the greeting. "Hello, Mr. Sue. It is good to have you back. How do you feel?"

"Betrayed."

"I meant; how does your head feel?"

"Revengeful. I need .... things from my .... room." He started to get up, but Suzette and Bridgette pushed him back down.

"Not so fast, my friend. You have a hole in your skull that I need to fix before you are going anywhere. Also, I would like to hear you say a whole sentence without stammering."

Mr. Sue smiled, "My head hurts."

"That's better. Do you feel sick?"

"No. You need to let me up. I need to go kill my nephew."

"I think Roland is taking care of that, and you are not going anywhere for at least a week or two here. No arguing, Mr. Sue. If the open hole in your skull gets infected, you will die. Understood? There are two Federal Marshals here that want to talk to you. Do you feel up for that? I could give you something for the pain."

"Please, Suzette, no drugs."

Marshal Pope only spent a few minutes with Mr. Sue. When he finished the interview, he had a signed complaint in hand, and all he needed to post Wang Wei and Randy Galveston as wanted men. It would be hard for them to hide anywhere west of the Mississippi.

The marshals left the next day. That night John buttonholed Eli after dinner and said, "We need to talk."

They sat under the ramada while everyone else retired for the night. Eli asked, "What's on your mind?"

"We have a problem. The water in the mine is getting hotter. When we started at the top, the water temperature was one hundred four degrees. When we drove the tunnel into the mountain, the water temperature there was one-hundred-ten degrees. Since we have been mining, the water temperature has gone up another four. That is in less than one year. The new shaft will reach down to the tunnel level in two to three more weeks, and that will vent the hot air out the top of the mountain. But the heat will increase as we sink deeper. I would guess that we will only be able to go, say, another two hundred feet. Then the bottom of the mine is going to be way too hot to work safely."

"The water getting hotter is a lot to think about," Eli said. Then he asked, "What about the flow rate?"

"That has increased slightly too. When we first drove the tunnel into the center of the mountain, the flow rate was twenty-seven gallons per minute. Then it went down to twenty-one as we drained the top of the mountain, just a little more than what we were getting from the hot spring on top before we mined it down. Now the flow rate is over thirty. What we have done is relieve five hundred feet of head on the hydro-system that feeds the spring. So, there is more flow, and it is hotter than before. More water isn't a problem. The steam pump we will use as we go deeper than the tunnel will pump up to seventy-five gallons per minute. We have already started a room to put the boiler underground, and we will go down with a spiral decline around the dinosaur dig to get the suction down so that we can dewater deeper. The shaft from the top will connect to the boiler room, so the fumes from the boiler will rise out of the top of the mountain."

Eli was thoughtful for a while, then brought up another point. "When we started down, and the gold got bigger, Mr. Sue said that the mine would get richer and then peter out at depth. Hard to say what that depth is, but up on top of the mountain, the gold was microscopic. Abby still has the hide that turned golden in the storm up on the wall above our bed. Now we are finding nuggets up to a quarter inch in size, and the ore coming out from the dinosaur dig is four to five times richer than the hot springs on top. What I am saying is, maybe we won't be going that much deeper before we have picked the eye out of this deposit."

"That is possible; a lot of the lode mines in California petered out at depth. We won't know until we reach the end of it. However, with the new winch and clamshell, we don't have to go down there by hand. We can dig at least a hundred feet deeper than the dinosaur from the top of the mountain. After that, we will have to lower the winch into the pit to continue down. All possible. I wanted you to know all the facts because we may have to make some hard decisions here in a while."

"Thanks, John. Let's get some sleep. Tomorrow we will get back to mining and do what we do best."

Eli didn't sleep well that night. He wasn't worried about the heat driving him out of the mine. He was worried if the gold petered out, what would become of the men who worked for him? He would have to talk to Roland about this, but by morning, he knew what he wanted to do. He would give the mine and mill to the men who were shareholders and let them continue mining the top of the mountain. He had made money up there, and the men should be able to do the same. He tried to sleep, but his mind churned between thoughts of going back home to Independence to rebuild the brewery business or going to San Francisco to a life of ease on Nob Hill. His father was a better patriarch than he would ever make. He was troubled by the thought that if he went back to Independence, there would be expectations he wouldn't be able to meet.

Somewhere in the night, Abby woke and listened to his concerns. She had some good advice, "Let it work itself out, Eli. It's okay not to have a plan for everything that will come around in the future." He didn't have to wait long to see that she was right.

John had started down on the circular ramp with the men using a hand-operated pump to keep the decline dry enough to work. The heat, however, was intense, and the men could only work a few minutes and then had to rotate out of the decline to cool down. The hand pump was made by the same company that had provided the bilge pump for *The Blessed.* It wasn't a perfect solution, but the shaft sinking from the top of the mountain would soon be deep enough to dewater the mine to hundreds of feet below the dinosaur.

Mr. Sue was back on the job but only for light-duty. Eli had him putting together a record for the month-to-month accounting of the gold production to date. The record was impressive: a few kilograms shy of thirteen hundred. In ounces, it totaled almost forty-one thousand, eight-hundred ounces; over eight hundred thousand dollars. Eli planned to hold a shareholder meeting that night and bring everyone up to date on where they stood financially.

His thoughts were interrupted with Eliza and Maria running into the refinery. Eliza was excited, and she almost screamed, "They found another bone in the decline! It's a big one! You have to come to see it." The two girls ran back to the portal. Eli and Mr. Sue followed behind but at a more casual pace.

They didn't go down the decline. The miners had Cliff propped up in front of the air blast from the blower. Cliff said, "I stayed down there a little too long – got too hot. What's down there is a leg bone so far. If it is a metatarsal bone as I suspect, it is from a smaller dinosaur than this one. Here is something else from down there that you might be interested in." The Professor dug in his pocket and came out with a gold nugget, almost the size of his fist. He handed it to Eli and Mr. Sue. Indeed, they were interested. It was the largest piece of gold yet found in their mountain. More than two pounds, there were at least thirty ounces in the large piece of gold. Eli was amazed and was hoping that there was a lot more down there.

Mr. Sue said, "There will be more, but it could also be close to the bottom of the mine we have been talking about."

Eli nodded his head but had a bigger concern at that moment, "Let's get the Professor out of here and into the clinic. Being down in that hot hole is a job for younger, tougher men. Cliff, I don't want you down there again until we can cool it down." Cliff wasn't paying attention; he was sick and throwing up.

Eliza piped up, "What about younger, tougher girls?"

Eli looked to the miners for their safety, "Five minutes at a time, no longer. And don't remove any bones until they are cataloged and surveyed properly." The girls looked at Eli like he didn't realize that he was looking at experts.

Cliff gave them a different job, though, to keep them safe and out of trouble, "Keep excavating this skull. Be careful around the teeth. If they are still attached, you don't want to break them off. The attachment to the jawbone will be very fragile." The skull was the last part of the dinosaur to extract from the red rock. The reassembled skeleton in Eliza's Secret Room was waiting for its head. "One other thing: you girls should have the honor of naming the skeleton. The name should be something elegant, something perhaps from your native languages, something you would like to see on the front-page headline on the *New York Times* or the *Alta California*. Give this some thought. Ask for help when you need it. Most important – use the library."

Long into each night, Eliza and Maria would work on the naming of the skeleton. During the day, they worked with the Professor on excavating the skull. They had the back of the skull supported with timber and were working their way forward to uncover the front of the upper jaw. The miners were getting excited. The noise of the clamshell could be heard through the wall of the cavern, digging down from up above. Each day the noise of the iron bucket could be heard louder and louder. John reassured everyone that it was coming down safely to the side of the dinosaur dig and would even be twenty feet north of the decline. Ever the engineer, his plan was a good one.

The sound of the clamshell was closer, but it was to the side of the cavern, no longer over their heads.

Work on the decline slowed. It was too hot at the bottom to let the men work any more than a few minutes at a time. The miners wanted to finish with the skull and suggested that they remove the skull and jawbone together as one block and finish separating them under the ramada. They were anxious to mine down on the cavern under where the skeleton lay. There were nuggets below, a belief shorn up by the Professor's finding the two-pound nugget at the bottom of the decline. Cliff decided that their idea was a good one. It took another few days and eight men to carry the skull out of the portal slung under a heavy pole. Four men in front and four men in back; Mr. Sue was calling cadence as they all walked in step with the precious fossil.

Under the ramada, the skull was laid on its side so the girls could remove the rock without having to support the top of the skull. Cliff and Lila supervised the work but didn't touch the fossil. They wanted Eliza and Maria to share the thrill of discovery as they removed the red rock from the fossilized bones. The girls worked with careful, meticulous energy, and within a week, all the teeth on one side of the jaw could be seen again for the first time in eons of geological time. Every night the girls worked on the name of the skeleton. Abby and Mary were pleased when they heard the girls discussing words for God, lizards, and creatures of every sort. One night, the girls didn't delve into the naming process, but Tio was in the shop at the refinery all that night working on something in secret.

The next day when the townsite gathered for breakfast under the ramada, there was a wooden sign in front of the fossil. It was a beautifully carved sign, stained red, with a name in large gold-leaf inlay. The name was **USENBESTIA**. Abby admired the way the two girls had brought their two cultures together in the name. She had to explain to the others, "*Usen* is the Apache word for God, the creator of the Apache and all of the worlds, including the world of the *pindah-lickoyee*, the white-eyes. *Bestia* is the Spanish word for a beast. The literal meaning would be God-beast, but even the most illiterate of the Apache or the Spanish would call it God's Beast." With her hand on the fossil, she welcomed the fossil into the modern world, "Welcome, Usenbestia, we are going to help you fulfill your destiny."

Abby didn't have to wait long for that destiny to unfold right before her eyes. A few days later, the girls were removing the soft rock from inside the skull and working their way down the left side of the upper jaw. All the teeth so far were still intact. The Professor told them that it was rare to find the teeth attached to the jawbones. They were working to uncover the front left fang. The right one was already free, and it was six inches long. Eliza held a small chisel and tapped the red rock at the top of the left tooth lightly with a wooden maul. A piece of the soft red rock fell away. Underneath where it had been, was the top of the left tooth. Abby gasped, "It is solid gold." She sent Henry to fetch Eli and Cliff from the mine.

By the time the Professor arrived, the girls had half the rest of the tooth uncovered. "This site continues to amaze me beyond belief. Eliza, Maria, you may just have become the most famous apprentices in the world. Is that reporter still around?"

Abby answered, "I think he is down in Wickenburg or Vulture City. He said he would be in the area for some time, gathering more background on Wang Wei."

Cliff said, "Let's send for him. There is a story here that is a lot more significant than a robbery at a gold mine."

Eli had just arrived and overheard the conversation. Bimisi, he went by Ben now, had come out of the mine with him. Eli turned to Ben and told him, "Ben, saddle my horse and go find the reporter, Ed Sigler. Bring him back here, but don't tell him about the tooth. I want him to see it for himself. He will need his first impression for his story." Eli flipped his youngest son a quarter for a trip to the candy store, and Ben saddled up and rode like the wind, proud to be trusted on his own for an important mission.

Eli had to get back to the mine. John and the miners were trying to break through to the vertical shaft. All-day long, the miners had been sawing sets of timber that would be used to shore up a room adjacent to the vertical shaft for the boiler. The boiler and pump would take over the job of dewatering the mine. The men who operated the hand pump couldn't wait. The miners were also building air doors to control the ventilation of the tunnel and the museum cavern once the connection to the surface was complete. The Professor was concerned that drawing in desert air through Tio's tunnel would adversely affect the Usenbestia skeleton.

It was late afternoon when a swing of a miner's pick broke through to the open air of the vertical shaft. John let the miners enlarge the hole but then backed them off until he could measure and survey the exact location of the shaft and add it to his drawings of the mine. He wanted the boiler room located out of the throat of the hot springs where they expected to find more large nuggets. He explained, "There is no need to put the boiler room in the middle of the high-grade ore. Even if we have to come in from the other side, it will be worth the time it takes." That night Eli, Mr. Sue, and John laid out a tunnel that would start one hundred feet back along the main tunnel and terminate in a room for the boiler twenty feet on the east side of the vertical shaft.

The next morning the men were a bit miffed that they had to drive another hundred feet of drift instead of mining their way into the heart of the ore body. It wasn't hard, though, for them to see the wisdom of not sterilizing high-grade ore in the throat of the hot spring for the sake of the boiler room. They decided to work three shifts a day to drive the new drift and complete the room for the boiler. After that, they would break through to the vertical shaft from that side and lay the steam pipe for the water pump.

In the meantime, Mr. Sue and the surface crew constructed another air door to isolate and control the air from the cavern created during the excavation of Usenbestia. The draft up the vertical shaft was going to be significant. While the cool air drawn in through the tunnel was welcome, John, as always, was planning. When the boiler was in place, the air turbine would be relocated underground, where its output would increase with removing the backpressure of the six-hundred-foot run in from the portal. They would recover all the air pipes and direct cool air streams to the hottest faces under excavation by the miners.

John spent his evenings plotting the progress on his mine map and sketching up his thoughts as to how to mine the heart of the deposit. They needed to mine without a major collapse of the low-grade ore above the dinosaur cavern. The clamshell had excavated to a depth of one hundred feet below the Usenbestia cavern, and they were still recovering large nuggets at that depth. Everyone was excited to get at the high-grade ore beneath the cavern. However, there had to be more development work before removing the heart of the deposit. The main problem was: if the roof started spalling off large slabs, it would be impossible to work under it without the constant threat of being crushed to death. He had to find the bottom of the high-grade ore and drive another decline to get under it. The only safe way to remove the rest of the treasure was from the bottom.

When John shared his planning with Eli, Roland, and Mr. Sue, they all agreed that John's plan would be the direction they would take. It would extend the development of the mine for possibly another year. Walking away with their winnings, though, was much more important than dying in the mine under a caved ceiling. The soft ore in the throat of the deposit was a blessing to mine, yielding to pick and shovel. However, the rock was not strong enough to support the weight of the low-grade ore above. John planned to enlarge the dinosaur cavern and shape the ceiling like the inside of a parabolic cone. A lot of work in the low-grade ore was ahead of the miners, but worth it if they could mine all the high grade without a major collapse.

John could see his retirement in sight. The clamshell would find the bottom of the deposit and quit deepening the shaft. It would turn to only hauling ore to the surface. They would mine a dump pocket where the miners first broke through to the vertical shaft. The main tunnel would then be used only for men and materials, and to drain the water pumped out of the bottom of the mine. Within a week, they completed the installation of the boiler underground. The steam pipe ran to the bottom of the decline, and the steam pump took over the job of dewatering the workings. The blower moved into the tunnel, and a steady stream of cool air brought temperatures at the face of the decline down to tolerable levels. The men could work for hours instead of minutes. The cavern was being excavated up and outward from the dinosaur cavern in the shape of the cone that would support the roof. The ore was removed from the cavern and brought up from the decline; the miners dumped the ore down the ore shoot, and the hoist lifted it to the surface. Mr. Sue measured the gold production in kilograms per hour rather than days, weeks, or months as before.

The clamshell found the bottom of the rich nugget laden heart of the deposit. It was one hundred fifty feet below the dinosaur cavern. Two more complete skeletons were under excavation in the decline. The skeletons were smaller than Usenbestia, and this time Cliff had Eliza and Maria do the entire excavation. Tio kept reassembling the skeletons in the museum room, and occasionally he would make his way down the decline to spend the day with Maria. Plans were made to move the skeletons to the museum at the Jesuit College, and the professor was going to take Eliza and Maria into the paleontology program at the college if they wanted to go. Lia asked Cliff, "What about Tio?"

The Professor said, "Tio has a job for life in the workshop at the museum, and he can go with Maria everywhere in the world her career will take her." Lia wasn't looking forward to leaving Red Mountain, but John was telling them that it would take around another year to mine and process the heart of the deposit. Some hard decisions were coming down the road for all of them.

By the end of 1864, a quarter of the high-grade deposit was removed and processed. The Dragon Tooth Gold Mine was on its way to becoming a million-ounce producer. The mine wouldn't double the fortune of the young Callahan family, but it was going to come close. Eli was sending Roland back to San Francisco to draft the documents to turn the mine over to the men and women that had been with him from the beginning. He didn't know yet what he and Abby would do after the high-grade played out. John and Mary were planning to retire on Nob Hill. Suzette and Bridgette made plans to return to teaching positions at the University of San Francisco.

Everyone had a plan But Eli and Abby. Jacques was the only other unknown. There was no news from him now for over a year. For all they knew, he could be dead.

Jacques

Christmas came again and with it, the end of 1864. It was New Year's Day and a rare-late morning for everyone. Suzette lay cuddled in the arms of her lover; fitful dreams were playing on the edges of her consciousness. Each dream sequence was more vivid than the last until she was reliving the reality of some of the worse battles back on the Santa Fe Trail. Bridgette held her close, waiting for the inevitable end to the nightmare. The end always came with Suzette waking, sometimes with a scream and her heart pounding. One time, Suzette bolted upright and started fighting Bridgette, thinking that the Indians had taken her and were on the verge of brutal-multiple rapes, followed by a merciless execution.

Mr. Sue had some experience with this kind of trauma. He told Bridgette to let the nightmares play out to their ends. Be there for her when she wakes up and get her to talk about the dreams while she still remembers them. It is a mechanism the mind has to relive horrific events in a way that lets a person put bad experiences behind them. This nightmare was going to be a bad one. It had been playing out in Suzette's mind for some time. Despite the cold room of the winter night, Suzette soaked the bedding in sweat. Her muscles were cramping, and she was starting to shake as each new scenario appeared like real life, just below the surface of consciousness. In the end, Suzette was sitting up in bed, trying to draw her revolver from the nonexistent holster on her hip. Bridgette never let her fall asleep within reach of a weapon of any sort.

Suzette wasn't the only member of the Callahan family that had nightmares. Jacques relived the battle of Gettysburg on Cemetery Ridge almost every night. After going east with the California Brigade, Jacques had joined Colonel Hancock's regiment as a scout and followed him through every battle from Williamsburg to the Boydton Plank Road. This fitful night, he was at the notch in the stone wall on Cemetery Ridge with General Hancock and his men. Wave after wave of ragged and weary gray soldiers attacked the hill. The fighting was some of the worst for both sides in the Civil War, but the waves of Confederate troops kept coming as the Union artillery slaughtered thousands in the open fields west of the hill. Wave after wave.

Jacques is a scout, but in the desperate fighting, he is at the stone wall on the front line with the Union soldiers. His Henry rifle is too hot to touch. General Hancock's aide crouches down behind the wall loading for Jacques.

Piles of gray soldiers lay before them, but the desperate Confederates keep coming. The air is full of the acrid smell of gun smoke, blood, fear, and death. Jacques reaches for another rifle, but the aide is dead. He looks back to the front and sees a rifle thrown like a harpoon sailing over the dead bodies in front of him, the bayonet aimed at his heart. He tries to sidestep but can't lift his feet. His body is locked in the slow-motion of fear. The bayonet pierces his heart, and he wakes up screaming in the West Texas chaparral. He sleeps alone; none of the unit he is with dares to be near the troubled young man when he wakes from a nightmare. The nightmare fades, one of many; he dies over and over again in General Lee's last attempt to break the Union lines and take Washington, D.C.

After Boydton, Jacques was sent west to hunt down and kill the Confederate raider Quantrill. General Hancock recognized that Jacques was on the verge of losing his mind after watching thousands of men die on the battlefields. Jacques was invaluable as a scout, but he was joining in the fighting, and his mental ability to cope with the endless killing was nearing an inevitable, tragic end. In the battle of the Boydton Plank Road, Jacques had lost control and kept killing Confederates long after the battle was over. He slaughtered more than a score of prisoners before General Hancock, and his staff was able to stop him. The General knew that Jacques was all used up. Jacques had been with him since he was a major, and the General considered him family. He made a life-saving decision for his young friend.

Hancock sent his Chief of Scouts west to hunt Quantrill, away from the front lines. Jacques participated in every battle the General was involved in since the beginning of the war, but with the luck-of-the-Irish, the young lad escaped every conflict unscathed. Almost impossible considering that the casualties were now numbering over one hundred thousand on both sides of the conflict. General Hancock didn't understand how one man could always escape death, while tens of thousands fell around him. It was as if he carried a protective shield around him going into every battle.

But the General was no fool; he knew that Jacques didn't escape. The young Irishman gathered more emotional damaged in every battle. Jacques was as pathological of a killer as any soldier Hancock had ever seen. The General sent Jacques west because the men didn't want to be around him anymore. It was his Sargent Major who convinced his general that his Chief of Scouts was on the verge of cracking up. Everyone feared that the proficient killer would turn his trauma loose on his own when he finally broke down.

When in battle, Jacques didn't foam at the mouth, but he killed with impunity as efficient as any berserkers born and bred to the cause of death. With Lee's defeat at Gettysburg, the war would be over soon. Jacques' service as a scout had been invaluable to Hancock through every battle. The General took his Sargent Major's advice; he sent the young man west while Jacques still had control of himself.

In the breaking light of the east Texas dawn, Jacques gathered up his bedroll, saddled his horse, and rode back into the ranks of the Union soldiers. It was common for him to spend his nights away from the unit, either hunting Confederates or Indian sympathizers to kill, or just sleeping alone to awake in his nightmares. Jacques knew he was close to insanity. He was holding on, though, soldiering mechanically forward, one day at a time.

The tide of war was in full flow against the South. It was only a matter of time before General Lee would have to surrender. General Johnson was still fighting in Tennessee, but like Lee, he was out of supplies, men, and, more importantly, the will to keep fighting. The handwriting was on the wall for the old general and every other Confederate soldier. The gallant cause of the South faded into the background long ago as the brutality of the war dominated the stage. The tribes that assisted the Confederates in Texas and the Indian Territories were vying for peace.

The Union Army was following Quantrill into Tennessee. Jacques followed them as far as Independence. There he laid down his weapons, sat next to his mother's grave, and wept. It was Hannah who found him there, staring into space as silent tears streamed down his cheeks. Hanna came like clockwork every few days to put fresh flowers on Anna's grave. She didn't recognize the bedraggled, bearded soldier until he stood up embarrassed to be seen crying. "Jacques! Jacques!" Hannah held him at arm's length until recognition replaced the unwarranted look of fear in the young man's eyes. Hannah took Jacques into her arms. His unit was preparing to march east. Hannah took Jacques down to her home next to where the hospital used to stand. Jacques's unit marched out of Independence, but Jacques didn't rally to the bugle call. The Civil War was finally over for the battle-ravaged scout.

Hannah could see that the babe she delivered was no longer a young man. War hardened and haggard, Jacques looked and acted like an old-broken man. He would drift off in the middle of a sentence and stare into space until he returned from one of his many horrible memories of the war. Hannah had seen hundreds of men and boys returning from the front lines missing limbs or crippled from wounds. Jacques was physically whole but damaged as deep as any other war-torn veteran.

Hanna lived with several orphans from the Callahan homesteads. Rufus had died fighting Quantrill when the guerilla fighters tried to take him back into slavery. Many of the blacks at Callahan Meadows died the same way, fighting to remain free as Quantrill and his men ravaged The Complex. There was nothing left there. Between the tornado that had killed Aaden and Anna, an invasion by the southern Colonel Price, and Quantrill's destruction, the forest was reclaiming the Callahan empire. The railroad had been torn up for iron. Quantrill burned all the homesteads, and the guerilla fighter and his renegades had pulled down the remnants of the stone buildings. Unattended, the forest was reclaiming the lush orchards that supplied the brewery. In Independence, Quantrill destroyed the hospital, Anna's school, and Denise's mansion in his attempt to purge northern Missouri of Union sympathizers.

Jacques wanted to rejoin his unit and kill the rebel guerilla, but Hannah recognized that her young friend needed some serious mental help. She convinced Jacques to stay. They would have to wait until later in the summer for the official word of the Confederate surrender, but they would wait together. Jessica had written that she would be returning to Independence as soon as the war was over. Hannah worried that Jessica would need the same kind of help as Jacques.

Everyone in Independence took heart when Lincoln won his second term in office back in November. He was the right President to end the war and start the process of healing the torn nation. Southern sympathizers in Northern Missouri were already trying to make life difficult for blacks. The war was going to end. Lincoln's relentless little general, General Grant, was willing to fight the war of attrition to the end. Hannah knew, though, that the radical-racial hatred would never end. She now had a project far more important than the rescue of orphans from the war. She had Jacques to make well again. She had Lily and Ben safe in San Francisco. She had Jessica and her husband Jackson to wait for, and the rest of the Callahan family somewhere lost in the west. She still had a lot of work left to do.

Jacques slept in peace for the first few nights with Hannah keeping watch. Exhaustion and a full stomach let him rest in dreamless sleep. Then the nightmares started again. It took weeks, but Hannah got Jacques to talk about the war. She had him start at the beginning with his leaving

Independence and heading west on the Santa Fe Trail. It took days in the telling for Jacques to get to the skirmishes in the woods and the battles with Hancock. Hannah cooked, cared for the orphans, and listened. For Jacques, it was therapy. A confession in detail of every battle, every man he killed, every friend he lost. Being able to remember the detail of every event was the mark of a strong mind. When every event recalled was horrific, it could drive the gifted mind to distraction and suicide.

At first, Jacques often lapsed, staring into space, quiet until a relived memory passed. If he stayed away too long, Hannah would gently bring him back. She wasn't a psychologist. However, she had been through this many a time at bedsides in the hospital. After a while, Jacques' lapses of consciousness grew fewer. Hannah considered this a sign of improvement.

Early April, news came that General Lee had surrendered to Grant at Appomattox after his final battle of the war. Days later, Johnson surrendered, and the war was officially over. Great hope swept the nation. President Lincoln could finally start the process of reuniting the southern states. That hope turned back to despair when news of his assassination came just one week later. Lincoln, the great man, the iron will and wisdom that led the Union to victory; it was beyond belief that he was dead at the hand of a coward. The nation was adrift in a sea of unknowns. Johnson, who succeeded Lincoln, was little more than a Southern sympathizer. He didn't favor protection for the liberated slaves. He never expressed any definite plans for the reunification of the South, even though his official position was for a rapid reunion with the provision imposed by Congress that the southern states accept the complete abolishment of slavery.

A telegram arrived from Jessica. She was on her way home. First by train to Ohio and then down the river. Travel by land was possible but not yet safe; hundreds of thousands of soldiers released from duty on both sides, were hungry and desperate, finding their way home. Hannah read the telegram over and over. She was as close to Jessica as she was to her daughter Lily. Jacques found her crying in her kitchen, the telegram in her hand. He read the telegram, then smiled and put his hand on Hannah's shoulder. It was the first time Hannah saw him smile. It was the first time since his return that he acted like the Jacques she helped raise from an infant. The country was awash with uncertainty, but if there was hope for Jacques, there was hope for every member of the devastated generation that fought the war. Jessica was coming home. Hannah suddenly realized a worry. Jessica didn't mention Jackson. Could that mean the worst?

The middle of summer arrived and brought Jessica with it. She wore a flower print dress, white with purple flowers, with a broad-brimmed straw hat on her head to shield her from the sun. She carried a carpetbag and pulled a small trunk on wheels behind her. Jacques was in Hannah's garden, pulling weeds when he saw her a block away. He didn't recognize her at first, but the woman looked familiar. He called Hannah, and she walked out onto the front porch of her little house. Hannah recognized Jessica immediately and shouted, "It's Jessica! It's Jessica! Go help her with that trunk."

Jessica dropped her luggage and ran the rest of the way to Hannah's open arms. Both women were sobbing, holding each other in the tight embrace for a long time. They were still holding each other when Jacques brought up the bags. Jessica was the first to speak, "Hannah, I can put my arms all the way around you!"

"The war-diet has been good for this fat old black woman. Where's Jackson, honey?"

Jessica stopped weeping quietly and broke down crying. When she could talk again, it was difficult for her to utter the words. "Jackson went down to Petersburg with an ambulance crew, and he never came back, and his unit searched, but they didn't find him among the dead. The ambulance wagon took a direct hit from an exploding shell and blew apart. The rest of the medics with Jackson were killed and lay scattered around the wreckage. Another medic from the hospital told me it was a bloody mess. The bloody mess in the wreckage of the wagon had to have been Jackson." She turned to Jacques, "Thank God you're alive. Where are your brothers and your sister?"

"I left them on a mountain in New Mexico Territory five years ago. They are either there or with Denise in San Francisco. I am sorry about Jackson. At least he didn't suffer." Jacques spoke his piece without expression without emotion. He turned and carried Jessica's things into the house.

Hannah said, "He is not well. He was unhurt but suffers from his memories. He is better now, but when he first came back, I was worried that he would take his own life. Maybe you can help him. There is guilt from surviving when tens of thousands died around him — a good many by his hand. There is something else. Something deep. I think it is shame. We haven't uncovered that one yet. I think he participated in some of the atrocities the newspapers reported."

Jessica nodded her head and started to look around. "The hospital is gone?"

"Yes, that circus tent is where the wounded veterans stay. I do what I can there, but most of them take care of themselves. Food is scarce. Every yard in town has a garden. The men in the tent have a whole field planted a couple of blocks south. I wouldn't go down there unless you want to see how amputees tend to a farm. One man is missing both legs and one arm. He pulls himself up and down the rows with a hoe. The town is full of damaged men. Almost every family with a little extra space has taken in a veteran or a refugee. The North is celebrating in the streets with parades and fireworks. They should come to places like this and see what the real outcome of the war has given us." Hannah paused, then asked, "Jessica, why did you have to walk up from the river?"

"There were several buckboards at the landing, but none of them would '*take money from a nigger*' no matter how much I offered."

Hannah said, "There are a lot of Southerners here full of prejudice and hatred. You have to be careful, honey. They are getting bolder and trying all kinds of evil to keep the blacks in slavery. What are you going to do now? We need a doctor here. Jacques needs something to do. What if you open a clinic for the vets. The carriage house behind Denise's mansion is still standing. Dr. Jessica Callahan, what do you think?"

Jessica wasn't thinking. She had a lot to relate. "I wouldn't say that I practiced medicine during the war. You see those men down in the tent? That's what I did. After every major battle, there was a pile of arms and legs outside my operating room. Jacques isn't the only one with nightmares. At least I don't feel guilty. I don't ever want to see another bone saw in my life. Let's go over and look at the carriage house tomorrow. Right now, I'm starving, and I need to rest. It will probably take some time for Jacques to get comfortable with talking to me. I have seen a lot of men with his problem. Of the few that were lucky enough to survive an amputation or infection and wind up in the recovery ward, all had emotional problems." Jacques was back in the garden, leaning on his hoe and staring into space.

Food wasn't a problem for Hannah. The veterans down in the tent kept her well supplied in vegetables and the occasional piece of venison or feral pig from the forest. It was a rare day that Hannah had any meat to cook, but today was one of those days. She had a huge pot of venison stew cooking on the stove and bread in the oven. Butter was like gold. Every milk cow in Missouri provided food for hungry soldiers or was killed by Union soldiers to deprive Confederate marauders of rations. The repair of the railroad from Jefferson City was almost complete, so soon, commerce and agriculture would start up again along the scorched corridor of northern Missouri.

The three old friends ate in silence, then Hannah asked, "Jessica, where are the Jones children?"

The tears returned to Jessica's eyes. "When the soldiers took me away, the children were down at *The Complex.* I don't know where they are. I don't know if they are alive."

Jacques reached over the table and put his hand over Jessica's. "If they are alive down there, I will find them. I overheard you two talking about a clinic in the carriage house. I think that is a good idea. We need to go to the bank and see if I can get some money. I need a horse, and you are going to need some medical supplies." Jacques hesitated, like one of his terrible memories bubbled up to the surface while he was talking, but then went on. "I'll get a horse and go down to our land as soon as I can."

Hannah filled with hope. Not for a clinic. She needed to see some sign that Jacques was going to be his Callahan self again. This moment was the first time Jacques expressed an interest in doing anything other than staring into space or weeding the garden. Jessica sensed Hannah's relief and said, "Thank you, Jacques. There is a lot of work out ahead of us here. Anything you could do will be greatly appreciated."

Jacques asked, "Who is the banker in town these days? I need to go see him."

Hannah smiled at him, "You are not going to the bank, looking like that. He will look at you and see one more deserter that has passed through here. You need a bath, a haircut, a shave, and new clothes. Do you realize that you have on a tattered pair of Union trousers and a Confederate shirt? Look at your feet. You have been walking around in mismatched boots. You can't go to the bank looking like that. Jessica and I will draw you a bath. I have a little money. We will see if we can buy you some clothes and restore you into a Callahan."

It took a couple of days of grooming, but in the end, Jacques looked like a clean, squared away young man. He was walking around, standing tall. The droop of his shoulders was gone. He stopped staring into space. The nightmares were still there almost every night, but they weren't as severe. It was time to go to the bank.

The three of them were walking to the bank. It was a beautiful morning in early fall. The summer heat was giving way into cooler days and cold nights. The forest was beginning to don its fall colors, and flocks of ducks and geese were migrating south. All around the square, men and women were rebuilding homes. The proud Independence City Hall was still standing. The square was empty. Gone were the days of thousands heading west on the Santa Fe Trail. Gone were the outfitters who supplied them. Hannah wanted to go up past Anna's grave. It was time Jacques paid his respects and put another part of his upbringing back into perspective. From a block away, they could see that the gravesite had been disturbed. There were some men there shoveling dirt back over the coffin. One of the men was as old as Hannah; his name was Andrew Sheridan. He had been one of the last teachers at Anna's school before Quantrill burned it to the ground. He greeted the visitors. "Hello, Hannah. My God! Is that Jessica and one of the Callahan boys?"

"Yes, Andrew, right on both. Jessica and Jacques. What's going on here?"

"Graverobbers, Hannah. We found the coffin open, and the alabaster horse with the silver knight was gone. I'm sorry, Hannah. We'll put this back in order. There are too many desperate men here. They will do anything for a buck. Be careful; there are a lot of slavers and Confederate deserters returning here along with the legitimate veterans from both sides. Jacques, we knew you were with Hancock from the beginning from the only letter you ever wrote to Rufus. You survived. Welcome back. I hope you stay; we could use your help around here."

Jacques intended to stay, and the first thing he was going to help with was tracking down the men who violated his mother's grave. The alabaster knight was a well-known piece of art. It would show up somewhere. He would post a reward for its return and then backtrack it to the robbers. He jumped over the wrought iron fence and took the shovel from Mr. Sheridan. "We were on our way to the bank, but that can wait until I help fix this desecration. At least they didn't destroy the headstones or the fence." With that, Jacques undertook the long process of reconstruction with the first shovel full of dirt over his mother's coffin. Hannah and Jessica stood hand-in-hand and watched until Jacques and the men finished the restoration of the grave.

The next day, they went to the bank early and were waiting for it to open when one of the clerks walked up the steps and unlocked the door. He was a wispy little man and looked like a teller with a black vest over a white silk shirt. He wore black trousers and good shoes; he didn't suffer badly through the war. He wore a name tag that said, Wilson Hicks. Before he opened the door, he turned and said, "We don't have any cash here if you are waiting for money."

"I need to see the bank manager," Jacques said.

The little man let them in and took them back to the manager's office. "Mr. Thurman Jones is the manager. He will be in shortly. Make yourselves comfortable. I will put on the coffee."

Thurman Jones arrived just as the coffee finished, and the aroma filled the room. The bank even had real sugar and cream; both were rare these days. Mr. Jones introduced himself. He was missing his left arm. He noticed Jacques staring where his arm should have been. "Antietam, and call me Thurman. What can I do for you?"

Hannah opened her bag and took out a tin of tea. "This is hypericum; it is for phantom pain. I grow it in the veterans' garden. It relieves the symptoms of phantom pain. I heard about your arm; if you have pain there, this will help."

Thurman took the tin of tea and called out to his teller. "Wilson, come make me some tea, please."

Hannah said, "It works best if you drink it before you go to bed. If it works for you, I have plenty; but give me the tin back when it is empty. Those are hard to come by."

Thurman said, "Thank you, Hannah." Then he looked at Jessica and said, "You don't remember me, do you, Jessica? You removed my appendix six years ago." Jacques opened his mouth to speak, but Thurman cut him off. "I know who you are. One of the Callahan twins, but I don't know which one. It doesn't matter; I have something for you." He opened the desk drawer and took out the alabaster horse and silver knight, and slid it across the top of his desk to Jacques.

Jacques looked at the statuette in wonder, "I'm Jacques. Where did you get this?"

"From Christian Commerly. He runs the pawnshop. He got it from the men who operate the pram service from the ferry dock up to town. They are all unscrupulous laggards. We don't have evidence, but everyone knows they rode in here with Quantrill and stayed after the raids. Commerly was in here first thing yesterday morning. He couldn't wait to get rid of your mother's statue. I gave him a hundred dollars for it."

Jacques couldn't conceal his shock. "I came in here this morning to borrow some money. Now I find out I already owe you a hundred dollars. I think I am good for it, but Denise moved all our funds to San Francisco when we headed west."

Thurman laughed. Wilson returned with the tea. He gulped it down, then he said. "Jacques, you are more than good for it. Right now, I would venture that you are the wealthiest man in Independence, if not all of Missouri. A while back, your sister sent a request through your banker in San Francisco. She wanted an estimate of how much it would cost to reconstruct everything destroyed in the war. I got estimates for rebuilding the school, the hospital, and the mansion. No one would tackle estimating what it would cost to rebuild the brewery."

Thurman went on. "I have three million dollars on the books that your sister authorized for the reconstruction. No work has started. I couldn't find a project manager I could trust. You look like a young man who needs a job. It is yours if you want it."

Astonished with news of his siblings, Jacques asked, "Where are they?"

"Out in what is now the Arizona Territory. Your brother Eli, or his wife, that is, discovered one of the richest gold mines ever. The gold all went into the mint in San Francisco. It helped fund a good portion of the last years of the war. Right now, your family has something north of sixty million dollars, and the gold mine is still producing. You remember your father's friend, Charles Coryn; he handled your father's fortune well. You and your brothers and sister were wealthy before the gold mine. You need to write to them and let them know you are still alive."

"I will do that, but right now, I need some cash, and Wilson said you don't have any in the bank. I also need a building that the veterans in the amputee camp can make their home. Also, contact the contractors that gave you the estimates, and let's get the work started. I'll be the project manager, but I will need some help. I have no idea how to go about that."

Thurman said, "I'll give you Wilson out there. He was the Chief Financial Officer for the Delta Lines before the war started. He isn't an engineer, but he has the most important skill for the job, and that is his absolute honesty. There is something else I want you to read before you leave here. It's in the vault. It is hard to open. Quantrill's raiders did their best to get it open, but there wasn't a skilled safecracker among them. They sprung the door a little with a black powder blast trying to get it open. Vigilantes from town killed them all on the steps outside while they were waiting for the blast to go off."

They walked out of the office and over to the safe door. Wilson was struggling with the combination and the handle. Jacques reached around him and gave the handle a turn and a strong jerk. The door opened about an inch. Wilson had a crowbar to open it further. Jacques pulled it all the way open. Thurman took a key out of his pocket and opened a box. Inside there were birth certificates, death certificates, deeds, and the original Articles of Incorporation for Callahan Meadows. The names of all the shareholders in his father's corporation were listed there and dated.

Thurman said, "I don't know if any of these people are still alive. Quantrill killed all the homesteaders he could find. Hannah, you have three orphans. They are heirs. I'm sure their fathers and mothers are on this list. There may be more around town, but be careful; you will have a lot of young men and women claiming they were born down at *The Complex.*"

"There's one more thing here," Thurman said. "See that row of ledgers along the shelf back there. I understand that your grandmother put them in here before she left to go to California. They are all the ledgers from your father's business. When you have a safe place for all this stuff, you are welcome to take it out of here. It is all yours." Thurman opened another drawer in the safe and counted out three hundred dollars in Federal notes of all denominations. "This is all I can give you for now, but in a week I will have the bank full of money again with a shipment of currency from the mint in Philidelphia."

Jacques shook hands with Thurman and Wilson, and as they left the bank, he gave most of the money to Hannah. "I only need enough to buy a Navy Colt and a Henry rifle. I have some business to conduct with Christian Commerly and the men down at the river."

Hannah said, "Jacques, the killing is over. I will have the veterans take care of the men down at the river and the pawnshop. You stay out of it. You are a Callahan, and while you killed hundreds of men in the war, that's different; a Callahan is not a cold-blooded killer."

Jacques drew remorseful and asked, "You forget about the prisoners on the Boydton Plank Road, Hannah?"

"Temporary insanity, Jacques. You need to share some stories with the veterans over in the camp. A lot of them were involved in the same sort of thing." Jacques looked at Hannah like she might be right. It was still going to take some time for him to put it behind him.

The three friends left the bank and bought: two horses and saddles, two Colt revolvers, bedrolls, and a small tent. The next day Jacques and Jessica rode down the road to *The Complex*. They spent three days down in the forest looking for survivors, but only found one man and woman rebuilding a cabin. Jacques recognized the man; he had been the foreman at the sawmill. The man had taken the name Callahan as his own. He recognized Jacques immediately and proudly introduced himself and his wife as Tunnis and Betty Callahan. Jessica stayed with Betty, and Tunis took Jacques into the forest to show him the remains of the locomotive.

When Jacques and Jessica returned to Independence, the three men down at the river were missing, and the veterans were running the pram service. Commerly had burned to death, smoking in bed. As Jacques posted his letter to his family, he thought he would indeed need to get to know the veterans much better. Contractors were waiting for him at the bank. The reconstruction of the Callahan empire was soon to be underway.

Dragon's Roar

The end of 1864 were exciting times for the Red Mountain community. Eli sat at the head of the table on New Year's Day with his family and all the miners and their families gathered around the ramada. Bridgette sat beside Suzette. Connor had returned Ragini from India, and Moses was there with her. Moses and Ragini married in Yuma as soon Connor reunited the happy couple. John and Mary sat at the table with Mr. Sue and Professor Laity, and Lila sat with the girls. The toddlers were under the table, enjoying the attention and treats handed down from above.

Eli had a lot to say; everyone grew quiet to listen. He started in a loud, serious voice. "I can't begin to express how proud I am of every one of you for everything we have achieved here over the last four years. When Abby and I first came here, we had no idea that we had stumbled onto the richest gold mine in the Territories. From that simple start with a pick and shovel and a gold pan, you people have built something here that has changed your lives forever. I can't tell you how proud I am that we have stuck together and not suffered the woes of others that have struck it rich and squandered the wealth that easy money brings."

"While we have been here working, the world has changed around us. Before long, we will all be making decisions to either stay here or go back into that world. None of you will go back into the world the same as you arrived at Red Mountain. I know you single men need to go find some wives." Everyone chuckled. "Roland and I have decided it is time for all of you to know where you stand. Since the beginning, all of you have been accumulating money from the sale of the gold in accounts in your names in the Bank of San Francisco. When we incorporated Red Mountain Mining, Roland reserved sixty percent of the stock for our family. That sixty percent will now be shared equally between the four of us, John, Moses, and Mr. Sue."

"The forty percent is divided equally among you twenty men that were the strong backs that made all this happen. What's a two percent share worth? Right now, each of you has four-hundred thousand dollars in your account in San Francisco. I wanted all of you to know where you stood before we went any farther, mining the heart out of the mountain. All of you know that as we remove the high-grade ore, the more the risk of a major cave-in. No one is holding a gun to your head and making you stay here. You are free to go if you want. Roland and I are staying until the end of the high-grade. We will mine it all out, or the mine will cave in, and we will be through. There is a risk, and I want all of you to think hard about taking that risk or walking away safe."

Everyone was quiet for a long time; even the toddlers under the table could sense that the mood was heavy and joined in the long silence. The six men that Moses brought with him from the river stepped forward. The oldest of them, already gray at the temples, spoke for the group. "Eli, you lifted us out of slavery, worked shoulder to shoulder with us inside this mountain. We came here with nothing, and you have made us rich. We ain't leaving until you do." The rest of the men stepped forward in agreement. The few wives among them, especially the miners' wives, stood by and hugged their men. They, too, knew the risk but understood and shared the loyalty to Eli.

Eli didn't take that kind of loyalty for granted, he went on, "Professor and Lila, you have brought more integrity to this mountain than anyone else here. Roland has written to Jim Parish to put an endowment in place for the Paleontology Department of the Jesuit College." The Professor started to protest, but Eli quieted him with a gesture of his hand, patting the air in front of him. "We have moved two million dollars into a trust to fund the endowment. You can use the money any way you see fit. The only thing we want in return is the best education possible for Maria and Eliza. The four of you can move into the mansion on Nob Hill and stay there for as long as you want." Cliff and Lila were quiet; both had tears in their eyes. All the men applauded. Eli said, "Now, I think it's time to eat, drink and be merry." Red Mountain did just that well into the night.

The next morning John and the miners were huddled around the table in the ramada with Eli. They were deep into a mine planning session. The spiral ramp had got them to the bottom of the nugget lode — the crosscut at the bottom of the spiral connected to the vertical shaft. The men, however, brought up a legitimate concern. There was no escape route from the bottom of the mine. John posed two alternatives: one was another decline starting far enough back in the tunnel to intercept the crosscut at the bottom of the mine; the other a vertical winze somewhere in the vicinity of the underground boiler room. The men opted for the winze even though it would be harder to construct. They didn't like the idea that a long decline would not be an easy route to evacuate through in the event of a caving emergency. The winze was a good solution. The original winch motor from the top of the mountain would have to be brought down and disassembled for moving in through the tunnel. The mill crew and the men who operated the clamshell from the top of the mountain volunteered to do that job. The miners would start on the cavern for the winch motor.

The men wanted to get right at work now that a logical plan was in place. Mary stopped them with a huge pan of ham and eggs. Abby and Lia were passing out plates and coffee cups. Mary said, "You guys need to sit down and eat. I know most of you go to work with no breakfast. Not today; I know you won't stop for lunch, so eat up. The mountain and the gold nuggets aren't going anywhere." Roland and Mr. Sue had already eaten their share in the kitchen while Mary was cooking. They headed over to the refinery.

Suzette and Bridgette saddled their horses. They were going into Wickenburg to a building they had constructed to house a small clinic and a few beds. Every day they had miners from Vulture City coming up to the clinic at Red Mountain. The clinic in town would save the sick and hurt from having to make the journey up to their clinic. The plan was for them to spend two days a week at the clinic in Wickenburg. They would spend more time there if the patients needed care beyond a one or two day visit. The clinic was under construction on Frontier Street in Wickenburg. A two-story hotel was going up next to the clinic. Suzette booked a room for a year in advance before the foundation of the hotel was even out of the ground.

On this visit to their project in town, they were only going to talk to the foreman of the carpenters and then ride down to Vulture City. While Suzette was talking to the foreman, a stage pulled into town. Bridgette was watching but was mostly disinterested in the passengers. Disinterest turned to dread when she recognized Fillmore stepping down from the stage. The driver and his helper unloaded two large trunks, and Fillmore sat down on them, waiting for some help to move him up to the boarding house several doors up the street. Bridgette turned away from him and twisted her flaming red hair into a ball and clamped her hat down over it. She clamped onto Suzette's arm and guided her around the corner of the clinic where Fillmore couldn't see them.

Suzette looked at Bridgette and said, "What's the matter?"

Bridgette's voice was only a shaky whisper, "It's Fillmore. He just got off the stage with two large trunks, and it looks like he is planning to stay."

Suzette looked around the corner and said, "Just what this town needs. Another quack, but he will be some real competition for Sawbones down in

Vulture city." Suzette summoned a boy who was following them around and gave him a nickel to bring their horses around from the front of the clinic. They saddled up and rode down Frontier Street, leaving Wickenburg as fast as they could before Fillmore had a chance to recognize them. It would be easier to plan some revenge on Fillmore if he didn't know they were close.

Suzette and Bridgette visited Sawbones down in Vulture city regularly. Sawbones deferred all cases requiring minor surgery to Suzette. This day, there was a miner in his office with a bad compound fracture of his forearm. Sawbones had sedated the man and then sent a lad riding hard up to Red Mountain to get Suzette. The lad must have passed them while they were in Wickenburg. Bridgette said, "It will be dark by the time we finish this."

Suzette responded, "We'll send word to Henry. We can stay with him tonight and ride back in the morning. I want to talk to him about Fillmore anyway." She had Sawbones walk over to Wickenburg's house and let him know that he would have some guests for the night. The broken forearm was difficult to put back together. It was well into the evening before the girls finished. Sawbones was a likable man, even though he wasn't a very good doctor, being drunk most of the time didn't help either. He was good for Vulture City, though, and Vulture City was good for him. His name was Hershel Pearson, but almost no one knew him by any other name than Sawbones. He accompanied Suzette and Bridgette over to Wickenburg's house and stayed with them for dinner. Over a dinner of wild javelina, Suzette and Bridgette related the story of Fillmore in detail. Both Henry and Hershel agreed that they would try to hire Filmore for the clinic. Suzette and Bridgette slept well that night, knowing that they would soon have total control of Filmore.

The next day, Red Mountain was a beehive of activity. The old winch motor was brought down from the top of the mountain. Down was a lot easier than up. Moses was there with a dozen mules to do the heavy pulling. The winch was brought around to the portal, and the mill men were busy taking it apart. It would be taken through the tunnel and reassembled in the underground boiler room. The miners were busy underground enlarging the back of the boiler room to accommodate the winch and also mining out a raise and a crosscut that would hold the pulleys for the cables. The clamshell was simple. Moses had it down the mountain by the end of the day, and it didn't need to be disassembled to take it in through the portal.

Suzette and Bridgette returned home that evening. They were anxious to tell Eli and Roland about Fillmore's arrival in Wickenburg. Mr. Sue listened in and then reminded Suzette about her vow to *Do no Harm*. As with Jenkins and his partner, Roland told the girls that they didn't have to do anything. He would take care of Fillmore. He was sure that he would have an opportunity to do so. Bridgette was uncertain if she wanted Roland's help. She wanted to kill Fillmore herself. Roland said, "You can help if you want, but we can't afford to lose either one of you. Let's sit on it for a while. If Fillmore sets up shop, he will be around to deal with at our leisure." Roland could see that Filmore's arrival had affected Bridgette deeply. She had never expected to run across her abuser again.

The Callahans, the Goulds, and Mr. Sue sat under the ramada and watched a spectacular full moon rise through crystal clear early spring air. Moses had brought a bundle of newspapers up from Yuma, and the families were reading by lantern light. The nation's capital and all the major cities back east were celebrating Lincoln's election to a second term. Petersburg and Richmond were under siege, and Grant was moving the Army of the Potomac in for the kill with two hundred and fifty thousand troops. They were most concerned about one soldier in particular and combed the newspapers for any reports of General Hancock's whereabouts. The moon was high in the eastern sky by the time Eli was satisfied that there was nothing in the papers that would ease their minds about Jacques.

The next day was again all about mining. Eli was with his men, and they started digging down to start the winze. As usual, he was stripped to the waist and shoulder to shoulder with his men. The men were digging with purpose; they would soon be taking out the heart of the mountain, and expectations ran high that what John called the *Nugget Pod* would yield as much as a million more ounces of gold. The crew from the mill were learning how to saw timber sets that would shore up the winze. There would be ladders down to the crosscut on the bottom. The bottom of the winze would also connect with a drift to the vertical shaft; a third way out if all others were blocked. It would take about two months to finish the development work for the escape route, but it was worth it. The escape route afforded a lavish amount of peace of mind. It was also important to John and Eli that they had done the best they could to ensure the safety of the men in the event of a major collapse.

Eliza and Maria were finishing with the excavation of the other two dinosaurs. Tio assembled the skeletons in Eliza's Cavern as the girls brought out the pieces. The Professor was in awe of Tio's work in the cavern. Lit by lanterns in key positions, the skeletons of the dinosaurs cast eerie shadows up on the ceiling and walls. Walking in from Tio's tunnel, it was easy to imagine one's self back in prehistoric times. Soon, when the girls finished their dig, the skeletons would be disassembled, boxed up, and shipped to the museum in San Francisco. Eliza, Maria, and Tio would be going with Professor Laity and Lila; Suzette was not looking forward to being separated from her daughter again. Eli had to keep reminding her that her daughter wasn't a girl anymore. She was a young woman entitled to an education and a life of her own. Suzette had done her motherhood, and she had done it well. It was time to let the two girls spread their wings.

Two months passed faster than anyone could fathom. News of the end of the war arrived, and like every community left standing in America, Red Mountain celebrated the end of the war. For the Callahans and their close friends, however, they celebrated but were reserved waiting to hear about Jacques.

The hard work in the mine made the days slip by with a lot of sweat underground and exhausted men sleeping like the dead before rising to another day's work. With unceasing effort, the bottom of the winze advanced and connected to the crosscut. The spiral decline ended in a drift that circled the bottom of the ore body. The miners drove another crosscut across the diameter of the circle. At the top of the ore body, the roof of the *Usenbestia* cavern was mined to the shape of a perfect cone. The bottom of the cone was forty feet in diameter. It wasn't as wide as the ore body, but it was as far as John dared go without further support. All was ready; mining the rich ore in earnest was a historic day for the Dragon Tooth Gold Mine.

Mr. Sue recorded the day in his log of the mine production. He had a lot of time on his hands as the mill only ran a few hours a day to process the development muck from the mine. He spent his days reading and in training for his inevitable battle with his nephew. Moses arrived with a supply train full of boxes and packing materials to ship the dinosaurs to San Francisco. Ed Sigler arrived with him with a cameraman to photograph the skeletons in place. Every detail of the cavern was recorded, and planning for the construction of an identical cavern was completed for the museum at the Jesuit College. Every detail of Tio's display of the three skeletons would greet visitors entering the cavern in San Francisco to include the lantern light and the shadows on the ceiling. He had arranged the two smaller skeletons in what appeared to be a loving embrace with their necks entwined; mouths opened to the heavens. Everyone thought the artistry was remarkable. No one could know what went through Tio's mind, but they could see that it made him happier than usual when someone walked into the cavern for the first time and experienced awe. Every day, people came up from Wickenburg to escape the late summer heat and stand in awe in the cool air of the cavern, looking at the skeletons and wondering about their origins.

Moses had a lot more than crates and burlap in this shipment. He had a letter; the address read The Callahan Family – C/O Moses -- Yuma Crossing – Arizona Territory. The return address read J. – Independence, MO. Moses brought it to Suzette in the clinic. She held it in her hands like it was the Holy Grail, then covered her mouth with one hand and broke down crying. The long-awaited word from Jacques was in her hands. She trembled out of fear as to what the letter would say. When she got control of herself, she sent for Eli, Roland, John, and Mr. Sue. Mary and Abby joined Suzette and Bridgette under the ramada and waited for the men. The letter sat on a cutting board in the middle of the table like a coiled snake ready to strike. Suzette feared the worse. But Mary put her arm around her and said, "He's alive, child. Don't fear the worse. If he could write, and you say it looks like his hand on the address, he may have survived uninjured. I am not going to make up a dark picture to worry about until we read what he has to say."

The men arrived from the mine one by one. Mr. Sue was first, and he sat down in the middle of the table and put his hand on the letter. "I will read it to you." Suzette covered his hand with hers and had him wait for the others. Eli arrived dirty from the mine with his shirt over his shoulder, with sweat gleaming on his muscled shoulders. John and Roland came together. Mary came out of the kitchen with an urn of coffee and a plate of cookies. John had a drawing under his arm and Roland, a ledger book as usual. With everyone settled at the table, Mr. Sue slit the envelope open with a long fingernail and removed the one-page letter. He unfolded the letter, looked around the table, and started to read.

Dear Family,

Forgive me for not writing sooner. I have been far less than myself these last two years. I am with Hannah in Independence. Physically, I am unhurt, but I was close to insanity when Hannah found me at our mother's grave. I am better now. You shouldn't worry about me. I have been working with the veterans here, and I have been to the bank.

The reconstruction of everything in Independence is underway. Jessica has returned from the war hospitals back east and is rebuilding the hospital. Jackson never returned from the siege of Petersburg. Rufus died fighting Quantrill's raiders.

On a happier note, when you finish whatever you are doing out west, your home here in Missouri will be ready for your return. I'm still a Callahan, and we are going to be making whiskey again by next year. I need men we can trust. If you have some, bring them with you.

J.

Suzette had been holding her breath. Both Mary and Bridgette had an arm around her; Abby and Lia were reaching across the table, holding her hands. Suzette wasn't sobbing but sitting with her eyes shut tight, breathing deeply, trying not to collapse with relief. Finally, she asked. "What did he mean that he is still a Callahan?"

Mr. Sue said, "He wouldn't be the first man to return from a war on the verge of insanity. Some never recover. Some don't even know who they are for the rest of their lives. Jacques is going to recover. Probably completely, but if I am not wrong, he will be remembering thousands dying around him for the rest of his life. If you want to go there, I can go with you."

It was time for all of them to rethink their plans. Going back to Missouri never crossed their minds since the four of them left. Jacques's letter changed all that. Eli looked at Abby, who nodded a secret approval and said, "I'm not going back until we finish with the mine." Abby let go of Suzette and squeezed his hand. Roland knew Lia would want to go to San Francisco to stay close to Maria and Tio. They would have a lot to talk about before making up their minds. Roland still had Red Mountain Mining, their interests in the Banning/Moses freight company, and their share of the Vulture Gold Mine to manage. Whatever he decided, he wouldn't decide on his own. He and Lia would decide together. For now, he was the only one that thought about writing back to his twin. Roland was always good with the details.

Suzette was having difficulty holding back a decision that she made after Mr. Sue finished reading the letter. She didn't want to blurt out that she would go as soon as possible without first talking it over with Bridgette. She would have that conversation when they were alone. Bridgette looked at Suzette with intense feelings. She was expecting Suzette to say she would also head east, but Suzette reassured her with a hug and whispered in her ear, "We'll talk about it tonight."

Eli asked John and Mr. Sue, "How long would it take to make ten thousand ounces in bars stamped three-nines fine with our name on them. I want to ship that much to the bank in Independence to make that bank solid. I don't like what I read in the papers about Johnson's lack of a definite plan for reconstruction. The war has only been over for a short while, and already, the South is running at the whim of Army commanders and carpetbaggers. Roland tells me that we are in for a depression, and there are going to be a lot of bank failures. We need to back up the bank in Independence with more than a piece of paper from Jim Parish.

John was thoughtful and took a while to answer. Mr. Sue was sliding the beads on his abacus. Eli could hear the gears grinding away as the two men collaborated on their answer. Finally, Mr. Sue answered, "No problem on the supply, we have plenty of gold. The choke point is refining to three nines. We can only finish about two-hundred-fifty ounces a day to three nines. It will take more than a month to have your shipment ready. I will have the girls start rolling out the ribbons for the salt melts today. It will take at least two melts for each bar; three would be better. We can accumulate small bars and then pour thousand-ounce bars to finish. That will reduce the number of bullion assays down to ten to guarantee the shipment at three nines."

Moses well understood the risk of shipping gold east beyond the reaches of the Banning/Callahan Freight Company. Sensing the planning was coming to a close, he said, "When it is time to ship the gold, Regini and I will take it there along with anyone else that wants to go back. Suzette turned to Moses, and the look on her face confirmed that she would be going. Moses smiled at her and knew what she was thinking. He gave a small affirmative nod, and

Suzette smiled back. Everyone stood up and stretched. It was time to go back to work.

What became known as the *Paleontology Team* was busy packing up the skeletons. The Professor and his wife, Tio, and the girls were the only ones allowed to touch the fossils. Moses and his men helped with the packing and carried out each crate after it was sealed and numbered, and replaced it with a new one. Roland, through Jim Parish, had insured the shipment with Lloyds of London for two million dollars. That was as high as the conservative London insurance company would go, but the fossils were priceless, especially the skull with the golden tooth. Ed Sigler's photographs of the cavern and his articles on the dinosaurs and the girls that excavated them had made them all world famous. The crates, the team, and Roland and Lia with little Anna would all go from Los Angeles to San Francisco on a Banning armored steamship. They would be leaving early in the fall after the summer heat left the desert.

Inside the mine, John had four vertical raises being mined upward from the bottom crosscuts. He had rails in the crosscuts and ore chutes to fill mine cars, all by gravity. Peeples had taken over the sawing of mine timbers from the forest by Prescott, and every day, wagons full of square set mine timbers arrived at the portal. Abby's boys took over moving the timbers to the winze where they were lowered down to the crosscut. The miners took them from there as they kept expanding the stopes. It was going to take well into the next year, but if they could recover all of the high-grade ore from the mine, the Dragon Tooth Mine would be a million-ounce producer or better. Mr. Sue was very pleased with the totals that kept building in his log.

The four stopes that John had on his mine plan were going to raise and connect to the floor of the dragon cavern. It was one-hundred and fifty feet up to the cavern. John called this *Phase One* of his mine plans. Once interconnected, the four stopes would become ore chutes, and the ore remaining in the cavern would be mined down from the top. This John called *Phase* 2. It would take six months to complete the mine that far and would remove on the order of twenty-seven thousand tons of the high grade. After that, John planned to keep expanding the domed top of the cavern out a few feet at a time and mining that new bench all the way to the bottom. If they didn't suffer any spawling of the ceiling or collapse of the sidewalls of the stopes, he would keep going until the heavy nugget part of the load was completely mined out. Maria had named the gold load, *garganta del dragón*, the *Throat of the Dragon*.

The day after they had read the letter from Jacques, Suzette and Bridgette announced that they were going to Wickenburg to check on the clinic. When the paleontology shipment was ready, they would leave with Roland and go as far as Yuma with the Paleontology Team, and take the Butterfield Stage east to Santa Fe. They would transfer there to the Overland Stage and ride it to wherever the railhead from the east now ended and then ride the train into Independence. Traveling night and day on the stagecoaches, they would be in Independence in less than two weeks, maybe less depending on where they met the railroad.

Eli asked, "What about Fillmore?"

Bridgette answered for both of them, "We're putting him behind us. The clinic in Wickenburg needs a doctor. Maybe the town will hire him to stay on there until we get back. We, and *I* especially, don't care anymore." Bridgette put special emphasis on the *I*.

Roland added his two cents, "I had Henry hire Fillmore for the clinic. He doesn't know he is working for you and Suzette. You girls can deal with him when you get back."

Eli asked another question, "What about us? Who will take care of our injured? What if we have a major mine disaster?"

Mary spoke up, "I can take care of all the minor injuries. Just don't have an accident that requires surgery. Otherwise, you're going to have to rely on Fillmore. I think it's important that Suzette and Bridgette go. Jacques needs to know that his family is behind him. I noticed in his letter; he didn't know if you would come back. To me, the whole letter expressed a lot of doubt about your feelings, and he is hoping that putting your home back together in Independence will bring you back. Go, the two of you. If you have to stay there, don't come back!"

The last part of Mary's statement startled Suzette. She hadn't thought of not coming back. But Mary was right. None of them intended to stay at Red Mountain forever. Roland could see Suzette was deep in thought. He brought her back to the reality of the moment, "You better pack. Moses will be here this afternoon, and we are leaving in a few days. We will take the River Route to Yuma so that I can talk to Henry about keeping the clinic financed and Fillmore employed."

Eli was one step ahead of everyone. "Suzette, you and Bridgette don't have to ride the stages to Independence. I'm going to have Moses take you there with the gold shipment. You will have to wait a month or more, but Moses and Ragini will see you safely across, and that way, you can take your horses with you. You will be safe and traveling along the route of the Banning stage line. You will be back in Independence in a few weeks to a month. Roland and I will have a letter for you to carry to Jacques. I will let you read it and then seal it up. I want to reassure him that he is in charge of the reconstruction, and I won't usurp his authority if and when I get back there."

Suzette hugged her brother and said, "Thank you. That is a better plan than we had. We'll be packed and ready to go when the gold is ready. Bridgette and I will ride down to Wickenburg today to talk to Fillmore. Don't worry; I am not going to kill him. Both of us need to finish with him, upfront and personal. We will be back by tonight."

Suzette didn't have time to think about how her abrupt decision to leave would play out and was relieved that they would have a little more time. It was a month or more before they would leave; she was already thinking about what she would pack. With the thought of not coming back, she decided she would take her footlocker with her prized possessions and a satchel with changes of clothing needed during the journey. They talked about it on their way to Wickenburg. Bridgette didn't know where her future was taking her, and she didn't have a footlocker full of personal things. She would only take a suitcase and a satchel; her whole worldly possessions packed in two bags. Both of them would carry their revolvers and their Henry rifles. The west was still the west, despite being able to cross in an armored stagecoach rather than a wagon train. The hostile Indians east of Santa Fe were no longer a threat, but there were issues of veterans and deserters returning from the war.

It took several days for the men to pack and load all the crates for the archeology team. The crate with the skull and gold tooth would be loaded last into one of the armored wagons. The rest of the crates went as common freight, but heavily guarded none the less.

Suzette had talked Mr. Sue into staying with Eli. She worried that Mr. Sue, despite his patience, still had to deal with his nephew. Suzette hugged him with tears in her eyes and kissed him on both cheeks when he agreed to stay with Eli at least till all the gold for the shipment to Independence was refined and ready to go. She couldn't talk as Roland waited for Lia and little Anna at the door of the first stagecoach. She turned and buried her face in Eli's shoulder. He held her for a minute and then passed her to Abby and Mary. Roland had his family loaded into the first stagecoach. He shook hands with Eli, John, and Mr. Sue. "I'll be back," he said as he stepped into the coach.

Eli walked over to Abby, who held Eliza in her arms with tears streaming from her eyes. Suzette watched with Mary and John as Abby passed Eliza and Marie into the loving care of Clifford and Lila. Suzette wasn't crying. She put her arm around Mary and said, "You are right; it isn't easier, but I am handling it better. I am not worried about her; I am worried about me. I may never see her again. I am not ready for that."

Mary walked her to the corral, where Bridgette was ready with their horses. Mary said, "You will never be ready to say goodbye forever. That's a part of motherhood, Suzette. Don't ever let it go; it is a part of who you are now." Mary kissed both of the young women. It was her turn to weep, and the girls left her there in the corral as they mounted up and rode to the front of the wagon train to ride scout for Moses as far as Wickenburg..

Moses satisfied that everyone and all his teamsters and swampers were aboard, climbed onto the lead armored wagon, and cracked his whip. The mules were anxious to be on their way. They stepped out in a healthy trot. Moses pulled them back into a walk; it was a long way to the Gila River, and they didn't need to get there in one day.

The Callahans accepted that part of their family was separated again. On the other hand, they also accepted that a very important reunion would be happening before long. Little Anna was at the window of the coach, waving goodbye. Everyone waved back and watched the coach until it was out of sight. John and Mr. Sue went back to the mine. Eli stayed with his family for the rest of the day. They talked well into the night, and after the two boys were asleep, he and Abby climbed the mountain under the light of a gibbous moon. The mountaintop was completely changed since their arrival five years ago. They sat on the eastern slope for a long time, just holding one another. Eli finally said, "You know; if the world was truly flat, I think you could see Independence from here."

Abby kissed her husband and said, "I think you can see it from here, anyway." They stayed on the mountain till dawn then walked down hand in hand. It didn't matter that their family was again scattered all over North America. Whatever the future brought their way, they would be together.

They would build to that future together, man and wife till the end of their days.

Filmore

There was the promise of a beautiful pink sunrise on an early summer morning at Red Mountain. Eli was the only one up with a cup of coffee of his own making. He watched Suzette stumble out of her house in a silk kimono she used for a bathrobe. It was white silk with several blue and gold-plaid silk streamers down the edges of the front, tied with a blue and gold sash. There was an elegant peacock embroidered on the back. She came back from the kitchen with a cup of Eli's bad coffee and sat down next to him. She asked, "You know what day this is?"

"Yes, it's June fourth, your birthday."

"You know what I want?"

"Yes. You want to go home and find Jacques and help him if you can."

"Another thing, I want you to send for Lily."

"I already did. Lili and Ben should be here in another week."

"Eli, you are scaring me. Have you developed some clairvoyance of your own, or are we both thinking about the same things?"

"I don't think I am clairvoyant. It just makes sense. John and the men won't quit mining until they recover all the high-grade ore from the mine. Lili was able to tell there was something great in the mine when she sensed the skeletons. I am hoping that she will be able to sense the danger and tell me something about it. The more ore we take out from the bottom of the mine, the more the danger of the cave-in that will possibly kill some of us and shut us down for good. If the mine caves without us in there, we can continue to draw the caved ore from the bottom. I think Lily can help us with this."

"But there is something else. I am worried about you and Bridgette making the trip back to Independence without me even though you won't be on your own. I have Moses coming back with an extra armored wagon and enough supply wagons to get you to Independence. I'm going to ship the gold with you and have you deposit it into the bank in Independence. With Moses taking you there, you will be safe, and you can take your horses with you."

Suzette was amazed, "You are clairvoyant. I didn't want to leave my horse, and Bridgette has grown fond of her gelding. But as far as going with Moses, we have discussed this before. Why are you bringing it up again?"

"There is another option. You could go to San Francisco or Los Angeles and take a trip around the world to get home. You could stop in Paris and talk to the doctors there that are reading your publications. Even if you take the Santa Fe trail home, you should still consider going to Paris. It will be good for you. If you do that, I want you to go to where your mother came from and look for relatives; it would be good to know the other side of the family. Denise never mentioned brothers or sisters, but it likely she had some uncles and aunts. Also, I would like to know what it was like there. Maybe someday I will go there myself when the mine runs out of nuggets."

"One more thing. The war is over, but the country still isn't safe. There are millions of people, soldiers, and civilians that are now without direction or support without the war effort to keep them employed or tell them what to do. There are already desperate people showing up here. It has to be a lot worse back east. Until the South is productive again, there are going to be a lot of hungry people down there."

"Then there is the issue of the freed slaves. They will be fine; they can feed themselves. But the south is full of disenfranchised whites that aren't happy with emancipation. It is one thing to say they are free. It is quite another to treat them as equals. There will be a lot of trouble, even in the North. I don't want you in the middle of that. Johnson is no Lincoln. As a president, he doesn't have the vision Lincoln had for reconstruction. Lincoln picked him as his running mate to placate southern sympathizers. He acts like a sympathizer himself. It's going to take years to make things right again."

"Suzette put her arm around her brother, "You have been talking all this over with Roland, haven't you."

"Yes, promise me you won't get involved in the politics of reconstruction when you get to Independence. I expect there will be plenty there for you to do. I want the hospital rebuilt completely. Jessica can run it, and you can be the chief surgeon."

"Don't worry about us we'll stay out of the way of the carpetbaggers and as far away from politics as we can. What about the rest of you?"

"Abby and I will come with the children when the mine closes. I expect in another year. We can come on the stage lines; the routes should be safe by then. If we wait long enough, we could even take the train. Roland made a heavy investment in both the Pacific and Union Railroad companies. It would be for the children. You know I have never been on one myself, and Abby walked out here from New York."

"Mr. Sue is getting ready to go to San Francisco and deal with his nephew. Roland and Lia will go back there after the next baby is born. That won't be very long from now. I am sure she would like you to stay until she delivers.

A couple of months wouldn't matter, would it? I am pretty sure Jacques is in good hands with Hannah. We haven't received another letter, but that doesn't worry me. He didn't write for years during the war."

The sunrise was one of the most spectacular they had ever seen. Red Mountain was more than a camp now, and it was beginning to stir. The rich odor of bacon frying filled the air mixed with bread and biscuits backing. Mary was up and brought them some decent coffee. Bridgette joined them at the table. She handed Suzette a small box and said, "Happy Birthday."

"Suzette asked, "Can I open it now?" Bridgette nodded her head, yes. The box held two rings — hammered gold with pink and green flowers made from copper and chrome gold alloys.

Brigette said, "For us when we leave here. They will at least keep the honorable men from hitting on us."

Suzette hugged her lover and said, "We can wear them now," and she slipped the ring onto the ring finger of her left hand. She handed Brigette's back to her and asked, "Where did you get these?"

"Mr. Sue made them for us. He is getting to be quite the artist. The alloys were something he read about in a book Moses brought him. By the way, he said he would be leaving soon. He is going to walk to San Francisco. He says he's going to walk up there barefooted because he is getting soft. Have you noticed he hadn't worn shoes for several weeks now when he isn't working in the refinery?"

"No, I haven't been paying attention. I've been reading the last stack of medical journals Moses brought us.

Eli said, "I noticed. He is training to fight. He is going to kill his nephew, and he is going to do that traditionally, in hand to hand combat. No weapons, no staffs, just skill, and determination. He says there can only be one Dragon at a time."

Suzette asked, "How will you run the refinery without him?"

"Roland, John, and I will take care of it until he comes back, if he comes back. Wang Wei will have an army behind him. It is a matter of honor, though. Mr. Sue will challenge him to single combat, similar to a duel. They will fight to the death. The winner will be the Dragon and wear the sash. Hopefully, that will be Mr. Sue. Wang Wei doesn't know he is alive. Chinatown is in for a big surprise."

"Can you talk him out of this fight to the death?"

Eli answered, "No, that is the way of their things. You can't stop thousands of years of culture with a single conversation."

Bridgette asked, "What will Mr. Sue do after he wins." Her loyalty and confidence in her friend were as bright as the morning sun rising in the east.

"He will come back if we are still here. Otherwise, he says he will walk to Independence and get a job as a cook."

Suzette got up from the table and said, "I have to get dressed. I want to talk to him before he leaves. There is a lot I need to learn from him before he goes." Bridgette went with her back to their house. They walked hand-in-hand, admiring their rings. Both had deep concerns about the implications.

The beautiful sunrise gave way to the inevitable hot day. Dust devils rose to ride the light wind from the southwest. All in all, it was going to be a good day for the turkey vultures. There were already more than thirty within sight or Red Mountain riding the thermals.

Eli was still under the ramada, and John Gould and Mr. Sue had joined them for a mine planning session. Suzette and Bridgette came out of their house. The two young women wore identical outfits. Eli could see that they dressed for a ride, but more than that, both had reddened their lips and powdered their faces, their riding clothes appeared to be their finest. Both wore matching soft buckskin breeches, white long-sleeved cotton blouses with blue and gold embroidered patterns that circled the cuffs and leather vests with blue and gold trim that matched the pattern on their cuffs. Even their boots were identical with silver-tipped toes and highly polished black leather with a diamond stitched pattern in white thread. Each wore a clean white *Boss of the Plains* Stenson. There was a loop under the back of the hat brim, and they wore their hair in ponytails pulled through the loop. The only difference, Suzette wore her Lafourche on her hip as usual, and Bridgette carried the Colt Suzette gave her when they left Los Angeles five years earlier. The gun belts and holsters, however, were identical and decorated with black Mojave rattlesnake skins. Eli had to ask, "Where are you girls headed?"

Bridgette answered, "We are going to Wickenburg to see a certain town doctor."

Mary Gould overheard her from the kitchen door. She stood in the doorway, wiping her hands on a small towel and said, "Dressed like that, you could have a lot of unwanted attention follow you home. I hope you don't come back with something you don't want."

Mr. Sue knew about Dr. Fillmore. He looked at the two women and said, "Remember, you can't kill him."

Suzette said, "Don't worry, Mr. Sue; we aren't going to kill him. We are just going to let him know who is paying his salary and who owns the clinic where he is employed. Along the way, we might shake him up a bit, but we won't kill him. When we leave here, I want him to come out here regularly one day a week and take care of our employees. I'm going to make sure that Red Mountain is his only priority in case of an emergency."

Henry, Abby's oldest adopted boy, had their horses saddled and ready to go. They rode the horses at a walk into Wickenburg; they didn't want to mess up their good clothes riding hard raising dust. When they got to town, they tied their horses to the hitching rail in front of the clinic. It was late in the morning, and they learned from the receptionist in the front office of the clinic that Dr. Fillmore was already in the Nugget Bar drinking and playing poker. The girls smiled and walked down the street to pay their respects.

Dr. Fillmore was sitting with his back to the door at a round poker table for eight players. There were two empty seats on the far side of the table. Suzette and Bridgette took the seats. Fillmore didn't recognize them at first, but as recognition settled in, he turned a little pale but didn't say anything. He looked long and hard at Suzette, and then he took a poor looking revolver out of his belt and laid it on the table. One of the miners to Fillmore's right asked jokingly, "What's the matter Doc, you afraid of pretty girls. Fillmore shifted his glare from Suzette to the miner. Suzette didn't take her eyes off Filmore's gun hand until he put the revolver on the table. Had he pointed it at either of them, he would have been dead before he could cock the rusty piece. Suzette's vow of *do no harm* did not include a clause covering self-defense. Every frontier doctor carried a gun; it would be suicide to do otherwise.

Suzette and Bridgette both took out a handful of Red Mountain gold coins from their vest pockets and laid them on the table. Bridgette said, "Deal us in."

Suzette asked, "Could we play twenty-one? I assume all you men know the game." One of the miners had been treated by the ladies up in the Red Mountain clinic for a crushed hand. He got up and left with his money. He went over and ordered a cold beer from Curley Bob Curtis, the bartender.

Curley Bob was also one of Suzette's patients. He asked the miner, "Dave, you afraid the women are going to take your money?"

"No, I was afraid to sit too close to the line of fire. Filmore could hit someone by accident." Both men knew of Suzette and Bridgette's prowess with the sidearms. Their gun hands were as good as their finesse with a scalpel. They had a covert chuckle as the miner to Dr. Fillmore's right offered to deal.

When Suzette got her first card, she picked it up and looked disgusted. "Curley Bob, this has to be the most bedraggled deck of cards in all of the Arizona Territory. Even the miners in Weaver Creek have better cards than these. You must have a new deck back there? You got any with the dragons on the backs. I would pay for them if you got them. Also, I want a beer and one for Bridgette too. How about you guys, you all want a drink? How about you, Dr. Fillmore? You want something a little stronger. Perhaps some of your magic elixir?"

Fillmore turned a little red but didn't show any signs of being nervous. "Whiskey, please." At least he was courteous.

Curley Bob brought over the drinks on a tray along with a new deck of cards. Suzette gave him a ten-dollar gold piece. Suzette broke open the deck, fanned the cards and dealt the first round. Twenty-One was her mother's game, and she had taught her daughter well. Suzette started the count of the face cards showing on the table along with the tens and aces in her head. Keeping track while carrying on a conversation was an art, but Suzette handled it with ease.

Bridgette bet a dollar on her hand, and the man next to her raised the bet fifty cents. The next man raised it another fifty cents, and it was two dollars to Fillmore. He saw the two dollars but didn't raise. Neither did the man to his left. Suzette put in her two dollars and asked without looking at her cards if Bridgette wanted another card. Bridget signaled for a hit, and so did the two men to her left. Fillmore raised another dollar and stood with the cards he had. So did the man to his left. Again, Suzette didn't look at her cards but drew another from the deck. The three miners thought she didn't know how to play, but when the bet came back to Fillmore, he bet another dollar. The man to his left folded, and then Suzette raised the bet five dollars, still without looking at her cards. Both men said at the same time, "Are you nuts? You haven't even looked at your cards!"

Suzette smiled at the two men sweetly and said, "Gents, that's why it's called gambling. What have you got?" Bridgette was the first to turn up; she had seventeen. The next man had stood on fifteen. The man next to

Fillmore's right had twenty-two. Suzette figured math was not his forte. Filmore had nineteen. The man to his left turned over eighteen. With a flare, Suzette turned her cards over for the first time. She had twenty. "Thanks, that was a lucky pot, not a parlor trick and not sleight of hand."

Bridgette won the next hand, and Fillmore won the one after that, but the betting was light. The deck was heavy on tens, and so far, only one ace was played. Suzette nodded at Bridgette, and she opened on the first card with five dollars. Suzette knew she had an ace. Fillmore was the only man that stayed in; he matched the bet but didn't raise. Bridgette got her second card and bet another five. Fillmore hesitated and then put in his money and called. Suzette reminded him that he couldn't call until she had an opportunity to raise, stay in seeing the bet, or fold; she folded. Bridgette looked at her cards and then pushed all the money she had into the pot. Fillmore only had twenty-five dollars, so Bridgette took some of her money back to match Fillmore's bet. Fillmore said, "I call."

Bridgette had twenty-one, the ace of hearts and the king spades. Suzette thought to herself, *How appropriate.* Fillmore had twenty, a king and a Jack. He watched his money disappear into Bridgette's vest pocket. The three other men said they were done and went over to Curley Bob to spend the last of their money across the bar. Fillmore sat at the table and said, "I don't think you came into town to take my money in a card game. Why are you here?"

Suzette needed to tell him, "We wanted to tell you that we own the clinic where you work. I give Henry the money to pay your salary. And I want two things from you. First, Bridgette and I are going to Independence before long, and I want you to take over our practice at Red Mountain while we are gone. I want you to go out there one day a week and be on call all the time if there is an emergency. Understood?"

Fillmore countered, "How do I know you aren't lying to me? I work for Wickenburg, and the Vulture Mine is my priority for emergencies."

Bridgette found her voice, "Not anymore. You have been working for us since the day you arrived. You just didn't know it, and we wanted to keep it that way until now. Ask Henry; we will let him know about the change in your priorities when we leave here."

Dr. Fillmore asked, "What's the second thing.

Suzette looked at him with a coquettish smile, "We want the formula for the aphrodisiac."

Fillmore was incredulous, "You want what?' He was yelling, but Henry Wickenburg walked in the door, and he settled down. Henry saw the girls and came over to the table to say hello. Fillmore back on track, asked, "Henry, do these two women own the clinic here in town?"

Wickenburg answered, "Yes, not only this one but the one at Red Mountain. Not only that, Dr. Suzette owns about ten percent of the mine, and Nurse Bridgette owns somewhere around two and a half. Both of them are very rich. By the way, never play cards with them. They clean me out every time my wife and I have them over for dinner." Henry walked over to Curley Bob to order a drink.

Dr. Fillmore said, "I don't remember the formula."

Suzette smiled at him and said, "Do I have to improve your memory with a lead injection." Fillmore looked at his gun, still sitting on the table.

Bridgette looked at Fillmore and said, "I wouldn't try that. She can draw and shoot you before you could even pick up and cock that antique. It doesn't even look like you take care of it. Maybe it wouldn't even go off if you pulled the trigger. I know you would never forget the formula. I know you purchased some ingredients from Asia. I even watched you mix it once. Don't try to bullshit us, or you will be sewing up cowboys on some rodeo circuit in Texas before you know it."

Dr. Fillmore sat quietly for a moment and then said, "I'll write it out and have it ready for you by the time you leave town. Why do you want it if I may ask?"

Suzette said, "Not to do harm, like you. Let's leave it at that; we want to experiment with a few more affectionate encounters."

Fillmore finally got it, "You both dress the same and you wear wedding rings. Are you married?"

Bridgette answered, "In a sense yes, but not in a relationship that is recognized by church or state."

Dr. Fillmore raised his eyebrows, "I'll be damned. Your lesbians!" He settled in his chair for a while and then got up. "Come by the clinic in a half hour. I'll have the formula written out for you. I even have a complimentary bottle of the magic stuff left that you can have. Enjoy yourselves and good luck with your relationship, in a way, it's not so bad. No disease. No pregnancy. I contracted syphilis from a whore in the Mother Lode. I live celibate now, in a remission period of this episodic disease. Bridgette, I will always have fond memories of our time together, and I wish you only the best. Dr. Callahan, you are a smart woman. Maybe you can find a cure for this horrible petulance. Don't stay away too long. I may put myself down with an overdose of laudanum if I get the bone aches at night." With that, Dr. Fillmore got up and put his rusty gun back in his belt. When he shuffled out of the bar, he looked like the saddest human being on earth. It was easy to see that the syphilis was progressing and ravishing what he had left of his once healthy body. As much as the women hated the man, they couldn't help but feel sorry for him. Both were sure he would kill himself before he reached the last, devastating insanity phase of the disease. *Syphilis is not an easy way to go*; they both thought as they held hands under the table.

It was a block to the confectionary. Suzette would take a big bag of hard candy of every sort back to the children at Red Mountain. By the time they were ready to go to the clinic for the formula, both were having second thoughts about knowing the formula. Sexually, they were both satisfied and happy with their arrangement. Fillmore had become addicted to using it, and now was paying with his life for his indiscrete sex. The price was too high to warrant experimentation.

They stopped at the clinic to say goodbye to Dr. Fillmore knowing it would be the last time they saw him. They left without the formula or the free sample. It was a long, quiet ride back to Red Mountain. They had a new worry — a potential epidemic of a deadly venereal disease. Suzette had to warn the community. Fillmore could have infected some of the whores in town before he knew he was a walking dead man. They would call a town meeting to spread the word as soon as they could arrange it.

Chinatown

Not every spring day in San Francisco is laden with the heavy fog from the ocean. When it is foggy, it is not like the dense, cold of winter fog, but lighter and sometimes refreshing and welcome. It was such a morning when Mr. Sue entered the Chinatown from the south end of DuPont Street. He walked stooped, shuffling in his soft shoes like an older man. His clothes were tattered, his few possessions in a bag over his shoulder. He didn't carry his staff like a soldier; he used it as a walking stick. Nobody paid him even the slightest attention. He was just another Asian, invisible as he walked into the embrace of his people. He looked around; the street to the north was indistinguishable from any street in Asia.

Much had changed since he first landed in San Francisco before the California Gold Rush. As he threaded his way through the narrow street, the aromas of the cooking fires of his homeland welcomed him. Unlike the rest of the city, the street was hopelessly crowded but clean, at least free of the horse manure that was the backbone of the food and materials distribution system in the rest of the city. In Chinatown, everything moved by rickshaw, wheelbarrow, or carts pushed or pulled by the Chinese.

He stopped in front of a pushcart selling dumplings. He bowed and said hello respectfully, and a woman his age gave him a free sample with a warm smile. Mr. Sue paid her five cents for a small paper box containing six dumplings, a small waxed paper container of soy sauce, and chopsticks. He sat down on a barrel next to the dumpling wagon, blending back into the sea of his countrymen and women. He preferred the shield of his autonomy, but he knew all would change as soon as he walked into his sister's presence. For this morning, though, he wanted to bask and be surrounded by the culture and languages of Asia.

The dumpling woman wanted to talk; she handed Mr. Sue a cup of tea. She asked, "Where are you from?"

Mr. Sue smiled at her and said, "China." The woman laughed and asked in three dialects: Mandarin, Cantonese, and the dialect of her province, Hunan. Mr. Sue was going to answer, also in several dialects, but his attention focused on a group of adolescent boys patrolling the street. *Inevitable,* Mr. Sue thought as he watched the boys extorting money from the shopkeepers. The aroma of burning opium wafted out from a darkened hallway. Young women were taking up their positions at the doors to parlors. The dumpling woman gave one of the boys a silver dollar as he held out his hand. Mr. Sue pretended not to notice and waited till the boys moved down the street. Then he asked in Mandarin, the language of the elite, the educated, the political leaders, "Who are they?" The dumpling woman lowered her voice and bent to speak, so only Mr. Sue could hear, "Chang Tong." She spat on the sidewalk to emphasize her disdain. "We call them, *Tiger Cubs*, but they are nothing more than hú jiǎ hǔ wēi (a fox borrowing a tiger's fierceness)."

"Who is their leader?"

"Filth and disgrace, Wang Wei." Again, she spat. Then in the dialect of Hunan, she asked, "Where will you be for lunch? Where will you be for your supper? Where will you be tonight?"

Mr. Sue felt flattered. He expected treatment suited to a traveler, fresh in from somewhere, but he answered, "If I can, I will come back here." He smiled at the dumpling woman. She wasn't bad looking. Like all Asian women in San Francisco, her face was smooth, not lined like the faces of the weary. To Mr. Sue's expert eye, she looked somewhat like a Korean woman or a Manchurian. The San Francisco fog did wonders for disguising a woman's age. Mr. Sue gave her a silver dollar, sealing the tryst and securing lodging for the night that would maintain his secrecy.

She pressed his forearm as he turned to walk away and said, "Be careful."

Mr. Sue wondered if she had recognized him or if he had met her before as he walked further up the street. It was possible. When he came to America with his sister, there were less than six hundred Chinese here. The gold rush, the war, and now the railroad changed all that. Chinatown numbered in the thousands and was busy with another day. Merchants were putting out their wares, and San Francisco's lower-class workers were emerging from the buildings and walking to their jobs; janitors, maids, factory workers of all sorts, laborers with shovels and hoes, rickshaws, wheelbarrows and carts pushed by men and women of all ages. The rest of San Francisco came alive later in the morning; life teemed in Chinatown at dawn. San Francisco came to life a little later. *Each day breathes its own breath,* thought Mr. Sue. Today would be no different than any other day for the Chinese people.

Mr. Sue walked the whole length of Chinatown and several of the side streets; he talked to no one, but he saw everything. He returned to the south end of DuPont Street for lunch. The woman closed the dumpling stand and took him to a dim sum restaurant named *The Pearl*. As they sat down at a table for two on the left wall of the small restaurant, four elderly men stopped their conversation and stared at Mr. Sue. One bowed his head in recognition. Mr. Sue grew tense, and the dumpling woman put her hand over his clenched fist and said, "Don't worry, you are safe here. You will see these men again tonight. For now, eat." Young girls, no more than eight or nine, passed by the table with the dim sum offerings. Mr. Sue ate and ate heartily, glad to revel in the cuisine of his homeland.

Some young toughs came in off the street and sat down for lunch. As the girls passed by with the carts, the boys fondled them and touched them in their most intimate places. The girls were too afraid to resist. No one else in the restaurant made any move to stop them. When one boy lifted the silk skirt of the youngest girl, Mr. Sue reached his limit of tolerance. He got up from the table and took his staff in hand from where it leaned against the wall. Without a word, he walked up to the table of four boys and knocked the one that had lifted the young girl's skirt over backward with a blow to his forehead. The boy went over in his chair and hadn't reached the floor by the time Mr. Sue put two more of the startled teenagers down with a left and right stroke of the other end of the staff. The last boy stood up and was going to speak with a knife held in his right hand. Mr. Sue batted the knife away with his staff and then picked the boy up by the throat with one hand. He carried him to the back door of the restaurant and threw him in the garbage cart to the side of the door. "Tell Wang Wei that this place is off-limits to him and his scum, like you, forever."

The boy found his voice and his courage as he shook loose from the crush of Mr. Sue's grip. "We will kill you! You hear me?" He shouted at Mr. Sue's back as he walked back into the restaurant. "We will kill you, whoever you are. We will kill you!" As his threat fell on deaf ears, his voice got high and desperate; it almost cracked before he pulled himself out of the garbage and ran away.

The older men had pulled the three boys up off the floor and threw them out the front door. After some men and women left, they locked the door and sat back down to finish eating. The leader of their group said, "Welcome back, Dragon. Your nephew," he paused and spat on the floor, "told us you were dead. We assume you want to stay hidden for a while. Wang Wei has at least a hundred young boys like that. He has taken over all the criminal enterprise in Chinatown and collects protection money from all the honest businessmen and women. Your sister is the only one safe now. If you want, we can arrange for you to surprise her tonight with your alive and well presence at a meeting of our secret society."

"I would like that, but I don't want to put anyone in danger."

"Don't worry, no one here is in danger. Look outside."

More than two hundred men and women of all ages, most armed with staffs, were gathering outside the restaurant. There were more in the alley at the back door. "I am Zhang Yong and the leader of our secret society. This woman you befriended is Zhang Xiu Ying." Zhang Yong bowed his head at the woman to recognize and honor her. "She is smart and cagey. She is close to your sister. She will bring her here for a meeting tonight. We know you will have to kill Wang Wei. It will be hard for her, but she will know it too when she sees you. Wang Wei hides somewhere in Chinatown and runs his criminal businesses with his adolescent henchmen, his *Tiger Cubs*. They are easily swayed into his thinking and rebel against a life only offering labor and servitude. Recruitment is easy. Crime is easy. Life is hard, as usual. When you kill Wang Wei, someone will take his place as he did when he killed the last *dai low* to take his place. There is someone here that owns him. No one knows who that is. If we knew, we would kill him – or her. But that person is vapor, thin air, non-existent in our numbers. Whoever owns Wang Wei, brought the Kwan Chang Tong with him from our homeland. Like you, the ones of us that came here early came to escape the Kwan Chang and the oppression and violence of the emperors. Now it is here among us. We will stop it if we can, but it won't stop unless we find the head of the cobra and chop it off."

Mr. Sue looked at the elders. He looked at the people in the street. He looked at the girls huddling behind their mother, who ran the restaurant. He made his decisions. "I can find him. I can help you. I want to leave now, but I want to remain invisible."

Zhang Xiu rose from her table and took Mr. Sue by the hand. "This way," she said. There were stairs in the kitchen that led to the upper stories and then the roof. They crossed the rooves and went down the stairs in the last building south on Dupont Street. Mr. Sue left Zhang Xiu at the back door of the laundry they had come down into and walked away. He left Chinatown. He walked to the center of the city. He entered City Hall and found the records department. He had to convince the matron of the city archives that he was literate, but by the time City Hall was ready to close, he knew who the secret leader and Wang Wei's boss was. He just needed to prove it, and for that, he had a plan.

Mr. Sue slipped back into Chinatown as the sun was settling into the ocean. Zhang Xiu was waiting for him in front of the restaurant. She said in perfect English but quietly, "Good evening, General Sue. I am glad you are back." She took him by the hand and led him to a tenement building on Kearny Street. They entered and climbed to the fourth floor. Men and women guarded the front door of the building and all the landings in the stairwell. The building was heavy with the cooking aromas of a hundred families mixed with the smells of close living conditions. Children played in the halls; babies cried behind half-opened doors. Half of the upper floor was an open hall. Men and women of all ages sat quietly on rows of small barrels, stools, and chairs. The girls from the restaurant were serving green tea and rice candies. As Mr. Sue entered with Zhang Xiu, the doors closed behind them.

Lǎo Yong rose from his chair and introduced Mr. Sue as General Sue, *The Dragon*. Then he told everyone, including Mr. Sue, to be patient for a few more minutes. There were murmurs and looks of awe from the gathering. It went on for a few minutes, and then the doors opened. Mr. Sue's sister was led in by the other three men of Lǎo Yong's cabal. She was indignant and raving on about being commandeered by her friends. She was almost shouting when she saw the crowd, "I don't want to attend a secret meeting. It is dangerous! I want to go back home." She was opening her mouth to voice another demand and then she saw her brother at the front of the room. Her jaw dropped, and her eyes widened. Her hands flew up to cover her mouth. She stood motionless, and fear gripped her as she realized that Mr. Sue was alive and there would be only one reason he would be in Chinatown, and that would be to kill her son. She was led to a seat in the front row and told to sit. She sat quiet and unbelieving that her brother was still alive. Her brother was still the Last Dragon. Her son was already a dead man and didn't know it. She didn't know where her son was. She knew him now by reputation alone.

Lǎo Yong addressed Mr. Sue. "General Sue, we are at your disposal. We need your help, and as we told you this morning, we will stand with you. But more than anything, we need your leadership. By being here tonight, we assume you came back to help us take back our community. Please." Lǎo

Yong swept his arm and invited Mr. Sue to assume leadership of the meeting and the men and women of their close-knit group.

Mr. Sue stood and bowed to his sister, he spoke in Cantonese, the more common language of the streets. "Xiǎo Ping, I am sorry I had returned here for one and only one purpose. That was to kill Wang Wei. He has dishonored you and our family. It is unfortunate, but by his dishonorable actions, he has to die. Since arriving this morning, though, I have discovered a more important cause than simply killing one dishonorable young man. We Chinese suffer oppression anywhere we have immigrated. It is bad enough to be looked down upon and abused by the white man of this country while we do his labor and make his cities and farms work to house and feed them. Now we have spawned a problem in our midst that makes life even harder. You all know what I mean. You see your young men in the streets every day extorting money and doing violence to anyone who dares oppose them. I am sorry to say, those youngsters work for one man, or so it appears, but Wang Wei is not the problem. He dances to the tune of a group of powerful men for whom he works. Therein lies the problem. We need to cut off the head of the snake. Otherwise, there will be another Wang Wei, and another one after that, and another one again and again."

The crowd got unruly and wanted to know who the top dog was. "I know who the head man is, and he has a council of three others. We need to kill them all, and I know how to go about it. Xiǎo Ping, are you with us or against us? I need to know. Your son, my nephew, is not going to survive this. I won't have to kill him; his boss is going to do that for me. The cadre that he reports to, however, will need some expert assassination. That I will orchestrate and help you to the end. After that, it will be up to the community to stay clean. There will always be saloons, gambling, prostitution and such. There doesn't have to be organized crime, especially among ourselves."

Xiǎo Ping got up and said, "Brother, do what you have to do. I have no son." She turned and walked with dignity to leave the room; a mother who disowned her son; a mother who would feel a sense of failure the rest of her life. Mr. Sue felt sorry for her. So did the rest of the elders in the room. Even if she was able to warn her son, there was nothing she could do to change his fate. The Dragon, the real Dragon, was after him. Like his battles and quests in China, he wouldn't rest until Wang Wei was dead.

Mr. Sue finished the general meeting and retired with Lao Yong and twenty of his trusted men. He told them how they were going to bring down the criminal element that terrorized their streets. It would start the next night and start slow at first. He joked that rehabilitating a hundred *Tiber Cubs* was going to take some time. The young teenagers that had parents were going to be taken off the streets and handed back to their parents. The orphans were going to be a more difficult problem. Mr. Sue volunteered to march them to Independence. That is where he was going after this unpleasant business was finished. He was getting ready to leave the meeting and find an opium den to sleep in or a *gong si fong* to remain invisible, but Zhang Xiu took him by the hand and led him down to her apartment. She lived alone, the sign of an important and successful woman in the community. Mr. Sue didn't object. It had been a long time since he shared the warmth and comfort of a woman's bed.

The next morning, he slipped away in the dark. He walked to Knob Hill and went to the back door of the mansion that Mrs. Mercier set up for her family. He knocked quietly on the door of the kitchen and was welcomed inside as a long-lost friend. Uncle Tio was at the table consuming a mountain of pancakes, he tipped over his chair, and spilled his coffee jumping up to grab Mr. Sue in his signature bear hug. Without a word, he ran out and up the stairs to wake Maria and Eliza. Professor Laity was up and saw Tio in the hall. Tio was too excited to talk, but he pointed down the stairs and at the kitchen. The Professor went down and welcomed Mr. Sue. Tio came down with the girls a few minutes later. Mr. Sue caught himself thinking about a great contrast that troubled him. Here, he felt in the presence of family. In Chinatown and even with his sister, he felt only sadness and his task at hand. He would spend that day with his family. He wanted to see the dinosaur museum. He wanted to see the girls at school. He didn't want to think about the days and weeks ahead. The only part of that scenario that brought a smile to his lips was thinking about Zhang Xiu. He wasn't sure what he would do about that. By nightfall, he was back in Chinatown.

Roland read the morning newspapers in the study. He heard the growing bedlam in the kitchen. He closed the paper on a story about some violence in Chinatown and walked to the back of the house to investigate. It was easy to see there was a party in progress, and the reason for the party was also obvious. He walked over and hugged Mr. Sue. "You're here sooner than I expected. Is everything okay at the mine."

Mr. Sue smiled, "Yes, I didn't leave until Moses left out with the gold shipment and the two doctors. What are you doing here?"

Roland looked a bit flustered and also a bit bored at the same time. "Lia and I are going to stay here until the baby comes. That's probably four more months or more. I am going crazy; I need something to do."

Mr. Sue lit up with inspiration. "I know you have a big investment in the two railroads building across America. When I leave here, I'm going up the railroad from Oakland, and then I'm going to walk to Independence. Why don't you come with me up the railroad? I want to see the camps and the work my people are doing. We can get to Carson City, and you can come back on the stage. What say you? It will help pass the time."

Roland was ecstatic, "I would love to go up there with you. How will I know when you are leaving?"

Mr. Sue smiled again, "Watch the papers. You will know when it is time. I will meet you at the ferry dock." The two men shook hands. Mr. Sue said his goodbyes, especially to Tio and the children. Lia was still asleep when he quietly left through the back door of the kitchen.

That night Wang Wei's world started to fall apart. Six of his young hoodlums disappeared. Worse than that, the money they collected on their rounds of the bars, brothels, and gambling halls disappeared with them. At first, Wang Wei thought they had run away. That was impossible though. Where would they go? It was inconceivable that they were off starting a protection service of their own. His control of the streets was ruthless, and any competition was met with immediate lethal force. His boys knew that. They were the instrument of the lethal force. Most of them had already killed their first victims, a rite of passage. Wang Wei made up the money lost from his funds; he didn't want to report to his boss that he had a problem.

The next night another squad of his boys disappeared. Again, Wang Wei wondered what was going on and again made up the losses from his own money. He couldn't go on like this forever. His funds were limited. He lived a good life, and it cost money. He had to pay the boys; he had to pay the madams. When they came around, he had to pay the police. In a week, he would be broke. He could crawl back to his mother and ask for money, but he doubted that she would give him any after the way he treated her for almost a year now. The young woman who lay beside him tried to get him to relax, but he pushed her aside. He dressed and strapped on his guns. He would go out on the streets. Something was going on out there, and he was going to sort it out for himself.

The streets were relatively quiet — most of the bars and brothels having closed for the night. There were no whores in the doorways or windows. The fog was rolling in, and he was cold. His soldiers, the ones that remained, had mostly finished their rounds and were bedded down for the night. He had a few guards out, and he stopped to talk to each one, asking about the missing boys. None of them had seen anything. But his guards weren't the only ones on the streets. Men and women were on every corner with their backs to the walls and stalls, looking like they were asleep but watching his every move, an invisible spy network in plain sight. By the next morning, they knew where Wang Wei lived, hidden no more from their watchful eyes. They also knew where all his soldiers slept. Now the watching would become more focused. Sooner or later, Wang Wei was going to have to report to his boss. The sooner, the better; once the identity of Wang Wei's boss was confirmed, the real battle for Chinatown could begin.

Mr. Sue and his twenty soldiers no longer had to take the young thugs off the street. They waited till the next night and raided each of the dens of the Tiger Cubs. No one knew where *The Twenty*, as they were becoming known as, took the young boys. Mr. Sue and Zhang Xiu had arranged for the captured Cubs to be held in the basement of the Ah Toy brothel. More than forty of them were sitting in the dark of the basement, not knowing where they were and, in some cases, not even knowing what happened to them. The pressure on Wang Wei was reaching a breaking point, and he still didn't know who his enemy was. When he was down to only twenty of his minions and out of money, he strapped on his set of Navy Colt 0.44 revolvers, gathered his youngsters around him, and set out to see his boss. As usual, he thought the darkness of the night would keep him shrouded in secrecy. As usual, he was wrong.

Mr. Sue and Lǎo Tong shambled along the street; two old men that Wang Wei paid no attention. With two revolvers on his hips, Wang Wei looked ridiculous and out of place, an armed Chinaman as he emerged from the warehouse he called his home and headquarters. He was dressed in the traditional loose-fitting blue clothes and wore the gun belt over a quilted tunic he wore to shelter from the cold of the night. He buttoned up the tunic after he was sure the Tiger Cubs had seen the guns. He walked to the north of Chinatown several blocks to the biggest illicit establishment in San

Francisco's Barbary Coast. The harmless old men watched as Wang Wei posted his guards at the door of the Hunan Haven. From across Columbus Avenue, Mr. Sue was waiting for lanterns to light the top floor of the office building next to the Hunan Haven. It didn't take long, the penthouse at the top of the four-story building was dimly lit at first but then shown brilliantly as flaming dragon pyres blazed to life on the balcony that surrounded the penthouse that occupied all of the top floor. Dramatic but stupid, Wang Wei was being treated as a guest of honor. His host was no surprise to Mr. Sue. The man Wang Wei talked with on the balcony was a Chinese/Korean named Sik Yeon. It was the last time Wang Wei would talk to the owner of almost all the illegal businesses on the west coast of America. The conversation only lasted ten minutes, and as the dragon pyres were being extinguished, Wang Wei emerged from the front door of the Hunan Haven.

Mr. Sue and Lǎo Tong didn't follow him. They didn't have to. A white man left the front door of the office building. He was dressed in a black-wool trench coat and wore a derby hat and strolled casually after Wang Wei and his troops. Three young Koreans came out of the Hunan Haven and ran west towards Knob Hill. Lǎo Tong asked, "What's going on?"

Mr. Sue smiled and answered, "Sik is summoning the other heads of the hydra. Time for patience; they will be here soon."

Within an hour, three ornate carriages arrived. Mr. Sue and Lǎo Tong sat on the sidewalk across from the front door of the gambling hall. Zhang Xiu joined them from the shadows. One of the men who got out and went into the Haven was a man who Mr. Sue had seen in the Arizona Territory. He was a friend of the banker, Jim Parish. All three drivers were Chinese. Zhang Xiu walked across the street and quickly learned the names of the other two arrivals and where they lived. The three men that arrived in the carriages were also having their last conversation with Sik Yeon. Zhang Xiu put her fingers to her lips and whistled three short-shrill notes. Three two-man teams emerged from the alley to their right and sat down on the sidewalk near the carriages. The dragon pyres stayed dark for this meeting. The Triad didn't want attention.

It took another hour, but the three men walked out of the front door of the office building and strolled as friends the short distance to the carriages. The drivers were holding their doors, ready to pick up the wooden loading steps and depart as soon as their charges were comfortably seated inside. As silently as cats, the two-man teams crossed the sidewalk and boarded the luggage shelves on the back of the carriages. It was not only the Triad's last conversation with Sik Yeon; it was also their last ride home. It would be dawn in another hour, but they wouldn't live to see it.

The next day was not only the last day of Wang Wei's life but also a bad day for his Tiger Cubs. He was escorting one of his remaining collection squads around Chinatown. It was mid-morning, and so far, things were going well, no signs of trouble. They entered the dead-end alley that led to the door of Ah Toy's brothel. They rang the bell, and the door opened. A middle-aged woman answered the door. She wasn't Ah Toy; she wasn't Chinese either; she was white. The young man in the front of the collection squad was confused, but he held out his hand for payment anyway. The woman raised her closed fist as if to pay him. Suddenly, the hand held an Italian stiletto; the woman stabbed the boy in the heart. The door slammed in the face of the other three before the dead Cub hit the cobblestones. Wang Wei pulled his tunic open and drew a pistol. He shot at the door handle until the gun was empty. He kicked the door, but it didn't fly open as he expected. What did fly was buckshot from the second story windows up and down the alley. Wang Wei was left standing alone with his second gun in hand, wondering why the attackers didn't kill him too. *This was a mysterious and deadly side of Chinatown*, he thought, *I'm not coming back here.* He didn't know just how true that was.

As he turned to leave the alley, the man in the derby was standing at the entrance waiting for him. He stood there in his black coat, his hands in plain sight. He turned his palms outward with his fingers spread to assure the armed man approaching him that he was harmless. As Wang Wei stepped out of the alley, an eight-pointed shuriken flew through the air at the speed of a plunging eagle, and slit Wang Wei's throat deep from one side to the other. He fell to his knees with his life's blood gushing out in front of him. The shuriken lodged in a sign that pointed the way back to Ah Toy's establishment. The man with the derby checked for blood on his shoes and then turned and walked away. He left the shuriken lodged in the sign; the assassin already faded into the gathering crowd.

The man with the derby walked to the Hunan Haven, sat down at the bar, and ordered beer with a shot of whiskey. He was waiting for Wang Wei's replacement, the next *dai low.* He would wait a long time; no one wanted the job until the "troubles" were over. The woman with the stiletto arrived and sat next to him; she had no interest in the next *dai low.* The bartender slid a glass of cold sarsaparilla down the bar; it stopped expertly right in front of her hand. She quaffed it in two swallows, slid three small stacks of gold coins off the bar, and turned to leave. Six men carrying *Luparas* met her at the door. They chatted openly about their morning's work as if they had been fishing for red snapper rather than killing. Together, they walked back to Little Italy.

That night, Lǎo Tong's secret society met again on the top floor of Zhang Xiu's apartment building. Lǎo Tong called the meeting to order and told the society that there were only a few of Wang Wei's soldiers left, and they were scattering. The *Triad* of Sik Yeon was dead. Wang Wei was dead. He assured his society that it was not *The Twenty* that killed the Tiger Cubs. Sik had hired the Sicilians to do his dirty work for him. Race meant nothing to organized crime.

Sik was the only one left, and he was unreachable in the penthouse above the Hunan Haven. They needed a plan. Would they burn him out? The danger was too great that a fire would spread from Sik's office/fortress to the rest of the city. Could they wait him out? He never had a need that would bring him out of his penthouse. Zhang Xiu and Ah Toy sat in the front row and were working in whispers, formulating a plan. Zhang Xiu stood up and said she wanted to address the assembly. She said, "The women will handle this one. We need only one thing from you, General Sue."

The rest of the evening was spent drinking tea and eating rice candy. The mood of the society was light-hearted. Even if the women didn't kill Sik Yeon, they had brought about a great change in Chinatown. The men of *The Twenty* took responsibility for dealing with the boys in Ah Toy's basement. They couldn't keep them there forever. Some of the society members had one or two sons locked up in that basement. Lǎo Tong assured the parents that they would make every effort to repatriate the young hoodlums back into the families and upstanding side of the community. Ah Toy was off in a corner, talking quietly to Mr. Sue.

They let a week go by, hoping that Sik Yeon was starting to feel comfortable that the troubles were over. Then early one afternoon, the women dressed for action. Ah Toy, with six of the most beautiful Asian girls in San Francisco, walked hand in hand with Zhang Xiu to the front door of the Hunan Haven. They entered and told the doorman that they wanted a private audience with Sik Yeon. He told them that wasn't likely to happen and that they should make themselves at home in the gambling hall or the bar. If they wanted jobs in the brothel, he had immediate openings they could fill. Ah Toy put her arm around the man's neck and kissed him. She whispered in his ear, "Tell your boss I am here to make him an offer he won't be able to refuse. Tell him I can end his troubles and make his little empire richer than ever before." If lust wasn't a strong enough draw, money, the other quest of Sik's life, might do the trick. Ah Toy was right. In ten minutes, a man emerged from the door next to the bar and escorted them through the hall joining the office building.

The walk up the six stories took some time. Ah Toy didn't want to arrive with her girls sweaty or out of breath. The younger women had no trouble with the stairs. It was Zhang Xiu and Ah Toy that had to take their time. When they reached the top, two heavily armed men guarded the doors to the penthouse. They looked the women over for weapons, but the women didn't carry purses, and their attire didn't provide many hiding places. The men had a good time patting the beautiful girls down. They had no interest in the two older women. They opened the door to the penthouse with an ornate brass key. Like palace guards, they swung the heavy double doors open. Sik Yeon was there in his foyer to greet them. "Ah Toy, it's been too long." Sik kissed her on the cheek and then led them into the penthouse.

There was a lot of glass; in fact, it was mostly glass with only a small living quarter in the southwest corner, the least interesting view. The moon was full, and the bay was spectacular, with hundreds of ships loading and unloading by lantern light. The port never rested; ships had to be ready to meet the next tide. A man dressed as a Chinese steward walked along the balcony that circled the penthouse lighting the dragon pyres. There was champagne to be opened and poured. The man lighting the dragon pyres came in and did that. He lit a wood fire laid in a raised fire pit in the center of the room, and then he left. Sik Yeon was alone with the women. The girls drank the champagne, ate the crab cakes and sampled the rest of the hors d'oeuvres. They discovered that caviar on small toast rounds topped with crème fraiche was the best food they ever ate. Sik Yeon knew how to entertain. Zhang Xiu and Ah Toy took Sik Yeon by the arms and said they wanted to see the bay. They walked out the doors on the east side of the penthouse. Ah Toy looked back through the glass to see if her girls were behind them. She told Sik that she was cold and walked down to the dragon pyre near the northeast corner to stay warm.

There was no fog, but the night air was cold. Zhang Xiu walked Sik down to join Ah Toy by the dragon. She looked over to the roof of a four-story building a block to the east and then stopped and leaned against the wall in front of the dragon. The fire in the bowl the dragon held was warm and welcome. The smell of kerosene fumes filled the air around the balcony. Ah Toy stepped over to the wall. Sik was now between the two women. Zhang Xiu turned and leaned over the railing. "What's that?" she said, pointing at something down on the street below. Sik leaned over to see what she was pointing at and his head exploded. A bullet ricocheted off the balustrade of the roof above and whizzed away in the night. The shot that killed Sik didn't attract the attention of anyone in the building. The crack of the rifle shot that killed Sik echoed off the thick stone walls of the office building.

Ah Toy signaled her girls, and two of them went out the doors of the penthouse to keep the guards happy. They carried a bottle of champagne and two glasses. They turned the deadbolt on the heavy doors and pushed them opened with a smile. The guards smiled back and pulled the doors closed behind them. The rest of the girls carried Sik's corpse into the living quarter, undressed him, and put him into his bed. They covered the ghastly head with a pillow and then cleaned up the blood trail that led from the balcony to the bed. Ah Toy and Zhang Xiu feasted on the caviar and talked about women things. They talked about their lives, their loves, and their futures. As the girls finished up, they joined the two older women and ate the rest of the food. In about an hour, the two girls from outside came back in. The top of one dress hung torn down to her waist. The girl walked shamelessly with her ample breasts exposed. Ah Toy took the antimacassar off the back of one of the sofas and fashioned a stole so the girl could leave the building without attracting attention.

They waited till almost dawn and then left the penthouse. The two guards were asleep in the armchairs to either side of the door. They went down the stairs, quiet as cats stalking prey. They found more guards at the front door of the office building. Ah Toy got them to open the heavy doors to let them out. The women walked out into the first light of dawn, crossed Columbus Avenue, and walked back into Chinatown. Mr. Sue took Zhang Xia's hand and said, "I want to talk to you." They fell a little behind the Ah Toy entourage, out of earshot, and Mr. Sue went on, "I am leaving this morning. I am going to walk to Independence, Missouri. It is a long way, probably two thousand miles. I want you to come with me."

Zhang Xiu's grip on his hand tightened. "I don't want you to leave me here. I will go with you. I have no family, only a handful of friends like Lǎo Tong and his sister who runs the restaurant, and her girls. I can walk to Missouri with you, but is that the only way to get there?"

"No," replied Mr. Sue. "There are stagecoaches, boats, and freight wagons. Which would you prefer?"

"A stage would be nice. Does the stagecoach let Chinese ride inside?"

"Only if you're rich. We'll go by stage." Another side of the mysterious Mr. Sue came to light.

Zhang Xia had one more question, "I know you may not want to tell me, but who fired the shot that killed Sik Yeon? There are no riflemen among the Chinese here, and you were down on the street watching."

Mr. Sue was quiet for another block, then he said quietly, "There were two children in my father's family that were trained to shoot the rifle."

"And the shuriken?"

"Yes, that too."

Going Home

Suzette was anxious to leave and start the journey back to Independence. She worked with Mr. Sue and Abby every day, refining the gold for the shipment that would go with her. Bridgette helped when she could, but there were still patients that needed care every day in the clinic. Summer held the desert in its deadly grip, and refining the gold was hot and tedious work. The only reward was watching the stack of refined bars growing in the safe. One more week and they would be ready to pour the one-thousand-ounce bars. Twenty bars, almost four hundred thousand dollars in value; they could pour four a day. When the stack of small bars in the safe reached seventy-five, Suzette asked, "Can we start pouring the bars for the shipment?"

Mr. Sue was ready; he had a new crucible for the melting. He said they could start the next day after the refining of the smaller bars was completed for the day. The furnace would be empty, and it wouldn't take long to melt the gold for the first set of 0.999 bars. Refining the gold to three nines was a slow process, and weeks passed as Mr. Sue's inventory of refined bars increased.

Suzette and Bridgette saw Moses arrive with his wagons when the bars were almost ready. Only one more bullion assay remained before Mr. Sue stamped the last of the bars. Moses was anxious to start east too; Ragini was on her way to India with Connor, and he wanted to be back in Los Angeles when she returned. He was also anxious because summer was passing, and he wanted to take the roads to the north, up through Prescott to Flagstaff before the winter snows set in. The Callahan/Banning stage line had stage stops into Colorado and even farther north into Montana. They would be spending the nights at the stage stops until they turned east into Kansas. Somewhere east of Topeka, Moses expected to find the end of the Atchison, Topeka & Santa Fe Railway. He planned to put all the wagons on the train and ride east to Independence in style. Had the war not interrupted the construction of the railroad, it would have already reached Colorado. They would be somewhere beyond three-hundred miles of Kansas to cross before they would find the end of the tracks.

Finally, Mr. Sue poured the last of the bars and started his last bullion assay. Despite the anxiety of the travelers, Mr. Sue would not stamp the last set of bars until the bullion assay finished at 0.999 fine. The results were good, and as the hammer fell on the die to imprint the last nine, all was ready for their departure. Patches and Bridgette's mare waited in a wagon that had high sides and the ribs from a Calistoga if shade was needed. Besides the armored stage, there were two other wagons in the line-up. Both contained oats for the mules and tents and cookware for camping on the open trail in Kansas. They would be staying at stage stops for most of the journey. Moses had even sent extra teams forward so that the team pulling the heavy armored stage could be changed out when needed.

Farewells are always difficult; this departure was no exception. Mary, Abby, and the girls cried openly as Moses, and his drivers carried the strongboxes for the gold and stowed them under the floor of the armored stage. Suzette asked Mary, "Will I see you in Independence?"

Mary answered, "I don't think so, child. We have children in California. There is a fishing village up the coast from San Francisco called Fort Bragg. I want to retire there. John wants to retire in San Francisco. We'll work it out when the time comes like we always do."

It was harder to say goodbye to Mr. Sue than Eli and Abby. Suzette knew she would see her brother and his wife again in Independence; Mr. Sue, she wasn't so sure she would see him again. He was ready to leave too. She knew he would walk west as soon as the wagon train was out of sight. "Mr. Sue reassured her, "Don't worry little one, when I finish with my nephew, I will come back here or walk to Independence. Only time will tell, but I will find you wherever you are."

Suzette and Bridgette did their last rounds of farewell hugs and boarded the stage. Eli handed her his letter to Jacques, kissed his sister goodbye, and closed the door. Moses nodded at his driver, the whip cracked, and the mules took the first step in the long trek east. Suzette felt some trepidation, unease at what she would find when they reached Independence. *Odd*, she thought, *I didn't feel this way when I ran away from home.* Five years ago, however, only the wilderness of the west lay ahead of her. Now the Civil War changed everything; millions of people didn't know what the next day would bring.

Suzette wasn't the only woman feeling trepidation. Ragini was uneasy ever since the *Adrianna* left the safety of Hong Cong. Connor had both guns set amidships on the main deck, one forward of the main hatch and one behind it. Her unease heightened when he tested the guns against a limestone pillar on the shore of the South China Sea. She knew pirates roamed the waters between Dutch Indonesia and Malaysia; she hoped they could make it into the Bay of Bengal without encountering them. The pirates hunted in wolf packs with an odd assortment of Chinese junks, smaller boats, and boarding crafts. In addition to the big guns, Connor had three of the swivel guns from *The Blessed* mounted, one each on the side gunwales and one on the stern transom. Even though the *Adrianna* was well-armed, it would be easy for the smaller boats to overtake the lumbering freighter. Ammunition for the swivel guns was in limited supply, only three to four rounds for each gun. An encounter was still unwanted, but one would prove deadly for the pirates. Hopefully, one cargo ship, no matter how elegant she looked, wouldn't be worth the loss of life it would take to board her. Regardless, Santiago had given Ragini a throwing knife, and she practiced with it daily.

Ragini was also in the dark as to what Connor would do after they reached Madras. He said that he would leave her there, and Moses gave her plenty of money in gold coins so that she could buy her passage back to the states. She knew that Connor was worried that his family in the states was going their separate ways for a while. He also told her that he wasn't sure he would stay in Ireland. Maybe he would go back to Los Angeles or Independence. There were a lot of unknowns on her mind that added to her unease. She couldn't sleep the night they entered the Malacca Strait; she spent the night on deck and finally dozed off on the forecastle before dawn.

One more day to reach the Sea of Bengal, and the *Adrianna* was making good headway sailing untroubled on the westerly trades. When the sun rose, however, all was not peaceful. There were at least ten small ships about three miles behind them. There was only one reason the small ships could be this far out in the sea lanes, pirates, and a lot of them. It would take most of the day for the small fleet of motley ships to overtake the *Adrianna*, but Connor had no intention of letting them get near.

Towards the end of the noon watch, the pirate fleet had advanced to within a mile and a half of the two big guns. The *Adrianna* wasn't as fleet of foot as *The Blessed*, but Santiago brought her around in the wind, and the starboard gun crew aimed and fired at the biggest junk. It wasn't a difficult shot, and the gun crew hit the junk dead on the bow. The round exploded inside, and the front third of the junk disappeared in a raining cloud of wood and debris. Santiago put the ship back on course, and Connor waited to see what the pirates would do. Smoke billowed from the forecastle deck of the second biggest junk; the feeble shot hit the water a thousand yards aft, it wasn't even an exploding shell. Connor looked at the fleet using one of the aiming telescopes from *The Blessed*. Most likely, the old junk carried a single lantaka cannon discarded by the Dutch before Connor was even born. It seemed a shame to waste an artillery round on a ship he could probably out sail, but the lantaka could be deadly at close range. He couldn't afford to let the pirate get close.

Connor ordered, "Hard a port." When the port gun came to bear, the second junk went to the bottom. Still, the remainder of the pirate fleet came ahead. Most of the remaining boats were padawakangs of various ages. Sails that may have been red when they were new had faded to pink with age; the fan like ribs of the sails held tattered sails, some were bent and bowed with age. Sheer numbers might let them get close, but not for a while. Connor held the course, and the port gun sank two more. Six boats left; one was faster than the others. Connor let it close to a hundred yards. The swivel guns raked the deck, and the hapless boat started to turn in a circle, the helmsman dead behind the wheel.

These pirates were either dumb or desperate. Perhaps they were just mad, having a cargo ship cut their numbers by more than half. Connor surprised them; he had Santiago turn to starboard and sail back at the small fleet. He let the fastest pirate pass him, and the starboard gun demolished the two boats that brought up the rear. The boat he passed saw their opportunity and turned to board. The swivel guns cleared the deck, and when the small boat came alongside, Ragini lit and hurled a bottle of kerosene onto the deck. As flames started to consume the boat, several pirates that were below when the swivel guns raked the deck, dove into the sea to escape the flames. Connor threw them an empty keg for a float and bid them goodbye. The last two boats turned to flee. Connor only wanted one to survive to tell the tale. He could almost see the look of fear on the pirate faces as he brought the port gun to bear. Men were diving off of both boats as the gun crew demolished the boat on the right. The survivor, an elegant looking little ketch, probably commandeered from a wealthy traveler, dropped its sails to pick up survivors. They would have quite a story to tell back at their den. There would be a lot fewer pirates to listen to the tale, but the day of destruction would be long remembered up and down the Malacca Strait.

The decimation of the pirates in the Malacca Strait wouldn't be the only memorable event that year. San Francisco was abuzz with the news of the killings in Chinatown; the deaths of four men who the port city considered pillars of the community shocked the city. No one in Chinatown was shocked. Those citizens, the invisible people, knew the reason behind the killings. Roland stepped out of the Mercier carriage at the end of Market Street and walked to the piers where the ferries docked. He was dressed to travel. His Colt revolver was on his hip, bulging the heavy jacket that hung open over his shoulders. He carried his Henry rifle in one hand and a satchel in the other. He saw Mr. Sue sitting on the pier with a Chinese woman and some young boys; joyous laughter bubbled up from the group as the woman pulled a good-sized red snapper from the water. Mr. Sue saw Roland and stood up to introduce the woman, "This is Zhang Xiu Ying. She will be going with us."

Roland greeted the woman with a polite bow and smiled his approval. He never could understand how Mr. Sue was able to remain celibate for so long. Mr. Sue asked, "How is Lia?"

"A little distressed that I will be away for some weeks. Lia is in good hands, though, with Dr. Lange taking care of her down at the college. When she gets close to delivery, Tio will take her down there and stay with her. I should be back by then with no problem. Let's get going; I want to see the railroad; I hear the eminent Theodore Dehone Judah is up in the Sierras inspecting the trestles and overseeing the tunnel construction."

Mr. Sue said goodbye to the boys and pulled three tickets from his black tunic for the ferry to Benicia. The next ferry was due in ten minutes. Here was Roland's first encounter with the discrimination against the Chinese. Mr. Sue and Zhang were asked to wait in a separate line reserved for Chinese, blacks, and any other people of color. Roland showed the man the tickets. All were for first-class passage, with coffee and Danish served in the upper lounge. The man supervising the quay reluctantly opened the rope to the first-class. Mr. Sue smiled at the man who was nothing more than a drone doing his job, and said, "Thank you sir, but I would rather be with my people."

Roland went up to the lounge, but he didn't stay long. He had counted all the people in the Chinese quay. He bought all the Danish and ordered two urns of tea. The porters objected to carrying the refreshments down to what they considered steerage but followed along as Roland left the lounge and walked down the stairs to the lower deck. There were several drivers on the lower deck calming their horses as ferry whistle blew, and the deck rumbled under their hooves as the boat left the pier. The drivers were more than a bit miffed that they didn't get a Danish as the porters passed out the food and poured tea among the Chinese. Roland told them, "Talk to your bosses." The drivers saw that he was armed and wisely chose not to make an issue of it.

In Benicia, they encountered the same problem. Chinese were not allowed to ride in the best stagecoaches to Sacramento. The ban was a standing rule, no matter how much money a Chinese offered for a ticket. Roland bought three of the cheapest fares offered. The clerk behind the ticket window looked at him with disgust as he pushed the tickets out from under the brass bars of the ticket booth. The clerk muttered, "You're going to regret this, mister."

Roland and his two Chinese friends rode to Sacramento on a flat, opened-cargo wagon outfitted with benches. He held a toddler on his lap all the way because there weren't sideboards or a gate across the back to keep a child from falling off. The toddler's mother was grateful with a baby nursing at her breast and another on the way. Mr. Sue and Zhang were both fluent in Cantonese and talked to each of the travelers on the two-day trip to Sacramento. Most of the men were traveling to the railroad camps in the mountains. The women were all going to the towns along the way, seeking work in the hotels, restaurants, and brothels that serviced the workforce.

Roland's back was killing him after two days of sitting on the hard bench. The overnight on the floor of a dilapidated shed on the edge of the Sacramento Valley did nothing to ease the pain. The driver had a cot but faired only a little better than the Chinese. Roland remembered his trip to California City on the small sternwheeler with Lia. It amazed him that over twenty-thousand people had traveled to Sacramento either on the open wagons or crammed into the bottom decks of the riverboats. When they crossed the Sacramento River at Rio Vista, Roland couldn't wait to reach a hotel with a comfortable bed. He wouldn't leave his friends, though. They would have to find a hotel in Sacramento that accommodated Chinese guests. The search wasn't difficult; a woman that was the proprietress of a restaurant on Front Street directed them to a Japanese hotel called the *Lotus Blossom*. The hotel offered hot baths, comfortable beds, and a dining room with an extensive menu in Japanese and English. Mr. Sue and Zhang booked two rooms and noticed that Roland's relief was palpable.

Roland wasn't the only one in need of relief. When Suzette and Bridgette reached Santa Fe, they were battered and tired from the ride in the armored stagecoach. They were also tired of the putrid outhouses at the stage stops, the miserable food, and the lascivious stares of the hands that worked around the stations. At one stop outside of Bernalillio, there was the usual putrid outhouse with a peephole sawed in the side. As Suzette hurried to finish her business, she looked over and saw a blue eye looking through the hole. She had decided to give the boy a thrill. There was only one blue-eyed person in the station crew. He was a white boy, about fifteen years old. She stood up and faced the hole before pulling up her breeches to give the boy a good look at the promised land. The blue eye disappeared, and an erect penis thrust through the peephole took its place. She slapped the boy's member as hard as she could and received her rewarded, a deafening scream and a line of obscene invective as footsteps scurried away. Brigette and Moses saw the entire incident and laughed until they cried.

Santa Fe was a pleasant layover for two days, free from the dust of the trail, poor food, and the flies that infested the stage stops. Suzette and Bridgette stayed in a room on the plaza, and Moses and his drivers stayed in a livery west of town, caring for the mules and guarding the gold. The first order of business for the two women was hot baths and a good meal. After donning their last clean clothes and turning all the rest of their trail duds over to the hotel laundry, Suzette took Bridgette out to revisit some of the sights around the old Spanish town.

Suzette took Bridgette to visit Mademoiselle Lynnette but discovered that she had moved back to France. One of the women who worked for Mademoiselle Lynnette now owned the salon and gave Suzette the address where she could write her in Paris. Saddened that she couldn't see the woman who helped her, she related the story of buying the Henry rifles and her encounter with the pornographer. They walked to the bank, and she told Bridgette the story of arriving at the bank to deposit Bent's silver. The banker remembered her, and when Suzette asked about Marie's grandparents, he told her that they purchased a home on the north side of town. Abuela's eyes were wide with astonishment when she answered the door of a small but elegant cottage. Suzette was glad they weren't in Bernalillio; she didn't have the time or inclination to endure another fiesta at the winery.

The best of the trip home came when they left the last station on the Banning/Callahan stage line north of Raton pass. Now the two women rode their horses since Moses couldn't change out the mules pulling the heavy stage, he had to travel slower. Suzette loved the solitude of traveling on the Santa Fe trail again, but the changes along the way were many. Moses had swung them north, up to Dodge City, because he knew the Atchison/Topeka was building to it from the east. He learned that the railroad was only one-hundred-twenty miles east of the wild and dangerous cattle town. They were glad only to be passing through; even in the middle of the day, there were gunshots from the middle of Dodge. It would be four or five more days, and then they would be riding on the railroad. Everyone was excited; the railroad ride would be a first for all of them.

Connor was also experiencing firsts in the ancient port city of Madras. He wasn't expecting that most of the city was nothing more than a slum. There was one paved boulevard leading up from the port, but every other street was nothing more than a dirt lane, lined with dilapidated sheds that served as homes for several families. The crowding was oppressive; the press of the people overwhelming with the odor of unwashed bodies and open sewer ditches that ran to the sea, overlain with the specter of starving people everywhere. At every step, there were the hands of children begging, a new foreigner in their midst, hope-against-hope a traveler new to the area would take pity on them.

Ragini kept a constant barrage of invective against the beggars, but the children, paper-thin with every rib and vertebrae trying to break through their skin, still badgered Connor in the hope of a coin or a morsel of food. Ragini could see that Madras was in crisis. She spoke loudly, almost shouting over the clamoring children, "There is famine here, and it is severe. There should be food carts and the smell of cooking from the houses. The children too weak to get up and beg will die soon."

Connor could see that it would take more than a food cart to fix the problem. Men were moving down to the port with bodies of children, and the elderly loaded like cordwood for disposal in the sea. The starved population of Madras couldn't afford even the traditional funeral pyre for the dead. He asked Ragini, "What causes this?"

"Sometimes, it is the lack of rain; more often, it is the British mandating agricultural products for export." She explained further, "Indian exports of opium, rice, wheat, indigo, jute, and cotton are a key component of the economy of the British empire. Sometimes, when the lack of rain and oppressive policies occur together, the results are deadly. The British don't care about the people; they think there are too many people in India anyway. All they care about is their damnable Empire. If people in Britain eat, they can't see the problems in the rest of the world. Someday there will be a revolution, but it won't be the work of the children dying in the streets. India needs a charismatic leader. India needs a George Washington. India needs to take control of itself."

Connor looked up the boulevard; there was a square with a stone building flying the British flag in front. Armed guards patrolled the streets around the square. No Indians were allowed on the square. The soldiers looked tough, and Connor thought that people would die if they stepped on the grass. Ragini assured him that many people died storming the government building at the start of a famine. When the people got as weak as they witnessed walking up from the port, they just lay around until death takes them away from the misery. Ragini talked to a petty official, and she was allowed to walk with Connor to a hotel for foreigners behind the government building. She could not stay in that hotel, but there was a decent Indian hotel across the street where she could stay. She took Connor to the registration desk and said, "Have a good rest. Tomorrow, meet me across the street, and we will walk down to where my family lived."

Connor was the quintessential Irishman in a British enclave. He had his supper in the hotel bar and sat alone and quietly listened to the conversations around him. He didn't hear a word about the famine, the death stalking all the people in the streets, or any measures to relive the misery. The talk centered on the rainfall, the production of the farms, and news from England. Queen Victoria had caught a cold in the spring, Charles Dickens survived a train wreck in Staplehurst, and there was a new book that took the nation by surprise – *Alice's Adventures in Wonderland*. Most of the Brits thought the book was nothing more than literary nonsense; however, some thought it was an unfavorable satire on the monarchy and argued for the deportation of the author, Lewis Carroll, to a penal colony. Connor would have to get a copy of the book when he reached England and decide for himself. He thought about little Anna; he would have a copy under his arm the next time he saw her. He wondered about Roland and Lia. Strangely he felt homesick, but not for Ireland. He decided on the spot to go back to America; he would find his family in Missouri and read Alice in Wonderland to his grandniece.

While Lia took little Anna on day trips around San Francisco, Roland was riding up the Central Pacific rail bed. The railroad was under construction every mile he traveled east of Sacramento. Mr. Sue and Zhang refused horses when Roland purchased an old stud to carry him up the Sierras. Roland would wait for the couple above Auburn. Talking to the construction bosses, he learned that Mr. Judah camped near Newcastle. It would take another day for Mr. Sue and Zhang to reach Auburn, so he decided to ride the short distance up the railbed to find the railroad magnate. He found Judah's camp and Judah himself seated at a table covered with reports and requisitions under a tarp stretched for a sunshade. The sun was still hot; it would be cooler as he went farther up the Sierras. Judah had a staff that took care of feeding him and moving the camp along with two bodyguards to keep him safe.

Roland introduced himself, and Judah rose to shake his hand, smiling profusely and holding Roland's hand a little too long. "Welcome, Mr. Callahan. It is rare to see an investor out here on the railroad. Most of the investors like working from a bar in San Francisco or New York. This man is Charles Crocker, one of our founders and in charge of all the construction. Roland shook Crocker's hand, but Crocker was more business-like, didn't effuse excessive cordiality, and didn't hold the handshake longer than a polite encounter deserved. Roland was more interested in the construction, but Judah kept control of the conversation. He asked, "Mr. Callahan, have you talked to Stanford?"

"No, Jim Parish purchased the stock for our family trust. I didn't have any reason to take up his time. I am mostly interested in the construction of the trestles and the tunnels. I hear you have twenty-thousand Chinese up here. It must take overwhelming logistics to keep this operation going."

Judah seized the opportunity to be authoritative, correct the younger man, and bring up the subject of money, "We only have twelve thousand regardless of what the newspapers say and, yes, it does take a monumental effort to maintain supplies. I'm going to have to ask the government for more support. Huntington is back east, talking to congress and more investors. Would you have an interest in increasing your family's holdings?"

Roland was pensive, "Maybe, I want to look over the construction first. I know the war has slowed both you and the Union Pacific down considerably. I read that the Irish are going to strike for more wages, and (Roland chuckled) better whiskey." Judah and Crocker laughed with him. "How much do the Chinese make? Do you pay for their room and board?"

Crocker was quick to answer, "Hell no. We pay them twenty-six dollars a month; they buy their food and camp along the roadbed. By the way, we have twelve thousand, and there is another twelve thousand waiting to take their place if they were to go on strike. The two crews laying track are all white men, and they get paid more and also get sustenance and better tents for the camps. Winter is coming. We have to buy some heaters for their tents."

Roland nodded his head as if he agreed, pursed his lips, and just muttered, "Humm! I see. How far is it to the first tunnel?"

Crocker said, "I'll take you over there; it's only a hundred yards around that point."

Roland looked over the tunnel operation. It wasn't a long tunnel like the ones he read about further up the Sierras. Roland watched the Chinese with hand drills and sledgehammers. One man held and turned the drill after every stroke of the hammer. His partner swung with precision and struck the drill with an eight-pound sledgehammer. Crocker took Roland by the arm and turned him back toward the entrance, "We have to get out of here. They are coming up with the explosives. Transporting and loading explosives is the most dangerous part of the work. I never stay around to watch them load the holes. We pay those workers thirty-five dollars a month."

"What do you blast with?" Roland asked.

"We mostly use black powder, but we are experimenting with nitroglycerin, especially at the higher elevations where we can keep it frozen. It is more powerful and a lot more dangerous if it thaws out. We still have accidents with black powder. I think it is from static electricity or just these dumb Chinese being careless. Let's get out of here. See the labor running for cover. They are the smart ones."

Roland walked the short distance to the portal. Looking down the railroad bed, he could see waves of laborers closing back on the roadbed after the explosives wagon passed. He walked back to Judah's camp, mounted up and rode back to Auburn to wait for Mr. Sue and Zhang.

Roland spent the night in a hotel on Lincoln Avenue. Like Connor in Madras, he ate in the bar and listened to the conversation. One of the drunks was a peddler that sold the new explosives. He was boasting that his boss had mastered bottling and sealing the nitro in glass tubes that inserted directly into the drill holes. Another young man who seemed to know a lot about chemistry said he could make it on-site, eliminating the danger of transporting the explosive liquid, and the process was cheap. Here was a fellow in whom Roland could take an interest. The man was James Howden, and Roland spent the evening, and the next morning at breakfast, talking to him. He had a lot to share with Mr. Sue and Zhang when he saw them walking up Lincoln Avenue later that afternoon.

On the other side of the Pacific, Ragini waited for Connor to cross the street from the government complex. Madras moaned awake to another day of devastating famine. As Connor crossed the street, he could see the impact famine had on the city. The morgue carts were already busy; the streets weren't alive like a thriving commercial center, people awoke and looked first to see who was still alive in their households and then checked on their close neighbors to see who was still alive. Ragini was grim, Connor could see the lugubrious mood that was going to greet him before he was halfway across the street. Ragini greeted him but had no good news from spending the night listening to her people.

The pearl merchant she dealt with years ago to buy her way out of India was long passed away. She learned that his son now ran the business but had her doubts that he would know any of her family. Ragini asked one last time, "Are you sure you want to go down there with me. It won't be safe; the fishermen will take you for a Brit. I can go alone. You can wait for me at the hotel. I should be back in a few hours."

Connor insisted on going with her. Ragini agreed if they took a carriage, a coach would be better, Connor would be less visible. He agreed on a coach, and they walked to the front of Fort St. George, where coaches for hire waited for the wealthy. It was about six and a half miles to Thiruvotriyur. The farther they got from the heart of the city and closer to the fishing villages on the coast, the less the devastation from the famine. The people close to the countryside and the ocean knew how to feed themselves. As the coach approached Thiruvotriyur, Ragini was fraught with dread. She wasn't seeing neighborhoods that were familiar to her. *Strange*, she thought until they came to a vast empty area that stretched down to the sea. The home she grew up in, along with the homes of several thousand people were completely gone. New shacks and hovels lined the edges of the open area, like a fungus of humanity growing inward to fill the void. Connor and Ragini got out of the coach and asked the driver, "What happened here?"

The diver answered in the sing-song English of someone whose first language was Hindi, "Jvariy Tarang, years ago."

Ragini stood and stared at the ocean in disbelief for a long time. Her entire family, an extended family of more than a hundred, was either dead or scattered by the indiscriminate whim of the ocean; the ocean that gave them life and sustenance, and then with one cruel stroke, took it away. Connor gently took Ragini by the arm and put her back into the coach. Before he hoisted himself up through the door, he said to the driver, "Take us back to the harbor at Madras." The driver nodded his understanding. Connor thought, *this man has made this trip many times already, and the ending is always the same.*

When they reached the harbor, Connor asked the driver, "Why didn't you tell us that Thiruvotriyur was gone?"

The driver answered with genuine sadness, "It wouldn't have changed anything. Everyone has to see for themselves." Connor paid the driver and thanked him. Santiago had seen the coach arrive on the quay. Amos was rowing into shore to retrieve his Captain and his stepmother. He didn't know that Ragini was an orphan just like himself, but he would be finding out much more about her on their way to England.

In the Sierra Nevada foothills, Roland was learning much more about the plight of the Chinese working on the railroad. Mr. Sue and Zhang had a lot to report over a meal in a Chinese restaurant on Lincoln Street in Auburn. For the most part, the workers were healthy, the cooks boiled water and delivered tea to the crews throughout the day. Cholera and yellow fever didn't stalk the Chinese like they did the Irish working west on the other end of the railroad. The men also washed up at the cook sheds every day when they finished their work. The main problem was the nature of the work. Quarrying out the tunnels is as dangerous as underground mining. Cutting the timber and sawing the logs to build the trestles was equally dangerous. The railroad paid more for the more dangerous work. There were always young men that would take the jobs, trying to earn enough money for a return voyage to China. The most dangerous job was blasting. The tunnel crews blasted with nitroglycerin for the hard granite of the upper Sierras, much more powerful than black powder and also much more dangerous. A man could make it explode by wetting his thumb and snapping his fingers. Roland was going to leave word at the hotel for James Howden to visit Mr. Judah in Newcastle. Here was something Roland could change to improve the safety of the workers. He was glad that the rock in Red Mountain did not need nitroglycerin.

Mr. Sue and Zhang walked hand-in-hand up the railroad bed. Roland rode his horse to Newcastle. Mr. Judah was at his desk under the shade of the tarp. After the pleasantries, Roland got right down to business. Judah's need for more investment money would make him easy to manipulate, and Roland took full advantage. Mr. Judah, there is a young man down at the hotel in

Auburn that is coming up to meet you. His name is James Howden. He knows how to make nitro on-site, and I want you to put him to work. I will put more money into the railroad, and I will back Mr. Howden to set him up with the chemicals he will need at the end of the line. What do you say?"

Judah was silent for a moment, and then he said, "I will have to check with Crocker and the construction boss, Stonebridge; they may not want to change the routine."

"Let me make myself a little clearer. Those men work for you, and you can let them make their decisions after they hear Howden out; that is if they make the right decision. I want the chemicals he needs moving up from San Francisco as soon as you can wire down to the company that supplies the mint. I'll be back down there in a couple of weeks, and I will talk to Stanford. I trust he will be able to tell me all is going well with Mr. Howden. Good day, Mr. Judah." Roland extended his hand to end the meeting.

The railroad magnate was no fool; he knew he couldn't turn his back on money walking in the door. He had made more difficult changes than this for the sake of keeping investors.

Roland, Mr. Sue, and Zhang worked their way up the roadbed to Donner Pass. The earthmoving, the trestle building, and the tunnel boring was an impressive operation. All along the way, they talked to the Chinese. All along the way, they heard the same stories. Blasting and timbering were the two most dangerous jobs. Roland decided he would have to look into the timber industry some other time. At Donner Pass, he put Mr. Sue and Zhang on a stage to Carson City. From there, they would catch the overland stage to St. Joseph, Missouri. Roland said his goodbyes and rode back down the mountains. He had a wife to attend to in San Francisco.

East of Dodge City, Moses gave out a whoop as they crested a hill and saw a locomotive sitting at the end-of-tracks. Several hundred men, all white men, were working on the railroad. Teams of oxen with box scrapers were clearing the grass and topsoil from the prairie ahead of the railbed. More men moved with mules and wagons, hauling ballast rock forward to cover the cleared ground. Other teams delivered ties, and forty men carried a rail forward. As Moses passed the railhead, hammers rang, men cursed, and sweat flowed freely. He was sorry he didn't pass on the upwind side. He needed to find the rail boss and arrange for a train ride east. The Irish looked with derision at the black men driving the wagons but forgot about that when Suzette and Bridgette stepped down from the armored coach. Somehow it was okay for two good looking, and two wealthy women, to have black men moving them across the prairie. Moses talked to the boss. They would have to go ten miles further east to the camp and supply yard. There they could load the wagons on empty flat cars, and Moses and his crew could ride on the open cars. The women could be accommodated in the caboose, as long as they didn't mind riding with the train crew.

The women didn't mind, when they boarded the caboose of the empty supply train that would take them east, they found a small galley, a meager water supply, and most importantly, a privy; even though the privy was nothing more than a place to sit with an open hole down to the tracks. Suzette didn't care; she was going home. She couldn't believe that she would be there in a little over one more day. In a way, she was glad; in another, she was sad. She regretted that she couldn't visit all the friends she made crossing on the trail. She wanted to see Mr. and Mrs. Mahaffie in Olathe. She wanted to show Bridgette the church where she killed Chico de Diablo. All that would have to wait till later. For the moment, finding Jacques was the only thing on her mind.

Epilogue

Five years and thousands of miles behind them, the young Callahan family had waited patiently for the start of the new year, and the end of the war. 1865 brought the promise of peace and reconstruction. President Lincoln had led the nation through the Civil War and had pushed Grant to finish it. Grant, with the Army of the Potomac, in command of two-hundred-fifty thousand, moved to break the back of the defenses of Petersburg and Richmond. Tens of thousands of black troops moved to the front and fought with determination to keep the freedom Lincoln had granted. The war finally reached its inevitable end. The South lay in ruin, but the racial hatred that underlay the war regardless of the high minded ideal of state's rights was destined to last for hundreds if not thousands of years.

There was still a lot of work out ahead of them, but the Callahans were young and hardened by five years in what most of the nation still regarded as hostile wilderness. Before they went their separate ways from Red Mountain, they contemplated the future and what it would hold for them. They weren't the only ones making plans. All over the South, white aristocrats were licking their wounds and planning how to keep the blacks suppressed after the war. Their counterparts in the North were planning how to control the South with marshal law backed by the US Army. The war with the South ended, but the conflict between the cultures of the North and the South would continue for centuries.

The young Callahans still had all this on their minds as they left Red Mountain. Some of them for the last time.

··· *End of Volume 3* ···

www.ingramcontent.com/pod-product-compliance
Lightning Source LLC
Chambersburg PA
CBHW060554310726
48982CB00008B/1117/J

* 9 7 8 1 7 3 3 6 6 5 0 1 8 *